Of Lilies And Lies

Stirling Harbor 1

Margaux Porter

Pocket Publishing LLC

Copyright

Contents

This book is dedicated to my husband and children. Without their love and support this never would have happened. My husband let me slave for long hours over words. My children only complained a little when I would ask them to wait so I could finish a thought.
They are the bright light in my heart, the gold of my kintsugi.

A special thank you to:
All the wonderful people who helped make this possible.
My girl squad, who sure as hell know how to make me feel good when we get together.
The people who have beta read my book, cheered me on, offered me guidance, or just became amazing friends.
And you.
Thank you for taking a chance on a baby author.

Acknowledgements

Developmental Edits: Miranda at
www.writingevolution.co.uk/
Line Edits: Beth at www.vbproofreads.com
Copy Edits: Brooklyn at www.bhauthorservices.com/
Proofreader: Alyssa Skaggs at
Instagram.com/alyssasbookservices
Object Cover Design: Ana at theasdesigns.com

Content Warnings

Because your mental health is important to me, I'd like to point out the trigger warnings that are in this book. This is not an exhaustive list, and I am certain I have missed a few. Please review this carefully, if there is anything you feel could cause you pain, please don't read it.

If you want me to clarify something to make certain it's the right fit for you, email me at any time margaux@margauxporter.com, or find me on IG/TIKTOK/FB and ask me.

Trigger Warnings for Of Lilies And Lies

Anxiety, Abusive relationship (past), Attempted murder, Death, Gun Violence, Infertility, Miscarriage, PTSD, Rape (not depicted, but mentioned in conversation), Sexual Abuse/Assault (past- , some depicted), Stalking, Surprise Pregnancy, Violence

One

Kit - Los Angeles, California

I KNOW THIS ISN'T the time or place for a laugh, but I could really use a good one. Not the funny ha-ha kind, more of the break-the-tension kind. The laughter that loosens tight shoulders or relieves massive weights, like the kind pressing down on my stomach. Most people would cry in a situation like this, but I was taught a long time ago that crying is a weakness.

So even though I'm standing at a gravesite, burying my husband at twenty-nine, I won't cry. Instead, I'll wait for the California sun to dip behind a cloud so I can stop squinting at headstones.

It's beautiful here; the stones are painted in gold and white and silver lines. It's over-the-top and ridiculous. But no one asked me what I thought about slabs with precious minerals stuck in them.

A strong voice pulls my attention.

"His strength and resilience are something he instilled in his loved ones. His devotion and grace showed those around him the road to travel in life." He pauses a moment, his hand over his bible, like what he's saying isn't blasphemy. "And he led with love and compassion." Pastor Clark's warm voice washes over us all. Always calm and clear, it should soothe me.

Not today.

Jaw tight, I hold back a bitter laugh and somehow keep my hands from forming fists. I mash my back teeth together, struggling to keep the energy pouring through me reined in.

Ethan's strength was in his fist, and he sure instilled the fear of that strength in me more than once.

Leading with love and compassion? I begged for compassion repeatedly and received none. Not once.

And love? More like ownership.

These people are blind to the person he was. Ignorant. But it's not my place to tell them, just like I won't mention those stupid headstones.

Ethan came from money. And this place? It's a burial ground for the elite.

I tune out and scan the cemetery.

Colette is to my right, soaking up Pastor Clark's words. I should pay attention, but if I look at the casket, I might puke.

The complete antithesis of my mother-in-law's resilience and grace, those traits were instilled with hard fists and fast punches. Hers are innate. She does everything to perfection, like paying attention. Something everyone around her should be doing. That includes me.

The cemetery is shaded in a dense canopy of green everywhere except in this exact spot. It's out in the open, the harsh sun glimmering over the group and causing shivers as it mixes with the coolness in the air.

Why would she choose this spot?

The canopy would be perfect for keeping out the sun. As it is, I'm under a tent designed to let in most of the rays while providing a false sense of security. Much like my life. It wouldn't be so bad, except I'm forced to stand on feet that have been squished into pumps designed to torment people—so perfect for this funeral.

I'd rather be anywhere but here. In the sun. And wind. Shivering in my too-thin shawl.

But this spot is perfect for Ethan. His presence will forever be solidified by the money surrounding him.

And it's all shit. Serious and utter shit.

It's been more than two years since he disappeared. Colette said we couldn't have his funeral until all the legal stuff was finished. Today we're having his celebration of life, casket included. I hold back another bitter laugh because only a few of us are in on the joke.

Shivers snake up my spine like *he* just walked over my grave somewhere.

Colette's cool hand slides over mine, uncurling my fist, forcing me to appear relaxed. She has a sweet smile plastered on her face, despite the occasional tear sliding under her enormous sunglasses.

But I don't have to see her eyes to know the message she's sending me. *Pay attention, Katherine.*

I am, Colette, I swear.

I focus my attention on the pastor and nod.

She squeezes my hand like she approves or like she can make everything better. But her attempt is futile—like this funeral. I can still feel him, hear him, and smell him.

Ethan is so ingrained in me that nothing will shake him loose.

He's like an amputated leg. The appendage is gone, but the memories remain. And sometimes, when the nerves hit right, hurt flares in a spot where toes should be.

That's Ethan. My phantom limb. The nerve forever pinched and twisted, painful in every waking moment of my life.

A wave of dizziness hits me, and pinpricks move up my arms and into my neck and cheeks. My pinched toes tingle and lose their feeling as my breathing accelerates. Classic symptoms of an anxiety attack.

Not here. Please, not here.

I can't fall apart in front of these people. Ethan Finney never showed weakness, and I can't either.

In and out.

Breathe.

This would be so much easier if I could slip my hand into my coat pocket and grab the pill I stashed there.

I could slide it up to my mouth, swallow it down with spit—even though I tell my patients never to do that—and finish this funeral numb to everyone and everything. Then I could silence my brain to black noise instead of the utter shit the pastor is saying.

But I can't because Finney women do not fade to black. We are the essence of society, the steel backbone, and even in his death, I must play a part.

The pressure on my hand increases from time to time like Colette is checking in to make sure I'm paying attention. *Yes, Colette. I am.*

I slide my hand over my wrist and push my sleeve back the tiniest fraction to sneak a peek at my watch. The pastor has been at this for twenty minutes already.

Distracting myself, I look around.

The crowd of over five hundred creates a sea of black around Ethan's plot. Colette is prominent in society, and most people are here to show their respect for her. They are tear-free, waiting for the eulogy to end so they can swoop in like vultures. Then they'll fight to be the first to offer condolences, ensuring that Colette continues to line their charities' pockets.

And a lone woman is crying silently on the outskirts of the mass. Maybe she's his secretary, but honestly, I don't care.

A sea of people, and not one of them is here for me. Colette is the only person I have a relationship with. The rest are all faces I've seen at luncheons, galas, or the few business dinners I was allowed to attend.

I don't remember any of them—not the names nor their faces. They won't remember me because they can't tell me apart from the next big shot's wife. They met the woman Ethan made me into. Katherine, the beautiful blond trophy wife he kept in a gilded cage.

That's not who I am.

I've lost all traces of the woman I was before and all traces of the life I once knew. Even the blond hair is fake, but the thought of letting my natural red grow out is enough to cause a panic attack on an easy day.

"How are you doing, Katherine?" Colette's voice is soft and buttery under the drone of the pastor. It's in stark contrast to how she holds herself: erect, icy. She's perfect from head to toe in a designer dress, pearl necklace, and matching earrings—the epitome of a lady in carriage and presence.

Colette pulls me close, whispering against my cheek. "I know how you hate these large gatherings, darling, but you're keeping your composure well. Keep your back straight, shoulders back, and chin high. You're a good girl."

Spine of steel. Prove to the world that I'm fine.

I want to scoff but bite my tongue instead as I force my brows and face to relax.

"Mrs. Finney." The pastor extends his hand to Colette, and she walks to the pile of dirt.

She grabs a handful, her body trembling as she prepares her last goodbyes to Ethan. The dirt slips from her hand. Her whisper is almost too faint to catch. "I love you, Ethan." She moves to the side, daintily wiping her hand with a lace handkerchief.

She didn't even know him. If she had, she wouldn't mourn him this way.

The pastor's voice booms. "Mrs. Finney." My turn now.

I grab a pile of the dark-brown earth; the soil fills my hand, weighing it down. I squeeze tight, letting the grains slip out and fall as I move my hand over his casket.

The dirt slides between my fingers, dropping noiselessly in the silence of the secluded cemetery.

When I'm done, Colette grabs my hand like we're part of a cohesive unit and pulls me toward the family sedan. We're let in, and for the first time all afternoon, I relax. My mind blanks as the sunlight hits my face, and we weave between buildings on our way to Colette's home.

It's a small reprieve from the first set of vultures we couldn't bypass at the gravesite. When we reach the house, there will be a mass of people offering condolences, and I'll nod and accept it like his death was the worst thing to happen in my life.

No, that all came before he was gone.

We pull up to the enormous two-story house inside the prestigious gated community. A home designed for parties, galas.

Babies.

That never happened.

When the car stops, Colette touches my hand before her gentle voice invades my brain. "Come inside. Get freshened up. When you're ready, meet me in the entryway so we can greet guests."

I stop at the base of the stairs. White flashes in my peripheral, and my gaze moves to it.

My body freezes as the fragrance hits me, curling around me like a billow of smoke, caressing my skin, sliding against the fabric of my black dress.

My pulse spikes, and ice picks attack my body. My vision blurs as my legs turn to jelly. The impact with the floor is jarring, and pain blooms in my wrists, then shoots up my arms.

Lilies.

The door closes with a snick, and shoes click against the floor. The crinkle of paper makes all feeling drain from my face and my heart race.

Flowers. He brought home flowers.

My gaze is glued to his hands as he walks into the kitchen with one arm visible and his hand clenched in a fist. The other is behind his back.

Pulse skipping, I wait for him to swing the bouquet around. I don't dare meet his gaze because it tells me nothing. And he doesn't like the defiance.

My fingers tingle as I wait. His breath harsh in the room, the click of the clock slowly counts down.

Tick. Tick. Tick.

What color are the flowers? White or pink?

Please be white. Please be white. I can't take another pink bouquet this week.

I don't dare look at the flowers on the table behind him. If I don't acknowledge that this is the second time this week, the retribution may be swifter.

"Katherine." Constrained. Cold. Bitter.

I swallow around the tightness in my throat, striving to keep my voice light. "Hello, love." Not that he's my love. That ship capsized long ago, but he wants to believe that we are in love, so I have to say it.

He nods, his foot tapping as time stretches.

I brace myself. They're pink. I know they're pink. What did I do this time? The gala was last week, but we've only been shopping since. What would warrant the punishment this time?

Shit, if I can't think of a plausible excuse, this is going to hurt. Sweat beads along my temples.

The sensation in my fingers disappears as the pink from the bouquet slides into view.

"Tell me why, Katherine."

I am well and truly screwed. Run.

Run, Katherine.

Shaking my head, I skirt around the counter and head for the door. Moving as fast as I can, I race down the hall, his footsteps pounding after me.

If I stop...if he catches me...it'll be worse. Keep running.

Don't stop.

Breathe.

Survive.

Bedroom, lock the door.

My lungs tight and chest heavy, I swing into the bedroom, turning to slam the door.

His fist connects, and pain blossoms in my stomach. I hunch over, the air leaving me as agony shoots up into my diaphragm.

My lungs spasm. The pain splintering me into pieces.

My throat is still tight, like sucking through a straw as I sip in as much air as possible. I wrap my arms around myself, guarding my stomach.

Get away.

The tink of metal is loud in the room, followed by the rush of leather through belt loops.

Finally, I catch a breath. I gasp out frantically. "Please, Ethan, give me a moment. I'll—"

"Too late, Katherine."

The strap connects. Sharp pain, like a knife, slices into my back. I can't stifle the cry that bursts out of my mouth as I drop to the floor.

Not soon enough, everything turns black.

‾⋯ ⋅ ‾ ⋅‾ ‾ ⋅ ⋅‾⋅ ⋅‾ ⋅‾⋅ ⋅‾⋅⋅ ‾⋅‾‾   ‾⋯ ⋅‾⋅ ‾‾‾ ‾⋅‾ ⋅ ‾⋅

Dr. Willow Brigham's office is in a remote section of town, per my mother-in-law's request. Her secretary waves me in.

"Katherine, please come in. How are you today?" She's a hippy at heart. She eats peanuts from the bowl on her desk, wears Jesus sandals even when there is a downpour, and prefers to have her patients call her Willow. Uncomfortable with that, I opted for Dr. Willow.

I settle into my favorite spot while she watches me. Although that's her job, the scrutiny sets me a little on edge.

I brace myself, forcing the restlessness out by linking my fingers together, then jump in with what has changed. That's what she likes. "Ethan's funeral was Saturday."

She smiles, her pen tapping her lips. "How does that make you feel?"

"Happy, but only slightly." I nibble my bottom lip, wringing my hands. "I feel guilty for being happy. Should this guilt be so overwhelming?"

Dr. Willow writes in her notebook and smiles. "You tell me. Do you have a reason to feel guilty?"

Yes. I'm a horrible excuse for a human who wanted nothing to do with planning his funeral. I can't say that; despite her being trained not to judge, she might.

"Katherine, therapy only works if you make it work."

I understand this. You can lead a horse to water and all that. "I didn't help with any of the planning. Colette arranged everything. And as his wife, I should have done something. It was too easy to let her plan it all to make the funeral perfect. She even picked out my outfit and sent it to the condo."

"Did you like it?"

I grimace before pressing my lips together for a second. "No." I twist my fingers tightly around my thumb, letting the tip turn white for a moment before releasing and letting the blood flow back through. Weird, this always brings me peace—a fraction of it, at least—resting my brain, allowing me to breathe easier.

"Why?"

I shrug.

She waits.

I admire her tenacity. But I wish she didn't still have to use these tactics to make me talk. Six years of abuse means therapy's not a simple fix. I have to open up to heal. Am I prepared to let her in? Not at all, and that causes my skin to prickle and my heart to race.

"Ethan would have wanted me to wear it." I watch Dr. Willow. "Not listening to him resulted in consequences—punishment."

"Did that happen often?" She scribbles on her paper, making notes.

My heart jumps into my throat, threatening to cut off my airway. She's still in the dark about some of our history. Despite not knowing everything, she has reduced my anxiety dramatically. And for that, I'll be forever grateful. If I want to heal, I have to tell her everything.

But then she'll see me for the weak, stupid woman I truly am. Freedom would be more than anything I can imagine, but I'm stuck here.

Stuck.

Stuck with the memories, the painful nightmares. Fear was my constant companion during and after my marriage.

Dr. Willow shifts in her seat and clears her throat, leaning closer, invading my space like sunlight slips into corners—silent but bright. "Katherine, if you want to heal, I can help you. But only on your terms. We've kept the pace slow, and we can continue to, but I think you're ready to push past those barriers you keep around yourself."

She watches me, her smile bright, soft, and gentle. She's right. She hasn't pushed me because I think she senses that I'm not ready. Despite needing to heal, I haven't made myself open up completely.

Dr. Willow tilts her head, and at that moment, with her gentle smile and her open expression, she reminds me of my mom. Patient, warm, radiating understanding. Before I can stop myself, the truth tumbles out.

"I miss my parents, my sister Rosemary, and my little brother Jack." The words are forced around that same lump in my throat and I squeeze my fingers tight, forcing my leg to stop bobbing.

"What happened to them?"

If I answer, if I tell her the truth, she's going to see me for what I am—a coward.

I wipe my palms on my thighs, keeping my view on my hands. Her question lingers in the air like a weight ready to drop.

Why can't I just open my mouth and say what needs to be said?

Just get it out.

"I pushed them away." It comes out small, like it's the size of my confidence. But the words need to bleed out, to flow, and I need to let them. Nerves rack me, and the bobbing of my leg takes over as I nibble on my thumbnail.

It is going to take more than her calm voice to urge me to talk. Every piece of me has to give in. Courage. I have to have courage.

Just like I tell my patients: be strong, you can do this, be brave.

"I met Ethan when I was twenty." *Good start, Kit. Keep going.* "The café I worked at was near his office. He was in one day for a lunch meeting. He was older than me, worldly, sophisticated, refined. He had this presence that filled the room. It was tangible. I was dumb and mesmerized."

Needing to connect my thoughts, I study the room until I'm ready to go on. "I told him my name, and soon I was Katherine, no longer the fun Kit I had been my whole life. Katherine was mature, elegant. Worldly like him. He enthralled me, enchanted me, and eventually shit on me."

Damn it. She'll never say so, but I'm still the biggest idiot on the planet. I fell for his bullshit and never recovered. And I only have myself to blame. Me and my foolish, stupidly naïve heart.

"He was hypnotizing. I thought I was in love. We got engaged and married quickly. The first bruise showed up just before the wedding. He was contrite, said it would never happen again, and I believed him. Soon, the lie became apparent, but it was too late."

Her pen bobs up and down, but she catches my gaze. Sorrow is etched in every line of her face.

"I wasn't strong enough." This is the challenging part, the truth that rips me apart in the middle of the night. "The last time I saw my parents was five years ago. They showed up without notice. I didn't have time to hide the bruises on my arms and wrists. We went out for supper, pretending nothing had happened, and when we got back, my dad confronted Ethan. Ethan, of course, denied the beating. When they left, Ethan said that was the last time we'd see them."

Those were the last of the visible bruises.

She stays silent as I continue, making sure to look me in the eye and nod in recognition. If she says anything, I'll falter, and I'm already fighting against the pounding pulse in my chest and the urge to run.

I duck my head. I can't look at her if I want to continue. "I fought—hard. I tried to leave, but the recovery was worse. When he realized I'd keep fighting, he threatened my family. His warning was enough. They never stopped calling, texting, or sending letters, though. They never stopped."

I glance at the clock, my hands, her desk. Now she knows. My skin prickles, my heart spasms, and if there is so much as an ounce of sympathy from her, I'll break down. She's holding back tears when I look up, and it makes me ache.

Son of a bitch.

I swallow past the tightness in my throat. "I was weak."

"No, saving yourself is not a weakness. You did what you had to do to survive." She is gentle in her approach, pausing, but keeping her attention on me.

I can't go on. I have nothing else to give today. The confessions make me want to melt into a puddle on the floor, to disappear into nothing and hide.

My fingers ache. Numbness creeps into them despite my constant twisting. I suck in breaths, struggling past the growing lump trying to suffocate me. Physically, Dr. Willow and I are the only ones here, but Ethan's ghost is heavy. The memory of him pulling at my clothes, dragging me by my hair, and shoving me against the wall. His spirit is a constant presence.

Trembling, I try to shake the memory loose, but a pit forms in my stomach, rolling, threatening to erupt, to spew out the poison the only way my body can—violently. I flex my fingers and calves, trying to return feeling to them. The air in the room is heavy and thick as I try to draw it into the tiny hole that is now my throat. It's not enough. It burns, wheezing on the way in and out.

I shift back, opening up my lungs to let air in.

"Grounding, Katherine. Deep breaths in through your mouth, out through your nose to the count of four. Find a cheerful place. Pick one of those and start. You can control your anxiety. Help yourself."

She's right. Focus on what I see, hear, and smell. I work through the room.

There is a painting on the wall of the ocean and a sailboat. The room smells like lavender and vanilla. Around me is the tick of the clock, the hum of the fan, and the tap of my foot.

I go through them again, ending when I focus on Dr. Willow. Better, but not perfect. I'll go through the technique as often as I need to heal.

"You did well working through that, Katherine. What brought on the panic?"

"Memories. The trigger is always memories. Can I ask you for a favor?" I bite my bottom lip, lacing my fingers and pulling. Acid churns in my gut. She'll say yes. Still, I work up the courage to ask.

"Of course. If I can do it, I will."

"I want you to call me Kit. It's a nickname from my childhood. Katherine is his name for me, and I miss the person I used to be." A buzz pours through me, filling every crevice of my body, scattering goose bumps down my arms. My frantic heartbeat eases, and my stomach settles. Pieces of me shift back into place. A bit of my heart, some of my soul, a sliver of sanity.

"Absolutely. Kit, it is." She scratches in her notebook before smiling at me again. "Why haven't you reached out to your family?"

"He could return at any moment."

"Dead people don't come back."

Logically, my brain accepts this. When a person dies, that's it. The end. The body goes into the ground. Confusion knits her brow, and she opens her mouth to speak. But I shake my head, and she stops.

"They never found his body."

May

Two

Greer–Stirling Harbor, Maine

I RIFFLE THROUGH THE papers at my desk, the figures and designs blurring in front of me. This order will take a month, two max, to finish. Three other clients are waiting, and two projects need to be bid on, but those are all on hold until I finish this.

"Simon, when is the project for Gideon Richards due?"

Starting a business with my brother might not have been the wisest decision. Still, he's the best at what he does. I can't complain since Winters Woodworking would not make it without him.

I pull out the Richards project, unable to stop the smile that breaks out across my face or the puff of my chest. This intricate design is my best commercial work. Wall art with inner mechanisms, gears, and locks that will open hidden compartments inside the wall. Once Richards sets the passwords, this thing will be like Fort Knox.

Despite being proud of the piece, every part of me is on edge. I'm itchy and twitchy, and it's annoying as fuck. The restless energy that helps me create remarkable work has been setting me off lately.

It's like I've been hollowed out. Maybe I'm allergic to something. But I haven't changed anything in my diet or routine. So whatever the fuck it is, it's a mystery to me.

Where the fuck is Simon?

A slight shuffle outside the door catches my attention. "Simon?" He's probably flirting with the secretary. Really, he'll hit on anything with a vagina.

Leaning to the right, I look out into the hall. He's there at the desk, leaning over as he chats with the purple-haired secretary.

He's wearing his man bun today. Why does that make me want to laugh? The grin I'm trying to hide escapes. Man buns are the epitome of douche to me. They're ridiculous, like he's a genie ready to pop out of a tiny lamp and grant one lucky person three wishes. I wish he'd get his ass in here so we could plan the upcoming week.

Juliet's cheeks turn pink, and I scowl before cocking my brow at Simon. If her blush is any sign, Simon is going to land us in a heap of trouble. I move toward the door, lean against the doorjamb, and cross my arms.

"Romeo! Leave Juliet alone and help me figure out the Richards project." I don't need his help, but he enjoys feeling needed, so I oblige. I scowl, heading back to my chair without waiting to see if he follows.

His shit kickers clip-clop into the room, but I keep my focus on the papers. "You spoke to Gideon. When was he hoping to have this project done?"

"Hello to you too." Simon flops into the chair. He clears his throat and paints on the face he uses when he's using his "Greer" voice. "Oh, hello, Simon. Man, it's good to see you. How was your vacation?"

"Simon, your vacations are always the same. I don't need to ask."

"Were you there spying on me? This one was different. Besides, you don't know what a real vacation is like. You haven't had one in ten years."

I lean forward and study him, taking in the purple under his eye, the faint marks on his neck, and the scruff on his fists.

"Okay, let's check off the facts." I raise my hand, holding up my fingers so I can tick off each one. "You met a woman."

His grin and sparkling orbs confirm I'm right.

"You got into a fight somewhere." He nods but has the decency to look chagrined.

"Fuck, Simon, I don't need you getting arrested somewhere up north." But I can't help myself from asking, "What did they do this time?"

"They started the fight. Ask anyone there, including the officer. These old geezers were roughing up a kid, Greer. He bumped into an older guy and spilled beer everywhere. When they started pushing him around, I stepped in. One of them hit me, so I hit back. The damn place is a biker bar, for Christ's sake. People are going to spill beer."

"What the fuck, kid? Why do you pick the weirdest places?" I shake my head and pinch the bridge of my nose. He's always getting into trouble. When we were kids, I was always stuck getting him out of it.

"Being ten minutes younger than you doesn't make me a kid, only the more youthful, more handsome twin." Simon smirks.

I lean back in my chair, steepling my fingers under my chin. "Congratulations on doing the right thing, Simon. Looks like you got laid as well."

"Well, I don't kiss and tell."

That's true. I have no idea who's warming his bed this month. He hasn't mentioned anyone since Eden died. Not that they were married, but still, it gets to him.

"Did Theo enjoy hanging out with Mom and Dad?"

"Are you kidding? Candy at every meal and late bedtimes? Mom and Dad spoiled the shit out of that kid, but they love him, and he loves Grandma and Grandpa."

"He needs a mom." He tries hard to be both Mom and Dad in their house, but we grew up with the best mom, and everyone should experience that.

"Damn, don't you fucking start. Mom has been pushing me to date again. I'm not ready, and Theo and I make an exceptional father-son team."

At least Mom is focusing on him for a change. I've been in a relationship with Nora for a long time, and Mom is always asking when we'll give her grandbabies. At this point, it's probably time to pop the question.

Five years.

Is five years enough? Social norms would say yes. And she fits into my life. She'll make a wonderful wife because she's exceptional. She's great with children—however many we end up having.

This is the next step.

Maybe that's why I'm itchy. Maybe it's time to move on to the next step with her.

Has she been dropping hints I haven't picked up on? Either way, she'll want to pick out her own ring. I'll ask, and then we can look together.

Simon's movements pull my gaze to him as he rubs at the back of his neck. Are those...*Ugh. Hickeys.* So fucking gross. "Simon, hickeys are disgusting."

"I can't help it if a woman wants to express her desire and devotion with her mouth."

"How are we twins?"

Simon's laugh reverberates through the room. "I have no idea, considering you're a cold fish. You could have a life, be adventurous, you know—swim in the warm current."

"I'm a warm fish, plenty alive and happy to go with the flow." I grin, shuffling through the pages before me to get inspiration for the next project.

Simon mumbles to himself. "Is that what Nora says?"

I ignore him and change the subject. "When is the Richards project due?"

"They want the design by June. He's got the room open for the hidden compartments."

A few weeks to finish, and then we can put it in the house. This thing is going to be wicked when it's done. I've never created a work of art like this.

It's an immense piece for Gideon Richards's wall. The background is a mixture of wood squares cut in varying heights with subtle changes. The focus of the composition sticks out an inch further than the background—The Scales of Justice for the Honorable Gideon Richards. The wood grains and varying heights are striking. It would be an incredible piece to showcase.

"How are we coming with the new marketing campaign?"

"I have a few things to iron out on the promotion for fall, but otherwise, marketing's done. I've got a calendar in the workroom with all the projects we'll have this summer, along with their due dates." He's passionate about his work, the same way I get when I'm elbow-deep in wood shavings.

He loves the social aspect of this job, and I'm thankful as fuck because being the face of Winters Woodworking gives me the heebie-jeebies.

"Great. Thank you. Now get back to work." I smile at him as he gives me a sarcastic seated bow.

I pull out a pencil and grab Richards's design, but Simon doesn't make any move to leave the office. He drums on the armrest of his chair, his foot tapping annoyingly—he does it to piss me off.

It works, given that I want to snap at him. Instead, I drop my pencil and quirk my brow, my lips tight. He playfully taps again, his other hand moving to hide his smile.

I have no time for these games today. Usually, I don't mind because his brain is a freaking marketer's dream, and he can conjure up gold better than an alchemist. But today, I'm ready to kick his ass if he keeps up with this shit.

I hold back the growl. "Spill it."

Simon perks up in the chair. His fingers stop, and his tapping ends. "We need to go out like we used to. Once a month."

That's it? I let out a long sigh and relax my shoulders. "Simon, I'll do whatever you want. Please, go get some work done."

He stays, looking at me like he's a dog and I'm holding his bone.

I do my best to ignore him, turning back to the stack of papers in front of me, but under his gaze, tension crawls up my neck. I glance at the clock, then at Simon, then at the clock again. While he bites his lip, stifling his laughter.

He clears his throat. "Are you going to Mom and Dad's next weekend? You've missed the last few, and Mom asked. She won't like it if you ditch out again."

Fuck, he's not leaving until he gets what he wants.

Goodbye, productive afternoon. Hello, demon Simon.

I bite back another irritated growl. "I have three hours left of work today. Is this what you want to talk about?"

"Don't fool yourself. You'll stay late like always. So are you?"

Not tonight. I've got impromptu plans I need to focus on. So at five o'clock sharp, I'm locking the doors. "No, I've got a meeting in LA Monday morning. I need three things to finish this piece, and only Tokohachi Inc. makes what I want."

"You could order it online."

"I'm taking the component it's supposed to fit with. If it doesn't work, I'm not wasting weeks with communication and mail. I'm not sure when I'll be back."

"Greer, it's only a few hours, and you can bring Nora." He pouts a little—must have learned that from Theo—before batting his lashes at me. Then he winks before grinning again.

"If I'm back by Saturday, I'll go. I'll ask Nora if she's free. Are you bringing someone?"

"Nope, still single."

"You could bring Juliet." *Not that I'm promoting work relationships.*

"She's fun to flirt with, but no, I'm not interested."

"Are you sure? Seems like she might be." We both shift to glance at her. Gaze stuck on Simon, a blush creeps up her cheeks, and she looks back at her computer screen. "Maybe you should stop flirting with the secretaries. Then we could keep one."

"Oh, I'm not the reason they quit. I flirt, but they all realize it's nothing more than that. Your grumpy-as-fuck face is the reason they quit. Maybe if you smiled from time to time, they'd stick around longer. And I'd recommend learning their names."

"What does that mean?" I know their names.

Simon bares his teeth, his mouth wide, then closes it. "That is not a smile. It's an animalistic mating ritual for people without emotions. Your usual grouchiness has amplified to assholery the last few months. Juliet's name is Dawn, and she's been here two weeks—one week longer than the last one. So, if you want her to stick around long enough to finish

21

training, figure out what is poking your ass and pull it out. Maybe if you give your asshole a break, you'll stop being one." With that, he walks out, leaving me with my mouth open.

"If I was an asshole, would I have remembered her birthday yesterday?"

Simon pokes his head in the doorway, his lips pressed together, fighting back a smile. "Martha's birthday was yesterday." He gives me a grin. "And she left two months ago."

The empty vase grinds against the glossy wooden tabletop as I push it between two candles. When those are lit, I lower the dimmer for the chandelier above me to set the mood.

Today is our anniversary—fitting for a proposal, in my opinion. I haven't purchased a ring, but it's fine. Nora never makes a fuss about these kinds of things.

Honestly, I lucked out with her. If I don't want to do what she's got planned, I do something else, and she doesn't make a big deal out of it.

Not everything in my life is at a point where I feel comfortable moving to the next step. Money isn't the issue. Although we're still stabilizing things, the business is up and running. But there isn't enough time in the day to get everything done.

I could hire another designer, but that's the part of the job that brings me the most joy.

But with Nora, I can continue to work like I have been because we're both dedicated.

Everything I've done with my life and my job was with the goal of being able to support my family. And I'm almost 100 percent there. Another few years, and it'll be perfect. Nora gets that. She respects the time I put into my business, and in the future, when we have a family, I know she'll be there to pick up my slack at home when I'm putting in the hours it will take to support her and our children.

With that last thought, I rub my hands together, looking around my kitchen. Roast in the oven, with carrots and green beans—her favorites. Sides of rice and salad are ready to go—she hates potatoes.

This is good, I have everything set.

The door clicks, and heels tap against the floor. "Smells good in here. I hope dinner's ready because I'm starving."

"In the kitchen." I situate myself on the floor, one knee propped. I hold up the bouquet of red roses I purchased on the way home from work so they're the first thing she'll see.

I think I did pretty damn good throwing this proposal thing together.

Her face is bright, but her smile fades as she looks at me. Her brows almost touch her hairline, and her hand is raised to her mouth. "Is this...?"

I smile brightly. "Nora, what started as a beautiful friendship, a mutual agreement to partner each other to galas and fundraisers and whatever else our mothers requested, has grown into something more. Something lifelong, I hope. I cherish you more than any other woman. I'm hoping you'll continue to be my friend in all life's galas. Will you be my forever plus one?"

I shove the flowers toward her. "I don't have a ring. You can pick out the one you'd like."

Her face falls, her stare dropping to the bouquet.

I cock my brow and wait. Her silence sparking a slight shift towards indigestion in my stomach.

I get to my feet and hand her the flowers. "You're overwhelmed. I get it." I press my lips to her cool, clammy cheek. "You're happy, right?"

She doesn't say anything as I lead her to the table and pull out her chair. She's stiff but sits.

"Say something." Maybe she doesn't like the flowers. I picked the most expensive ones. Roses and seven other flower and leaf things that have names I don't know. The fragrance is overwhelming for me, but all women like roses, right? "Is it the flowers?"

She shakes her head like she's in a daze. Then gently lays the bouquet on the table before turning to me.

"Greer, why do you want to get married?" Her brows scrunch as she stares me down.

"It's time. And I'm almost where I need to be with the business. A few more years, and I'll be able to devote more time to family. We've been together for five years, so my parents and your parents expect it."

She stares at me, lips pinched tight before she asks. "What do you think of marriage?"

"Marriage is great. Find someone who ticks all your boxes—which you do, by the way—get married, have children, grow old together."

"What boxes do I tick, Greer?" Her face tightens as she watches me, her thumbs working around themselves.

Odd. She never fidgets. Ever.

"Honestly, I expected you to say yes. We'd eat the dinner, end up in bed, and then start planning a wedding."

She nods, still watching me, her nostrils kind of flaring. "What boxes do I tick, Greer?"

"Are you mad?"

"Kind of. What boxes do I tick?" If her eyes could shoot daggers, they would at this point.

Am I in another dimension? "Why are you mad?"

"I just worked twelve hours on a case I'm losing. I'm hungry and tired, and my feet hurt. And you proposed to me because I *tick all your boxes.*" She uses air quotes with the last part of that.

"I didn't say that. I said I wanted you to be my forever plus one."

"Plus one, the person who makes the party less boring, not the person you love most in the world." She stands and plants her hands on her hips, and sparks almost shoot from her ears.

"Why are you getting so upset? They're words, Nora."

She huffs. "Every woman wants to be proposed to with sweet words. We want to be told how much you love us and that you can't live without us."

What the fuck is going on? Do I need to take cover? I hedge around the love word. "I care for you deeply."

"It's not enough." She shakes her head slightly and crosses her arms over her chest.

"What is that supposed to mean?"

"I want more. I want passion. A life full of travel and adventure. I don't want to stay in Stirling Harbor." Her admission is soft, like I'm a child, and she's trying to break the news to me gently.

"My job is here. I've worked hard to make it successful. I've had my adventures, now I'm ready to settle down and start a family."

She stares at me for a moment, her face paling.

When she breaks the silence, her words are a blow. "I don't want kids, Greer."

I struggle to keep my face neutral. What the actual fuck? "We talked about what we wanted out of life, remember? I said I wanted kids, and you—"

"Do you remember what I said?"

Shit, what did she say? We were at the table, drinking wine and laughing. I said I wanted kids, and she said...

Fuck, I don't remember.

She clears her throat. "I told you I didn't want kids. Ever." She pauses a moment, a pitying look on her face. "Do you remember what you were doing when we had that conversation?"

I remember the laughing, the casual conversation about work, then a design struck, and I grabbed a napkin to draw it out...

Fuck. Gritting my teeth, I swipe my hands through my hair.

When I look up again, she's nodding. "You were drawing something on a napkin. Inspiration, you said. When I asked if you heard me, you said yes. You told me it wasn't a problem."

Her voice softens. "Greer, I care for you, I do. But this"—she waves her hand between us—"isn't working. We want different things."

"You might change your mind."

"Will you change yours?"

I shake my head. I know I won't. I've always wanted a family.

"I won't change mine either. I don't want kids to hold me back and tie me down. I want to buy into my firm one day, have the freedom to get up and go, and do what I want when I want. I can't have that with kids. At least not without some resentment."

"So it's my fault?" Fuck.

"No, we're both to blame. I've been too complacent, and you've been too distracted to wonder how our relationship worked. Your drive for perfection runs as deep as mine. It's hard to balance the careers you and I have and family life."

She stops moving, looks at the table, and then at me. "It never occurred to you why I was okay with you working all the time?"

"No. I figured when it was time, you would slow down and want children."

"Wouldn't you slow down too?"

Something hot and heavy twists in my gut. "No." I'm not sure I can, anyway. I've been so focused on getting this company off the ground that I've done little else.

Been little else.

Needed little else.

Dad provided for us. He built a business from ashes, showing me what it takes. Determination, dedication. Focus.

I've been focused.

She touches my arm, and I look her way. Her mouth parts and her words are soft. "I think it's time we broke up, Greer." The smile she gives me is sad.

The air leaves me in a rush. "I'm sor—"

"Please don't. Neither of us needs to apologize."

"Okay." It still lodges in my throat like I should say it.

"I'll grab a few things now and stop by in a few days to pack up the rest. Do you want to come by my place and grab your things? I don't know that you have much."

It had never occurred to me to bring anything over to her place, so it's probably a toothbrush and a change of clothes. "You can box it up, donate it, whatever you'd like. If I can't remember it, I don't need it."

When she's finished packing things in the bedroom and bathroom, she hugs me tight, her body warm against mine, and kisses my cheek. When she's done she pulls out her keys to give mine back. It jangles as she struggles to get it off the ring.

I reach out to take it, wanting to help, but she pulls back.

She stares me down. "I can do this. You don't need to swoop in and save me like you always do."

I nod and stick my hands in my pockets, giving her space. My palms itch as she struggles to get that fucking key off. I bite my lips and grind my jaw into dust, but she finally does it.

Do I really swoop in and save people like she says?

"Here." Her hand shakes a bit as she slips it into my palm.

"I'm sorry, Nora."

She tilts her head, her brow raised. "Why are you sorry?"

"I feel like I failed you somehow, screwed up this relationship."

Her face softens. "Figure out what's important, Greer. And then give it some of your time." She places her palm on my cheek and leans up to kiss it, her lips warm and smooth.

She pulls away. "You'll be fine. I'll be fine. We'll both move on and find people who make us absolutely dizzy with joy."

"I know you will, Nora. You'll bounce back easy." There is a heaviness in my chest as I let it all settle over me.

"So, when you see me with another man, are you going to fly into a jealous rage?" Her laugh is forced, brittle around us as she tries to lighten the mood.

I drop my head and smile around the tightness in my chest. "I'll lament our breakup for eons. You will be the one that got away. The one I pine after as my old, wrinkly balls shrivel up, and I die a childless, bitter old man."

"Oh god. That's depressing. Promise me something, okay?"

"What's that?"

"When you meet a woman who jolts your whole being into existence, promise me you won't run from it. Give yourself the time you need to get to know her. When you meet her, you'll be so...unsure. But loving her will be the most rewarding thing you ever do."

June

Three

Kit

THE CALI HEAT CAUSES sweat to roll down my back in rivulets. The weather has been cooperating, and this is the perfect time to get down to the shore to hike. I'll finish filling up my gas and get to the shore after my appointment. I need the quiet, the time with nature, so I can work on keeping my emotional shit together. Especially after coloring my hair.

I hold myself back from touching the natural-looking red that now frames my face. It was a huge decision, and my pulse still skyrockets from time to time. But after taking back my name, I needed more.

Now I just need to figure out how to calm the rest of my life.

With my hand on the gas pump, I take in my surroundings. Cars, trucks, kids with surfboards, and a big hulk of a man at the car a few spots over. Usually, I can ignore men, but today, something says to look.

His shaggy chestnut-brown hair brushes his collar. Thick brows and eyelashes set in a square face. He's tall and solid with enormous hands, one of which is flexing as it clenches the pump lever.

Attractive hands. Hands that could own a girl in all the right ways.

He's lost in his own world, his body tight, the shirt a second skin over a taut, muscled body.

My pulse races, and a zing travels up my spine as his hand squeezes the lever again. His hips shift as he disengages the pump, and a shiver runs through me at the sight.

What in the hell was that?

I give myself a little shake, but I don't stop watching him. He looks up, checking out something above me.

Holy shit, who has eyes like that?

Amber. Sinfully delicious.

Butterflies attack my belly. My hand drops from the gas pump. He turns back to his vehicle and twists on his gas cap, then looks back over again, this time his intense dark gaze locks on me. They widen, and his smile hits me smack in the chest. My heart summersalts.

Stop staring, Kit.

What is happening to my body?

He's too beautiful. It makes my insides ache, which hasn't happened in a long time. Heat creeps up my cheeks, and I twist back to my pump. It finally clicks, and I finish up quickly, then head toward the station doors.

I'm escaping; I can't help it at this point.

I reach out to grasp the handle, but an enormous hand gets there first, curling over the bar and pulling it open.

"Let me get that for you. It's a lovely day out, isn't it?"

My heart jumps into my throat. The gravel in his voice ricochets down my back, pinging through my spine as goose bumps scatter along my arms. His northeastern accent rumbles easily, settling deep in the pit of my stomach. Gruff, sharp, fast, and achingly familiar.

I glance up. His irises are my favorite color, with their deep red-brown base and gold flecks. And he's got lashes to die for. Why do men get the double row of long dark lashes? It's not fair.

I slide back so he can go through the door first. But he pulls the door open wide and gestures with an arm for me to step through. "I insist."

Oh, electricity zings down my spine again. His voice lights me up inside, and the intensity of his gaze is way too distracting. And his mouth? Every time he opens it, I stare, waiting for his lips to glisten from the brush of his tongue.

"Really, it's fine." I motion in front of me.

He smiles, his jaw slightly clenched. "My mom taught me to open doors for ladies, so why don't you head in?" His face softens.

My insides do that dropping thing again, and I stand there frozen, waiting for...something. He clears his throat, jarring me from my thoughts, and I step forward and let my weight propel me through the door.

On my second step, my ankle buckles, my foot twisting at the odd angle underneath it. Something hard bumps into me, and I'm knocked off balance.

I tumble toward the pavement, but my descent stops a hairsbreadth from the ground, and I'm jerked up. Heat rushes up my neck, flooding my cheeks.

His hands are strong on my arms as he sets me to rights.

I stare a moment as he watches me until a hint of a smile plays on his lips. Why is he smiling? Oh, he's waiting for me to move. "Shit, I'm so sorry." After a pause, I step away, giving us both some space. Did I step on him? "I'm sorry. Did I hurt you?"

A deep chuckle follows my question. "Nah, a little thing like you can't do too much damage."

I give him a half smile and head to the back.

The refreshment section cools off some of my body as I open a door for something to drink.

Everything in me wants to turn, to look at him again. If I turn back to look, that would make me weird. But I want to know if he's still there. Or interested, and I'm not sure I'm ready for that right now.

I've ignored every man on the planet since Ethan disappeared, so why is he so different?

The intrigue killing me I finally give in and peek over my shoulder, trying to be casual. His gaze meets mine. White-hot heat flows through me, blooming in my cheeks and now my ears. He's coming over. My pulse spikes, and I whirl back to the selection of drinks in the refrigerator.

"Anything worth getting in there?" Those sharp vowels tickle my insides.

Home. He sounds like home.

"Uh, I'm going with water. What about you?" I try to ignore the butterflies flying through my abdomen right now. Men should not look that good.

Why am I doing this? What the hell is wrong with me? I don't flirt, and here I am, looking through my lashes at a stranger.

"Nothing for me. Figured I'd offer you some help if you needed it." He holds out his big hand. "Greer."

Shivers dance along my skin as his fingers close around mine. His nostrils flare, and his pupils widen. As I suck in a much-needed breath, the amber turns molten, like liquid lava flowing in his irises.

"I'm Kit." He's still holding my hand, his thumb brushing back and forth.

All the oxygen has been stolen from the room.

Sparks radiate from that simple touch. He's taking up all the space in the place. It's like his body pulses with an energy all its own, destroying the ambiance in the room and rebuilding it in his favor.

"Is that short for Kitten?"

His voice is delicious. Deep and resonant, it bounces around in my stomach and spreads warmth into places that have been frigid for years. Bypassing his question, I ask my own. "Are you here on business?"

"What gave it away? I thought I fit in pretty well with the long hair." He shoves his hand through it, and it flows around him like a halo before settling. Damn it, even his hair is better than mine.

The smile I'm tightly holding on to slips out, as well as a bit of a laugh. He lets go of my hand, and instantly, I'm sorry we aren't touching anymore.

"You sound like my dad." And Mom and Rosemary and Jack. I shift a little closer.

"Your dad is from the Home of Harbors?" He scoots a smidge closer, too, and my heart beats triple time in my chest.

I haven't heard the nickname for Stirling Harbor in ages. Not that I would have known him in my past life. It's an enormous city with lots of suburbs. "Yeah, thereabouts." Dad and Mom live on the outskirts of Stirling Harbor, but he doesn't need to know that.

"You don't sound like you're from Maine. Did you move here when you were young?"

"Something like that." My phone beeps, pulling my attention from him momentarily. I pull it out of my pocket, glancing at the reminder. *Shit, I'm supposed to see Dr. Willow in thirty minutes.* "I have to get going. It was nice to meet you, Greer."

"It was nice to meet you too."

If he smelled like sea salt and gasoline, he'd be perfect. As deep as I can, I inhale his scent.

Oh. My. God.

He smells better than that. Mint, woods, and desire. What sorcery is this?

He steps closer, slowly crowding into my space.

He's too close now. My pulse races, and my body instantly tightens. A shock of ice moves through my veins.

I'm okay as long as he doesn't crowd me.

He keeps moving like he has no intention of stopping, much like my heart. My pulse has officially taken over as I resist the urge to flee.

Space, I need a bit of space right now.

I frantically search for the door. I need to get out of here. "Well, I hope you enjoy LA. Safe travels."

His brows draw in confusion. "Nice to meet you too, Kit."

I quickly pay and head to my car. Finally alone, I force my tight muscles to relax, then buckle my seatbelt and start the engine. It takes a few minutes for my pulse to settle and the warmth to return to my fingers. Though the energy that radiated off him and the thickness of the air around him lingers.

Shit, he makes me ache for home, makes me yearn for my family. My loneliness here has never been more cemented.

Rat-a-tat-tat.

I jerk. My heart races in my chest when I catch sight of a shadow at my window. The pulse that was normal a moment ago ratchets up again before I look up.

34

It's the amber-eyed Mainer. I can't pull my gaze away. Pretty sure I look like an idiot staring.

He waits...and waits. Smirking, he pantomimes rolling down the window. I slowly put my hand on the button and crack it halfway. Then I stare some more.

He has a straight nose, slightly flaring nostrils, and a firm jawline. Maybe even a dimple on at least one of his bearded cheeks.

"I'm only here for a few more days. Have coffee with me. Show me a mom-and-pop seafood place. We can see if it rivals Maine's lobsters." His smile is sweet, like he's trying to hold back.

"I don't think it's a good idea."

"Are you married?"

I bite my lip. "No." Never again.

"Engaged?"

"Nope."

"Have a boyfriend?"

"Not right now."

He observes me for a moment, the gold flecks changing. "Girlfriend?"

Laughter spills out before I can hold it back. "No. No girlfriend."

"Maybe one day?" The amber sparkles.

"Not for me." I can't help but grin, watching the color of his irises continue to change.

"Then coffee?"

I give him a tight smile and push my hair back behind my ears. "I'm sorry, Greer, but no." I don't know if I'm ready for that or if I'll ever be.

I roll up my window, not waiting for an answer. He steps back, giving his head a small shake and crossing his arms.

Damn, now his muscles are on display. He's a big guy. His shoulders are broad, tapering to narrow hips. He looks edible in his fading gray shirt and loose jeans. Big men aren't all bad, but they are strong. Ethan was strong.

Ethan.

Ice douses my inner joy, and shivers shoot up my spine, but not the good kind.

Belly in knots, I pull out of the parking lot. Greer shows up in my rearview, a pensive look on his face. My attention keeps straying back to him as I drive away. Just as the last of him leaves my view, my heart drops.

Why does leaving him make me hurt?

I'm weird, I know this, but the increase in temperature makes me love my hot tea even more. It makes me think of home. Something I've been doing more and more recently. June is cooler there, and hot tea is something my family drank year-round in Maine. Did Greer get tea at the gas station?

Stop thinking of him.

But he makes me miss home.

I stand at the counter, my cup ready, while my phone blasts out the sultry jazz of Etta James. I can't help but sway my hips a little while I wait for the tea kettle to whistle.

With tea in hand, I sing off-key while picking a book from my mini library. A romance novel I've read a thousand times. I settle on the couch with it while sipping.

How do people live without it? This is the stuff of the gods.

My shoulders have finally relaxed after the first chapter when the phone flashes. I frown but pick up the reciever. "Hello."

"Mrs. Finney, there's a visitor to see you. Should I send them up?"

"Not Colette?"

"No, ma'am."

"I'll come down." A moment later I'm in the elevator. Who would visit me? I reach the first floor, and I step out to find a woman standing at the desk with her back to me. She's carrying a little girl at her hip.

I approach slowly. The woman's hair is blond and long, but I don't recognize her. When I get closer, she turns to look at me.

"Hello, how can I...help you?" Why does she look so familiar? She's the most gorgeous woman I've seen in ages. Her blond hair is silky and straight, just like Ethan forced me to keep mine for years, and her irises are gray. The little girl on her hip has a mess of blond curls, her face hidden against the woman's chest.

"Hi." The woman shifts her child, taking me in.

As silence stretches between us, I try not to show my discomfort. After a moment, I glance over, smiling at the child in her arms. Her little face is still pressed against the woman's body, her cheeks and mouth barely visible. "Can I help you?" I'm repeating myself, but I don't know what else to do.

"I, uh...this is a bad idea. I should go. I'm sorry." The woman makes to leave, her body stiff and her brow furrowed, a tormented look pasted on her face. Her discomfort makes me ache to fix whatever is going wrong. If there is one thing I've held on to in my life with Ethan, it's my compassion and empathy.

I reach out to her, wanting to offer comfort of some sort. "What do you have to be sorry for?"

The woman wavers, her body swaying as she struggles with the child on her hip.

"Why don't we sit down?" I direct her over to the table and chairs in the entryway's café area. "I can get you a tea. Or Coffee?"

"Oh. Yes, please. Coffee. Shoot, you're...nice." The woman whispers the last word, her voice catching as her face falls and tears blur in her gray eyes. "This is so much harder now." She tucks her chin and pinches her nose with her free hand.

37

"You grab a seat, and I'll be right back." I order her a coffee and get myself a decaf tea so I have something to hold on to. Walking back to the table with warm cups, I study her. I know her face, but I can't place her.

Nodding at her drink, I set it in front of her, then sit. "You seem...well, let's start with the simple stuff. I'm Kit."

"I'm Francesca. This is Harper."

She watches me with deep intensity. When I smile, Francesca reaches for the cup with a shaky hand. Okay, a bit weird. But instead of heeding the urge to flee, I sit across from her and force myself to look calm—relaxing my body, crossing my legs, and leaving my arms open.

She angles her head towards Harper. "Is it okay if she uses the table to color? I've brought everything for her."

"Of course. You have a beautiful name, and so does Harper." I wait and smile, watching as her face twists. She shifts on her feet and, eventually, nods to herself.

She hands a coloring book and crayons over to Harper, who hides behind her mop of curls. Grabbing a crayon, the little girl attacks the book with as much enthusiasm as she would a bowl of ice cream. I look back at Francesca, who's sitting on the edge of her seat, her hands twisting in her lap. After a moment or two, she gathers her nerves and looks at me.

"Did Ethan...did he ever mention me?"

I rack my brain. Where would Ethan know her from? My skin prickles, but I shake my head with a frown, studying Harper while she colors. Her characteristics are predominantly her mother's, but there are hints of another face I know well, and it steals my breath. Goose bumps pepper my arms.

She speaks again, pulling my attention back to her. "I don't know how to start. I've rehearsed a thousand times what I would say. I was going to introduce myself in April, but I didn't think it was a good time."

The funeral.

She smiles at me, apology written all over her face. "I was a bartender." She shrugs, her smile sad and tight. "He wore me down. We'd been together two years before I found out he was married, and by then, I was in love...and..."

Francesca raises her head, stricken as she gestures to Harper, who is coloring a picture of a princess in a castle. "He, uh...I'm so sorry." She swipes at the tear running down her cheek. "And when I got pregnant...It wasn't my intention. I wasn't trying to trap him. The birth control failed." Her voice hitches, and she gives up on swiping at the flood of tears falling down her face.

I can't tear myself away from the heartbreak in her eyes as her shoulders shake in silent anguish.

"You were at the funeral." A tiny ball, that's what I want to be right now. Tucked into a void of nothing.

I wrap my arms around myself, blocking the pain radiating off her. My stomach roils as the truth sinks in. I squeeze tighter, fighting off the ache in my heart at seeing Ethan's child.

"Yes, I had to go. I-I know this is hard, but I loved him and had to say goodbye."

Harper looks up, and Ethan peers back at me. Tensing, I brace myself for the glare and condescension that were ever-present in the familiar gaze. But she smiles, her crystal-blue irises warm and sparkly as she tucks her hair behind her ear and focuses back on her book, coloring the princess furiously.

I stare at her a moment, forcing my heart to slow. She's not Ethan. There is goodness and warmth in her.

"No, he never mentioned you." I barely get it out though tightness in my throat, as if his ghost is gripping me around the neck. Did he love Francesca the way he *loved* me?

I can't hold back the pants as I imagine Ethan grabbing her arms, or worse, Harper's. The blood leaves my toes and hands, making them tingle. It travels up my legs and arms as darkness creeps in from my peripheral vision.

My chest locks, and I choke out, "I need a moment."

Without waiting for confirmation, I rush to the bathroom, bracing my hands on the counter as my legs go numb. I lean over, anchoring myself so I won't fall. Ground myself. I breathe in and out to the count of four each.

I'm reflected in the mirror, my pale face, the stalls behind me. The sterile perfume of the soap, and the air freshener. The cool air from the fan above.

It takes a few times, but eventually, my pulse slows, and calmness washes over me. The veil over my vision recedes while feeling returns to my extremities.

Will there ever be a time when I don't have to repeat these techniques over and over before they work?

I take an extra moment to calm myself, splashing my face with cold water before returning to Francesca. She's watching me with concern etched across her brow, her fingers tight and white like she's trying to stop herself from reaching out to me.

I have to know everything. I have to know now so I can process it all, so I can rip it off like a Band-Aid. On shaky legs, I move back to the chair and sit. Please, don't let her have suffered the way I did.

"What was your relationship like?" The threat of nausea churns in my belly, but I press on.

Francesca looks at Harper, lifting her hand to ruffle it through her daughter's curls. Her face softens, and she shines with warmth. "It was perfect. When he found out I was pregnant, he was so happy." She glances at me, that apology on her face again, the words on her lips.

I wave her off as I shake my head, signaling to go on.

"He doted on me. We were in bliss for months. I kept waiting for him to ask me to marry him. He never did, so one day, I asked him. He said no, obviously. I was furious, heartbroken. I stopped seeing him for a while, but I loved him. I wanted to be with him. I wanted Harper to know her father."

She clears her throat, a red flush painting her cheeks. "Do you have any pictures of him I could have? I have one, but nothing from his childhood or before we met. I'd like her to have photos of her father."

Well. That is not what I was expecting.

I look at the table, giving myself a minute. All the sensations amp up, my heart rate, the suffocation, they all fight to break through again, making it a struggle to get enough air.

Focus, Kit. Focus on the breaths.

What if he put his hands on her?

Don't think about it.

Ground yourself.

"I know it's a lot to ask."

I hold my hand out, needing another moment to collect myself. When the pain and constriction in my chest ease, I look at Harper.

I love children. That they would be a part of my life was a given. I've always imagined my life with a handful of my own. Blaming her for what someone else did is pointless. Ethan cheated them out of a normal life as much as he cheated me.

But why? Why did he stay with me if he was so in love with her? So happy?

It's something I'll never have answers to. If I let it, the whys will suck me down into a murky pit that sinks every piece of my soul. So, I tuck it away to review later.

"When was she born?"

"November third. She'll be three then. She has so much of her father—his eyes, the long middle toe, the goofy hiker's thumb." Her voice trills while looking at Harper.

Her brows shoot up, and her face falls before the color leaves her cheeks. Bringing her hands up to her mouth, she whispers, "I'm sorry, so sorry...I'm so insensitive. Here I am talking about our child, and this is...this is..."

"Yeah, this is difficult." I don't know her. She doesn't need to know any of my personal stuff. The terror, the pleas, my deepest secrets.

I reach for my teacup and sip the warm liquid. It becomes my shield, bracing me for the hurt, the ache deep inside from knowing that I can't have children. Is that what made us different?

The sharp pang of agony returns, hitting me deep in the gut.

And this woman? She's so bubbly, bright, and radiates joy. Could Ethan have treated her differently?

My stomach rebels, but I force myself to ask. "Did he ever hurt you?"

Something like pain flashes across her face, fierce and fleeting. Then she pales and paints a happy mask on. "No. Never. He was a good man."

Ice pours through my veins. *Lie.*

He hurt her, and even though he's gone, she's still lying for him. The way she recovers quickly, and the smile that paints her face, still bright and joyful, tells me it probably wasn't more than a few times. Once, maybe? "Are you okay?"

"What? Yes, of course. I'm fine." She smiles at me again. "He never hurt me." She ducks her head, taking a sip of her coffee. "He even took me to meet his mom. When she found out I was pregnant—"

"You met Colette while Ethan was alive?" I set my cup on the table and lean forward in my chair. Furrowing my brow, I stare at her, my mouth open like a fish out of water, gasping for air.

"Her and Ethan's brother. Neither introduction went well."

"What?" Ethan didn't have a brother.

"You didn't know about him?"

I shake my head as my body curls in on itself. "No, he never mentioned a brother."

What. The. Fuck?

Ethan probably didn't think I was worthy of knowing. Then again, I never knew about his affair. Or where he was every night.

"I didn't know they were brothers until Ethan pulled him away from me one night. I was tending bar, and he came in. He flirted with me, then touched my back, and Ethan was outraged."

"I can't wrap my head around all of this. Ethan has a brother." The brother, the affair, and all the lies are bubbling, building. I swallow against the crushing sensation in my chest, forcing it back down.

"I met him for two minutes before Ethan pushed him out of the bar, and then I never saw him again. Dougan, Mitchell, Nigel...something old like that. I don't remember."

But having a brother is significant, whether or not she thinks it is.

What other secrets did he keep from me?

Francesca touches my arm. "This is a lot to take in. Me, my daughter, and now a brother. I'm so sorry."

I nod, frowning. It is, and I need a moment to digest everything. My body tightens, my chest caving in as I twist my hands together.

When I can breathe without pain and think without the ache, I look at her, ready to hear the rest. "What happened when you met Colette?"

Francesca's lips tighten at the corner, her voice dropping as she focuses on the tabletop in front of her. "She didn't acknowledge me. She kicked me out of her house and told Ethan to 'get rid of it.' He was livid until she mentioned you. His demeanor changed, and he screamed something that made little sense to me. Still doesn't."

At this point, I'm not sure what anything means anymore. My world is upside down. I'm on the verge of needing some sort of medical intervention if my lungs seize one more time.

Ethan had a brother, and Colette lied to me. For years. Damn it. My heart spasms, breaking a bit.

Colette's all I have left, and she didn't tell me. "What did he say?"

"He told his mom it was so 'We could be a family.'"

What in the world? I shake my head, my brows knitting. "I have no idea what that means."

She nods. "I wasn't sure you would. Was he introducing me to his mom so we could be a family? But then what about you? I'll never have answers. I never saw her again, and he refused to talk about it."

"Colette has a deeply ingrained sense of social propriety. An affair would have changed her social standing. Although, I don't know how, since everyone has affairs in their group. Not that I agree with how she treated you. But keeping up with appearances is everything to her."

And maybe I can give her something to keep her happy memories alive. It's not much, but if she wants the photos, she can have them.

I pat her hand and then stand.

"I have pictures. Let me round some up, and I'll give them to you."

July

Four

Kit

ETHAN'S STEPS SOUND BEHIND me as I stand at the granite counter, cutting vegetables for our salad. Sweat drips down my face from the California heat. Raising my knife hand, I brush at the moisture with my sleeve. Hair flops in my face, and I push at it, wincing as my bruised wrist presses against my hairline.

I keep my head down as he presses close. He sets his arms around me, caging me against the countertop. The white lilies held in his right hand, his fist still wrapped around them, settle.

He brought me lilies.

I tense when he leans in close, breathing me in, pressing his body against mine. His lips touch the base of my neck.

A heavy sigh brushes against my ear. He wraps himself around me—his left hand on my hip and his right around my chest, settling on my breast. Then he licks below my ear, making me shiver.

"I got carried away, Katherine. You're too beautiful. The thought of someone else flirting with you, touching what's mine, makes me crazy." He nuzzles my ear, and my body coils tighter. His lips shift against my neck in what I assume is a smile. "Put your lilies in water."

I swallow as he massages my breast, goose bumps forming along my arms. His hand roughens. My stomach clenches. I fight against nausea, knowing what's coming. "We'll save dinner for later. Come to bed."

I hate that memory. It wakes me up most nights, but I'm fighting my way through the agony of it. It's getting better, but since the gas station incident, it replays more and more. Which is why I'm sitting in Dr. Willow's lobby, waiting for her door to open.

"Kit, please come in." Dr. Willow gestures me into the room, and I settle into my favorite spot. When I look up, she's smiling, her expression bright. "I still love the red." She points to my hair.

I touch the waves and give her a half smile.

She nods, moving to her spot. "I saw you were penciled in today. What brings you an extra day this week?"

Finally, a place where my racing mind can calm. Ever since the day at the gas station, all I've been thinking about is returning to Maine and Greer. I can go home. There is nothing for me here anymore.

"I'm on edge. Like there's something trying to rise to the surface to get out." I frown and press my fingers to my temples, rubbing gently. "The nightmares are worse." Is it because of Greer? I force my hands down, letting my leg bob as I wait for her to respond.

"What's happened since our last visit?"

So much. "I had a visitor at the house. Ethan's mistress."

Dr. Willow gasps. "What an asshole." Her voice is sharp and excited, bouncing around the room.

My laughter spills free. And I can't stop it. It's bubbling out of me like a fountain without end.

"I'm so sorry. I can usually keep it together. Please forgive me." She frowns before her face softens. "That was so inappropriate."

I force my muscles to relax, trying to stem my laughter, and swipe at the tickle on my cheeks. They're wet? I pull my hand back and rub the wetness that coats my fingertips. I'm crying? Why now? I haven't cried in ages.

I shut her out for a moment, scrunching my lids as another round plops down my cheeks while my heart drops into my stomach.

And whatever barrier I built to hold back my emotions unleashes.

A sob radiates up from my toes, shaking every part of me. I'm leaking like a sieve. Every single painful memory slides down my cheek, one tear at a time.

She touches my arm, and I jump, peering up to find Dr. Willow in my space.

"I can't stop it." I gasp between snot, tears, and trembles.

"Oh, Kit. Can I break protocol and hug you?"

I nod, aching with the need to be held.

She envelops me in warmth, holding me close. It almost hurts. My lungs ache, my arms twitch, and I want to shove her off me, but I force it down and make myself lean into her embrace.

Her hold is fierce and tight and firm, and it's been so long since I've been touched like this. I've missed the genuine affection of hugs. And I take it all, closing my eyes and letting the warmth fill me.

After some time, my sobs cease, and I move out of her arms and wipe the tears. I take a deep breath in, then blow it out, letting my body calm down and cool off.

"Welcome back." The lyrical and soothing quality of Dr. Willow's voice settles into my bones and roots me in peace.

She puts a tissue in my hand and scurries back, giving me the space I usually ask for.

"Tell me what brought that on." She grabs her notebook again.

"You were so honest in your response. I couldn't stop the laughter, and then I was crying. I'm not sure why it started, but I haven't laughed—or cried—like that in years."

"It was an emotional release caused by cortisol and adrenaline. When you're under high amounts of stress, high levels of the chemicals are produced. You've lived in a state of constant cortisol and adrenaline, which is normal for patients with PTSD. Laughing releases the hormones, as well as crying. Because your body was releasing stress, it sought the release that would unload the greatest number of hormones. In your case, crying."

"Thank god I can understand that." I laugh again, my body filling with warmth.

"And how do you feel now?"

I take inventory. The muscles in my shoulders are less tense. My body isn't primed to run. "Lighter. I'm not as drained."

She nods and smiles. "Good. Anything else happen in the last few weeks?"

I study my hands. What a question. Where do I even begin? I met Francesca, and I'm still unsure what to make of her. And Colette asked me to move in with her. The sadness that lingered on her face when I said no surprised me.

"Colette thought I was moving in with her. I'm not, but I feel bad about it. She's so sad." I try to ignore the pang in my chest. "I talked to a coworker about having her wife take me to the gun range. We've been practicing once a week. I'm finally getting comfortable holding it. I know it's weird, but I want to feel safe."

Looking at the floor, I bite my lip. I want to tell her about the man at the gas station who's been a prominent subject in my thoughts. The timbre of his voice flows through my head, warming up my body.

Shivers fill me when I think of his thumb moving over my hand. "I feel stagnant, stuck here. I've been agonizing for weeks about the possibility of going home. I've been waiting for the world to give me a sign, and I think it finally has."

She perks up. "Tell me about that."

"When I was pumping gas last week, there was a Mainer there. Hearing his accent, being near him, reminded me of home. Then later, he reminded me of Ethan."

"What about him did that?"

"He had this presence that ate up the energy in the room, larger than life. I panicked a bit when he got close to me. Probably looked like an idiot when I basically ran out of the store." Shit, I'm rambling. *Shut up, Kit.*

"You seem to be attracted to this type of guy."

"No. No way. I'm not looking for a relationship. I—"

"I don't mean him specifically. But his type of energy."

She waits, letting the silence in the room eat away at my psyche until it all bursts out.

"His energy, his build, his confidence, it all made my body tense. But then, when I think of him, his gruff talk and brusque nature, my whole body heats up, and I get a bit breathless. By no means am I ready to date again, but he makes me think of things I haven't thought of in a long time. He makes me feel warm."

"Is fear of him or what he represents?"

"What do you mean?"

"You have two responses when you think of him. Fear and attraction."

"It's what he represents." I chew on my lip again, fiddling with my fingers in my lap.

"What does he represent, Kit?"

"Power, dominance, another person controlling my life."

"What about the other part of it?"

"He makes me long for home." I swallow past the lump in my throat. If I don't leave California soon, I'll die here. There is nothing left of the woman I was in this shell of a body. If I stay, anything I am now will be sucked out of me, brittle and broken.

I'm shattered and cracked, but I'm putting my life back together with hope. Kind of like kintsugi, where the pieces of broken pottery get glued back together and painted with gold.

Kintsugi is beautiful, whereas I'm tattered and torn. My edges don't mesh completely. But perhaps by going home, I can learn to be whole again.

"Kit, you're strong. You can move on."

"I'm scared shitless." Goose bumps scatter down my arms, and I stare at the floor.

"Hmm." She waits, letting me work through my anxiety on my own. I need to. She could do it for me, but if I go home, she won't be there to help me.

"I'm scared I'm not strong enough to do this. I want to go home. Mom and Dad's voices ring through my head. Rosemary flits through my mind. Jack is like a distant memory. He was a kid when I left home."

Shaking out my hands, I focus on the rug design.

"I ache to be with them. I'm barely living because of the anxiety attacks and nightmares choking me awake each night. And I'm sick of being terrified he's going to come back."

I sigh, leaning forward again, adrenaline running through me. The surging energy moves through my legs, making them bob, and I plant my hand on them to keep them still. How can Dr. Willow watch me so calmly when I want to jump out of my skin?

She leans forward. "Kit."

I take a moment before raising my gaze to Dr. Willow's. She's so close to my space. Filling me with brightness that I long to have all the time.

"You are strong enough. You prove it every day and will continue to do so with all the decisions you'll make on your own." Her voice is so melodic and smooth as she poses herself in a way for me to copy—arms loose, hands clasped gently, breathing slowly in and out. She's calm and peaceful.

It'll take a while, but I know I can get there.

She breaks the quiet with her soft voice. "What are you going to do first?"

I don't know. What is there for me here?

Nothing.

Colette. Francesca and Harper? If I'm honest with myself, I don't want to be anywhere near them right now. At least back home, I have people who know and love me.

I can get to know people again and find friends.

Greer's image pops into my mind, but I black him out, focusing on Dr. Willow.

I exhale, holding her gaze, gluing together broken pieces with first binding of gold. "I'm moving home. I'm leaving the house and most everything in it and going back to Stirling Harbor."

She watches me, intent but smiling. She nods gently. "Why?"

"Because when I find myself again, I want to do it without being haunted by my past."

Five

Kit

M<small>Y PALMS ARE SWEATY</small> as I stand on the doorstep of 413 Cherry Lane, Stirling Harbor, Maine. Mom and Dad's home, or what I hope is still their home. I had forgotten how cool July could be in Maine, but the moment I hit the border, the memories all came flooding back.

The last time I saw them, they saw the fresh bruises and the old ones. They fought to stay in my life, and I shoved them away. Pushed them out to keep them safe. The knot in my belly twists, growing, pushing until there is a lump in my throat.

I press the doorbell and hold my stomach, willing it to keep from expelling my dinner.

There is a rush on the other side of the door, and then it's thrown open. "Katherine?" My dad's deep timbre is whisper-soft in the night but harsh enough to make the crickets stop. "Oh, Kit, baby."

His image blurs as I stand there. He pulls me into him, and I stiffen as he holds me. It's stifling, but I force myself to bring my hands up to wrap around him. It's a lot easier to do than I thought it would be.

Trembles rack against me. He's shaking. My dad is shaking. I frown, pinching back pain as a ball of nausea forms in my belly.

He missed me.

Even if he never says it, it's right here in his arms, in his cheek against my head.

"Sue, love, Kit's here."

Dad's familiar scent hits me, and I draw it in, letting it melt into my arms and legs and ground me in security I haven't felt in ages.

"Harvey, what's—" Mom gasps behind us, and he keeps his arms around me as he waddles us inside the house so she can shut the door.

Tears want to fall, but I blink them away.

My mom's warm fingers lace through mine, fully cementing that I'm loved and safe, even after abandoning them years ago. Then she surrounds me, her body pressing against my back as my dad continues to hold on to me.

It's almost too much, but I latch on to it and tuck it deep into my soul so I can bring it back any time I feel alone or afraid or lost.

After several long moments, they both back up, giving me a bit of space at the right time.

I forgot how in sync they were with me. It's no wonder my mom's face fell when I lied years ago. They knew without a doubt that something was wrong.

My mom still holds my hand, and I want to squeeze back and then drop it, but I force myself to keep it, to feel the tension coiling until it doesn't anymore. Once I reach that point it doesn't physically hurt and I can breathe again without forcing it.

"Are you hungry? Do you want something to eat? I've got roast." Mom babbles beside me and I don't even try to hold back the soft chuckle. She hesitates and then smiles her guarded smile.

My body aches with the knowledge that I did this to them—caused them to be on edge and wary around me.

"How long was your drive, kiddo?"

I glance at Dad. His eyes shine with unshed tears, making me choke up a bit. I hold it back, forcing the blinks that'll take them away. "Somewhere around forty-five hours, give or take."

"Is it just you?" Mom squeezes my hand along with her husky words.

Holy shit, they don't know what happened.

I nod as we head into the living room. The house looks the same as it did when I left for California. The walls are white, pristine, with the TV in the center of the far wall. The same curtains drape at the windows. Pictures of events I wasn't a part of hang throughout.

The furniture is new but similar to the style my parents owned the last time I was here.

Our silence is loud in the room. As we sit, our hands part, and thousands of questions dance in the air between us. I can answer one, at least.

"He's dead." I think.

I'm still not entirely sure what happened to him.

Their mouths flop open and closed like fish gasping for air. My mom looks at my dad, and they both have the same expression on their face—*shock.*

After several moments where my parents do their best to hide their relief, my father speaks. "We're happy you're here. We've kept your room the same if you'd like to stay."

"I'd love to stay." It's silent again, the thickness in the room increasing with each passing moment.

The clock ticks.

The refrigerator knocks.

"When, uh, when did he die?" Mom asks, tucking her hands under her thighs like she's restraining herself.

I can see it on her face. She wants to grab me and never let go. I kind of want that, too, even if hugs make my skin crawl sometimes. More than anything, though? I'm tired. "November, almost three years ago. He went missing and hasn't returned."

The surprise on their faces is telling, and now their wheels are spinning, surely wondering what I've been doing since then.

"I'm sorry. I hope it's okay that I showed up. I should have called first." My stomach is in knots, twisting, churning, and the acid's still burning in my throat.

It's been so long since I've seen my parents. Maybe I don't know them like I thought I did. They are treading on eggshells, making sure they say nothing that will scare me away. The indecision lingers in the tension of their shoulders, the way my mom bites the inside of her cheek. In the set of their mouths and how they grip each other's hands so tight they're almost white.

I've caused them anguish, and they worry I'll do it again. That I've popped into their life only to disappear again.

"Always, baby. This is still your home. This is always a safe place for you."

I smile at that. Safe. I don't know if I'll ever be safe again, but I'm going to try.

"Is it okay if I grab my bag and freshen up? Then we can chat. I can't promise to answer all your questions, but I'll do my best."

Mom nods while Dad stands and heads toward the door. He stops, turning to us. "I'll get your bags. Will you be staying long?" There's an edge to his voice, the question hesitant.

I study him as he watches me. His face is the same it's always been, but now with crinkles from laughter or stress. Hard to know at this point. But he has aged.

"I'm staying indefinitely."

My mother laugh-gasps. Tears pooling, she smiles at me. I smile back. Then she's on me, her arms open, pulling me in as she squeezes me with all her strength. Something hot and wet hits my shoulder as she lays her cheek against mine.

Her silent sobbing slays me, opening something that makes my own tears flow. I held on to them for so long, but now I welcome the release. It's a while before we let go long enough for her to wipe away my tears.

"I have missed you so much, Kit-Kat." And with that, I know I'm home.

No matter what happens, no matter what comes, I can manage because Mom and Dad haven't changed.

"Give me your keys, baby girl. I'll put your bags in your room."

"I'll make tea. Green?"

"Decaf?"

"Always."

I walk around the living room when they disappear, taking in all the pictures. Rosemary got married at some point, and I missed it. Either she didn't send an invitation, or—most likely—it was another thing Ethan kept from me.

The tea kettle whistles, and the clinking of mugs chimes from the kitchen. I head that way, still looking at pictures.

"What are Rosemary and Jack doing now?" There are pictures of each of their college graduations on the wall near the kitchen.

"Rosemary is teaching second grade. I'm teaching fourth this year. We're both at your old elementary."

I nod, taking the cup that Mom holds out to me.

Dad grunts, carrying my bag through the door, its wheels banging against the floor. He winks at me when he walks past before a gigantic smile takes over his face on his way up the stairs to my bedroom. Warmth blooms under my breastbone. My bedroom is in the same spot, second floor, third room on the right.

Will the posters on the wall up there still be the same?

I watch Mom through the steam from my cup as she continues talking. "Jack got into NYU, and he's studying for his bar exam in Vermont. I keep hoping he'll meet someone. Well, you don't need to know that."

"I want to know that." I smile at her, and her face softens, gifting me with the brilliance of her happiness.

"Well, he's been up there for a year now. Rosemary is doing great, married an incredible man named Angelo. They have two kids. The youngest is just over a year now. They are beautiful."

She sits at the table, and I follow suit; then she asks, "Are you hungry, love?"

"No. I kind of lost my appetite on the way over."

"Nerves?"

I chuckle and nod. I sip my tea as Dad tromps back down the stairs then sits beside me, grabbing my free hand.

"Rosemary is going to be so happy you're home."

I hope so. She could be angry with me for abandoning her. Maybe when she learns why, she'll forgive me.

"I'm happy to be home."

"Kit, what happened?" Mom turns serious but sad.

"He traveled overseas for a work meeting and never returned. When Colette searched, we found nothing."

"Are you...happy he died?" Dad's voice is deep, the sound settling into my soul.

"Yeah, I am."

"I'm so sorry, baby. I'm so sorry we didn't save you."

They are sorry? I'm the one who picks shitty people to love. "I should be sorry. Every time you reached out, every time you called, I pushed you away. I wanted to keep you safe. I tried to leave Ethan many times, but when the pain didn't stop me, he threatened to kill you."

My mom puts a hand to her mouth, nodding.

My father bows his head before meeting my gaze. "He couldn't have hurt us, love."

I shake my head, raising my brows, imploring them to understand. They have no idea the type of man he was. "Yes, he could have. You don't know what he was capable of."

"Will you tell us?"

It's an opening, one that could allow me to unleash everything. But their utter faith in my ability to heal chokes me. It grips my throat like an invisible hand, subtly clenching, twisting, locking everything down.

"Maybe." One day, years from now when I know I'm safe.

They look at each other, and Mom reaches for my other hand. "Why didn't you come back?"

"It never felt safe." It still doesn't.

August

Six

Greer

I'VE BEEN BACK IN Stirling Harbor for months, and that woman keeps playing in my mind. It wasn't the red hair and freckles or the green eyes and subtle curves. No, when I shook her hand, my whole body lit up in a way I've never felt before.

I went back to the gas station a few times, but I never saw her again. Los Angeles is an enormous city, so going back was useless. And I only know her first name, nothing else.

A week in California, a week at that gas station, a week of agonizing about whether she'd be there. And here I am, still stuck on a woman I'll never see again.

"Violet, grab the salads and put them on the table out back." Mom orders from the kitchen.

I glance at her, forcing thoughts of Kit out of my mind. It's something I've been doing more often lately—pushing away thoughts of her. Focusing has become almost impossible, and my work is struggling because of it.

Stop thinking about her. Focus on what's happening here and now. Like Violet and Mom.

Violet must be around here somewhere. She's Mom's clone, down to the mothering and sassy attitude. My baby sister grew up when I wasn't looking. So did the rest of my family, if the noise is any indication.

It's already chaos out here, and a headache is on the horizon. I pinch the bridge of my nose to ward it off and scan the people around us.

Violet sashays in, happiness flitting around her like she's having a wonderful time. Simon grabs two beers from the fridge. She blows us each a kiss before scooting out the door with salads in hand.

"Have you been on any dates since Nora?"

"No." Only one woman has interested me.

"Are you losing your charm?" Simon winks at me, so I give him a half grin and shake my head. "What about the supply lady? She was flirting with you pretty hard the other day. What happened there?"

"Nothing."

"Nothing?"

"There is nothing to tell." I grind my teeth, ignoring Simon's amused expression.

He arches a brow at me. "Yeah, I can see that. You've been an even bigger dick lately. What is with you?"

"Not a damn thing, Simon. Leave it alone."

"Okay." He gives me the eye and then pointedly leaves while I stand here like an asshole.

What *is* with me?

The Richards project was two weeks late, and that never happens. I had everything to finish the piece, but I sat on it. I'd start working, then Kit would pop into my brain, and I'd be lost for an hour. That shit's been happening over and over. Something red will flash in my vision, and I think about her hair. Or someone makes a joke, and I wonder if it would make her laugh.

I've spent more time working out, trying to get rid of the energy flowing through me, than is probably normal for a person. My sixty-minute workouts have stretched to two, sometimes three hours. What I need to do is get everything back into perspective. Retrain my brain to concentrate on what is in front of me. Pull it away from Kit.

Fuck, there I go again. I force her out of my brain and look around the yard.

Maddox and Troy are deep in conversation, with Maddox doing most of the talking. Troy's grunts are occasionally heard through everyone else's laughter.

Dad is still at the grill. Mom and Violet are setting the table, while Asher and Han look at something on Asher's computer.

I head over to Dad.

"Hey, bud. How are things?" He flips a burger, rotates the hot dogs and brats, and closes the lid.

"Same as always." Restless. I scrub my hand down the back of my neck, trying to dispel some of that energy.

We stand quietly, me sipping my beer while dad drinks from a mug he's got sitting on the table next to the grill. Dad puts his hand on my shoulder, squeezing to get my attention, and I turn to him with a small smile. He studies me for a moment before frowning.

I know what he's going to ask and point to the burgers to distract him. "Almost ready?"

He squints at me, deciphering my comment. When he frowns again, I know I've dodged a bullet. "A few more minutes and they'll be done. You want to let your mom know?"

I head off to the big table set up on the lawn, knowing he was going to ask if I was okay.

I'm fucking fine, people.

I head towards mom. "We're almost ready for the meat, Mom."

"Excellent. Boys. Sit, Greer. I'll help your dad."

Everyone crowds around the table, their chatter loud in my ear. It's hard to believe it's been two years since Han and Troy joined our group, but they fit in pretty well with us as honorary brothers. They round out our family.

"I'm so glad you came tonight, Greer." Mom leans in close and kisses my head before sitting. "What's new? Tell me everything."

Everything? Yeah, I don't think so. "The same old stuff, Mom. Working on designs, Simon works on everything else. Living."

Simon sets his beer down. "Sure, and being a huge asshole while you do it."

"Language." Mom chastices at him.

Thank you, Simon. "I'm not an asshole."

Violet pokes my side.

I hold back a growl. "What gives?"

She smiles brightly. "I wanted to see if it's true. You usually hug me or laugh it off when I mess with you. Yup, more assholeish."

"That's not even a word. I'm sorry if I don't share every piece of my life with you all, but that doesn't make me an asshole."

"Oh my goodness, people, language." Mom glares at me before plopping a huge scoop of potato salad on my plate.

"Why am I the only one in trouble for language?" Jesus Christ.

"Is it Nora? Are you wanting to get back together?"

"No." Fuck, I don't want to discuss any of this in front of everyone.

"Thank god."

I'm not sure who said that, but it sure as shit doesn't bode well. "What was wrong with Nora?"

Violet leans close. "Nothing. But there was no angst or passion between the two of you."

"I'm done talking. Let's move on to something else."

Dad clears his throat and changes the subject. "How was the trip to California?"

"Fine until I met Kit, and then—" It slips out before I can stop her name.

"Who's Kit?" Violet questions.

Fuck. Why is the world revolving around me today? "No one." But that isn't true.

Kit was beautiful, with a sweet, husky laugh. And the glimmer in those greens. I don't know why, but I was pulled to her the second I saw her.

Violet points her fork at my chest, scrutinizing me. "You can't say it's no one and then make faces like that."

"I'm not making a face." I scowl at her, trying to ignore the goose bumps scattering along my arms and legs. Was I making a face?

"So who was she?"

"I'm not talking about this."

Simon scowls. "Someone special, maybe?" He quirks a brow at me while he shoves pasta salad in his mouth.

I grind my teeth and give him the death stare.

She could have been special. I wish I'd gotten the chance to know her.

"Hah! There's the look again." Simon winks as potatos make their way around his words.

"Shut it, Simon." I pull my hand down my face, trying to erase whatever they think they see.

Nothing. They see nothing.

Turning to Mom, I change the topic. "Any word on Harrison?"

She smiles, wistful. I'd feel guilty at triggering a heart-wrenching moment for her, but desperate times and all. "Maybe another year or two, and he'll be up for parole. Haven't heard anything else yet. We'll go see him in a few weeks."

From there, the topic bounces, mostly staying in safe territory. Once in a while, it moves back to me, but I bark out a response, and they let it go somewhere else.

The condensation builds on the outside of my beer bottle, the droplets like magnets—connecting, moving, joining into big fat blobs that fall down the glass. Hooking my thumbnail under the label, I pick at it.

Violet pulls the bottle out of my hands, her fingernails flicking against the pieces that have peeled off. "Stop fidgeting. Your leg is shaking the table so bad my water is almost sloshing up the side." She sets the beer back down and scrutinizes me.

"Sorry."

"You know you can tell us what's going on." They are all so open with each other, it's no surprise that she pushes.

Eight pairs of eyes look in my direction. Except Theo, who is inhaling a hotdog. I point to him. "Someone should cut that up. He's going to choke."

Simon reaches over and pulls the hot dog out of Theo's hands.

"Is it Nora?"

No, it's never Nora. "I'm fine."

I honestly don't miss Nora. I never worried about what she was thinking. If she had a girls' night out, it was okay. And if she didn't want to do what I was doing, we did our own thing.

Maybe I wasn't as invested in her as I thought I was.

I didn't want to know her the way I wanted to know Kit. I want to make her smile again, hear her laughter, see what makes her tick.

I want to know *her*.

"There it is again. Are you okay?"

I push back from the table, the scrape of my chair harsh on the cobblestone. "I don't know what you don't get about 'I'm fine.' But I am. So leave me the fuck alone."

I storm into the kitchen, aiming to grab another drink.

I back out of the fridge slowly, clutching the beer, when someone taps me on the shoulder. Simon grabs the bottle and pops the lid with the tool on the counter before handing it back.

"We didn't mean to push out there. I know you deal with things your own way, but when you are ready, I'm here. I'll listen."

Would another "I'm fine" be too much at this point? I purse my lips, fighting off the itch to grind my teeth.

"Thanks."

September

Seven

Kit

ROSEMARY'S COUNTER IS COLD against my palms as I lean against it, ignoring the loud thud of the knife as she chops veggies.

"Thanks for helping me pick stuff out for the new house." I grin. I own my home, paid for it outright, and only my name is on the deed. Something I never dreamed I'd do.

"Anything for my baby sister. Did they say when it would be delivered?" She dumps all the veggies into the pot of homemade spaghetti sauce.

"A week tops. I can't wait to get my room set up and live in my own place."

"You know you could have stayed with us, right?" Mom sets a pot to boil for the noodles.

"I know. But I need to do things for myself. It's been challenging, but it feels good. Even if my demons want me to live under the covers in my old room."

Mom squeezes me, her affection soothing. Every hug, every interaction, puts me more and more at ease. Almost two months, and I don't tense when they touch me or knock on the door or when they come into my vision.

I only needed two of Ethan's punches out of nowhere to get fidgety with random people coming from out of my line of site.

Everything is getting easier, but it would be so much better without the nightmares. I've woken up to Mom and Dad running into my room on more than one occasion, scaring them and myself.

"How have your nightmares been?" Mom gestures to the table, handing me plates.

"Better, actually. I think it's because I'm making my own decisions and doing things for myself. I'm managing the anxiety that accompanies each new adventure and working myself around it until I can get through it."

When they stay silent, I look over. Mom's face falls. Rosemary has her hand to her mouth. Mom slips around the counter, touching my arm. "It was that terrible?"

Dr. Willow said I need to let people in—tell them what happened so I can share the burden and heal myself.

I've had no one to depend on but myself for years, so opening up is hard. I especially hate the idea of letting them into the darkness of my old world. But it's time to let someone in. I don't have to tell them everything, but I can start with a few things.

"Yes, it was." I walk around the table, placing silverware.

Rosemary's strong arms circle me, and I tense for one moment before forcing myself to relax. I turn, wrap my arms around her waist, and lean my head on her shoulder. My mom's warm body presses against the length of my back as her arms wrap around me too.

"We're happy to listen if you want to tell us."

When we let go, losing their warmth is a bit jarring, as if my body's already forgetting what it's like. Placing everything on the table, I head to the couch on the other side of the room. "If I tell you, you can't tell Dad. I'm not ready for him to know yet."

How do I even start this? I stare at my hands, pulling courage from the pit of my stomach. Mom's hand settles on top of one of mine, squeezing assurance. Rosemary does the same to my other hand.

And I hold on tight.

"It started out wonderful. He was great." I tell them about how we met and how fooled I was. "Now I know it wasn't love. I was infatuated with him." I chew on my bottom lip.

Rosemary moves closer, her knees bumping into mine as she shifts.

"I didn't know how jealous he could be." At first, I thought jealousy was romantic and meant he loved me. But he was never in love with me. I was a possession, and he wasn't afraid to show the world who owned me. He knew how I should act, talk, and what I should wear. If I didn't do what he wanted, there were punishments.

Swallowing, I twirl my thumbs around each other. "Somewhere in there, I lost myself. What is so weird is that he actually loved someone else and had a child with her."

I glance up, staring anywhere but at my family. I'm too raw to look at their faces.

To see their shame.

I force past the lump in my throat. "The first year wasn't bad. In the second year, I learned to control wrong behavior. In the third year, I was terrified. He thrived on it, and I couldn't hide it." I slump forward, too exhausted to hold myself up.

Someone's hand brushes down my hair. I'm guessing it's Mom's. Over and over, it strokes, soothing me from the outside in.

"Kit?"

"I don't know if I can, Mom. It aches to think of what I lost." My abdomen clenches, nausea rolling deep in my belly. I suck in a deep breath, trying to settle my stomach.

"Hey, shhh, it's okay. It's all right, Kit-Kat. You don't have to talk about it now."

I can't stop the shakes or the tears from dropping. Trying to hide the sobs is useless. Still, I push a hand to my mouth. "I think I do." I gulp, wrapping my arms around myself and rocking back and forth. Then I force everything out, squeezing my eyes shut.

"It was hell. Think of hell and multiply that by a hundred. I learned to tiptoe around him, focusing on never setting him off. I didn't speak right or wear the right clothes. He wanted a trophy wife, and I lost forty pounds to be it. He plied me with beautiful intents and then molded me into something dark and twisted."

It's easier to let everything out than I ever imagined. I stuffed it all down for years, but tonight it pours out like muddy water. Even talking about Francesca and Colette.

"Kit, I don't know what to say. I hate that you suffered through it all alone." Rosemary's whisper fills the room.

It's hard, but I fight the urge to tell them about the hitting, scratching, hair pulling, biting, punching, and name-calling.

The rape.

They'll never see how he tore me down, piece by piece, until I was battered and bruised, and then rebuilt me in the image he wanted. Bloody but perfect—bloody perfect.

They'll never see the hours I spent on a treadmill or the way I counted every calorie. How I wasted my college education so I could do what he told me to.

I don't want them to see me almost broken. I want them to see me as strong, fierce, and independent—all the things I'm trying to be.

See me for the woman I am. Not the person Francesca and Colette will always remember—the quiet, submissive, cracked, bruised shell of a wife.

My family can see me healed.

I force my pulse to slow. "The weird part? He actually loved her. It wasn't about possession with her. I could see it on her face. She was happy with him. If he didn't want me, why wouldn't he let me go?"

I glance at my mom. She's so gentle, always so soft. Her brows are knitted together. Love shines from her as she holds out her hand for me again. I grab it, anchoring myself to her, to love. "What made him treat me like that?"

"Kit." Rosemary scoots closer, putting her arms around me again. We sit, tangled together, while the anguish that built up in my body eases a little.

"Baby, there is nothing wrong with you. That dick needed control of something because he lost it somewhere along the way."

"Was I an easy target?" The tears burn, and my nose prickles and is stuffy now.

"Love, no. You've always been a fighter. Sometimes they need that fight to prove to themselves that they're not weak. To prove they have control. You are a challenge, and...I can only guess, but he felt like he had to break you."

"He succeeded."

Mom's arms tighten. "No, baby, he didn't. Because you're here. You fought through it. You sought counseling. More than anything, you're opening yourself up. That's how you heal. Break the cycle. You've got this, love, and we'll be here every step you want us to be."

My heart thumps against my ribs, the ache slowly fading. A pleasing buzz washes over me, warming me up, and something bright enters my soul, seeping into crevices that were blackened and hiding away.

Mom wipes at my tears and cups my chin. "I don't usually swear, but fuck him, Kit. Fuck him."

She says it so violently that my brows shoot up, and I lose the sour in my belly as laughter bubbles up from inside. I pull her close and squeeze her hard.

"Thank you, Mom."

She kisses the top of my head, brushing her hand down my hair. "Who's ready for dinner?"

Greer

I grab a jar of peanut butter and toss it in my basket. My whole body feels like it's on pins and needles—like it's expecting something to jump-start it.

What the hell is happening to me? Maybe it's time to go to the doctor.

I should hire someone to do the grocery shopping for me. Going up and down the aisles and picking things for myself isn't hard, but it's a waste of time. Maybe I'll hire a housekeeper.

I grab a bag of potato chips and throw them in my basket. The restlessness makes me want to eat more junk food. Serotonin or endorphins or something—a false sense of happiness.

Is that what it is? Am I unhappy?

Laughter, lilting, sweet, and happy, hits me. I focus down the aisle. A redhead, beautiful and curvy, is talking to someone through an earbud. Her voice is husky and sultry without even trying. I take a step closer, having to know what she's saying.

My stomach flutters. A zing moves up my spine. Tingles rush through me, light and dizzy at the same time. I reach out, bracing myself on a tray of onions.

Weak knees.

I have weak fucking knees. I'm a fucking cliché.

What the hell is happening to me?

She laughs again. My pulse kicks up, beating a fast rhythm against my wristwatch. I can't tear my gaze from her, and I'm not sure I want to. And I'm moved by her, literally. My cock is stirring.

All right, time to get control of myself.

She moves on, and I make myself hang back. Shaking my hands, I force out these weird reactions, this desire to claim her somehow. Club her over the head and bring her back to my cave.

Yeah, that would go over well.

Oh, hell. My feet are moving of their own accord. I can't make them stop. I round the corner, hoping to glimpse her again.

I follow her like a stalker, not even watching where I'm going. I need to see her face.

I slam into someone—Mrs. Perkins—in the cereal aisle, tripping over her petite frame. "Mrs. Perkins!" I reach out and gently steady her. "I'm sorry. Are you okay?"

"I'm okay, boy. But you sure bulldozed me over in a rush like you are. What fire are you chasin', Son?" She pushes her gray bun back in place. Her bones crack as she bends down.

"I'll get it." I bend to pick up the cereal she dropped. "I apologize again, Mrs. Perkins."

"Oh, Son, it's all right. No harm, no foul. My old bones can take a handsome man like you bumping into me." She winks at me and gives me a once-over.

I hide my smirk, biting on my lip as this ninety-year-old grandma flirts with me. I set both boxes in her cart and turn, preparing to leave, but she grabs my arm.

"Tell your mom to call me for lunch. I missed her at church last weekend."

"I'll tell her to stop by."

She talks about church and my family, and I stand there listening, my skin prickling, my brain telling me to move. I don't even go to church, lady. And I need to find my redhead.

When appropriate, I nod and answer. I peek over her little gray bun, looking for my girl. My palms itch, wanting to find her and hold her hand, so I fist them.

Finally, Mrs. Perkins lets me go. I dash down the aisle and walk the back section. Now I *am* a stalker. I force myself to slow, to stop looking so I can finish my shopping. I clench my jaw as I ignore every instinct to look up and around for her.

I head to the checkouts, stopping in one of the shorter lines. Well, fuck, I can't stop myself as I scan the area. Merely looking around, checking out the crowd. Now I'm just fucking lying to myself.

A flash of red disappears down the freezer food section. I don't even try to stop myself as my feet lead me that way.

There she is, standing in front of the ice cream, her hair shining like a halo around her head. She watches her surroundings for a moment, then frowns before her face turns back into a smile.

But she hasn't noticed me through the crowd and noise. Everything about her is exactly like I remembered—magnificent.

Kit.

Eight

Kit

WITH A GRUNT, I grab a grocery basket and loop my arm through the handles, then adjust my earbud so I can hear Jack better.

His voice is so deep now, like Dad's. "The last place we rented was infested with cockroaches. Jill wouldn't stay, so we had to find something different."

I bust out a chuckle. "Your roommate's name is Jill?" Because that is...interesting.

His laughter booms in my ear. "One of them, yeah. The smart one. We get a lot of Jack and Jill jokes. We're going to put a bucket of water next to our door since the house is on the top of a hill."

We spend the next ten minutes bullshitting as I check out the flowers and fill my basket, but a weird niggling in the back of my neck causes me to stop. A shiver travels up my spine like someone is watching me. I whirl, panting, and search up and down the aisle. Backing up, I hit a cardboard display at the end. It crashes, and I jump.

"Kit? You still there?"

"Yup, yeah, I'm here." Nothing there other than an older couple bickering over which denture glue to buy and a big guy who raises his brows at me as I straighten. I quickly turn away. Why does it always feel like I'm being watched?

I pick up the cardboard boy and puppy, then shake out my fingers and glance around one more time. Other than the couple and the guy who is now actively avoiding my gaze, the aisle is empty. Not one person appears off.

I turn, brushing off the tingling as a fluke, and head to the ice cream aisle.

Embracing the cold, I lean down to get a better view of the options. "Hey, which flavor of ice cream should I get?"

"I'm a fan of coffee, myself." A deep, gravelly voice answers from behind me.

I whirl around at the sound, my hand flying to my chest.

He reaches around me, his big hand settling over the lid of a coffee ice cream.

My brother says, "Hey, my roommate needs me—he's stuck in the dryer. Jesus. I'll call you later. Bye, Kit."

"Yup, bye Jack." I pull the earbud from my ear and tuck it into my pocket.

I'm almost certain my mouth is open, and I look like a fool, but damn, I can't help myself.

Greer.

Seriously, he's here in the flesh, like my subconscious mind conjured him up. His big hand pulls out the ice cream. Those deep gold irises meet mine, twinkling as he places the container in his basket, then settles his hand in his pocket. His pants are tight, outlining his hand in his jeans, thumb out—among other big things.

Like really big things. BDE.

I dart my focus back up to his face. He smirks and shifts his feet.

Don't stray. Keep your eyes on his face. You can do it.

Though I can't stop myself from asking, "What are you doing here?" Because of all the grocery stores in Stirling Harbor, he's walked into mine. Or something like that. Thank you, Rick Blaine.

"Getting groceries." As simple as that. "I didn't think I'd see you again."

Neither did I, and I'm not sure what to make of it right now. He scans me from head to toe, his pupils widening, the amber glowing, and a wolf-like grin curls his lips.

My pulse kicks, thumping hard against my ribcage, waiting for whatever comes next.

Wait, he said he didn't think he'd see me again. That means he's thought of me. As much as I've thought of him?

Oh, shit. I don't know if I'm ready for this.

For him.

The way he sucks all the energy out of the room. That BDE again.

I turn back to the cooler, grab a container of ice cream, and put it in my basket. The urge to put it on my cheeks rushes through me.

He reaches over and picks it up. "Butter pecan?" And puts it back in the cooler. "That's the worst flavor of ice cream." Pulling out a coffee, he puts it in my basket. "I promise you'll like this. Have you ever had it?"

I bite my lip, refusing to answer. Pretty sure I can pick my own flavor at this point. That, and I think I've lost the ability to speak.

"Did you lose your tongue?" He leans in close. "I can help you find it."

My cheeks are blazing. His burned, woodsy scent halos around me, and for a brief moment, I pull it deep inside. Sin. He smells like sin—hot, delicious, earthy, bed sheets type of sin.

Stop. Snap out of it.

I mentally shake myself. "The butter pecan is for my sister." Which she wanted, so she's going to get it.

When I pull it back out, he grabs my hand. Shocks of electricity flow from him, buzzing through me from the inside out. I jerk back.

During clinicals, I touched men all the time, but it never felt like this. Charged. When he lets go, the sensation leaves too.

He cocks a brow, watching me before those luscious lips part. "Then I suggest she try the Bourbon Praline Pecan." The breadth of his enormous body moves closer, crowding, caging me in.

When he reaches around me, his arm brushing my shoulder, I freeze. The basket shifts on my arm as he sets it inside.

Air sticks in my lungs. He's too close.

The floor shakes under me. No, not the floor, my trembling legs. He watches me with concern as my throat constricts and my chest caves in. Space, I need space. I put my hands up, warding him off as his brow furrows.

76

He steps back, and I whirl around to put my head in the freezer and let the frigid air ease the rigidity in my throat. When I've put myself back together enough, I turn back around.

He's backed away, but I still want to lose my shit.

"Kit, you okay?" He has a brow up, worry etched in his features.

"I, uh, yeah. I'm fine. A bit overwhelmed at the moment, but fine."

And there we go.

The concern fades, and he smirks. "I overwhelmed you."

That damn sensual grin. Despite liking it, I clench my teeth and fight the urge to wipe it right off his face.

After grabbing the butter pecan, I put the Bourbon Praline back.

He watches me, the amber glowing. "I insist she try it." He switches out the ice creams again, placing the bourbon in my basket.

Grinding my teeth now, I smile, my lips pinching. "Thank you."

"You need a coffee one too."

"One is enough. It's only two of us eating ice cream." I turn, ready to move by him, but he grabs a second carton of coffee ice cream, the two in opposite hands, and holds one out temptingly.

Something about this guy irks me right now. "Bad day? Usually, it's women who drown their sorrows in fat and cream." Not that I want to be bitchy, but damn it, he's messing with my insides. Despite feeling caged in by him, I want him close.

I should be full-on, knee-deep in a panic attack—they never let go of me this easily. All this is making my angsty head dizzy with irritation.

But also with want.

Need.

"Nope." He moves the ice cream back and forth in my vision, trying to tempt me. It's his grin, though, that's the temptation. It's far too delicious, with his lips all puffy and luscious and surrounded by a beard. What would they feel like...

Danger, danger, don't soften.

Too late, my insides are already turning to goo, the knot of irritation easing. I try one more time to be formidable. "Do I have to be mean to you to get you to go away?"

He winks.

Stop making eye contact. Easier said than done, but I do it. If the heat coming off my cheeks is any sign of how red they are, they must be crimson. Abort mission, exit stage left, do something. I make my way to the checkout. He chuckles—that deep, resonant one—behind me in line.

It's a chore to fight the urge to look back, but I succeed.

Once I leave the store, I load everything in the back of my SUV and try to settle myself as I sit. I want to think about him, but don't want to at the same time. It would be so much easier if he didn't invade my thoughts.

Rat-a-tat-tat.

I jump, catching a dark shadow in my peripheral.

My heart thumps like crazy, and my palms get sweaty. I turn when the shadow moves.

Greer.

I stare as my pulse slows. Instead of basking in my ability to quickly move from panicked to calm, arousal settles deep down in my belly as his amber gaze glows. He motions me to roll down the window.

Just like he did in California.

I shake my head. Undeterred, he does it again, a sexy half smile peeking from behind his beard.

With a sigh, I push the button to lower the window. All the way this time.

"Did I forget something?" Despite wanting to brush him off, I can't help the soft, flirty way the words leave my mouth. Damn conspirator voice box.

"Have coffee with me."

"No. What if you're a serial killer?"

He shoots me a killer smile, and I'm almost dead on impact. I bite back the return smile that wants to erupt.

I cock my brow at him, giving him the look Ro gives her husband when she's irritated, and squeeze the steering wheel so tight my knuckles turn white. Otherwise, those rebellious hands will reach out and touch him.

They want to, badly.

He shoves a hand through the window. The scent of peonies instantly hits me. "You seemed to like these. I want you to have them."

My heart trips, softening as my mouth drops. I grasp the bouquet with trembling hands, trying to hide the stutter of my heart. The exact flowers I stopped to smell.

The last time I got flowers...Nope. I'm not going there. I turn off those thoughts, focusing on the pleasant hum starting low inside and flowing up.

Breathless, I offer my appreciation. "Thank you." I bring them to my nose, inhaling deeply as something crinkles outside the window.

"Maybe you'll change your mind about having coffee with me after you see what great taste I have." He hands me a carton of ice cream in a bag. "Try it."

I can't stop it. My mouth defies me, the corners kicking up. As pushy as he is, this is sweet. I set the ice cream down near the floor, alongside Ro's, before turning the cool air to my feet so they don't melt.

He rests his forearms above his head on the car's roof, watching me silently for several moments.

"Thank you. Goodbye, Greer." With a huge smile stuck on my face, I roll up my window. Once again, looking at him in the rearview mirror, I drive away. Even when he's out of sight, his heat lingers.

"The kids are in bed. Let's find something shitty and hot to watch so we can eat this ice cream before Angelo gets done."

When I'm settled on the couch, I shovel a colossal spoonful of coffee ice cream into my mouth. The flavor explodes on my tongue, sweet, nutty, and tangy like coffee should be. "This is delicious."

"Hell, yeah, it's good. This is Haagen-Daz ice cream, baby." She takes another mouthful. "Assuming they were out of the butter pecan? Not that I'm complaining." She flips the channels before settling on the movie about a Norse god, played by that Aussie actor. "Now, he's divine. Look at him. I mean, Angelo is hot, but Thor is mmm-hm."

I chuckle, shaking my spoon at the screen. "The guy at the supermarket would give him a run for his money."

Rosemary peeks at me, her brow up. "What did he look like?"

"Intense, dark, dreamy. His eyes were...smokin' hot. Gold and dark..." I shrug, unable to control the smile fighting through. I shove another spoonful into my mouth before my lips can move any more.

"Ooh. You talked to him? What did he say?"

I swallow quickly. "He asked me out a few times. His whole body puts off this aura of in charge...everywhere."

"Were you staring at his junk?" She waggles her brows.

I didn't.

I swear.

"His jeans weren't hiding much." Not that I pointedly looked, but dang it, it was hard to ignore. And I kind of didn't want to. Yeah I snuck a peak or three.

"Could you be more obvious?"

I shrug again and bite my lower lip to hide my smirk this time. So apparently, whatever libido I had has returned with a burn that rumbles under my skin. Right now, it's pleasant, and I hope it stays that way. I can work with pleasant. "He gave me flowers."

"Really? Awe. What was he like?"

I wring my hands together, twisting them tightly before letting go. Broody, demanding, a bit controlling, and in my space.

Like Ethan. Involuntary shivers rack my body before I tamp them down.

"You're frowning. What are you thinking about?" She tilts her head and studies me thoughtfully. "Ethan?"

I nod.

"Kit, whoever this guy is, he's not Ethan."

"I know he's not Ethan. But he could have similar tendencies. You never know."

"Actually, I do. Ethan was a shitbag who fucked you up, but not all men are like that. Angelo is deep and intense and dominating in a fucking good way. But only to me. It can be like that."

I snap my gaze up to Ro before knitting my brows together. I can't shut off the thoughts. Greer did some sweet things, even if he was domineering while doing them. But Ethan was charming in the beginning too.

She continues like I wasn't staring off into space. "He can be your seal breaker."

"There is no seal to break. That's been done."

"Yeah, but, Kit-Kat, it's been three *years*. It's like you're a virgin again. You need a little *unts, unts, unts* to get back into dating." Her hands dance seductively down her body. "You know, like when men jack off before the third date so they don't blow too early when it's time for the dessert."

My spoon stays poised at my mouth. "They don't do that."

"They sure as hell do."

I shake my head. "Please, watch the movie."

"Let's ask Angelo. You need to know these things if you are going to date."

I reach out to grab her, shaking my head wildly.

Rosemary shifts, "Hey, love? Ang?"

"Rosemary, *no.*" My stomach is in riots. "Please."

Angelo peeks around the corner. "Babe?"

Laughing, Rosemary shifts her gaze from me to Angelo. "Love you, sweetums."

He beams as he says, "Love you too."

I have to look away from the intimacy.

Rosemary turns to me after Angelo leaves, breaking the silence. "All kidding aside, I will back off if you say you aren't ready. And if you are ready, tell me, and I can help."

I nod at that. It would be nice to meet someone. And despite what Ethan did, I don't view all men badly. Maybe I'm okay with it. "He asked me for coffee."

She shifts toward me. "And you said no? Why?"

"He almost triggered an anxiety attack when he was too close, and then he was telling me what to do. He switched out my ice cream containers twice. I finally relented because I knew it would continue to be a battle."

I scrunch my brows together. "He's all big energy with his determination and presence, and I don't know. He's hot, but it's too much like Ethan."

Doesn't stop me from shoving another spoonful of the ice cream he insisted on into my mouth, though. Then I sputter around the ice cream. "I completely lose my cool around him. He's full of himself. I want to lash out and make his smirk drop. Or lick him."

"Those guys often have the biggest emotions, Kit. And not bad ones."

I don't know if I believe that.

Her face softens. "I was like that with Angelo at first." She puts her spoon down for a moment. "Angelo rubbed me the wrong way, and I kept telling myself I hated him. But when he kissed me, Kit, that was not hate. That was not hate at all."

"I want something like Mom and Dad have, or you and Angelo." I want to let someone in again, or at least try. And if it doesn't go well, there's no harm in giving myself more time.

"It's not too late. You can let someone in."

"Hmm, not someone intense. Someone easy, nerdy, like a male librarian. Do you think they exist? I've never seen one. Are they called librarians? That seems like a feminine term."

"Yes, you dope." She lobs a pillow at me, plopping it against my arm. "They are called librarians too."

"Hey, you can't pillow bomb me, especially when I'm eating delicious ice cream. That's a sacrifice that even you can't get behind." I pop another spoonful of the tasty treat before crisscrossing my legs under me. "He is gorgeous, though." The way his clothing fits his body flits through my mind. "He made me all warm and tingly. I couldn't catch my breath."

"Gross, Kit. I don't want to hear that from my baby sister."

"Are you kidding? All I've heard since I got back is you and Angelo behind closed doors. You can put up with my 'warm and tingly.'" I shake my spoon at Ro. "At least I didn't say 'moist.'"

"Oh, gross. One of the worst words on the planet."

"See. Moist. There's your payback. Now stop telling me about Angelo."

"Seriously, though, Kit? If you want to get back out there, I'd be willing to help."

Ugh, I keep the grimace off my face. "You mean a blind date? Ro, those are the worst. Worse than moist."

"But what better way to figure out what you don't like so you know what you do?" Rosemary winks at me.

I dip my spoon into my bowl.

Easy and calm is nice in theory, but can passion exist in a connection built on that foundation?

Greer is passionate. And strong. But I said no, and he respected that.

He didn't change, shift, or rage. Then again, Ethan had been easygoing and sweet in the beginning.

I scrape the bottom of my bowl and lick the spoon. The coffee flavor is delicious, annoyingly proving that he has remarkable taste.

"Kit, thanks for the ice cream." Angelo holds the container, standing by the door. Holding the carton up, he scoops out the last bite of the ice cream like kids slurp up their cereal.

Ro's excited voice pulls my attention. "Kit, there's a number on the bottom of that container."

"Yeah right." But my disbelief doesn't stop me from checking out the bottom of the carton.

Holy shit. I rush over and grab it from Angelo, holding it above my head so I can look at the writing scratched into the container without making a mess of the melted remains of the ice cream.

He seriously gave me his number.

"So." Rosemary grabs it and hands it back to Angelo. "Now that you have his number, what're you gonna do?"

Nine

Greer

I SHOVE MY HAIR out of my face before pushing the papers around my desk. My life is out of control.

Son of a bitch, I can't even concentrate enough to design something. This crazy sense of disquiet makes me want to crawl out of my skin.

The need to see Kit again, to touch her, get lost in her scent, is gnawing at me. I want to know her favorite color and how she tastes.

My need for her is visceral.

Who is this person I'm becoming? This is not like me, and I don't know how to stop it. I need something—action, movement, anything—that gets me up and out of my space.

I knock on Simon's office door, popping my head in. "Wanna hike?" I don't wait.

I've never been this focused on a woman. Nora had my attention, but never in this way. I enjoyed hanging out with her, but I long to see Kit again.

Nora made me laugh, but it wasn't a soul-deep laughter. She was logistically funny, making jokes she knew would be a hit. Everything was calculated.

Kit has made me chuckle or laugh straight from the gut. And it wasn't on purpose; it was the way she was all cute and unsure.

I like when she gets her dander up. Sometimes it looks like she might break a little, but then something inside her perks up. She straightens her back, and she gives me a little dig.

I like that. A lot.

She might actually challenge me a bit, and that is...*exhilarating.*

I left my number, but that doesn't mean she'll call.

Fuck.

I shake my hands out while I wait for Simon. He follows me out back, past the wood shop, and out to the forest area.

"We haven't been out here in a long time."

I nod. It's been years.

When we hit the trees and can't see the workshop anymore, Simon grabs my shoulder. "What's going on? You've been so..."

I shrug. He steps back and leans against a tree, giving me time to struggle through my thoughts.

"Will we be standing out here long, you think?" He grins at me after a moment.

"Give me one second."

"Sure."

When I don't say anything else, he kicks a rock my way. "Theo starts preschool next year. I don't know if I should leave him at the daycare he's at now or enroll him in an actual school."

"Do they teach him colors, letters, all that stuff at daycare?" I could almost groan with relief. Thank fuck, Simon knows how to read me; he jumps in and doesn't make me start the conversation.

"Yeah, they always have."

"Then keep him there."

I scrub my hands through my hair, scratching at the nape of my neck. Everywhere on my body is taut, like a rubber band pulled to its limit.

What if she never calls? What if she never saw it? I shake my head slightly. A hard lump forms in my stomach, pressing against everything like a massive bomb waiting to explode.

"When you give your number to a woman, how long does it take for her to call?" I shove my hands into my pockets to keep from fidgeting. It's been four days.

"Most people follow the universal three-day rule."

My heart stutters—I'm past that.

"You get a number, wait three days, and then call. If you call too early, you seem desperate. If you call too late, then you're not interested. It's a fine line between being a stalker and being an asshole."

"What do you do on a first date?" Nora and I didn't have conventional dates; they were planned functions. Truthfully, I'm not sure we ever had a real date.

Surprise paints his face before he recovers. "First dates are kind of tricky. And annoying. And they can be exhausting. It's all about figuring out if the connection is real."

Yeah, I forgot all of that. Especially how annoying people can be.

"Most of the time, it's not. It sucks. You are attracted and want to fuck like crazy, and once that's out of your system, you realize you have nothing to talk about." He shrugs and drops his gaze to the forest floor.

"Do you go on a lot of first dates?"

He chuckles and shakes his head. "If you don't know the person well, and you're worried about conversation, I'd recommend a movie, then dessert. That way, you have something to discuss at the end of the date. Then when you take her back to her place, you wait for the signal to kiss her."

"What the fuck is the signal?"

Simon laughs outright, staring at me like I have three heads. "How do you not know this?"

"Nora and I started as plus ones and continued on from there. I've never really dated anyone since college." So yeah, ten years, give or take.

"Well, the signal is, you know, the batting of the eyes. Staring longingly at your lips. She might twirl her hair, linger at the door."

My gut sours. What if I don't recognize the signal? Do I get another shot? Is the date over, and that's it?

"Do you have a date?" Simon's head is angled to the ground as he asks, but his gaze is locked on me.

"No. Just trying to figure things out."

He nods and checks his watch. "Shit, it's almost four. I've got to head back, or I'll be late picking up Theo." He steps close and pats my back. "If you need some pointers, let me know."

He acknowledges my nod, and then he disappears through the trees.

I roll my shoulders, stretching the tightness out by pulling one arm across my chest, then do the same with the other. Maybe I just need to walk more.

The trees make a canopy overhead, hiding me between the little flits of sunlight. I take the winding way back to the warehouse. The tall timbers are a balm to my soul, singing songs of what they could become, and I let it flow through me.

This is where I find inspiration.

If she doesn't call, it's okay. There is nothing I can do about it anyway, but I won't stress about it. I'll move on and figure out what else I need to do in my life to keep going.

I bite back a sigh.

My phone buzzes in my pocket. Probably Simon, letting me know he's leaving. I pull it out and check the number.

Unknown.

My heart sputters as I hit the answer button.

"Hello, this is Greer." Damn, please be her, please be her.

"Hi, Greer, this is Kit. "

Her sweet, husky voice fills my ears. A nice buzz shoots through my body, dizzying almost in it's intensity, as I smile at the surrounding trees. She fucking called, and now everything is frozen inside my chest.

My galloping heart is loud in my ears, and my body hums in the best way. I want to jump and punch the sky, I'm so fucking ecstatic. Instead, I force myself to focus.

"Hi." It escapes me as a sigh. I sound like an idiot.

Her laugh is sweet and lyrical. "Hi again. Uh. I found your number on the bottom of the ice cream container."

"Yeah, I put it there." What the fuck is wrong with me? Of course I did. "Did you like the coffee ice cream?" Did she even try it?

"Yeah, it was good, great even."

Now what? Do I just ask her? Energy radiates from my arms and legs, so I pace to keep from combusting.

After several silent moments, I clear my throat. Grow some fucking balls and spit it out. "Would you want to go on a date with me?"

She gasps, and I wait, my palms sweating and my heart racing.

Do I need to talk her into it? I will. "We can do something easy, like a movie. Then maybe grab some dessert afterward. What do you say?"

It's way too silent on her end.

Shit, she's going to say no.

It hits me like a punch to the gut.

"Yes."

Standing behind the line at the ticket booth, I glance at my watch. Kit should be here in ten minutes. The marquee sign of this old-fashioned theater glows bright, painting the sidewalk in blues and reds.

I've always loved this place. It's a relief to know that in a world where things are slowly dying out, it's still here.

I look back to the road, watching the bustle of cabs dropping people off.

Will she be nervous? Will she even show up?

Fucking nerves.

I shove my hands in my pockets to stop from running them through my hair.

I don't even know what's playing. I probably should have checked. I glance back, reading the signs behind the booth. Looks like we have two choices. Romantic comedy or thriller. What would she like best?

My gut twists.

I glance at my watch again, swallowing as the minute hand ticks closer and closer to seven.

A cab stops, the door opens, and she steps out, her hair loose around her face and glowing in the fading light.

Fuck, she's beautiful.

Where is the man who was completely in control when I first met her? Because he's long gone, and somehow I missed the memo that he was taking off.

"Greer, hi." An enchanting rose-colored blush creeps up her neck and cheeks.

What the fuck do I do? Lean in? Kiss her cheek? Give her a hug?

I thrust my hand out, keeping the other one shoved in my pocket. She stares at it for a moment, then a smile lights up her face, and she puts her hand in mine. Electricity sucker punches me, making me grin.

I pull her in and lightly kiss her cheek. She gets a slightly wonderous look on her face, her eyes as big as saucers as I lean back, keeping her hand. My heart beats erratically in my chest until her fingers curl around mine.

The action soothes every part of me. That restless energy that has bubbled through my body for these last few months eases.

"Hey." I smile at her. Maybe a little too long because a blush creeps up her cheeks again.

Not that I can help it. I'm mesmerized. The woman I've been thinking about for the last few months is standing in front of me. "Rom-com or suspense?"

"Rom-com." She bites her bottom lip and then clasps my hand a little tighter.

Damn, her hand feels so good in mine, and I don't want to let go. Trying not to sigh, I let go of her to pull my wallet out and ask the teller for two tickets.

"I'm sorry, sir. That show is sold out."

I glance at Kit, one brow raised in question.

OF LILIES AND LIES

She hedges, worry on her face, and then seems to decide. "We can do the other one."

After I pay the lady, I guide Kit in with my hand on her lower back. Her body is a bit too tense, ramrod straight, even. So I drop my hand in case it's me.

We pick out a snack and head into the theater. Her hands fumble in front of her. "Can we sit on the end?"

"Yeah, absolutely. You get claustrophobic in the middle?"

She smiles, not as bright as before, but redness creeps up her cheeks again. "Yeah, something like that."

"Do you want the inside or outside?"

"Outside, please."

When we're settled, I reach over, slipping my hand into hers. Electricity arcs again, and she tenses a moment but then relaxes and keeps our fingers entwined.

Stuffed in like this, it's hard for someone as tall as I am to get comfortable, but I settle into the seat, rubbing my thumb over the top of her hand.

During the previews, I drop my voice for the two of us. "I thought you were from California?"

She pauses, her smile faltering a bit before she beams at me. "I'm originally from here. I recently moved back home."

"Well, I'm glad you did." I smile big, making sure my dimples pop. She briefly watches my lips, and I barely stop the urge to lick the bottom one.

"Me too. It's been interesting seeing how Stirling Harbor has changed."

"Has it changed a lot?" Did she scootch closer? She has to be closer.

"More than I expected, but in a good way." The smile she gives me is enchanting.

"I'm thrilled you're here, Kit."

"Me too. Nervous, but me too." She gets all soft, and she squeezes my hand. "Do you know what this movie is about?" Her focus bounces back to my mouth briefly.

Now I can't stop it. I lick my bottom lip, and she almost shudders.

"Nope, I didn't look anything up. Did you?"

"I rarely deviate much from rom-coms. I might get scared." Her voice lilts, teasing a bit as she sparkles.

Her body shifts, lips parting as she fidgets in her skirt and presses her thighs together. My palms itch to touch her.

The electricity arcing between us pulls me closer to her, and I lean in. "If you get scared, I'll keep you safe."

She stares at me, breaths shallow. If I move an inch, I could slip my mouth against hers and finally taste her.

Her puff of air hits my lips.

The lights go dark.

She jumps back, squeezing my hand tightly. I smile, a chuckle escaping me. "It's just beginning. Scared already?"

Her laugh hits me as the boom of the credits begin. I can make out her small smile in the flashes of the screen.

The movie starts out clean and calm. As the suspense builds, her hold on my hand tightens, and her other hand latches on to my wrist.

She's almost hyperventilating when the action starts, and her fingers dig into mine. When the main male character gets into a brawl and blood flies everywhere, she turns and hides behind my shoulder. Her gasps slam into my heart, one after another.

"Are you okay?"

She shakes her head.

A woman in the movie screams.

Kit screams, her actions making me want to hyperventilate too. Peeking out from my shoulder, she looks at the screen.

The color leaves her face. Terror paints her expression.

Her body trembles so hard next to me.

The man on screen is slapping the woman around. Her body hits the bathroom wall.

"I need to—" Kit rises, her body shaking so hard she can barely stand.

"I gotcha. Grab my hand."

She struggles to take a step, her focus still stuck on the screen, so I slide one arm under her knees and the other around her back to carry her out of the theater. She doesn't fight me, but she's so fucking tense.

Her body curls into mine, and her head tucks into my neck.

I fucked this up.

My rushed steps pound on the concrete floor in my haste to escape the noise. The air outside is cool against my skin, even with her hot and jagged pants against my neck. "Is there something I can do? Someone I can call?"

She can't even speak, she's trembling so hard.

"Breathe, Kit. In, out." Fuck, how do I help her? Mom would know.

"Sir, is she okay?" A woman's voice pulls my attention. She's walking down the street with a man, stopping when they are close. I sit on the bench outside and set Kit next to me.

My pulse races, and my hands sweat. I'm helpless. And completely out of my element here. "I'm not sure. We were watching a movie, and in the middle, this happened."

The woman stops in front of us. "Is she having a panic attack? Honey, are you okay?"

Fuck if I know what it is. Kit is still too panicked to respond or even look at the woman.

The woman's face softens as she watches Kit. "I'm Dr. Everson. I'm a therapist. What's her name?"

"Kit."

The woman drops to her knees in front of Kit. Her hands gently draw Kit's into hers. "Hi, Kit, I'm Lori. Honey, we're going to breathe together, okay?"

Kit's eyes are clenched tight, but she squeezes Dr. Everson's hands.

"Okay, honey, now open your eyes for me, and tell me what you see."

She takes a moment, but when she does, they're glazed over. She looks everywhere but at me. That makes my heart ache. My body tenses next to her because I want to take her in my arms, but I have no fucking idea if she'll scream.

"What do you see, honey?"

"Streetlights, a cab." Her attention moves to the movie posters.

Shit, don't look there. My voice is strained over the lump in my throat. "No, Kit, look this way. Don't look at the posters."

"Greer."

The woman nods. "Wonderful, good job. Now, what do you hear?"

Kit's gaze locks on mine, her movements pained, her chest heaving. "Music, horns honking."

"Good. What do you smell?"

Shit, I smell shit and dank sewage.

"The ocean."

"Good, let's do it again."

The woman leads Kit through this three more times until Kit is breathing normally next to me.

Dr. Everson pats Kit's knee and stands with a smile on her face. "Is she your girlfriend?"

"This is our first date."

Surprise flickers on Dr. Everson's face, and she nods. "Okay. Well, when this happens, help her ground. Get her anxiety under control. Find the trigger and then remove it. Lots of love and patience." She gives Kit another once-over before turning back to me. "She's good."

Kit's face is blotchy from tears. Her lids red and swollen. She mouths *I'm sorry* to me before turning to the doctor. "Thank you. I..."

Dr. Everson nods, heading back to the man she was with. "You should get her home. Tylenol if she has a headache, then some rest, a bath, all that good stuff. Get her to relax, but no alcohol."

I nod.

When the woman leaves, I stay with Kit on the bench for a while.

After what feels like hours, she speaks. "I can't do this right now."

Fuck. My stomach jumps into my throat, punching holes in my lungs. *Fuck.*

"It was my fault. I didn't think that movie would..." *What, set her off? How would I know?* "Are you okay?"

She shakes her head, wrapping her arms around her abdomen, effectively distancing herself from me. "I can't, Greer. I'm so sorry. It isn't you. I'm...broken."

"Kit, we're all broken." I stand, reaching for her, but she jerks back. The ball in my gut explodes, and ice fills my veins. "I like you. We can go slow."

"No." She looks at me long and hard, and then steps close to the curb, signaling for a taxi. Her face falls as she looks at me again. Tears roll down her cheeks as a cab stops next to her. "I'm so sorry. I'm not ready."

My heart is in my throat, punching me with every beat as the cab door shuts and she drives away.

The taillights blend in with the rest of the cars, and my chest caves in. *How the fuck do I fix this?*

Ten

Kit

"It wasn't him, Rosemary. It was the movie, and I feel so stupid." I snuggle closer to her.

"So it wasn't the date?"

"No. It was the memories, the struggle, the tension and tightness in my chest, the feeling that Ethan is out there."

She studies me calmly. "Do you want to see him again?"

"Yes. No! I don't know. It was so embarrassing. I don't think I can face him again."

She looks at me like she wants to say something, her eyes moving back and forth between mine before her face drops and she nods.

My phone buzzes on the coffee table, and I grab it. Pulse spiking, my belly does cartwheels. "It's him." I look at Rosemary, panicked.

"The date?" Shit, I never did tell her his name.

"Yes, his name—"

"Answer it." She bites back a smile as she gestures for me to go ahead.

Frowning at her, my thumb hovers over the green "accept" on my phone. Goose bumps raise on my arms and legs, and ice paralyzes me while I stare at his name.

Greer.

Calling me.

I peer at Ro, shaking my head. Then slap my gaze back to the table, eyeing the phone like it's a snake ready to strike out and bite me.

I can't.

There is a shit ton wrong with me, and he shouldn't have to put up with it all. The ringing stops. "I feel stupid. I figured I'd eventually have a meltdown, but not during the first date."

"Of course you weren't okay. It was your first date after that piece of shit traumatized you. You were always going to get emotional. If the guy likes you, he won't mind. He probably called to ask you out again. The question is, are you going to accept?"

No. I can move on with another person, someone who is soft and straightforward. Someone who doesn't remind me of Ethan with his soul-sucking energy and larger-than-life attitude.

"No. Nope. I'm going on easy dates from now on. Men who don't like suspense or thriller movies."

Rosemary laughs, and I lean my head on her shoulder. "I'm attracted to him, Rosemary. But I'm not looking for someone like him."

She hums, kissing my head lightly while rubbing my arm. "It'll come in time, Kit. When you meet the right man, it'll all fall into place. Even if the universe has to nudge you a few times to get you there."

"What if I never get there?"

She pauses for a moment, pressing her cheek to the top of my head. "Maybe it takes a week, a month, or even a year, but that doesn't mean you don't deserve love and a family if that's what you want. Eventually, the dates won't be bad, the laughter will flow, love will spark, and you'll find your happiness."

"I would settle for a normal life with normal stress levels."

"Then that's what we'll aim for. I'll help, I promise, Kit. I'm here 100 percent of the way."

I keep my body snuggled against hers, letting the peace and calm cascade through me, settling the nerves that ratcheted up from the call.

My phone pings—one voicemail notification. I'm not going to listen. What if he's calling to say "thanks, but no thanks" to my brand of crazy? I don't know why, but that thought alone makes me want to cry.

She nudges me with her shoulder. "He left you a message."

"Thank you, Captain Obvious."

"Are you going to listen?"

"Eventually. I can't now. It's too fresh. I can't imagine what he thinks of me right now."

"Don't you at least want to tell him it wasn't his fault?"

"I did. At the end of the date, I said it's not you; it's me." I look at her with what I hope is a good representation of my chagrin.

"Oh, Jesus, Kit. You didn't! He's going to think it was his fault."

"It wasn't, though. It was the circumstances of the date, and it wasn't a line."

"How did you leave?"

"Calm, cool, and collected. I rode my bike." I shake my head. "How do you think I left? In a panic, hightailing it out of there in the back of a stinky cab with a driver who kept calling me 'Kitten.'"

She sighs next to me, resigned. "Okay, Kit."

I stare at my phone while the noise of the TV drowns out everything else. I tentatively grab it, clicking on the voicemail icon. He left me a message over a minute long.

What could he possibly have to say that would last over a minute?

Greer

Well, I fucked that up. I scrub my hand through my hair, rubbing away knots at the back of my neck. It's been a week, and she hasn't called, texted, or shown up at the supermarket. And I'm the fucking weirdo who has gone almost every day to pick out dinner. Even making it a point to go at random times, hoping I'd bump into her again.

The going out of my way to see if she's at the store, yeah, that's not me. But I can't seem to stop myself. I need to know that she made it through the evening and that everything is all right.

Simon pops his head in, a huge smile on his face. "Hey, Richards sent over an appreciation gift." He sidesteps the door, sliding into my office while holding a big box.

Let it be cognac or scotch.

It clanks when he sets it on the table, thank god. I'm not much of a drinker, but I want to drown myself in a bottle of scotch right about now.

Why is starting relationships so hard? More than that, why am I hung up on Kit? I should focus on moving on, but I've yet to meet anyone who intrigues me the way she does.

Is it me? Am I the issue? I don't think I'm too picky, but I guess it's possible.

Simon rips open the tape, his delighted groan echoing in the room, and draws out a bottle, which he tugs to his chest and holds like a fucking baby. "Richards sure knows appreciation. Look at the date on this."

I study the label with a raised brow. Holy shit, that must have cost a fortune.

"Macallan Sherry Oak, and there are ten bottles in here. Fuck, you did good work, Greer."

Simon continues to study the bottle, popping it open and inhaling the delicious ginger, toffee, and maybe a hint of nut.

Fuck, relaxing with a few fingers of expensive whiskey is going to be incredible.

Okay. Maybe more wallowing than relaxing.

Is it time to cut back? Make more of a presence in life? Not that I have a life at the moment, other than work.

This is everything I've known for the last ten years—working my ass off to build something that matters to me. That will one day keep my family afloat. I don't want to stop what I'm doing now and have it all flop, losing everything because I wasn't paying attention to the tiny details.

But if I don't cut back, I won't *have* the family one day. I glance at the clock, then at the pile of work I need to have completed in the next three months. I could start by not accepting every job that's offered my way and giving myself more time to complete them, but I don't think I can.

"I'll split these between the crew and us. Maybe we'll keep one here at the office for special clients."

Shit, I forgot he was here for a moment. I really am fucking cut off from the real world. This is another sign that I've been working too much.

I wave him off. "Whatever you want to do is fine."

"You okay? You've been off lately, but you look completely lost right now."

The grinding of my jaw is louder than his exhale. "Yeah, I'm fine."

"You're always fine. You know, if you ever need something, you can come to me. Things were weird after you started the business. You clammed up, and I didn't push you. I'm thinking I should have because you shut me out, and now we have this *work* relationship."

"I know." I give a halfhearted smile. But he's wrong. It was realizing that I had nothing to offer a person that changed things.

"Maybe it's time to try with everyone. Bring yourself back into the family unit."

The idea of being more open with my family, letting them into my private thoughts, makes me want to puke.

"I'll think about it."

He nods, setting a bottle down with a clank on my desk. "Well, I'm here if you need me."

The steady thump of his boots echoes as he leaves.

October

Eleven

Greer

THE SMOOTH BEER HITS my tongue as I watch Simon and Angelo throw darts. This is one of those monthly outings Simon told me we needed to embark on.

Fuck this shit.

To top things off, tomorrow is Halloween, and stupid fucks are treating tonight like it's the night to dress up. Slutty nurses, vampires, werewolves, and mummies. I'm pretty sure that woman's mummy costume is made of toilet paper and those sticker things that go over nipples. Everything else is outlined explicitly.

But I'm not interested.

I called Kit multiple times after our date. I left messages and texted her how sorry I was. She never replied. Any chance I had is dead in the water now. It's been a month. It's time to stop thinking about her and move on.

I push the hair out of my face and study the label on my bottle of beer, ignoring the look from the woman across the bar with a major crazy vibe. Kit wasn't like that. She's got some serious emotional trauma, but she's not crazy.

And I have no idea how to help with that. Not that it matters anymore.

"Greer?"

I glance up. Apparently, their game is over, and they've been standing there for who knows how long. Simon's laughing, biting off a smile, and Angelo smirks.

"What? I didn't catch what you said."

"Can't leave work at the office, can you?" Simon tips his glass of bourbon up and smirks, his lips kicking up at the corner the same way mine do. "You're predictable."

"I *was* thinking—something you should try—but it wasn't about work." I shift my gaze to my beer bottle and tap against the glass.

"Interesting. Angelo, Greer isn't thinking about work." He turns to Angelo, pretending to be ridiculous—which isn't hard for him. "Is it a woman?"

Angelo's brows shoot up. "If it's not work, then it's the only thing left *to* think about."

My gaze slides to Angelo, heat rushing into my cheeks like a hormonal tween.

"Holy shit, are you blushing? He's fucking blushing." Simon points at me like he did when we were teenagers.

"Seriously, Simon, put your damn finger down. Fucking child."

"I think the more important thing is that he *is* thinking about a woman." Angelo winks.

Heat rises to my ears now. Jesus, I'm a grown man. I rub my hand down my face, ridding myself of any evidence.

"Shit, you're right. That redhead?"

"What redhead?" Something sparks on Angelo's face before disappearing.

"Someone I've run into a few times. It's nothing."

"It's something. You've been ruminating over her for months." Simon chuckles.

With a cough to clear my throat, I change topics. "Are we set up for the weekend up north?" I need the time away. My body is restless, and my stomach is doing that stupid twisty thing again.

I'm in limbo, and I need control.

Beer gone, I signal for another. Whatever the thing with my body is, it got worse after my date with Kit. I'll be fine at the cabin, where there's always something to repair. It's an easy way to give my brain a break or spark inspiration. It also doesn't hurt that the weather is usually promising this time of year.

"Yup, we are all squared away. Angelo said Rosemary might bring her sister. She's finding herself, I guess." Simon signals for another drink.

"She *is* finding herself. It took a lot for her to get where she is. Ro hasn't said much about her life before moving back here, but she's been telling me all about the *datetastrophes* she's had. I didn't know men could be so helpless. Where does she find these dopes?"

"This should be good. Tell us." Simon's elbow hits me squarely in the gut, forcing the air out of my lungs. Of all the habits he's kept since childhood, this is the most annoying.

"I can't. I told Ro I wouldn't share. Besides, they aren't my stories."

"Just one, Ange. Then this guy will know what *not* to do when he meets his woman again."

My woman.

I don't need to hear about disastrous dates since I'm reliving my last one over and over. But I shake my head in defeat and lift my chin toward Angelo for the go-ahead.

He recounts a story about a picnic, a man who shared his food with his dog, and how she narrowly missed a dog hair-infused kiss.

Angelo smiles at me, nodding with an odd twinkle in his eyes. "Hopefully, she finds what she wants at the cabin. It's a perfect place to relax and figure things out. Are you heading up a day or two early?"

"Yup. Have to fix a few things around the place before everyone gets there."

Finishing his drink, Angelo looks at his phone. "Ro and her sister are around here somewhere. You want to meet her, Greer? I think you might like her."

"I've met Rosemary many times. I was at your wedding, and I like her." I'm being blatantly obtuse. Her sister wasn't at the wedding because of some family issues. And I have a feeling they are trying to set me up on a blind date of sorts, which I'm not ready for.

"I meant—"

"Nope, I don't need to be set up. Never was that type of person."

"I know. But Ro and I think you would be good for each other." He gets shifty and squinty for a moment, but then he pastes on his usual grin.

I pinch my lips, my brows shooting up. "No thanks, man. I'll meet her at the cabin. And don't tell her about me either. When we don't get along, I don't want it to be awkward." Besides, no one is going to send electricity arcing through my body, traveling through my veins, and exploding in my heart like Kit did.

Is that why it keeps eating at me?

"You don't get along with many women because you're a grumpy asshole. Even more so lately. You need to get laid."

I swing my gaze around the bar. The woman on the other side is still looking me over like I'm her next baby daddy, as are a few ladies looking between Simon and me, aching to be the filling of a Winter sandwich. Not that we've done that since college.

Sighing, I put money down for my tab and chin dip the two gimps.

"Already?" Simon groans.

"Yeah, I've got shit to prepare for the week." And I need to settle my body, my brain.

I need to get a hold of my life.

november

Twelve

Greer

"Happy Thanksgiving, my sweet boy." Smiling, Mom wipes her hands on her apron as I wait patiently for that fierce hug I want so much right now. The last week has done nothing to calm the irritation in my belly.

I'm still off, and my woodworking is shit because of it. The business end of things is suffering because I can't get my head around my fuck up. And I've ruined two ridiculously expensive pieces.

Mom wraps her arms around me, calming my heart and easing my headache. She pulls back, one hand on each of my arms, and gives me that look. "Tell me, Greer."

"What do you mean?" I step back and lean against the counter. It's a farce, truly, since I'm too tense to slouch convincingly against it.

"You tell me what I mean." Her face is soft, but her brows say she knows me inside and out.

"A lot of work stuff, Mom. Deadlines. You know." At the root of it all is Kit, but I don't want her to know that. Why can't I fucking let it go?

"Hmm." Her touch is cool against my cheek as she pats me, her focus on me shrewd. "Set the table and then come back in here."

Fuck. She knows I didn't give her the truth. And some sixth sense tells her that I'm about to burst.

Nevertheless, the punishment begins. She's a master at making people wait, letting them stew in their gastric juices until they realize their mistake and ask for forgiveness.

Her damn stall tactic worked so well when I was a kid. I could never hold out. My stomach would knot, my palms would sweat, and I'd be so

107

nauseated that by the time I was done with what she wanted, I'd spill the beans so I wouldn't puke.

"I'll tell you now."

"Nope, dishes first."

I grab the plates roughly, loading on silverware and balancing cups. I push through the swinging door and start setting the table. My gut sours, and bile climbs up my throat like it's an honesty ladder, wanting to spew out in a geyser of truth vomit.

I should have said I don't want to talk about it. Instead, I lied, and I'm not sure why I did. Now I'm going to be in torment for the rest of the night.

Where are the TUMS?

I close my eyes, groaning.

Fuck, I'm an ass. When I first saw Kit, my pulse raced, my stomach got those weird flutters, and I was hard as a rock. She had an ass I wanted to grab on to and sink into. She was—*is*—perfection with her freckles, fiery red hair, and curves for freaking miles.

I glance around, making sure it's clear before adjusting myself outside my pants. No sense in scaring Mom and embarrassing myself. *Roadkill, malaria, starving children.* That cools things down for now.

Bracing myself, I walk back into the kitchen. Her back is to me, and she's whisking something like crazy. Violet is next to her, grabbing buns out of the second oven.

"Violet, I think Mad is asking for you." Well, that one popped out of nowhere. Great, two lies in one day.

"Whatever. Tell him to do it himself. Big baby. Can't take care of things on his own sometimes." She huffs, her blond hair swinging as she shuffles out the door.

"Ma." I stand beside her. "I'm sorry for trying to brush you off." I look down at my feet.

"I know when things aren't right, so don't say 'It's nothing.' Don't lie to me."

She's right.

I rake my hands through my hair before straightening. "I met this woman, and...I don't know much about her."

"Hm." I watch as she whisks her gravy into perfection. That is my mom—even in imperfect moments, her love is limitless.

"But every time I see her, I just...I have no control over anything. She wants nothing to do with me, but I want to be near her. We went out, but the date ended badly. It wasn't anything I could change, but I called and apologized. I texted. I don't know what the fuck I'm doing."

"Language."

"Ma! You called yourself a bullshitter the other day."

"Yeah, well, I'm your mother, and it's my house. I'm allowed to swear in my home; you're not." Her smile is bright, her gaze twinkling with no remorse. "Is she from here?"

"Yeah. She recently moved back."

"Is she dating someone or married?" She pours the gravy into two bowls, then twirls to set them on the island.

"No. I asked."

Back to me, she sets her hands on her hips. "Well, that's a start. In time, you'll figure out the rest. You know, your father was like that when we met. He was always in my space, putting his hand on my back or touching my hand. I was already engaged."

"What? I never knew that."

"Nobody does. Your dad doesn't like to tell the story. He still thinks it's a weakness that made him go after me so hard. I was his secretary, but he knew from the beginning that he loved me. Me? I was slow to come around."

"How did Dad change your mind?"

Mom looks at me for several long moments, then cups my cheeks and angles my head down so she can see into my eyes. It makes me squirm when she does this, like she can see into my soul.

I hold still, letting her look deep, my gut doing that dropping thing again.

Being emotional is not my MO. Pretty sure I need a head check.

"That's the same thing I saw in your father, Greer. That longing look." She pulls me down to kiss my cheek before letting go. "He was too in my face all the time. Everything he did made me angry. I threatened to quit so many times, but the money was too good. Thank goodness." Her laughter lifts the sucker punch out of my stomach.

"He annoyed the hell out of me. I thought he was driving me crazy because he was my boss. I'd been working there for four months, traveling with him to meetings and whatnot. He fought with me in the car one day because it was his favorite thing. He riled me up whenever he got a chance. He told me later that when I fought back, he knew I cared for him.

"Anyway, there was a wreck up ahead on the road. A bad one. I watched as he stayed in control, stayed rational. He saved a man from a burning vehicle that day. It was a side of him I'd never seen. He was only irrational and chaotic with me because not having me drove him crazy."

She moves to pull the green bean casserole out of the oven. "When he got back in the car, his adrenaline was high. He leaned over and kissed me. It was never the same after that. When I broke my engagement, he proposed the next day."

The smile on her face is sly. "I made him wait a few months before I said yes, but he was a changed man after that. He was calmer but no less intense, no less controlling. But he only controlled himself. He encouraged me to be strong and do what was best for my heart as long as he was involved, too, and I loved that. He was calm and rational during life's storms. I love him so much more now."

I frown, hoping I was getting this right. "So he showed you how rational he could be and that changed it all for you?"

"It was what I needed to see. You know me." She shrugs. "I needed to know that someone could calm me down if needed, be my anchor."

An anchor.

Dr. Everson said I needed to keep Kit grounded. That restless energy eases a bit at the thought.

Is it possible that I can turn this around? "How do I know what she needs?"

"Find out why she's distancing herself from you. When you know that, maybe it will help you figure out how to keep her."

She kisses my cheek once more, giving me soft eyes again before turning back to the stove.

The room breaks out in chaos when the meal is ready, but I eat in relative silence, watching my parents, their smiles and laughter. Their love shines through in every exchange. They fight, but they also love hard.

I spin my fork in my hand. So I'm acting like Dad when he fell in love. I'm not in love, but I have never had this all-consuming, soul-sucking need to be around someone.

I grab a few plates to help clear the table. If I can get her to let me in, I sure as hell won't leave.

If I see her around again, I want to keep her.

Thirteen

Kit

"I LIKE THE ATMOSPHERE here." I grab a napkin and carefully wipe my mouth as I finish my meal. "It's a lovely restaurant." It's a rustic bistro that brews its own wine and serves an eclectic menu. The sort of place I would make my usual spot.

Carl peeks up from his plate, trying to claim my attention.

It's a Friday night, and this is my fourth blind date—all friends of Rosemary's friends. People I can't say no to. After the last one, I want to curl up on my couch, read a book, and eat sushi alone. Why did I agree to this? Oh, right, because my "dead" husband was a cheating, abusive, lying sack of shit, and I want to prove to myself that he didn't break me.

Not sure I've accomplished it yet, though. My independence is tentative, and my heart smarts anytime I think about his mistress. Who should be texting any day now to *check in*. I'll text back to be polite, but I can't, for the life of me, understand why she's interested in keeping in touch.

At least I have these dates. And the getaway that Rosemary and Angelo planned for us at his bosses' cabin. My bag is packed in my car so I can head straight there from here. Carl has to work the night shift, so the date should end early.

Damn you, Rosemary. Seriously, I gave her a timid okay to a date, and she pounced like an attack dog.

"Get to know people while you get to know yourself," she said.

"It'll be fun," she said.

They are not always fun.

But as much as I don't like them, they're teaching me a lot. Like that I love rock climbing and sushi, and I want a dog. I hate picnics in the park, men who are superstitious about sports (one date threatened to punch a guy if he didn't take the other team's jersey off), and peanuts in Thai food.

I've also started a list of dealbreakers: men who smoke, are late, or are dirty. I draw the line at twice-weekly showers (or less). Also, not wearing shoes. Who does that? I don't want to see their feet.

"Kit?" His hand casually brushes mine.

I jump, my attention coming back to him. He's a nice-looking guy—if a little plain. Brown eyes beneath dark, slanting brows, framed by black tortoiseshell glasses. His hair is thick and nicely groomed. He's only an inch or so taller than me, but he dresses nice and smells pretty good.

But he does nothing for me.

Not like Greer.

Just the memory of that man makes me shiver. I push the thought of him away like I've been pushing away the urge to listen to his voicemails. It's a constant battle, shoving down the need to hear them, especially when darkness falls, and I ache for the sound of his voice.

He probably called to say *hope you feel better* or something. But on the off chance that it was something worse, I refuse to play them.

If only Greer didn't test my limits. He takes away any sense of control I have. I want to push him and pull him close at the same time. It's those contradictory feelings that make me so wary.

And he saw me at my worst.

Giving Carl a slight smile, I tuck a strand of hair behind my ear. "Sorry, I was thinking about something else."

He smiles, giving me a warm look. Too bad his irises aren't sinful amber, then they would be perfect.

"I must not be engaging if your mind is wandering."

"It's not that. I've been applying for jobs and moving into a new home. I have a lot on my mind." Right, waiting for those interviews to turn into a job offer.

He strokes his fingertips over my hand as his smile turns seductive. "It's okay. When my friend set this up, I didn't know you were so stunning. I'm enjoying our date."

"I am too, Carl. We have a lot in common. Being a paramedic is such a crazy job, but you seem so calm and level-headed."

"I have to be. If I'm not, patients can lose their life."

"Much like nursing."

"Exactly like nursing." He rubs the top of my hand again, then flips it over. I watch as his fingers skitter along my palm. This is nice. As long as I don't compare it to the intense longing I experienced with Greer.

That keeps me awake at night. And okay, I may have once or twice—all right, *three* times this week—orgasmed to fantasies of him, fingers frantic, heart racing.

The Greer of my dreams is sweet, patient, and not intimidating at all. Most of the time. His hand twisted in my hair and tugged tight once, and instead of banishing the fantasy or relating it to my past, I let it play out to a delightful end. He keeps some of my nightmares at bay, helping me get more than a few hours of sleep at night.

Not thinking of Greer.

"Well, my shift starts in an hour, so we better part ways soon." Carl stands, pulling my chair back before grabbing my coat and holding it out for me. I smile to myself. He's charming, and the best date I've had so far.

His fingers graze mine, then loop around them. He catches my attention again before smiling. Sweet. But nothing rushes through me when he touches me.

Will this be how it always is now? I'll compare everyone to Greer and how he moved me?

He leads me to the door, holding my hand while I follow behind. He's gentle and even-tempered. His touch is pleasant. Easy. Simple.

When we reach my car, he pulls me in close, his hands settling at my waist. I tense, fighting back the need to move away.

I need to get used to this, the touches. Think of other things, focus on other things. I inhale, catching the scent of his smooth aftershave. It's a little intense but not overwhelming.

Is he going to kiss me? Spikes of ice shoot against my skin.

As long as I don't give him a signal, he'll figure it out. No signal. Straight face equals no kiss.

"Can I call you again, Kit?"

I try not to show my reluctance. How can I let him down easily? It's not you; it's me. I did that to Greer. This time, though, it's him. Maybe if I step back, get out of his arms first? Then say I need space.

I stare up at him, opening my mouth to tell him just that.

Sparks flicker across his face, his brows rise, and then he's leaning close, his lips briefly brushing mine.

No! Wait, I didn't give the signal. No.

He shifts a little closer, his keys poking me in the thigh—*hard*. I jerk back, and he follows, his lips brushing over mine again.

I turn my head to break contact. "Carl, your keys are poking me. Will you take a step back, please?" I need space. And probably a shower to rid myself of any lingering unease if it's not his keys.

"Oh, sorry." He shoves his hands into his pocket. "It's not my keys."

Please, no.

He pulls out an elaborately decorated vial with an etching on it. He smiles warmly at it and keeps it in his palm like he's waiting for me to ask about it.

"Is that a pepper shaker?" I hold out my hand, and he sets it in my palm while I stifle a laugh. "Why are you carrying pepper with you?"

Redness paints his cheeks. "That's not pepper. It's actually my mom."

I shove it back at him, my hands shaking as I rub them back and forth against my pants.

He fumbles with the vial. If my life was a movie, everything would slow down as it tumbles from his hand. But it isn't, and the vial moves quickly through the air.

He dives for it, missing, and the elaborate mother-holding device smashes into the hard pavement, the crystal shattering, the ash flying in every direction. I jump back, holding my breath as Carl falls to the ground.

"Oh my ever-loving god!" His screech is high-pitched as his hands sift through the ash. "My mother, you dropped my mother! Argh." His face pinches and reddens, and his eyes flash. Facing me with tears welling in his eyes. "Now I'll never have that piece of her again."

My heart twists at the agony I've caused. Shit. "I didn't mean to. I'm so sorry. So, so sorry." I keep one hand over my mouth, plugging my nose and taking a step back. As the "dust" settles, Carl openly weeps over the gray mess.

"Do you have a baggy or something? Anything?" His hands tremble, and I stand staring at the sight before me, of this man on his knees on the wet concrete as the slush eviscerates the dry ashes.

"I, uh...I'll go ask the bistro. I'll be right back." I rush into the store and bring back an eco-friendly takeaway container for him. He collects himself and starts shoveling the snowy ash mixture into the container with his hands. Not sure what else to do, I stand there waiting for him to finish. When he finally rises, I try to look into his eyes, but he evades me.

"Carl, I'm so sorry." My eyes stick to his face. I reach out to touch him, hoping to console him. Scratch that, I'm fairly certain his mom is still all over him. *Ugh.* Gross. I bring my hand back, trying to hide what I'm sure is a look of horror.

"I need to take her home and put her in the dehydrator. I think I got all of her." His voice is neutral and calm despite the tense set of his body and the tightness of his mouth. He takes a deep breath and forces all the air out, making weird noises at the end.

And I can't stop staring wide-eyed as his body relaxes and his smile returns. "I'm not, uh...She's my mother, and I'm remarkably close to her." He glances at me sheepishly through his lashes. He reaches his hand out to touch my cheek.

Ugh, no. No more touching after that.

I shift back, ducking under his hand. "Well, you better get home if you're going to do that and have time to get to work."

His eyes flash with hurt, but he leans in again to kiss me goodbye, stopping when he notices my face. He steps back. "Can I still call you?"

My face drops, and my belly tightens like it's preparing to run. I don't want to hurt his feelings, but damn it, carrying your mother around is eccentric and bizarre.

Why do I keep getting the unique people?

Shaking my head, I suck in a deep breath. *I hope there is no mother dust in that one.* "I don't think so, Carl. It was nice to meet you."

"All right, well. Goodbye, Kit."

Stepping into my car, avoiding all eye contact as he stands there with his mother in his hands, I pull my phone out of my purse and place it on the center console.

I start my SUV, set my GPS, and then sit while everything defrosts. A voicemail from Colette is waiting, so I hit play.

"Hello, darling. I hope you're doing well. Call me later this week and fill me in on how the interviews are going. All my love."

She's been so supportive since I returned home. It's helped to ease the ache of leaving her in California. I've mentioned Harper to her on several occasions, and so far, she's remained cold toward her.

I click on a text from Ro next.

Ro: *How'd it go?*

I peek at the windshield. Seeing Carl gone, I grab my phone and call her. She picks up on the second ring, and I jump in. "Damn it, Rosemary, where do you get these people? Carl actually brought his mother's ashes to our date. Seriously. It has to be a practical joke."

"What? I didn't know he'd do that!" Her voice and laughter muffle like she's hiding behind her hand. "Are you heading up to the cabin yet?"

"I was going to stop at home and shower first. I got some...stuff...all over me."

"Don't worry about that. You can shower when you get there. We're going to be leaving soon. Make sure you don't delay too long. There's supposed to be a storm starting tonight."

"How bad of a storm? Are we talking Canada storm or a regular one?"

"I think some heavy snowfall to start, but maybe winds and stuff starting tomorrow."

"Got it. I'm set to go. GPS says I'm about an hour and a half away."

"And you're sure you're safe to drive?"

"I didn't have any alcohol if that's what you're asking."

She hums. "We should be right behind you."

We say goodbye, and I click off before putting my car in drive and heading north.

I squint through snow so dense it looks like it's flying upward as it hits my windshield. It's been two hours already, and my GPS says I've got another three minutes to go if I were traveling the speed limit. At least the wind isn't howling yet.

"Hey, phone, call Rosemary."

She answers on the third ring sounding more than sleepy. "Hello."

"Hey. You sound passed out, is Angelo driving?"

"Oh shit, no. Kit, the snow started coming down hard here. He didn't want to drive in it, so we're waiting until morning. Did you make it yet?"

Well, shoot. "No, and I should have waited too. I can barely make out what's in front of me." I hit the wipers, kicking them up a notch, then flick on the high beams, which don't help.

"I'm sorry, Kit. I didn't think it would be that bad."

"It wasn't bad when I started out. It only got heavy in the last five minutes. Everyone else is there, right?"

"Uh, honestly, I'm not sure. I know Angelo's boss is up there. Don't forget I texted you the code to get in."

"What's his name again?"

The connection gets fuzzy as she says a name.

"What was that?"

"Sccc...rr."

Then the line dies. Great. I have no bars, and I'm not sure if anyone is up there. What if everyone else stayed behind because of the snowstorm?

Well past midnight, I turn onto a back-country road. There isn't a single tire track in sight.

I pull up to the cabin. Darkness pools in on all sides as I try to make out the monstrosity in front of me. This isn't a freaking cabin. This is a mansion in the middle of nowhere. Who the hell owns this place?

I park and dial Rosemary.

Beep, beep, beep.

Ugh. Of course there isn't a signal out here with the snow falling in blankets. Typing out the text anyway, I tell her I made it and click send.

This is just my luck.

With a sigh, I turn off my vehicle, then twist in the seat to grab my bag. I pat around the seat and floor, finding only air. Frantic, I hike half my body back there to search. Where's my bag? A heavy weight drops deep into my belly.

I forgot my bag. Shit, shit, shit. No, I swear I put it in the car.

I don't want to sleep with Carl's mother all weekend and don't want anyone else to have to sleep with her, either. Maybe I can find an extra set of clothes inside because sleeping naked with a bunch of people I don't know nearby is not an option. Shit.

Well, get on with it.

At the door, the world is eerily quiet. The wind blows, and a *shclrp* with a random plop sounds behind me. I jump, turning around. The *schlrp* sounds behind me again, and a massive patch of snow slides off the roof and hits the ground not five feet from me.

Shit, get inside. I punch in the code and dash in before an alarm sounds.

As I shut the door, a deafening *crack* sounds outside, and everything turns black.

Please let it be a fluke. Being in a house without power, with people I don't know, is kind of stupid. Okay, maybe I am stupid. I did drive out to Bumfuck, Egypt, in a snowstorm no one knew was coming—thank you, Canada.

I twirl to face the room I'm in.

Pitch-black. The house is completely dark. The only sound is the howl from the snowstorm.

I flip on my phone's flashlight and take a look around. I'm in the entryway, which is approximately the size of my entire home.

I creep forward, and when I round a corner, the little light from my phone teases at the place's rustic atmosphere. Large fluffy couches and light-colored chairs sit in a drop-down family room. The slowly dying embers in a stone fireplace paint the softest of glows.

Sweet, that's a good sign. At least someone has been here in the last few hours, and I haven't seen a speck of blood on the floor or walls, so it's not a murder scene.

"Hey, uh." Well, shit. I still don't know his name. "Bossman? Hello?" Yeah, stupid, but I can't think of anything better.

I kind of want to be a dick and call him shit for brains. Who drives out in this craptastic weather? But then again, I just drove through the storm to be here. Rosemary owes me for this. She's the only reason I came on this *weekend up north*, and she isn't even here.

Well, she isn't the only reason. I needed to get away. My calls with Colette have been okay, but then she ends by asking me to move back to California.

Every. Single. Time.

She's lonely, but she needs to move on like I'm trying to. We are still family, but I wish she'd stop asking.

She could reach out to Francesca. I'd *love* for her to take over communication with my late husband's mistress. I sent a box of pictures and heirlooms to Francesca, and she's been texting or calling every week since.

When I showed Rosemary how many texts I'd gotten this week, she said Francesca seemed a bit obsessed. Maybe she is. Who am I to judge, though? She's got her demons, and I have mine.

Luckily, mine is dead. I'm here trying to exorcise the ghost.

I don't know whether I'm running to something or away from it.

Ethan.

Still out there, hiding, wearing me down, waiting to catch me unaware so he can pounce. My gut instincts say he isn't dead, and I have a hard time ignoring that. Or the little chills I get once in a while like I'm being watched when I think I'm alone.

I make my way through the home, finding a kitchen, a bathroom, and a poolroom, but no other signs of life. After a full circle, I'm back in the entryway. I only saw one bedroom on the first floor, so I take the stairs hugging the left wall to find a place to settle in for the night.

I shine my light down the hallway, my belly souring, my blood pumping harshly through my ears. My skin prickles as I walk through the darkness.

Why did I drive up here alone?

Focus Kit. Find someone, find a bed, anything. And if you can't do that, go back downstairs and throw another log on the fire because you're going to need the heat.

Damn, this place is scary, though. My heart races as I trek down the hall to the first open door. I peer in, my flashlight swinging from corner to corner, casting shadows everywhere.

A man appears in the darkness.

I squeak, shoving my hand over my mouth. I tremble as the man remains where he is, almost impossible to see in the darkness. I point my flashlight at him, and he disappears.

A shadow. I exhale.

Of course.

I give myself a mental shake, fortifying myself, and sweep the light over the room, highlighting a tall chair—the "man." *Oh, for the love of Pete, I'm losing my mind over a stinking shadow.*

Forcing my pulse to slow, I give myself a moment. *Get a grip, Kit. There's nothing here to fear.* Except, every room is empty, and despite calling out, I get no response. This is the perfect plot for my husband to reappear and murder me.

What if I am here alone? The last room is the only one left to check. I flash my light down that way. This door, unlike the others, is almost closed.

I've looked everywhere else. If bossman is here, this is where he is. *Do I knock?*

I rap my knuckles on the hardwood and wait.

No response.

I do it again, my heart picking up pace again.

I push open the door. It creaks so loud it almost shatters my ear drums. "Hey...guy?" The silence greets me as I step into the room and flash my light toward the bed.

I frown. Well, shit, someone was here if the wrinkly sheets have anything to say about it.

What in the ever-loving hell? I'm going to kill Rosemary. Frowning, I approach the bed. "Hell—*oh* shit!"

A hand reaches out from the shadows.

A scream rips from my throat as I'm lifted and thrown onto the bed. I land on my back, bouncing a moment before a big, thick body lands on top of me. Massive thighs cage in my arms, and a rough hand settles around my neck, squeezing enough to make me panic but not enough to cut off my air.

A stiff, raspy voice grates out, "Who the fuck are you, and why are you in my house?"

I scream.

Fourteen

Greer

I SLAP MY HANDS over my ears. The noise from below me is too high-pitched to be a man's. Fuck, I need lights. Scrambling off, I flip on the bedside lamp. Nothing.

I swipe my phone off the nightstand and open the app that turns the backup generators on. I don't know how Asher fucking did it—something about giving the generator its own solar-powered Wi-Fi so we have access to it all the time—but I'm thankful I don't have to go out in the snow to get it going anymore.

I give it a moment, grossly aware of the whimpering coming from the bed, and then flick on the light. It casts the room in a soft glow, giving me the chance to see my intruder. The lump in my sheets is trembling and growing noisier by the minute.

Fiery red waves cascade over the bed, and the curves of a woman are curled into the fetal position, her body shaking.

I approach slowly.

Oh, fuck. Freckles everywhere. Red hair.

Kit.

Shit, is this a panic attack? Tears stream down her face, her eyelids are clenched together, and she's got her arms wrapped around herself while she makes the most awful sound of misery I've ever heard. "No...no...no."

I triggered this.

My stomach tumbles to the floor, my hands hanging helplessly.

Her body trembles, and sweat coats her skin. Still, I step closer.

"Kit? Oh, fuck. I'm sorry, so sorry."

I reach out to touch her but pull back when she flinches. Her eyes stay screwed shut, but somehow, she senses me. Her sobbing hits me in the chest, smacking me with her hurt, making bile rise in my throat.

She pulls her hands up to her face, muttering words like *shit* and *please, no,* and *Ethan*. By some miracle, she's not talking about me, and whoever Ethan is, he's fucking dead.

"Kit, it's Greer. Can you hear me?" My focus on her, I lean in close to the bed. Please snap out of it.

She's gasping and gagging. I can't stop my cringe when she vomits on the bed. Her body is cold and rigid when I pick her up and shuttle her to my bathroom.

"No...Ethan, no. Don't...don't hurt..." She pulls herself into a smaller ball. I shuffle her in my arms, holding her.

Shower—that's the best option.

I turn it on, shifting her with one arm and a knee to hold her up. She retches again, and I tip her up quickly. *Please don't choke.* Twice she vomits down the front of her clothes before the steam from the shower is visible. The hold I have on her is sure as I step inside.

"Kit, baby, shhh. Deep breaths. In, out." My body is shaking, damn it. I hope I'm not fucking her up more.

On the floor in the shower, I wrap her up in my arms, trying not to hold too tight. She needs to calm. "Kit, shhh, it's Greer. I'm so sorry. Can you take a deep breath?" She continues to sob, her body shaking so hard she almost slips out of my arms.

I settle her, tucking her head under my chin, her hips in my lap, and her legs off to the side. The water cleans away the mess as I stroke her hair softly, rocking her, crooning about how good she's doing.

Telling her to take deep breaths and that she's beautiful.

That I'm so sorry.

Grounding. The doctor from outside the movie theater said to try grounding. "Kit, can you tell me three things you see?" I wait, asking a few more times, but she continues to sob. Fuck it. This is useless when she can't hear me through her pain.

Maybe if I did what Mom did when I was a kid, that would help. Strained but steady, I start with a hum, then work up to singing.

I go through "I Will Follow You Into The Dark" twice.

Her sobbing slows, so I keep singing, the melody slow and sweet.

Her body sags against mine, the shock receding under the spray. Starting again, I sing softer until everything slows to a normal rhythm.

My legs go numb, and my arms ache, but still, I don't move. Eventually, her body adjusts slightly.

"Kit?" I peek down at her.

She jolts, her deep green eyes focusing, widening when she finally notices me. "Greer." Realizing where she is, she pushes against my chest, attempting to get out of my arms.

"Shhh, Kit. Give me a minute...just sit. I'm not decent." And I'm noticing her soaking wet clothes and how they cling to her luscious body. Nope, this is not the time. *Don't be a dick.*

"Why are we in the shower? How the hell did I get here? How the hell did *you* get here?" She struggles in earnest. Her voice rises. "Greer, why are you here?"

"Sit, and I'll tell you. I...Please stop moving, Kit." Her squirms are driving me crazy, and despite it being a shitty time, my body doesn't care. I hold her a little closer, praying she will stop shifting against me.

It's too much. Her body is soft and warm, and even after what happened in the last hour, my body is reminding me of how right she is against me.

"Greer, is that...uh..."

"Kit. Please." I drop my wet head against hers, gritting my teeth. Finally, she stops moving.

"Why are we in the shower?"

"What's the last thing you remember?"

She blinks a few times. "I remember walking into the last room in the hall."

"I didn't know anyone was in the house. I sleep pretty hard." I swallow against the tightness in my throat. "You must have opened the door to my room, and somehow it woke me up. Then when you walked in the door, I pushed you onto the bed and held you down. I thought you were an intruder. I'm sorry. You must have had a panic attack or something, screaming and yelling about someone named Ethan."

Fighting the urge to tuck her hair behind her ear, I continue. "I think you were in shock. We're in the shower because you puked a lot, and I didn't know where else to go. I'm naked because I sleep naked, and I didn't think to put clothes on."

I lean back, tilting my head so I can see her.

She peeks up at my face, roaming over it. "So you attacked me and then sat in here with me until my freak-out stopped?"

"Yup, that sums it up. Don't forget I'm naked." I smile deep, my dimples popping, hoping it helps calm her.

Dark-red hair paints her cheeks, and I finally give in to the urge and tuck that stray strand of hair behind her ear. "Any of it coming back yet?"

She nods, studying me. "The power was out. Otherwise, I would have flipped on lights." She pauses a moment, her brows furrowing. "Did you call me baby?"

Of everything that happened, that's what she remembers? My laughter spills out, filling the shower. "I may have gotten carried away, but honestly, it felt right. You want to tell me about it?"

"Not really. Do we have to stay in the shower?"

"Shut your eyes, and I'll get out." I want her to look at me, but I don't want to upset her. I wait until I can stand her up and then head out the door, grabbing a towel and wrapping it around myself.

"I'm decent. There's a towel out here for you. When you're ready, I'll meet you downstairs." Her face is comical as she keeps one eye squinted shut, the other open a sliver.

"Greer? Is it okay if I clean up while I'm in here? And can I borrow some clothes?"

"Give me yours, and I'll put them in the laundry."

"I'm not letting you see me naked."

"Kit, I'll be a perfect gentleman and only sneak a small peek." She gasps, sending those saw blades buzzing in my belly. She's so cute. "I won't even open my eyes. Put them in my hands."

Squeezing my eyes tight, I wait for what seems like forever before the shower door creaks open. I hold my hands out, and the sopping-wet clothes are in my arms before the door clicks shut.

Now I have at least ten minutes to strip the bed and change the sheets before heading downstairs to wait.

What the hell happened to her?

Kit

"Your clothes should be ready by morning." Greer's deep voice calls from the living area. "And I have a lot of questions."

So do I. Like how do I face him? And can I hide on the stairs for the rest of the night?

I threw up on his bed. He had to change the sheets. If he didn't think I was an idiot before, he has to now.

My hands tremble, and I shake them out, the energy dancing up my legs and into my arms. I will my body to calm.

"Are you coming in?"

That gravelly deliciousness shouldn't call to me like a siren song, but it does. And even though I'm afraid of what he thinks of me, my feet move of their own volition.

Okay, focus on anything but the need to run. Look at the room.

My attention zeroes in on Greer.

So much for focusing on the room, disloyal eyes.

He is sitting on one of the cream-colored sofas directly across the fireplace. His long legs stretch out before him. He's wearing gray sweatpants but no shirt, his hands resting behind his head. His chest is broad and covered with a dusting of hair, with a swirling mosaic of black lines running from his shoulder to his elbow.

He has restarted the fire. Not that we need it, because he effortlessly absorbs all the energy in the room while making it hot as hades in here.

The cabin is rustic and open, with what looks like a large kitchen connected to a dining area. A sunken living room is two steps down from the platform entryway and tastefully decorated with muted colors. The main wall is a deep blue, with grays and creams accenting it. The fireplace has slate rocks in varying shades stacked to the ceiling. It's like being under the ocean in a calming wave.

I swallow as I step down and make my way over to the couch. Drawn by the intensity of his gaze and the warmth of the blaze, I'm pulled to the spot next to him. If I want, I can reach out and touch him; he's so close.

Dressed in one of his shirts and sweatpants, I try to settle. After everything, I'm surprisingly calm but wary of what I need to say next.

I need to apologize again.

He arches a brow, his voice soft and gentle. "You okay?"

"Yeah. I need to say this, so don't say anything until I finish. Okay?" His face is earnest as he keeps his gaze on me and nods. "I'm so sorry. For this, tonight, and the movie. I freaked out on you twice. And each time, you've been nothing but kind to me. And I puked on you."

He opens his mouth. "I—"

"Quiet, or I won't get this out." Maybe this woman who's telling him what to do will stick around for a while. I like her.

His brows shoot up, but he presses his lips together then gives me an encouraging smile.

"When you look at me, I don't want you to see something broken or damaged. I don't want you to think you have to fix or save me."

He gives me a slow once-over. "I'm looking. And I think you look good in my old college shirt. It's a little big, but I like it. I promise, Kit. I won't hold those against you. We all have our demons. Some are just harder to see."

Heat paints my cheeks, and I sag against the seat.

He doesn't think I'm crazy. He might even like me.

Like I like him? I've tried to deny it, but everything about him appeals to me on some primal level.

I tuck my hands under my thighs, pretending they're cold. If I don't keep myself in check, I'll be touching him to see if his skin feels as warm as it looks.

He scratches the back of his neck before looking away for a moment. "Do you need some sleep first? Or can I ask my questions?"

"Oh, I'm up. I'll probably have an adrenaline crash here soon, so you've got about thirty minutes."

"Thirty minutes. That's precise."

I shift my gaze away and shrug. "I'm pretty familiar with the cycle." I push a wet strand of hair behind my ear and peek at him from under my lashes. "You can ask."

Greer's face softens, but his brows knit together. "First, why are you here?"

"I'm supposed to be here. Everyone is coming up this weekend for the cabin get-together." I give him the side-eye. His grimace makes my stomach drop. "Am I not supposed to be here?"

"Who is everybody? I don't know if I know anyone you know."

"My sister Rosemary and her husband—"

Clarity dawns on his face. "Angelo. He works for me. You're Katherine."

"Yup, that's my real name."

He chuckles softly, shaking his head. All the while, he stares at me, sending tingles zipping down my spine.

Holy hell, he can slay me. If he keeps staring, he will see through to my soul. And the arousal? It's delicious and thick, warming me from the inside out.

He's all out laughing now, this deep rumble of a sound. I want to roll around in it, soak it up, and then bottle it to use later when I'm feeling sad.

"What?" I lean forward, shifting my hands and tucking them between my thighs. All the better to contain those traitorous bastards. They want to stroke his skin to see if it's as silky as it looks. He needs to put a shirt on, and I need to focus on what he's saying.

"Angelo kept trying to get me to meet you. I think they may have taken matters into their own hands. I needed a break. I've felt kind of"—he smirks, watching my hands before he shifts and peeks back up at me—"burned out and needed a week to myself."

Well, now it makes sense. *Damn it, Rosemary.*

She's been setting me up on dates with duds for weeks, and now I know why. "I'm intruding on your time. So they tricked me? I talked to Rosemary on my drive here. She said they were leaving in the morning because of the storm."

"Yeah. They won't be here until later next week. And you're stuck here for at least the rest of the night."

"Well, I figured I'd be here all weekend, but I thought I'd have my sister here too. Hopefully, it will be clear enough to drive out."

He nods toward the window where it's dark still. "The snow is really coming down out there."

I make my way to the window and pull back the drapes. It's still black outside, but I can make out the heavy snowflakes hitting close to the windowpane.

"This sucks." I grumble, and he laughs.

A shadow appears in the glass behind me. "Is it so bad to be stuck here with me?"

I'm having a hard time not eating him up in the reflection. I fist my hands to keep from reaching out and touching him. It's like they have a mind of their own tonight. "No, but it's not what I had planned for the weekend. It's pretty out there, though."

"Absolutely beautiful." He's looking at my image in the glass.

He makes my body sing with desire. My cheeks are already reacting to his words.

Needing space, I shuffle to the side. He is so close; I can almost taste him standing next to me. While Rosemary and Angelo might trust him, I'm not sure I'm ready for this step.

But *he* is the beautiful one.

I'm transfixed as he crosses his arms over his broad chest. Sparks fill me, warmth flooding my core and my cheeks. He watches me like he's trying to figure me out.

"Whew, the fire is warm." I shift away from him, moving back to the couch. I need to cool down a bit.

There's enough oxygen in the room, but it's hard to breathe.

I bite the inside of my cheek, trying to kill off my need, and tuck my feet under me again. He sits down, too, closer this time, with his thigh brushing against my knee.

"Are you saying I'm stuck here for a while?" I wiggle my toes closer.

I can't get my heart to slow down with him continually creeping into my space. He's like a beautiful sunset on a rotten day.

"At least until the snowplows come this way." He yawns, and I stifle my own. "Who is Ethan?"

I blink at him. He deserves some sort of explanation, especially after how he took care of me. My heart is aching, telling me to crack. I clear my throat, swallowing down the lump in my throat.

"Ethan was my husband." I wrap my fingers around themselves, pushing myself deeper into the couch.

"Was?"

"He died three years ago, but he's always been there, haunting me."

"What does that mean?"

A prickling burn licks down my spine, shocking me as it moves into my fingers.

It isn't his right to know, and I don't have to answer that question. I shrug one shoulder, grinding my teeth together, tucking what he wants to know inside my cheek.

When I don't answer, he asks another. "How did he die?"

"No one knows. There is no evidence of his death, not even a body. Nothing. He was on a work trip to Brazil. There was a flash flood, and his body got swept out into the ocean."

"Tell me about him."

"I'd rather not." I shift my gaze to the carpet, letting it blur the longer I stare. "I left that part of my life behind. It took years to get the courage, and I try to revisit the memories as little as possible."

"Why did you have a panic attack when I touched you? Is it because he hurt you?"

"You sure know how to let things go, don't you?" My gut tightens, and I glare at him as I rub my arms. "I said it's a part of my life I don't want to talk about with you. I don't know you." My body is rigid, ready to flee at the first sign of his eventual explosion of anger.

He holds up his hands, an innocent look etched on his features. When he brings his hands back down, his face falls for a moment. "I want to get to know you."

"Why? So you can revel in my stellar attitude."

"So I can revel in being beside you."

Really? My body melts a little at that, and I stifle the urge to fan myself. I'm downright steamy now.

He smiles and shifts his body a little. "How about I tell you about me first? I'm methodical. I'm working on expanding my business overseas. I bought a house recently, and I plan to renovate that next spring. I've got a trip planned for April that will take me to Japan. I'm working on a mockup for a part I created."

I nod.

That's all great, but how do I know he's not going to hurt me? How do I even ask that? I can't come out and ask, "Have you ever beaten a girlfriend? How do you manage your frustration and anger? Will you come to hate me once you realize I'm not the perfect woman?"

Sweat pools in my palms, and I grind my teeth together, fighting to find the right words. I want to trust him, but I need to know who he is deep down.

Asking Ethan *anything* was like setting off a bomb, regardless of what I asked or how I phrased it.

With Ethan, the sky was never blue; it was azure, cornflower, or slightly gray. The weather wasn't hot; it was sweltering, scorching, or boiling. And I wasn't perfect unless I was perfectly made up and silent.

"Tell me about you."

I jerk, the sound of his voice jarring me from my spiral. Frozen, I wait for him to lay into me for daydreaming, but his smile is warm and friendly.

I rub up and down my arm and will my muscles to relax. Then I shrug. "There isn't much to tell." Truthfully, I have no clue who I am sometimes.

He taps my thigh. "What's your favorite thing to do?"

I frown, my shoulders stiffening again. I don't know. I was beginning to figure all that out with those stupid dates Rosemary set up.

He breaks the silence when I don't respond. "I like woodworking. Reading. On rare occasions, I play basketball. Loved football in high school. I love hiking and being outside. Any of those?"

Shit. I don't know. And he's about to realize what a mess I am. I spent six years unbecoming the person I was to please Ethan.

If we were out in public, I played the part of a trophy wife. With family, I was the doting wife, always catering to him. In private, I was the punching bag. Now I'm none of those things.

"I don't know. I'm..."

"You don't know what you like to do? You don't have a hobby?"

I shrug and look at where I've got my fingers twisted together in my lap.

"Come on, tell me one thing you like to do."

My heart hammers in my chest. "I...I don't..." All my thoughts fly out the window under his intense focus.

"Okay." He shrugs, a brow knitting. "How about an easy one? Where do you see yourself in a few years?"

The tightness in my chest increases, and I blink back tears. That question was harder than the last.

He softens. "Okay. Tell me a happy memory."

I huff out a breath, forcing myself to chuckle. A happy memory. Those are almost nonexistent. But somehow, I think of one. "It was a long time ago. Rosemary was going off to college, and we spent the night watching old movies, drinking sodas, and sneaking a few beers from Dad's stash. She was so happy—happy to snuggle up and spend the evening with me when she could have been out with her friends."

I peek at Greer from under my lashes, shifting, drawing my legs closer to myself.

"That's a sweet memory. What about one of you?"

"That was about me."

"That was about your sister and how she felt when she was leaving for college. Didn't you have a moment like that?"

I swallow the saliva pooling in my mouth, fighting the lightheadedness that threatens. "That was about me. I-I don't think I can do this." I shake my head and move to stand.

He puts his hands up, palms out. "It's okay. I wasn't trying to push or make you feel bad. I just want to get to know you. Stay, please. We can talk about other things."

I chew on my lip, watching his eyes. They are earnest and soft, the intensity gone. The tension in my shoulders eases, and I nod at him.

His body relaxes as he lets out a little smile. He shifts, looking at the fire and asking, "What have you done since you moved home? Tell me about your life now after, you know..."

I shake my head. What does he mean? "I've lived."

"And?"

I clench my jaw, fighting to hold back the tears I haven't let fall yet. The lump in my throat is big, and I swallow around it. "I've lived in fear that he would come back."

He turns his body toward me, open, wanting my trust. I'm not sure I'm ready to give it. "Kit, whatever you tell me can stay between us."

"I don't want to go there, Greer. Quit. Pushing." The hair on my nape stands on end as I glare at him.

"I think I got to know you pretty well tonight, Kit. I held you through whatever that was upstairs. I cleaned puke off you. I even sang to you. Can't get more intimate than that." He winks, his face softening like he's trying to diffuse my anger.

Damn him, it's working. My emotions have been absolutely bedlam tonight, sometimes sinking so low into the pit of despair that it's hard to climb out. But I did because of him.

Time to change the subject.

"You have a great singing voice. Have you always been a singer?" I force my shoulders to relax, the tension leaving me quicker than before.

"Oh, I trained with the boys' choir from the Swiss Alps." *Well, that's impressive.* "I was the best soprano on the squad. They had to remove my balls to do it, but it worked." He watches me with a smirk.

I grin and shake my head. "I believed you until you said they removed your balls. I can help with that, though."

"Nah, I like my balls where they are, thank you. Besides, I'm going to need them later."

"Uh, no, you're not."

He chuckles, every bit of him seeming to twinkle with his mirth. "Get your head out of my pants. I'm talking about children. I want them one day." He winks at me.

My stomach drops. He wants children.

Let it go, Kit. "Hmph."

"So what do you do, Kit?"

"With what?"

"Your life, your job, your free time."

"So far, no job. I was a pediatric nurse in California. Otherwise, I've been trying to fit back in with society."

"Were you a criminal?"

"What? No. I meant I'm finding my way back in Stirling Harbor."

"Nothing else?"

"Right, nothing else."

He shifts, his brow rising. "Angelo says you've had some pretty impressive dates lately."

Oh, for the love of Pete. Rosemary and Angelo should keep their mouths shut. "Yup, they've been great."

He's silent as he watches me, the flames dancing in his eyes.

"Okay, that's a lie. But I'm working on doing things outside my comfort level."

His other brow joins the first. "Like what?"

"Well, I've gone hiking and played with dogs. I've eaten at restaurants where I wouldn't normally eat."

"Did you find anything you liked?"

"I've been hiking a bit, and the more I go, the more I feel at peace. And I like the dogs."

"Great, that's a start."

I pause a moment, looking at him. He's seriously sitting here guiding me through small talk. "I love reading. Could spend hours at a library, oddly, just smelling books."

Well, the reading part is something I didn't remember from my childhood. I hide the smile that wants to erupt, focusing on the warmth blooming under my breastbone at the memories.

He shifts, briefly rubbing up against me, reminding my body of how much it likes being next to him. "What's your favorite book?"

I pull my attention away from his thigh and look into his fiery gaze. "*The Things They Carried*. It's kind of a love story, but not between two people."

"That is not a romance novel."

"What?"

"Yeah, no romance. That book is about war. War and how it affects people, and it's gory."

"It's about how trials and tribulations affect our thoughts on love and how we treat the ones we love." Okay, so maybe it's literary fiction, but it's also romantic.

He's pensive as he watches me, and then he finally responds. "I'm going to have to reread it. I don't remember much about love in it."

"Well, as a man, you would focus on the blood and gore."

"That's not true. I've read love stories."

"Name one." This is fun. I bite the inside of my cheek, trying to hide my smile.

"*Pride and Prejudice*."

"There is no way in hell you have read *Pride and Prejudice*."

"I have, at least a dozen times."

"Quote me a line."

"Angry people are not always wise." He grins at me, his eyes crinkling in the corners. He must not smile often. He has no lines or wrinkles around them.

"That's not in the book."

"It is. Have you even read it?"

"Of course I have!" I cross my arms again. "Another line."

"What are men to rocks and mountains?"

"Everyone knows that one. One more, make it a good one."

Greer sits for a moment, his brow furrowed. "'There is a stubbornness about me that never can bear to be frightened at the will of others. My courage always rises at every attempt to intimidate me.' Or something like that."

I cough, trying to stop the slight ache in my heart as it softens. "Do you relate more to Elizabeth in the beginning or Elizabeth in the end? Or maybe Mr. Darcy? You seem like you follow the rules. Like you're tied to a family legacy or something like that."

"Nope, not Elizabeth or Fitzwilliam."

I smile, not used to hearing Darcy referred to by his first name. I'm starting to believe Greer's a genuine fan.

"I'm satisfied with being myself, Kit. True to my nature of being a grumpy asshole—except when I'm around you. When I'm around you, I'm pulled to you. I'm bright, and if I don't orbit you, my light will die out. If I don't hang out in your radiance, the fire inside me will extinguish. I edge closer, hoping to feed off the flame or be consumed by it."

The air leaves me in a whoosh. That is incredibly poetic and hot.

But I can't.

"Greer, I...I'm trying to find myself again. I'm not ready for something like"—I wave one hand between us. "this. My life with Ethan was passionate in the beginning, and he consumed me. He sucked me in and took every piece of my soul. I can't do that again."

"I promise to leave your soul intact. I'm not sure what this is between us, Kit. All I know is it's something I've never experienced before." His focus dips to my lips, his pupils growing.

Tingles rove my body, my core clenches, and my heart stutters like crazy. The desire in his eyes roars to life as he scoots closer.

"Don't you wonder what it'll be like?" His voice drops an octave, that deep baritone dripping like chocolate.

"What?" I'm turning into a seductress, my voice husky like his.

"The first kiss. Our kiss. How it's going to feel."

My lips tingle like they already know, my heartbeat thrumming there.

"I'm going to kiss you." His hushed tone pulls all the oxygen from the room. Still, he waits, focusing on me like he's asking instead of telling.

The only thing I can do is swallow down the need filling me and nod.

Goose bumps scatter down my arms. I gasp as he leans forward slowly, giving me time to back away if I want.

I don't.

He moistens his bottom lip, and my body trembles, wanting that tongue on me. He gently grasps me behind my neck, his fingers dragging on my wet strands. Then he tugs, pulling me forward a tiny bit.

His breath hits my lips, and I close my eyes as he moves just enough for his lips to brush against mine. Soft. Lush. He licks the seam of my mouth. My lips part like they have a mind of their own.

I'm too focused on how it feels to tell them what to do.

He sucks the air from my lungs before giving it back, settling his mouth firmly on mine. His tongue slides inside, stroking against me before taking over. Rough palms cup my face, gently tilting my head where he wants it. Butterflies leap into my throat, and tingles rove up my spine.

He consumes me, making those butterflies in my belly take flight. I grab on to his wrists, gripping, holding on for dear life.

His thumbs brush against my cheeks. *Heavenly*. Each swipe of his tongue is like fireworks forming along my skin and bursting just before the finale. I push closer, my tongue stroking against his in return. His groan vibrates against my mouth.

Electricity travels between our lips, the sparks singeing my skin, burning my core, and I moan in need as he slows. He nibbles my lower lip before withdrawing, sighing against my mouth as he rests his forehead on mine.

"I didn't know it could feel like that." His breathing is ragged, making his words choppy.

"What?"

He lets go. His fingertips trailing along my jaw. "That all-consuming feeling they describe when you kiss someone meant to be yours."

Holy shit. Did he just stake a claim on me?

"I like it."

Before I have a chance to freak out, he stands and winks, his tenting sweatpants leaving nothing to the imagination. *Holy shit, he's packing.*

He smirks. "Eyes up here, Red." His laughter sends heat rushing to my cheeks. "I'm going to take a shower and get some water. Do you want some before I go?"

Some of him? Oh, yeah...

Water, Kit. He means water. "Yeah, water is good."

He disappears for a moment before bringing me back a chilled bottle. "Kit?"

I just stare at him and *hmmm.* My ability to communicate has disappeared. Primal sounds, and maybe gestures, are all I have left.

"I liked it a lot." He gives me a panty-melting smile before shooting up the stairs.

One thing is for sure. That was the best damn kiss I've ever had. Electric. All-consuming. Cleansing. Like he's washed away all the previous kisses and replaced them with a glimmer of hope.

Hope that maybe I can truly move on.

I relax my shoulders and melt, all the tension draining from my body. He is dominating and liberating, sweet and salty. A dichotomy.

As if his departure removes all the energy from the room, from me, my body becomes a puddle on the couch.

I pull a cover from the side of the couch over my body and let the thick, soft cotton and the fire's warmth stoke the longing stirred deep in my belly.

⌐··· · ·⌐ ··⌐ ⌐ ·· ··⌐· ··⌐ ·⌐·· ·⌐· ⌐·⌐⌐   ⌐··· ·⌐· ⌐⌐⌐ ⌐·⌐ · ⌐·

I'm weightless but moving, the motion pulling me out of sleep. I wake to him shifting me against his chest as he makes his way up the stairs.

"I can walk." It escapes muffled. His body heat is soothing. The rocking lulls me until I'm laid on a soft bed and tucked in. Then I shift.

"Shhh, settle, Kit. You're in the bedroom next to mine. I'm going to my room. Sleep."

Fifteen

Kit

"WHERE ARE YOU HIDING?" Ethan sings from down the hallway. My door creaks open, the light from the hallway slowly making a larger V as he pushes it wider.

"Katherine." His feet appear in the doorway. "I've checked all the other rooms. I know you're in here."

Please don't let him find me. I picked a shitty spot. My heart beats out of my chest, and I press my palm to it, trying to smother the sound.

His black leather shoes and the bottom of his black slacks are the only things visible from my hiding spot.

His shadow plays games with my mind, twisting around the floor like he's floating toward me. At least I see it coming this time. No hands flying out of nowhere to knock me off my feet.

The shadow moves closer, gliding demonically across the floor.

"Did you enjoy it? His hands on you?" His anger drags out the "you."

I gasp, my body prickling. He knows what happened.

Step after agonizing step, he moves closer. I slap my hand over my mouth so the sound doesn't give me away.

He stops at the foot of the bed, the tip of his shoes inches from me. The left one taps a rhythm I know by heart.

One, two, three. Tap.

One, two, three. Slap.

One, two, three. Punch.

There is movement on the bed, the ruffling of cloth, and then the heavy comforter floats to the floor.

"Hmm." His feet shift, taking a step back from the foot of the bed. His legs slowly bend, and his knees come into view. Then his torso and his shoulders. An evil smile plasters across his face as his eyes lock on mine.

"Found you."

"Kit?" Rough hands grip my shoulders, pulling me from sleep. I try to sit up, but something cages me in. My pulse rages inside my chest, tachy as all shit.

"No." I kick out, but some magical force holds my legs down. My arms are free, so I swing wildly, hitting the body on top of me as hard as I can.

"Oh, fuck." The pressure holding me down eases, and then it's gone altogether. "Kit, wake up. It's Greer."

I twist, tangled in a mess of blankets, and crack open a lid. Greer stands in a sliver of light coming through a mostly closed door. He's at the foot of the bed, his hands up, concern etched across his face.

"Kit?"

I sit up, struggling to get out of the cocoon binding me. Breathing harshly, I choke down the sobs that want to erupt.

"You're wrapped up in the blanket. Can I help you?"

I nod, unable to speak past the weight pressing down on my lungs.

He slowly and methodically untangles me as I do my best to calm down and shake the thoughts of Ethan from my mind.

My legs are free long before the agonizing needle pokes tell me that blood has returned to my limbs. I lay on the bed, my body finally returning to normal, tears streaming from my eyes.

"Kit. What can I do?"

When I can finally focus on him, he's squatting by the bed, watching me as I try to pull myself together. I shake my head, blowing the air out slowly, methodically.

"Can I hold you?"

My nose burns as my heart melts and my tears fall in earnest. I nod, and he works his enormous body into the bed, wrapping himself around

OF LILIES AND LIES

me like a cocoon. He pulls my arm up around his ribs and my thigh up over his hip.

Then I'm tucked close, my head under his chin. He sighs, all the air and tension leaving his body.

He is stable and together and doesn't have a clue how messed up I am inside. But he's here, holding on to me, asking for a chance to be let in.

He is perfect, and I'm not.

"Shhh, Kit. I got you." He's too sweet. It bubbles inside me, lodging into my heart. I sob, unable to hold it back anymore as my body breaks in his arms.

His thumb is rough as it strokes against my cheek, smearing the tear he's trying to wipe away.

"If you want to sleep, I'll stay."

I nod, my throat tight around the lump there. He is too gentle, too kind, and it's almost too much.

Almost.

But here in his arms, I feel safer than I've felt in years.

Delicious warmth wraps itself around me, pulling me from a place of peace.

Hot breath hits my forehead, and I bite my lip to keep from breaking out in a grin. He stayed the whole night. And he kept the nightmares away.

His arms are still wrapped around me, and my hands are tucked between us. I want to touch him— to slide my fingers up and graze his skin, to rake my nails through his beard, to hear him moan again.

I study his features. I want to bite that plump bottom lip. The top is thinner with a wide cupid's bow. Last night, they were divine—thick and firm at the right time but soft and plush when it was time to lick them.

His nose is straight and long—prominent. Masculine. Like his thick black brows. The only thing faintly feminine about him are those thicker lashes.

His beard is neat and thick. Brushing his shoulders, his hair is a deep chestnut. He has a square jaw and a wide neck. I dig the facial hair so much, I have to fight back the urge to scratch it with my nails.

What would his scruff feel like against my skin, my neck, my thighs? Oh, yes please. His head between my thighs is an image I want to see in real life. His tongue was magic with that first kiss, so I have no doubts it'll be magical in other places too.

He stretches against me and inhales deeply, a smile playing on his lips before he leans in and sets his lips on mine.

I can barely take it; my skin lights up as he sucks gently on my bottom lip with a sleepy kiss.

He pulls back, and I grab on, holding his face to mine as I open my mouth. I want to taste him. My pulse jumps in delight when he growls against me.

His hold on me tightens, his hands splaying against my back as his tongue darts out to play with mine. And it is intoxicating. I can't stop myself from arching against him.

His hand is rough as it moves to my waist, gripping, pulling, and trying to get closer. The other tangles in my hair to keep me in place.

Yes, this. I need this. I break the kiss, breathless as goose bumps scatter along my arms. His lips move to my chin and down my throat, sucking gently at my clavicle.

Holy shit, yes. It's a rush. We are rushing things, but I'm lost to it and unsure I can stop. Of all the things I've done since I've been home, this tops all of them.

He brushes the underside of my breast, and all the breath leaves me in a whoosh as I wait for the thrum of his fingers over my nipple.

My arousal pours through me, pulsing so strong I'm going to combust. His fingers are rough as they brush over the tight bud, and that alone is enough to send me spiraling.

He rolls us, his body moving over me, his weight pushing me into the bed.

The last time I felt the heavy weight of someone on top of me was with Ethan.

Ethan. Nausea pools in my belly at the thought.

I tense as his hand moves against my breast again. His big body blocks out the light from the bathroom, and the darkness haunts me, the corners of the room hiding demons I can't see. I can barely breathe with the weight of the past crushing me.

I'm not ready for this.

I push against his shoulders, and he immediately pulls back, concern etched in every line of his face. I must show panic because he's off me instantly. Rolling back beside me, he holds me loosely, his arm draped over my middle. I test my arms to see if I can move, and he gives me another inch.

I focus on my heartbeat, making it calm, taking the time to accept that his hold is kind and gentle. I'm not trapped. The rubber band around my lungs is gone. The tension inside me eases with each reminder.

"Fuck. Kit, I'm so sorry."

My heart aches. "It wasn't you. I want it. I just need time, Greer."

He nods. "What was it?"

I swallow past the lump in my throat while he brushes his hands up and down my back soothingly. I scoot closer. "I haven't been intimate with anyone since Ethan. It was a shock feeling you so close, so heavy on me."

"Okay. You have the reins here."

I smile at him, my brain niggling at me as he nuzzles against me. There are so many differences but also so many similarities. I see Ethan less and less when Greer is around, but I still feel him.

"We still have a few hours until morning. Try to get some sleep."

He is way too good to me. He handles every freak-out with compassion and ease. How can a man so intense still be so gentle? Still have so much empathy?

Even at the start, Ethan couldn't fake empathy or compassion. I should've seen the signs then, but I'd been too swept up in the romance.

The lack of care when I was emotional, the way Ethan's grip was punishing, not tender. The way he pushed for sex, even when I wasn't ready.

Ethan focused on himself, never asking about me, my goals, or my dreams.

I've said no to Greer so many times, in so many ways, and not once has he been anything but caring. Physically, verbally, and emotionally, he has always respected me.

And he listens.

He wants to know me.

Greer's body relaxes against me as he falls asleep. In the faint light of the bathroom, I can make out the fan of his lashes and slightly open mouth as his puffs of air hit me.

He might not be like Ethan, but I'm still broken.

Sixteen

Kit

WHEN I LOOKED OUT the window earlier, the snow was still coming down hard, with no end in sight for the storm raging through the area. Greer's shower is running, and despite wanting another one to wash away the nightmare, I want to get my clothes clean and rewash his sheets. I need to find bleach first.

I make my way downstairs and head to the laundry. It takes a moment to find everything I need, and I've finished shoving everything in when Greer pops his head in, a bemused expression on his face. He points to the door I've just closed. "Why?"

"You don't want to know, trust me."

"One day?"

"Maybe." It might be one of those stories where we laugh thinking about Carl's mom in his bed.

He nods, standing against the doorjamb, his body relaxed. "Why don't we pick out a movie, and then we can replay that date we never got to finish."

The date I ruined with a panic attack. My pulse spikes, and acid bubbles in my stomach. I don't know if I can do another movie like that.

"It can be whatever you want. You can pick." He smiles softly, probably reading the panic on my face, and holds his hand out for me.

I stare at his large hand, my heart thumping wildly in my chest.

Something flashes in his eyes that's hard to place, but he shrugs and lowers his arm after a moment. "Come on. I'll give you a tour, then you can pick out a movie."

We spend an hour peeking in all the rooms until we land in an entertainment room with an enormous screen and large couches.

"Holy shit. You have everything here." Seriously, a workout room, a hot tub, a craft room. And this room filled with hundreds of books, movies, and games.

He shrugs. "It's my parents' place, but we all use it. Want to pick a movie?" He gestures to a wall lined with hundreds of DVDs.

I peruse the bookcase and the shelves lined with entertainment paraphernalia, running a finger along the fronts of the games. "You have a ton of UNO cards."

"What?" He sidles up next to me, his grin magic when he sees the abundance of cards. "Yeah, we get pretty intense with our family games."

The smile I've been fighting all morning breaks free, and he peeks at my lips.

Holy shit.

The air is heavy, like all the oxygen is sucked from the room. I want to jump into his arms and put my lips on his. Mouth dry, I swallow and try to miraculously impart moisture into it. Doesn't work. My pulse jumps erratically behind my chest, and I gasp through the tightness and take a step back.

I bump into the shelf but quickly steady myself and turn to look at the movies, putting some space between us.

He backs up too. Like he can sense the panic rising inside me. I force my body to relax.

I take a moment, letting my heart rate settle. Damn, he was so close. And I thought he was going to kiss me again.

Give me one of those wonderful, soul-sucking kisses.

But I can't do that right now. It's too much.

"I'll be right back." His voice comes out more distant than it had been. "I'll make some popcorn."

While he's gone, I scan the movies. I've never seen most of them. *Monty Python*, Seth Rogen movies, and a few chick flicks.

I have no idea which one to choose. One I know a guy would like? Or should I stick with what I'd pick for myself?

After several minutes, I hook my finger on a spine and pull down *The Proposal.*

"Pick one?"

I jump. "Jesus." My hand flies to my chest, and the movie drops to the floor, clattering louder than my heart right now. "For such a big guy, you are ridiculously quiet."

He bends down to grab the movie, his chuckle soft. "Dancing. Mom made all of us guys take it. She said it was to make us graceful."

"Like ballet?"

He grimaces. "Yeah, unfortunately."

Damn, he's an enigma right now. "Did you like it?"

"Hardly. But after practices on Fridays, we'd make up for it with rough-housing and breaking things—usually noses. Once or twice, it was a TV." His grin is so freaking gorgeous. I want to look at it all the time.

He studies the movie, looking at Ryan Reynolds and Sandra Bullock on the front. "Chick flick?"

I nod and lace my fingers behind my back as I bounce lightly on my toes. "Yup. Your mom's?"

"Definitely. Or Violet's."

He heads to the media player, and I fixate on his ass as he moves. It's exceptional, seriously. He peeks behind him, catching me before I quickly look away, heat creeping up my cheeks.

His soft chuckle sends sparks thrumming through me, and I delight in how it makes my body come to life.

"Pick a spot." He tips his head toward the couches.

Instinctively, I know that no matter where I sit, he'll sit right next to me. It should send me into a panic, but the energy zinging through my body at the thought is the kind that makes my heart flutter, not sink in fear.

He plops beside me, his thigh brushing my knee, just as I expected. "Flip open that armrest and hand me the three remotes." There's room for me to move, to hop up and escape if need be, but I'm letting myself settle in.

Breathe. He's relaxed, so I can relax too.

My body slowly melts into the cushion.

He points one remote straight up, and the shades on the windows roll down, then the lights dim to almost nothing. Handing that to me, he fiddles with the other two. The screen lights up, and the media player whirs to life. Greer grabs the bowl of popcorn and settles it between us.

Soon the movie is playing, and I'm eating perfectly buttered popcorn and falling in love with Ryan Reynolds again.

This date is so much better than the first one.

Greer

Kit fell asleep in the middle of the movie, which isn't surprising after the events of the last twenty-four hours. I should check on the generator, though, and make sure the Wi-Fi is still working.

A work check in would be good too. I head over to the desk and log in to my work site on my laptop, then spend the next hour poring over proposals.

Kit sleeps peacefully on the couch, occasionally moving around or ruffling something. When she wakes, she peeks at me and smothers a huge yawn with her hand. "What time is it?"

"Close to four." I smile. "You'll be lucky to sleep tonight."

She wipes away a small drool trail adorably. Warmth radiates from under my sternum at the sight of her. This is something I could get used to.

What is it about her that makes me want to stick around? Most people would see her panic and fear as red flags, but something keeps telling me to wait, to hold on. Because whatever is coming is worth it.

I see beauty and vulnerability. And that sparks my creativity, filling my mind with scrawling mantles, curved moldings, and intricate geometrical patterns in wood furniture. And I want to run to my drafting table and draw everything out.

She's beautifully broken.

"Earth to Greer."

She's standing in front of the desk, a small smile on her face as she looks at the pen and paper in my hand.

I clear my throat. "What were you saying?"

"I asked what you were working on."

Don't say work. "Emails." Doofus, that's still work.

She nods and gives me a half smile, then walks to the bookshelf and pulls down a book. "Do you often work on emails when you're on vacation?" She peeks over her shoulder at me with a hint of mirth in her eyes.

"Yes."

"What are you doing now?"

"Creating designs for two new proposals. Customers give me basic ideas about what they are looking for, and I create something that I think will fit their needs and style. Not to mention the commercial projects I'm bidding on."

"I didn't know woodworking was so involved." She looks down at a book, riffling through the pages. "Is this what you thought you'd be doing with your life?"

I ponder that a moment before responding. "I'm not sure I knew what I'd be doing with my life. I always thought I'd have a family and a good job. I figured that would make me happy. But I'm still trying to fit all the pieces together and find a balance."

"I wasn't allowed to work when Ethan was alive. I was a housewife. I read books, watched shows, cleaned the home, and made meals. There was no balance, so I guess I understand what you mean in a way."

Holy shit. I'm digesting everything she's said and getting ready to ask a question when she points to the window. "Do you think it's safe to head back home yet?"

No, I don't want you to leave. "I haven't plowed the driveway yet, and I doubt they've made it up this far. But I can check the department of transportation to see what the roads look like if you want."

"Sure."

In seconds, I'm on the website. The roads in our area are still labeled as unplowed and dangerous.

"Well, there is my answer." She smiles softly. "I'm going to head to the kitchen and start dinner."

I nod and watch the way her hips move as she leaves. Was the sway intentional? Probably not. I want to pounce on her, but I have to take it slow.

But that's not why I don't follow her out the door and offer to cook dinner together. That's not why I'm still at my drafting table, penciling out designs. Creating something new.

Maybe I need to be in here, drawing straight lines with a ruler so I don't get lost in the feelings Kit brings out in me. More importantly, I don't want to make Kit feel like she has to do anything she doesn't want to.

I told her she had the reigns, and I meant it.

Seventeen

Kit

"I'VE GOT TO RUN out to the woodshed. I might be a bit. If you need me, stick your head out and holler." He stops at the back door.

We are well and truly snowed in. He barely cut a path from the garage to the outbuilding, and that was after a few hours of shoveling. He didn't complain once, and I didn't complain about the hotness overload.

I nod, my attention on his body as he shoves his feet in his boots. He threads his arms into the sleeves of a heavy jacket and then pushes on gloves and a hat.

The man moves like a cat.

He grins at me and winks before he ducks out the door. A blast of chilly wind greets me, along with the click of the latch.

I pull my phone out of my pocket. Fully charged; thank you, Greer. I have a weak signal now that I'm in the house, but the Wi-Fi covers what my cell service doesn't.

Three text messages and two new voicemails.

Shit, I haven't checked in with Rosemary since I got here.

I open up my phone, clicking on the texts.

Ro: *I hope you made it up there okay.*

Ro: *Call me, please. Shit, you probably don't have a signal.*

Ro: *Angelo got a call from Greer saying you made it all right. Call me if you need me.*

I chuckle to myself. Yeah, I didn't die on the roads. She sucks. I should have known she was up to something when she said to hurry before the storm hit.

Jesus.

What a freaking disaster last night was. My stomach riots at the thought of puking in front of him.

And this...this ever-present desire to lose myself in Greer.

What in the hell is going on with me? I've lived the last three years in solitude, but I meet Greer, and suddenly everything is turned upside down.

Why? Why do I feel this way?

Maybe I need to know what he was thinking after the first date before I can figure out what is happening here.

Tapping the voicemail app, I find Greer's first message and hit play.

"Kit, hey. Are you okay? I'm so sorry. Was it the movie or me? Me, probably. I pushed too fast. I'm sorry if I pushed you into a date you weren't ready for. I hope you'll give me a second chance. We can do anything you want, any time. Just...Yeah. Okay. I hope you're okay, Kit. Talk soon, I hope. Bye."

He seemed so much more controlling when I met him than he does now. It's like something in him changed—even at the movie. When I would stiffen, he'd back off. Now he knows when to give space and when to push for more.

Can I trust this? Trust him? I want to; I want to let him in so badly. I want more of the desire, the laughter, and the understanding. And I want to feel his mouth on mine again.

I brush my lips with my fingers. The tingles are still there—the memory of his firm lips makes an ache form in my belly.

It could be so easy to let him consume me.

Could I let him in and still keep parts of myself? I don't have to give him everything, just enough to share joy. And would he be willing to let me continue exploring myself and be the person I want to be?

I tap on the second message and hit play.

"Hey, Kit. I'm so sorry. Please call me and tell me you are okay. That's all I'd like to know. Even just a text or something saying you're okay, I would appreciate it. I'm so sorry, Kit."

My heart does a little stutter in my chest. He didn't push, even in the last message.

It's hard to move past what Ethan ingrained in me. The assumption that he would be angry with me or blame me for the failed date. But he sounded so genuine on the phone.

Maybe it's time to get some other perspective. And give Rosemary a tongue lashing.

I grab the house phone and dial her number.

"Hello?" Her voice is soft and distant.

"Rosemary, it's Kit. Is now a good time?"

"Oh yeah, just, hold on one second." A door closes, and paper crackles. "Ah, sorry. Had to set down the bag I was holding. So you made it okay in the snow?"

"Yup, it was fine. I don't have much time. Can you tell me about Greer?"

"A bit, we aren't super close. What do you want to know?"

I settle deeper into the couch, tucking my legs under me and watching the door. "Whatever you can tell me."

"Angelo has worked for him for seven years now, I think."

"What is he like?"

"Quiet and broody. He's a thinker. But he's a good man, Kit. He's a caretaker when no one is watching. You should see the way he dotes on our kids."

Well, that isn't what I was expecting. "Why is he so quiet?" Because he doesn't seem that way with me.

"I'm not sure. But there is a sweet guy underneath the hard shell. Do you like him?"

Heat rushes into my cheeks. I do like him. And maybe that's the problem. "Yeah, he's nice. But I don't know. I'm so torn."

"I know it's hard to let go and trust in something you're not sure of. But sometimes you have to leap to grow."

"What if he breaks me? I really, I can't..." The breath catches in my throat. I can't do another life like I had before, taken, stolen, shattered.

"I can only tell you what I know, Kit. He's a good man. He's not like Ethan."

"This is so hard. I want to—I want to try, but Ro, it could kill me if it ends up being a repeat of before."

"Then take it slow. Let him in piece by piece, and if you ever feel like it's not working, you can stop. He'll stop. I know he will."

The silence eats at both of us as I take in her words. The hush stretches and it's clear she's waiting for me to say something. "Right."

"It's okay to give him a chance. And if it doesn't work out, that is okay too."

But does he really want to be stuck with someone like me? "So are we going to talk about what you and Angelo did?"

"In my defense, you didn't give Greer a chance. We knew that you would be good together, and after that first date...well, you weren't keen on giving him another shot."

That is true. I can't fault her logic. "I wish you hadn't felt the need to hide it."

"I won't do it again, Kit. I'm sorry that the storm happened, that wasn't planned. But getting you up there early was."

"Mm-hmm. Well, he hasn't killed me yet."

"Oh jesus. And he won't. It's okay if this doesn't work out. You're getting to know him. I gotta go now, though. Call you later?"

Warmth tickles my belly. "Sure. Thanks, Ro. Love you."

"Love you. See ya soon."

See ya soon? That's right. They'll be coming up after the weekend. And I won't be able to hide the way I feel about Greer from Rosemary.

The door creaks, and Greer stomps inside, knocking his boots free of snow and kicking them off. He dumps the wood in the holder by the fireplace, then looks up.

I've yet to see the hard shell Rosemary mentioned. He's been soft and sweet the entire time. "Did you call your sister?" He nods toward the phone.

"Yeah." I smile back, unable to take my attention off him as he walks back to drop off his winter gear by the entrance.

"Hope you gave her hell for sending you up here in a snowstorm."

Shit, once we started talking, I completely forgot. I shake my head slightly, keeping everything kind of close to the vest.

He clears his throat, barely biting back his smile. "I'm going to make some tea. Want some?"

"That would be nice."

He winks and heads into the kitchen, where the cupboards bang and the water faucet turns on.

He's making this easy. Not pushing, not pressing.

Another broken piece glues back together, shining, gold, and filling me with awe and warmth.

And that is so much more than I could have hoped for.

Greer

We get lulls here and there, but the snow keeps falling. When I can, I run out to the woodpile and stock up for the next run, but it's been a nonstop deluge since that first night. It's the lake effect. There is a constant source of moisture nearby, and the storm keeps recycling itself.

Last night Kit offered to wash dishes, so I dried them. Her mashed potatoes were better than Mom's, but I'm not telling my mother that. And the chicken was incredible. It beat my usual steamed chicken and vegetables.

She kept to herself after that. She read for a while, then we watched a show and laughed, but she hightailed it to bed pretty early, a book in hand.

Her screams woke me sometime around midnight again, and knowing what to expect this time, I held her until she calmed. I snuck out in the morning to give her privacy, but it's damn hard.

I want a repeat of that first night where we woke up with our lips on each other and our hands scrambling to touch skin. I can't keep my eyes off her when we're in the same room. She's funny and sweet, but she's got a fiery side that I hope will come out more.

She's still timid, but I think I'm doing the right thing, letting her lead conversations and guiding her when she flounders. I try not to push, and hopefully, it's helping her trust me.

Because I want in. For the first time in ages, I want to know what a woman is thinking and feeling.

She's strong, but she doesn't trust herself enough to believe it yet. And I want to help build that because there is something lurking there, something that tells me she's going to be unstoppable. Her strength is there, like a poorly cared for armoire that I have to strip down and polish back up to make it shine.

After my shower, I creep out of my room. It takes everything in me not to peek through her open door to see if she's still in bed. I pull a Fred Flintstone, slinking by on my tippy toes so I don't wake her.

All the inside work I needed to do, I finished the first few days I was up here. The snowstorm kind of snuck up on me, and outside chores are impossible right now. Another round of wood will be needed soon, and I'll check the plow to make sure it's gassed up and ready for when the snow stops.

I'll have to check the roads too. Last night the county roads still hadn't been plowed, so even if I'd gotten the driveway done, she'd still have had to stay.

I stop in the middle of the hallway. If I go left, I can head to the study, go to my drafting table and work on some more of that proposal. Right would lead me to the kitchen, and I could make her breakfast and maybe spend some time with her.

I know what I want to do, but my feet pull me in another direction.

I pad to the study, picking up my tools to resume working on the proposal. An hour later, a soft knock sounds against the door. How is she so beautiful in my sweatpants and a sweatshirt, her hair tucked up in a messy red bun? She's fiery and sinful, and I want to run my fingers across her skin and feel her body erupt with goose bumps as I pleasure her.

"Good morning. Work stuff?" She gestures to the table with papers strewn about.

I nod because it's about the only thing I can do right now. She stretches and shows a hint of skin, and now all I want is to see all of it.

I want to be in her so fucking bad. An intense longing pours through my veins, settling deep in my groin.

It's been a while since I've had sex, and between the kisses and the touching and waking up to her in my arms more than once, I'm primed. I've never felt so loaded in my life, and if I don't scratch the itch, I'll probably explode if she actually touches me.

Redness creeps up her cheeks, and she clears her throat. "It seems like you're in here every stray minute."

I shrug. "It's my happy place." Well, it used to be. Now I'm torn between coming to what I've always known and doing something different. Branching out and being more open.

The talks between us are easier now, and I want more of them. But then my brain opens its fat mouth and reminds me that if I get the chance to settle down with her, I need to make sure we never go without. That if I'm not working, I'm not supporting my potential family.

She steps through the doorway, her feet moving softly in the cozy silence. "Do you want breakfast? I'm going to make some French toast. Sound good?"

"Better than good. I haven't had it in forever."

"Well, you're in for a treat. These are mediocre at best. My mom always made the best ones. I don't know if it was the love she put into them or the whipped cream. Anyway, mine aren't my mother's." Her chuckle is small but still sweet.

"It'll be good. Everything you've made so far has been incredible."

"Well, I don't know about that." She points out the door, taking a step that way. "I'm going to get started. Come when you're ready."

Holy fuck, I could come right now with her soft looks and sweet actions. I want to rush to the door, pull her into my arms, and settle our lips together. I want the rest of the afternoon to play out in a bed, where we fuck like crazy and I make her scream. Then afterward we share secrets and laughter.

And she must read the room because the redness burns brighter on her cheeks, and she licks her bottom lip before she flees.

I clean up my things, put everything away neatly, grab a jar of syrup from the pantry, and then head to the kitchen. Already the smell is permeating the air: cinnamon, eggs, and butter. I can't wait to dig into a heaping pile.

She's standing at the stove, a spatula in hand, moving her hips side to side when I walk in. When she notices me, she stops and turns. "Welcome to your humble kitchen." With her free hand, she points to the stool by the island. "Sit down. I've got the first few done." She slides a few onto my plate, and I drizzle on the syrup.

"Homemade?" She points to the syrup.

"Yeah, we've got a ton of maple trees on the property."

"I've never made my own; you'll have to show me how to one day. Dig in when you're ready."

"Thank you." My mouth waters as I take a big whiff. "I'm going to annihilate these."

She laughs before turning back to the stove. "I thought we could get to know each other more this morning."

With force, I swallow down the bite. "Sure, what did you have in mind? A game of twenty questions, truth or dare?" When she turns back to me, I wiggle my brows at her while I say dare.

"Well, you know a bit about my past, so I wanted to know more about yours." She smiles, bringing her plate of French toast to the island. "Tell me about your last girlfriend or two."

I choke at her suggested topic.

"That bad of a relationship?"

I shake my head, pointing to my throat.

She slides a cup of milk my way, and I grasp it like a lifeline, letting it coat the stuck lump of food.

When I can breathe again, I smirk at her. "You almost had to do CPR there."

"I saved your life." Her smile is huge, and she takes a bite of her breakfast, licking away the syrup that coats her bottom lip. The way she eats is far from dainty, and I can't tear my gaze away. I like her this way.

"So about that girlfriend."

Right, the reason I almost choked to death in my kitchen. "How many do you want to know about?"

"Are there a lot?" Her brows are almost in her hairline, and she's watching me from the side.

"I've only had a few serious relationships since high school."

"Oh. Will you tell me about them?" Her focus is glued to me, only dipping back to her food to get another bite.

"Well, my last girlfriend was Nora. We broke up in April before I came out to California and met you." It changed my life, made me question my sanity, and made me restless.

Every. Fucking. Day.

"What was your relationship like?" She's genuinely curious, and it makes me want to answer instead of giving the response I usually give my family, which is politely telling them to mind their own fucking business.

"Nora was driven at work. She is a lawyer at one of the law firms here in Stirling. We both worked long hours and didn't mind when the other was busy."

"What did you guys do for fun?"

"Nothing. I worked, and she worked. We both focused on making our financial foundation rock solid and were together when it was needed."

She smiles and gives me a bit of a laugh. "You didn't do dates or whatever people do on dates?"

"No. Mostly just social functions, but for the most part, we were to-gether without ever being together." Fuck. How I thought we would work well as a couple is beyond me at this point. And it never occurred to me to question our long absences from each other.

Or to care.

"That sounds kind of lonely. Is that how it was with the other ones?"

I set my fork down, my appetite gone now. Half the plate of French toast is gone, but I don't think I can swallow another bite. Not because I'm not hungry. I was starving when I walked in. But now all my shortcomings are at the forefront of my mind.

"I was with women who were social and wanted a partner around all the time. And I was, for the most part."

She eyes my plate, then looks at me. "Not hungry anymore?"

"I've been thinking a lot lately about how I focus so much on work. Maybe I should try to do other things. My relationship with Nora just ...saying that we weren't together much out loud made me realize how much time I spent working."

She nods. "Why is that?"

I'm not sure I'm ready to embark on that part of my history. I stall for time. "Maybe we can talk more about it later. I have to finish up some stuff before I send it to my brother."

"Okay. Sorry if I pushed."

I point to her plate. "You done?" I grab her plate and mine and take them to the sink. "Thank you for breakfast. I'm going to work a little more, and then maybe we can watch another movie or find a show."

"Oh...okay." As I leave the room, her face falls, like she wanted to hang out with me.

"If you need anything, I'll be in the study."

And with that, I escape.

Eighteen

Kit

THE SNOW HAS BEEN falling for days. The trees have blankets of fluff across their branches, and it's completely covering my car.

It's been too easy spending the afternoons laughing at shows on the TV after finding something to eat.

Greer's been keeping his distance, though his eyes eat me up whenever I lean over the counter or after a shower when my hair is still wet. Twice he's caught me watching him from my peripherals. More like twice an hour.

Goose bumps are becoming permanent residents along my arms and legs. All too frequently, I swallow down that clenching need in my stomach—that knotting, pre-release spasm between my legs.

It's an easy routine too. He spends the day doing work around the house, and I clean up the kitchen, finish the laundry he began, and throw things together to eat. When I run out of things to do, I read a bit more of *Pride and Prejudice*, which he brought me from his room.

I mentioned how much I love having a fire roaring, and now he brings in more firewood at least once a day.

He's so sinfully delicious. I could watch him all day. He stomps back into the house and shakes out the snow, doing this shimmy that makes his hair spray everywhere. The wet drops hit me—because I can't stop myself from gravitating toward him—the wall, and the floor.

My body tenses. Electricity zings down my spine with every glance in his direction. I try to tamp down the need, the want of his hands on my body, but his touch is something I dream about—vividly.

"I wasn't expecting to be snowed in for so long." I smile when he looks at me. "A day or two at most, but this is crazy. How much longer do you think it will last?" It's been three days. Not that I'm complaining.

He grunts in response as he drops the logs he brought in with him, doing his shimmy again while I drown in a pool of drool. "Not sure. A day or two or ten. Never know up here. The lake supplies all the moisture we need for a good snowfall. I've been snowed in for a week before."

"Good thing we have enough food. Speaking of which, I made my specialty for dinner." Warmth pools in my chest when he follows me into the kitchen. I prepare a plate of veggie drawer lasagna and place it down at his spot.

"Is it poisoned?" He leans in close to sniff, and a smile lights his face.

"What? Why would you say that?" My brows scrunch together as I shake my head. I tuck into my plate, shoveling a portion of the sausage, noodle, and veggie goodness into my mouth.

"Things have been going so well, I figured at some point, you'd off me. I'm a notch below wealthy, you know."

"Why would I kill you off if I get nothing from it? We'd have to be married."

"Do you want to get married?"

"Like, now?" My brows rise, my gaze shooting to Greer.

"No, in the future."

"I don't know. I've been married, and it didn't...it wasn't..." I bite my lip and set my fork down.

"One of those things you don't want to talk about." He swallows tightly before quickly regaining his composed expression. Letting out a long sigh, he looks back at his plate.

I examine his face. He wants in, and I want to let him in. But if I do, I might not let him out again.

Worse, what if I let him in, and then he doesn't like what he finds? Ethan hated the real me. I didn't talk right, dress right, look right. For so long, I believed him. Believed there was something wrong with me, and that I wasn't good enough for anyone, let alone him.

And then I met Francesca.

Ethan didn't hate her. He didn't find anything to change. Was it because she could have his baby? Something I can never have.

They said it's not possible. Not after that. Not anymore. Will Greer think I am less because I can't do the one thing women were made to do?

That thought alone makes my stomach drop out.

The knot in my abdomen twists, and my lungs seize.

He places a hand on my back, and I jump. The slow rub of his big palm against my T-shirt makes me look up.

He radiates warmth and sincerity. "It's okay. Deep breath in and out."

He makes it sound so easy. But I do as he said, taking a slow breath, then another. My fingers warm up, and the knot eases. He picks me up, and I squeeze my eyes shut, letting him lead us to the couch and situate me on his lap with my feet dangling over the side.

My body responds, the tension melting away while his hands rest soothingly against my back and hip, his fingers brushing gently, unhurried, calm.

After a few minutes, his gravelly voice whispers, "Good?"

I'm more than good. I usually suffer my panic attacks alone. Ethan used to leave me after one started, or he'd stand and watch me, laughing or staring as I battled through them.

Greer's effect on me ties my stomach in knots and makes my pulse skitter, but in an edgy, want-him-close-to-me kind of way.

I slide my hand over his neck. Lacing my fingers into the hair at his nape, I play with it gently. He moans, so I scratch with my nails.

With my eyes squeezed shut, I let it flow out of me. "He was not a good husband. He was easily angered and possessive. Everything in our relationship was under his control. At first, it was subtle suggestions about my hair or weight, then my job. I never imagined he could be that type of man."

"He hurt you." His voice is tight, his body tense under my hands. I jerk back and search his face again. His gaze catches mine, molten amber pooling in his orbs.

The tension I see there isn't directed at me. His fury is on my behalf.

Instinctively, I pat his chest gently, a soft smile parting my lips. As I stare, my whole body relaxes into him. "Yes, he did. At times, I didn't know what I had done to set him off. Sometimes I flinch when people come near me because he would take me by surprise, throwing an arm out to hit me when I didn't even know he was there. Like he was hiding and waiting for my guard to lower before he let his rage fly. But it's over. I was lucky enough to survive."

"With a lot of fucking scars, Kit." His fingers clench against my skin rhythmically.

He means emotional scars, but there are physical ones too. "Yeah, with a lot of scars. Some deeper and more painful than others.

"Want to tell me one?" His thumb brushes against my hip.

I stiffen, holding back tears. He wants children. I clench my jaw, my hand poised on his, ready to push him away because I don't want him to know. Once he knows, it will change things—he could leave.

But he deserves to know what I can and can't do if he wants to be with me.

A baby with his beautiful amber eyes and my red hair. I won't carry the child, so it might be impossible.

A keen sense of loss hits me, the pain burning through me, settling in the deepest corners of my body. I cradle my belly, my fingers pressing deep.

Please don't let it change what he thinks of me.

Pulling air into my lungs, I hold it.

Then let it out and swallow.

My chin trembles, and the words come out thin, like a whispered secret. "I can't have children. Doctors think there's too much damage."

"Kit." Greer leans his head against mine, his arms pulling me closer for comfort. "Do you want to tell me what happened?"

I sit in silence. I want to spew my angst and aggression all over him so he'll understand my pain, know it as sharply as I do. Irrationally, I want to hit him with it.

But I can't. Instead, I look over his shoulder and focus on the wall. "I was pregnant. He was so happy, and I thought it would change him. I was naïve and still didn't know how cruel and possessive he would become. He came home from work angry. They lost a big shipment from overseas or something. I can't remember..."

I swallow, shaking my head gently. Memories like this are important to get out, but it's hard to relive them.

I have to let it go. It wasn't me, wasn't my fault.

"I made dinner. A new dish to try to offset the tension. He refused to eat. Drank his meal instead." I glance at Greer.

Grief. Agony. Loss. They all mean the same thing. I'll never carry a child of my own.

My fingers tingle as I shake them out. Bracing myself, I search Greer's eyes, looking for the disgust Ethan never failed to hide.

But they soften. They're filled with nothing but compassion.

The tension eases in my body, and I let Greer's kindness and warmth fill me. The openness is there, and something else that lingers. A spark of something that could grow if given the right kindling.

"I'm sorry. You don't have to continue."

A tear falls down my cheek. He's sorry? When he's looking at me as if I'm whole? Like a beautiful broken vase, healed with gold rather than swept up and thrown away. As if I'm kintsugi.

The constriction in my chest squeezes for too many reasons. I've never told anyone this. Not even my therapist.

And he wants to listen, to hear me. He doesn't want to fix me, or offer a way to move on, or try to make things better. He wants me to fall so he can catch me. So I do.

I let myself fall.

"He chased me down the hall. I tripped and slid into our glass cabinet. It exploded all over the floor. He grabbed me. I raised my hands to fight back, so he hit me hard enough to knock me to the floor. Some of the glass pieces were like icicles, poking up from the hardware."

My stomach spasms, the driving pain of the shards entering it all over again, the slick feel of them sliding out, the scorching blood seeping down my abdomen and pooling on the floor.

Greer's harsh breath draws my eyes up. His hands tighten against my skin. I focus back on him, lifting my shirt to show the many silvery scars from those long shards of glass, jaggedly crisscrossing by my pubic bone.

"I'm not a violent man, but I'm glad he's dead. How could he do that?" He brushes a thumb gently over the scars.

A bitter laugh escapes me, and I look at my hands again. "He asked me why I made whatever dish I had. When I said Chris from school had recommended it to me, he grabbed my arm. He'd assumed Chris was a man and started screaming at me for being attracted to him."

I can't stop the bitter chuckle—the half-disgusted laugh—that escapes me. I swipe furiously at the tears streaming down my cheeks.

"Some pieces are fuzzy when I think about it. I remember shaking loose from his arm, and then he started chasing me. That was when I still fought back."

I swallow past the burning lump in my throat. "I fought back. I hit, I kicked, I screamed. It breaks you a bit when you're calling, and there's no one to hear you. He was terrifying. His voice was emotionless as he said I belonged to him. No one else could have me; nothing would keep him from me, not even death.

"The doctors couldn't save the baby. After I healed, Ethan was adamant that we keep trying. I wasn't allowed to take birth control, but I never got pregnant again. They said there is probably too much scarring from the injury. I sought counseling after he died. It took years to come to terms with the trauma I suffered. This year, we started focusing on the anxiety."

"Oh, Jesus, Kit. No wonder you wanted nothing to do with me."

I shake my head. He can't even begin to understand. I want him passionately. It consumes me every time I see him. Every piece of me senses him, calls to him, and wants him in my life.

He hasn't shied away from my pain, my trauma. Hasn't told me I need time to heal, hasn't said that I'll get over it. He is my peace. And it makes me want him with every single piece of my broken and slowly mending soul.

And everything about him says I can trust him, believe in him.

Choose him.

My skin prickles with the agony of choices. Let him in, take a chance that this could be the best thing that ever happened to me.

Or the worst.

I search his face again, taking in the longing and the control. He smiles gently at me, reaching up to wipe away the stupid tears.

It's impossible for him to know how much that simple gesture means. Still, I try to explain it. "I want everything to do with you, but you terrify me. Suddenly, I want something powerfully. Everything I imagined to be dead inside me is sparking to life, Greer. All because of you."

His face turns smug, that wolfish smile curling his lips, but there is warmth and softness too.

"How long were you married?" His hands are soothing again.

"Four years."

"You suffered his abuse for four years?"

"Longer than that. He threatened my family and showed me pictures of them. He seemed to know everyone, good or bad." I've suffered for years since.

If he could breathe fire, I think he would be right now. "That is so fucked up. How do you move past everything?"

I slide my hand up to his neck. Then scratch my nails through the hair at his nape. "Slowly. Very slowly."

He squeezes me, and I rest my head under his chin, allowing my body to fit into his.

His warm body under me soothes me in a way I haven't felt in ages. It's like a balm to my soul, rebuilding cracks and fissures.

He's part of the gold that glues me back together.

I squint against the early light. The crisp chest hair under my cheek and nose is tickling me. He's slept with me every night now, his body shielding me from the nightmares plaguing me. Including last night, when we fell asleep on the couch. My sleep has never been so easy.

It's like we're cocooned in a magical bubble where all the awful shit in my life is slowly fading away. I don't want to face reality when this snowstorm ends.

I slowly lift my head, watching his chest rise and fall. He pulls me closer to him. His body shifts a tiny amount before relaxing again.

I'm tucked in the arms of this man in a cabin out in the middle of nowhere. Every night, he tends to me, warms me.

This is the first time in years that I haven't worried about my safety. It's intense, awing, startling.

He is so patient with me. When I got lost in the second kiss, he didn't complain when I pulled back and gave me space. He's able to tuck my body into his, and the closeness is something my body obviously has no problems with—even if my brain sometimes says *hold on*.

Tingles zing up my spine. He has to feel my heartbeat right now. It's almost painful in its intensity.

If I shift, I'll probably wake him, but I can't stop myself. I fit my hands under my chin, letting the pleasure and delight of an entire night's rest spread throughout my body.

I rub myself against his thigh.

The pressure is good. Too good.

He stirs under me, hardening against the leg I have over him. My eyes fly to his, catching his sleepy grin before meeting the burn of his hooded gaze. It glows with lust in the light, and he tightens his hands around me.

"Mmm, this is the best way to wake up." He snuggles further into the couch, pulling me with him.

I have no idea how to do this—how to show him what I want. With what I hope is a smoldering gaze, I look at him from under my lashes and nibble my lip.

Please take the hint.

His eyes blaze as he stares at my mouth. I must have done the right thing.

Cupping his jaw, I dig my fingers into his beard, scratching with my fingernails. His moan is delightful as he arches his neck.

I want more. I want to make him feel good. Sliding my hand into his hair, I bring his attention back to me before shifting over his body so our heads are even.

"Greer." I swallow and then lick my lips, angling my head so I'm a hair's breadth away from him.

He keeps quiet, his hands moving on my back, his thumbs brushing against the dimples above my ass. He subtly shifts, pressing his cock into me.

So good—*heavenly* to be this close to him. Safe, warm, cherished. I close my eyes, moaning at the contact. If I shift enough, he'll be right at my clit. Grinding against him, I bite my lips against the delicious pleasure dancing in my core.

One of his hands makes its way into my hair, tangling in the strands. I gasp, desire pooling deep in my belly when he gently tugs.

Oh, I like that.

It's possessive in a way I've never experienced before. It's not pulling like Ethan did. The way Greer does it centers on desire. He needs this as much as I do, so I keep my gaze on him. He's waiting for something.

Me.

To give a signal, to let him have me. Holy hell, do I want him to have me.

Fiercely.

Panting slightly, I puff out against his lips. "Greer, it's been years since I've been touched this way. Can we go really slow, and... you show me?"

"Show you what?" He swallows, his Adam's apple bobbing. How is that sexy?

"How it could be."

His free hand slides up and down my back. He caresses my ass, then moves around my hip to feather up to the underside of my breasts before he dips back to where his cock presses against me. I gasp.

He shifts, sitting up and pulling me with him so I straddle his hips. Face to face, there is nothing to hide behind.

"What do you want, Kit?" His voice is gritty as he moves his fingers back and forth over my sensitive skin.

I should be scared. Instead, I'm ready to jump headlong into whatever this is, because the touch of his hands on my body is more soothing than anything I've ever experienced.

It's perfect. I want the protection and the desire and the way he cherishes my body. So it's easy to answer.

"You."

His mouth moves on mine, brushing slowly, that plump bottom lip grazing against me. He applies pressure, settling in firmer against me for a moment. The tip of his tongue licks along the seam of my lips. It's delicious and wet, and the thrill fills me.

Arousal floods my body, filling up every nook and cranny, making me yearn.

He pauses for a moment, leaning back to search my eyes. "Okay?"

I nod. My body thrumming, begging him to keep going. I pull his mouth back to mine. The pressure of his lips forces mine open, and his tongue darts inside. He gently sucks air, creating suction against my mouth, and I want more of it. It's never been this consuming, not with anyone before.

This is perfection, the way he kisses, the pull of his lips, the way my body aches for him. It's everything I could have asked for in the first time since...*no*. Shut that thought down.

This is different. It's beautiful, full of more than curiosity or scratching an itch. More than owning another person.

This is a gift.

I want to drown in him, taste every part of him, and show him what he does to me. Show him how the brush of his hand turns me on, fills me with raging desire, and makes me human.

I'm not an object to him.

Moaning, I press down against him as he rocks his hips up, sliding his cock against me, softly nudging my clit. I shudder against him, aching deeply, goose bumps skating down my arms.

Yes. It's all-encompassing. And I need a smidge more.

His tongue tangles with mine. His hands move to my face, tilting it how he wants it so he can go deeper. Shit, it's intoxicating. His deep moan tells me he's losing himself to this. I rock back, grinding against him faster.

"Kit?" His hands tighten, his neck arching.

"Yes, it all feels so good." I cup his cheeks and bring his lips back to mine, sliding my tongue deep inside chasing his. I want to show him what he does to me, how he makes me lose my mind. How he takes everything inside me and transforms it into a mushy pile of want and need.

His hand trails down my neck, sliding across my breast, learning the shape of me. His fingers tremble slightly, thank god, because I'm utterly lost in the sensation of his hands on my body.

He closes his hand around my breast, and the pressure sends tingles through my body, making me tremble.

Good lord, it's like he knows my body better than I do.

I press my chest into his palm, burning from the inside out. His cock is driving me mad with its little thrusts. I'm so close. Only a little faster, and I'll fall, tumbling into that soul-fracturing orgasm my body wants.

Needs.

He slows. Can he feel me tensing, fighting for that tumble into the abyss? The pleasure dips, and my body laments the loss. I want to lash out at him, make him come back to me and finish what he started.

I don't know if I can go back to anything other than this.

Grabbing his arms, I pull him closer and arch against him. "Greer, I'm so close. Please..."

He leans up, sucking on my nipple through my shirt, the rough, wet texture so good. Then he takes it deep into his mouth as his hand continues south. His fingers brush against my skin. "You're so smooth and soft, Red. So beautiful. Can I touch you?"

"Shit, stop asking, just... *Oh.*" I pant, my heart racing out of my chest. I clutch his hair, holding him to my breast as he pulls my nipple in deep. "Yes, it feels so good."

Finally, finally, finally.

He slides his hand under the waistband of my sweatpants and parts my slit. The pleasure in my body builds, pulsing at the spot centered deep between my legs.

"Oh shit, Red, you are so fucking wet."

Those magical fingers slide up and down, circling my opening. He traces one finger over my slit, then two, before pulling out and sliding them into his mouth. He sucks hard, dragging them out with a pop. "And you taste so good." He tugs at my pants. "Kit, give me more."

Need pours through my veins because that was a fucking turn-on. It's amping up my desire, my need to see him, touch him, and taste him.

I lift my hips, helping him get my pants off. When they're gone, I straddle him again, trying to get him where I need the pressure. His fingers brush the hem of my shirt next. My heart stutters, and I grab his wrist. "Not that." He's already seen my scars, but I'm not ready for them to be a part of this.

He nods and gives me a quick kiss. Then he gently rolls me under him, careful to keep his weight off me. He's being so considerate. Validating that I'm important.

His lips mesh with mine again, our mouths fusing in a mash-up of want and need. And then his forehead is on mine, and we are gasping, our breaths mingling, hands still grasping.

Yes, I've never been this swept up with passion before. It's freeing, feeling beautiful and sexy. The way he stares at my body is reverent. It makes me want to let it consume me.

He looks at my pussy and licks his lips.

Then slips off me, settling himself on the floor in front of the couch. He pulls me around so my ass is on the edge of the cushions. His palms are on my knees, pushing them open before slowly sliding up. He grabs my hips and pulls me closer. He settles his hands on my inner thighs where they meet my hips, his thumbs brushing my lips there.

His eyes turn into liquid gold, the irises black and wide. When he looks up to check on me, I shiver at the intensity. He's making sure I'm as deep in this as he is.

I nod, wishing I knew what to do with my hands. I want to touch him but don't want to throw him off, so I grip the edge of the couch instead.

His thumbs dip into my seam, parting the lips. Pleasure skirts up my body. *Oh my god.* His hair brushes my thigh, and then there are hot puffs of air against my skin. Closer. He licks, flattening his tongue against me as he traces me from slit to clit.

"Holy shit, Greer." I think I'm seeing a divine light in the distance, and I'm not even religious.

He licks again, applying more pressure, his broad tongue devouring me, the toying pulses pushing against my lips. Something brushes my clit as his tongue dips inside me, tickling against my walls.

Oh my—wow.

I pant hard, the pleasure building, blinding. He is torturing me with his magic mouth, with his thumb rubbing my hard clit in a slow rhythm. I can't stop myself from arching against his face, from riding his tongue, chasing the bliss.

Bracing myself, I settle one foot on his shoulder and tense. He nips my ankle before sinking back into my pussy, thrusting into it with his tongue.

My body is so tight. His pressure is constant as he moves up to my clit, sucking on it gently while pushing a finger inside. Twisting it around, he pulls out, then drives back in with two.

I hiss as he curls his fingers, pressing against that hidden pleasure spot.

He sucks again, his mouth over my bean. It's incredible. His fingers dance inside me, the tension rising higher and higher. My legs tremble as his digits shift. My chest constricts. I'm going to explode and die because I can't catch my breath.

I'm almost there...

I break, spasming around his fingers, my wetness dripping down his hand. "Shit, shit, shit."

He continues stroking softly, extending my pleasure until the pressure fades. Then he kisses my leg before easing away.

My chest heaves as I return to earth. When he leans up, my body is still twitching, and I blindly grab for his cheeks to pull him close and nip his lip, tasting myself.

I didn't know I could fracture like that—in every part of my body—and still come back to life.

Opening my eyes, I focus on him, smiling because that was the best orgasm of my entire damn life. I lick his bottom lip slowly. "I thought we were going slow?" Because I don't want to anymore.

I want more.

"This is slow." He chuckles, and it bubbles through me. I smile back.

His smile lights up his face, his dimple popping. "What now?"

"Please tell me you have a condom."

Greer

Fuck, she's magnificent. And she tastes so damn good that I want to dip back into her pussy and lick her again.

Instead, I can't stop staring at her eyes, and I'm awed by what they reveal. This is more than physical for her too. "Are you going to wait here while I go get one?"

I need her lips again. Leaning forward, I take them, dipping my tongue out to lick her bottom lip. She wraps her legs around me, grinding against my dick as I suck her bottom lip into my mouth and bite gently. She's so responsive, and it's making me crazy to see her lose herself like this. I want every piece of her.

Every.

Responsive.

Piece.

She nips my lip then leans back. "I'm giving you one minute to go find one."

I want her consumed by passion, to be as deep into this as I am. So I grind against her again, loving her moans. I shift back reluctantly, not wanting to leave her. "Fuck that. You are coming with me. Wrap your legs around me."

When we're both on our feet, I scoop her up with one hand under her bottom and the other in her hair, then drag her lips back to mine.

She sucks on my bottom lip as I make my way up the stairs, my cock rubbing against her clit with every step. Fuck, her moans are driving me crazy.

I pause at the landing and push her against the wall, pressing my cock against her. She gasps as I drag my lips down her neck. *Fuck, there better be a condom in my drawer.*

"Faster, Greer. I need you."

Racing down the hall, I kick open my bedroom door before tossing her onto the bed. She bounces with a soft laugh, landing on her back with her knees slightly bent.

Fuck me.

She rests back on her elbows.

I yank open the drawer and dig around, touching everything but what I want. *Motherfucker.* "Shit, Kit. I don't have one. Someone has to have one in this house." I grab her again. "Wrap those legs around me, Red. We'll find one together."

"Hurry. I want you inside me."

I growl into her neck. "Tell me more."

She swallows, that shyness creeping back in. Fuck, that is sexy.

Breathy and full of desire. "I want you to slide into me; feel how wet I am..." She bites her lip, and a growl erupts from my throat.

I stop at the wall and thrust against her, delighted by the laughter tickling my ear. Her cheeks are red from the desire consuming us both. "I like when you talk dirty to me, Red. It's such a turn-on."

She leans in, biting my bottom lip and tugging it into her mouth.

Fucking erotic. "You are killing me."

In every room, she grinds against me as I search for condoms. Each room is fucking empty. My only consolation prize is dry humping her against every door.

In my life, it's never been this fucking spicy with a woman, and I'm consumed by the need to make this the best she's ever had.

I want to lay into her with abandon while cherishing her at the same time. Instead, I carry her back to my bedroom, sucking on her lips. Her frustrated groan hits me. *I know, trust me.* The need to be a part of her is about to kill me.

I lay her down and settle myself on my elbows above her. "A fucking cabin for adults and not a single fucking condom."

Leaning up, she bites my throat, and I arch to give her more access. Her tongue makes its way back to my mouth, pushing inside, applying subtle pressure.

She pushes on my shoulder, so I roll until she's sitting on top of me. Her body tenses when I slide my hands under the hem of her shirt. I stop, barely brushing her skin.

"This okay?" My thumbs coast over her nipples, which harden again.

She nods. I groan, gripping and kneading her breasts.

"Grind against me. Come again. I want to watch you." I grab her hips, pulling her naked pussy against my sweatpants. Wetness blooms all over them, soaking through the fabric as I gyrate her hips against my cock. "Fuck, you get so wet, Red. So fucking wet."

I move her hips faster. A flush creeps up her neck to her cheeks. She pants and rocks forcefully against me. "Greer, I need something more."

She slides her hands down her breasts, settling on her thighs. Her hand moves between her legs, right over her clit, then sinks between her lips, and she moves feverishly as she rocks.

My cock strains against her as I arch and rub against her entrance, teasing that opening. My heart thunders, pounding hard.

Our moans and gasps are harsh in the quiet. She's a goddess, and I'm so turned on that I can't stop my groans. "Show me how to work your clit."

Her cheeks redden, but she keeps her attention on me.

I push my fingers against hers, drawing them over her sopping-wet clit, noting her movements as she rubs furiously. Her body tightens over me again. She gasps, but her pace slows.

I grab her hips again and buck against her while sliding between her lips. My tip lodges into her opening through the fabric of my sweatpants, and she spasms as her body convulses again.

"That's it, Red, come all over me." Her moans go on forever, her body shuddering against mine as she comes down from her release. It's beautiful watching her refocus on me. Her hands go to my chest as she leans down, hiding in her hair.

I push her silky strands back and nudge her chin up so she's looking at me.

"Kit, you are so...arresting. Beautiful. Fuck." Pulling her face down, I brush her lips.

"You didn't come."

"I'll take care of it in the shower."

Smiling coyly, she leans down, her buttery smooth lips trailing across my chest. I moan as her hands follow, crossing my ribs and my pecs. Her lips are soft as they move across my skin. I'm torn between wanting her touch on me forever and wanting to end it all now because I need her. This.

More than I need air.

My dick is rock hard, filling with the desire pulsing through me. I wait, biting my lip as she scoots her hips back. Her lips trail down to my belly button. With her hands on my waistband, she peeks up at me.

I am floored. The green luminous in the lamplight. She pulls at my waistband, exposing the head of my cock and soaking up every inch of me. As she reaches the base, my cock springs free, shooting aggressively toward the ceiling. The purple head is angry with need, a drop of pre-cum dribbling off the tip and down my shaft.

I can't stop my grin at the look on her face. "Something wrong?"

"That's barely going to fit in my mouth. Good thing you couldn't find a condom. I wouldn't walk for a week."

I bark out a laugh, my cock bobbing against my stomach. She watches it dance, the green of her irises turning liquid before disappearing against the blown-out black of her pupils. Her hands rest on my thighs, brushing gently.

If she touches my cock, I'll explode. I'm so fucking primed and ready. She leans forward, her tongue slipping out to lick up my cum. "How do I taste?"

"Salty." She smirks and then pops my head into her mouth.

It's intense, the pleasure and pressure. Her lips are soft and perfectly wrapped around me. She grasps my dick and moans, running her tongue along the underside and swirling around. It's making me almost delirious. I've always had self-control in these situations, but I'm quickly losing it.

I tangle my hands in her hair. Her body tenses, and panic flickers across her face. "I won't push. I promise you are in charge."

She assesses me for a moment, something warring in her eyes. Finally, she nods and moans around me again. She slides her lips down to her hand and swallows before bobbing back up. Her lips butt against her hand, encasing my dick. I can almost imagine it's her pussy when I close my eyes.

Oh. Jesus Christ.

I moan, swallowing against the building pressure. My balls tighten. My spine tingles. "Kit, you take my cock so good."

She hums around me.

"Look at the way your lips grip me. So fucking perfect." And it's true. Her mouth closes around me as best she can as she glides down. It's one of the most erotic things I've ever seen.

"Fuck, that is perfect. I'm going to come soon."

She slides her mouth back down, further this time, gagging a little as I hit the back of her throat. She rebounds and does it again, this time not so far. Using her hand in tandem with her mouth, she works my cock, building the pressure.

My fingers pulse in her hair, tangling in her strands to pull her up. She shakes her head, sucking harder.

"You're sure?" I revel in the ecstasy, enjoying how her mouth circles my cock. The way she's taken charge of my dick.

Yes, yes, yes. The pressure is so good, her lips perfect, her tongue dancing in an agonizingly good way.

No one will ever compare.

I spread my legs wider. She adjusts and moans around me. The vibrations against my cock are all I need.

"That's it, baby, take my cock." And with that, I explode inside her hot, wet mouth. I jerk up once, twice, as I unleash all the restless energy I've had building. With her magic mouth, it's instantly gone.

She takes it all like a fucking champ, gliding up and down, swallowing what she can.

A small amount dribbles out of the corner of her mouth as she continues to work me, swallowing the last of it down. She settles back on her heels, her cheeks rosy, a shy smile lighting her face.

I lean down and pull her to my chest, tucking her head under my chin. I heave in air, trying to reduce the black dots in my vision.

She wraps her arms around me.

And for the first time, it's her choice.

My heart stutters, a pleasant hum filling every inch of me. "Fuck me, Kit."

"I tried to."

Laughing, I swat her ass gently. "Let's get cleaned up and then get something to eat."

Nineteen

Kit

"Tell me about your family." I shuffle my body in the chair as Greer scrambles eggs at the stove.

"What do you want to know?" He peeks at me from where he stands, his spatula gliding around the pan in a move that reminds me of the slow sweep of his hand down my torso.

Focus, questions.

"Are you an only child?"

"Oh, fuck no. My parents couldn't keep it in their pants. There are seven of us, but two aren't blood-related. Simon and I are the oldest, then Maddox, Harrison, Asher, Violet, and the two we pseudo-adopted, Troy and Han."

I stare at him with what I'm sure is an incredulous look on my face. "That is a lot of kids."

He chuckles, his body at ease in the kitchen. He continues talking, but I'm lost in the way his shoulders bunch as he moves the spatula, the muscles undulating under his shirt. I'm pretty sure I'm drooling at this point. He stops, his smile dazzling as he turns to me for a moment.

Shit, I stopped paying attention. Ask a question, don't make it obvious that I was ogling his body. "How old are you?"

He smirks like he knows what I was doing. "Older than you." The eggs sizzle, their aroma filling the air, and my stomach growls.

"Well, the way you act says differently." Winking at him, I try to soften the blow.

"I'll be thirty-four next month."

I exaggerate a surprised look on my face.

He laughs at it. "What? Expecting me to be younger with my delicious body and boyishly good charm?"

"Something like that." I chuckle as a plate of eggs, toast, and a few slices of bacon appear before me. I reach for the fork he's holding an inch out of reach.

He rears back. "If you want to eat, you'll have to tell me how much you like looking at my body."

"That's coercion. Besides, if you tell me I have to tell you, then how do you know if it's true?"

He slides around the island and leans in close, goose bumps erupt along my arms from his proximity. "It's not coercion if it's true." He leans back, handing me the fork.

"You were married for four years, and you've been a widow for three, which makes you older than twenty-five. Maybe twenty-seven?" He guesses as he rounds the island.

"Thirty." The first bite of eggs is delicious, and I spend a few silent moments eating in delight. "What do you do?" I shove a forkful of eggs in my mouth, salivating over him across the countertop.

"Simon and I own a woodworking business. I design everything, and he manages the day-to-day. We have a group of people working with us. We service a third of Stirling Harbor, and hopefully soon, some international." The coffee maker buzzes, and he pours himself a mug of coffee. "Do you want one?"

"Only if it's decaf."

"You're in luck. That's all I drink."

A pleased hum leaves me. Surprise, surprise. I'm finding so many things about him that I like, and we have a lot in common. We both like reading, hiking, being outdoors, stupid humor movies, and the actor Simon Pegg. People either love him or hate him, and there is no in-between. I find him hilarious, and luckily Greer enjoyed *Hot Fuzz* as much as I did.

It's getting harder not to like him, especially given the calm and peace he brings to my life. "Your eggs are delicious."

He smirks. "It's the secret ingredient."

"Which is...?"

"Still a secret." He winks at me, handing over a glass of steaming decaf.

I chew the last mouthful, carefully this time, as I reach for the cup. "I taste hints of oregano."

"Nope."

"Marjoram?"

He quirks his brow.

"Basil?"

"Now you're listing pizza sauce ingredients."

I chuckle. "Will you tell me if I promise to have some more *sausage*?" I waggle my brows.

Desire flares in his eyes, and he bites his lip before leaning over to take my mouth.

"Tempting. But I'm still not giving you my recipe." His body is delicious, all the muscles twisting and turning as he loads the dishwasher.

"What sort of things do you make? And how?"

"I make a bit of everything for the home, and then doll houses, cradles, that sort of thing." He turns to face me, leaning over the island. "I designed a machine to do precision cuts. As for the design? Usually, I listen to what people tell me they want. Most of the time, they are curves or geometric shapes. Once in a while, people let me design something based on a theme or a feeling they want captured. Or inspiration from the things around me."

"Show me?" My lips kick up in an uncontrolled smile.

Greer is silent for a moment, then grabs my hand, pulling me upstairs to his room. He leads me over to his nightstand. "On the sides here."

Layers upon layers of wood curve up and down in rolling waves. There is a lighthouse in the distance with the froth of the waves brushing a craggy shore. The ripples seem to move beneath my fingers. The texture is smooth through the grooves, then rough on the peaks, changing like the ocean. I beam at him.

"This is stunning." I can't stop running my fingers over it. "I can feel the power of the ocean."

When I look at him, my heart drops. He is absolutely resplendent, glowing under my praise with a brilliant smile, bright eyes, and those dimples. They are going to kill me. His chest puffs out, and he nods.

"That's my favorite lighthouse, Bass Harbor Head Lighthouse, about an hour north. You can see it off on the horizon from my favorite spot on the coast. My dad took us on a fishing trip up there when I was a kid. I remember looking up and seeing that lighthouse, and I was a goner. There has been nothing like it since." Something on his face says *until now*, and I drop my gaze back to the lighthouse, not ready to delve too deeply into how I'm feeling.

I trace my fingers over it again. "You made your own machine to do this? Holy shit, Greer. I'm a little intimidated."

His deep chuckle draws my attention. "Why?"

"You own your own business. You design machines and create remarkable artwork. It's like your life is all set." Standing, I face him. "And my life is such a chaotic mess. I have no plans for the future. It's...sad."

I head over to the window, needing a break from my wallowing and a change of subject. "Do you think the snow stopped?" I pull back the curtain to peer outside. "I hadn't thought to check when we first woke this morning. Thanks for saving me from my nightmares again, by the way."

He moves behind me. His chest barely touches me, but his warmth radiates into my skin. He slides his hands to my hips and leans in close, his mouth caressing the curve of my neck and shoulder. I shiver, closing my eyes. Butterflies take flight in my belly. His soft beard brushes my skin, and I revel in it and his buttery soft lips nibbling on the sensitive spot.

"I checked the DOT website, and it looks like they've started plowing the county roads. Hopefully, the road will be cleared by morning." Hot air puffs against my skin. "And I enjoyed saving you."

His fingers lock on my hips, the tips digging in, anchoring us both in place.

"I'm trying hard not to like you, Greer. You make it almost impossible."

"Then stop trying. Let this happen."

"I can't. I don't trust...me. You're not safe for my soul." I turn in his arms. "But I still want you."

We watch each other for several quiet moments. I want to trap the words I need to push free. But I can't keep them in. Not when I've finally tasted freedom. "I'm not ready for more than this, Greer. I can't lose myself again. I can't..." I stop, unsure how to say that the thought of being with him terrifies me.

My head says to do this alone, make all the decisions and discoveries myself. Give myself the time and freedom to *learn* me. But my heart? It needs to shut up right now. "And you have so much ahead of you." It's a cop-out. "I can't even make it through a week without having a breakdown."

"Kit." He drops his forehead on mine. "It's okay. I can take it as slow as you need me to. This can stay easy like it has been. Please give us a chance."

He makes this so hard.

"Let me show you how easy I can make it. Come shower with me." He holds his hand out.

I look into his eyes, always so warm, open, and eager. Trembling, I slide my hand into his. He raises it to his lips, biting down on my fingertips.

He doesn't let go as he leads me to his bathroom. He sets up the shower and then pulls me to him. His breath settles over me, his lips so close. I wait, wanting him to close the last millimeter. Finally, he moves forward, licking my bottom lip before sucking on it.

"How do you do that?"

He cocks a brow, questioning me.

"You touch me, and I go up in flames."

"Me too, Red. You're not alone in that." His fingers brush the hem of my shirt before tucking into the waistband of my sweats and pulling them down. As he kneels in front of me, I brace a hand on the counter for balance and step out. His hands skim the outside of my legs, then move up my thighs and hips.

He kisses me, his lips landing on my pussy, his nose nudging against me as his tongue flicks over my clit. I shiver and grab his shoulders to steady myself. The constant thrum he creates works its way through my body, building up.

I hold my breath, my body taut as he strokes my bean with the tip of his tongue, his fingers digging into my hips. He centers a soft kiss against me, then stands with the hem of my shirt in his hands.

I lick my lips and raise my hands high so he can bring the shirt up and over. My hair falls free, brushing my shoulders and down my back.

His eyes rove over my body, intense and taking in everything. He settles his hands at my hips while he waits for me to give him the go-ahead. I nod, and his fingers skim my breasts before palming their weight completely, his thumbs brushing over my nipples.

The zings and tingles amplify, shooting down my spine and into my core. He sucks my nipple into his mouth, and my pussy spasms, drenching my channel in wetness.

I thrust my fingers into his hair and arch against his mouth.

He releases my nipple and kisses his way back up to my neck. "You're fucking gorgeous, Kit. So fucking soft everywhere you're supposed to be. Hips made for grabbing." He punctuates his words by squeezing them.

My hips and thighs are large, my stomach soft, and my breasts full, and he seems to delight in them. I'm a mix between an hourglass and a pear, and it's everything I wanted to be.

My heart skips a beat. Stepping back out of his grasp, I point to his pants and beat-up T-shirt. "Off, now."

"Whew, bossy." He winks, then something pleasant fills his gaze, but I can't pin it down before it vanishes. Reaching back over his head, he pulls his shirt off and throws it to the side. His fingers trail down his chest to settle on his sweats. Then his pants are off, and that glorious cock springs free.

I pull him into the shower with me, closing my eyes as the hot stream hits my body. He turns me, pushing me against the tiled wall, eliciting a shiver as his body presses flush against mine.

His rough palms slide up, over my neck, and under my chin, forcing my head up. And then his lips crash down, devouring me, minty tongue tangling with mine, dancing sinfully. He dips in and out, mimicking the thrusting of his hips against me. The head of his cock brushes the soft swell of my belly.

He growls against my lips. "Fuck, I want to be in you so bad."

Shit, me too. But going bare? I'm not ready for *that* level of intimacy. I can keep a piece of myself; keep it slow this way.

Sliding my hand between us, I grab his long length, squeezing tightly. His eyes roll back in his head while his hips piston into my hand.

He kisses me frantically, sucking my lips and my tongue, and his hands touch me everywhere. Marking me as his. It's there in his hands and mouth, the way he moves. He's claiming a piece of my heart, even if he doesn't know it. His patience and acceptance are working their way into my soul.

It's slow this time. Our bodies getting to know each other, taking the time to savor one another. Long strokes across the skin, slow, tempestuous kisses. Our voices and harsh breaths mingle in the air as our pleasure builds.

I show him how much he means to me with my hands and mouth. He shudders against me with each pass, his moans bouncing off the walls as he explodes.

Then I'm weightless as he lifts me into the air. I wrap my legs around his hips and meet him kiss for kiss as he brings me to release again with his fingers.

When we can finally breathe slowly, he holds me close for a moment, his arms wrapping around me before dropping my feet to the ground. He turns me to face the wall, and I let my head rest against it as his hands run soap down my back. Suds puddle at my feet as the water washes them down.

He has magic hands. His thumbs and fingers knead into the tight muscles of my back and shoulders. His hands trace along my skin. "These look like belt or whip marks." His voice is shaky, almost disbelieving, and his fingers tremble.

Right. He can see it all. "They are." Both, actually, and why does it hurt less to talk about when his hands are on my skin?

"I forgot getting in the shower meant you'd see everything. I have many scars, Greer. Some are worse than others—some deeper. They all bury a hurt. But the physical ones are healed, and I'm working on the rest."

He runs his hands up my back, the warmth in my heart increasing tenfold with each brush of his hands over my traumas, both the physical and emotional ones.

I turn and wrap my arms around him. His kindness seeps inside me, gentle touch by gentle touch.

He soaps up my shoulders, around my breasts, and then my stomach before dropping to his knees and washing my hips and legs. His fingers whisper along the marks on my abdomen, lingering on the most wicked one. "What about this one?"

That one? "That one is deep, and try as I might, I don't know that it will ever heal." I lace my fingers through his hair when he leans his head against my stomach. Faint pressure draws my focus. His lips are pressed against it, kissing along its jagged edges.

Unshed tears burn my eyes. He's changing me.

Changing everything.

I don't want to let him go. I need the way he makes me relax, feeling protected and cherished.

A pleasant hum grows under my breastbone, but it's so different from all the other times. It radiates from his lips, touching all the dark places in my soul. I'm open. Open to the idea of more, and the anguish over having lost the ability to have children slowly fades with his touch.

He's giving up that ability, too, because this is more than a weekend thing. He knows what I can and can't give him, so he's not walking into this blindly.

Still, it makes me ache for what he would have to give up.

I smooth my fingers through his hair, holding on to him, trying to silently communicate how he's altering me.

The bomb of emotion detonates as his thumb brushes over the scar he kissed. His lips move to the other ones, pressing tenderly over the puckered silver skin as the loss of what we could have had rushes through me.

The tears I've been holding off no longer listen to me, and thankful for the stream of water that will hide them, I let them flow.

Greer

"Arms up."

She chuckles as I wrap the towel around her and tuck the end into the fabric under her armpit. I grab another one and work on drying her arms and legs before hopping back up to dry off her hair. I've never done this before—never taken care of someone this way—but after that shower and all the unspoken words that flowed in there, I had to do it.

Everything inside me wants to make her feel as good as she makes me feel. I've never been so compelled to stay with someone. It wars with my brain and makes me want to jump out of my skin because I don't want to go to work. I want to stay right here.

"What are we doing the rest of the night?"

"I'm going to check the transportation website again. They started plowing a few hours ago."

"Oh."

Her face drops, and I pull her close and press my lips to hers, not wanting to lose the energy from in the shower.

When I pull back, I drop my forehead onto hers. "That doesn't mean you have to leave tonight. Or even tomorrow. You can stay until the rest of the group shows up. It's up to you."

She pulls her bottom lip in with her teeth and nods. "All right."

I lead her to my bedroom and get her dressed in another set of my clothes. Once I pull the T-shirt over her head and get it situated, I slide my hands up her arms. "Do you want to rest for a bit? I'll wake you for dinner."

She slips over to the side of the bed. "What are you going to do?"

Sit at my drafting table and hide out so I don't ravish her again. As much as I want to crawl into bed with her, I also have some things to get done.

"Ahhh." She smiles at me, pulling the covers back to climb inside. "I have a better idea." She pats the bed next to her. "Lie here with me awhile and tell me stories about your childhood."

I scratch the back of my neck, hesitating. My feet are itching to make my way toward the door, to go down to the study and get back to work.

She pats again. "Stay out of the study today."

Gritting my teeth, I grab some shorts and pull them on before stomping to her side of the bed. "Scoot over."

She obliges happily, and I get in, lying flat. My mind races with all the things left out on the drafting table that need my attention—the emails I need to send, the letters piling up at the office.

A smooth hand travels down my chest, then another grabs my arm and lifts it out of the way so she can lie on my shoulder. Kit shushes softly, and miraculously, my body relaxes. I wrap my arm around her, settling my hand under her arm so I can feel her heartbeat. Steady, strong against my palm, grounding me in the moment.

One at a time, the thoughts racing through my mind shut off, and I focus on the sparks that flow out of her hand when she touches me.

I've never been a napper, but the rhythm of her hand and the steady beat of her heart releases something inside me. It isn't long before I'm lulled into a sense of security, and not long after that, she sleeps in my arms.

Why did I resist this?

Twenty

Kit

"MY FAMILY WILL BE up here in the next few days, along with Rosemary and Angelo. Are you sure you don't want to stay?"

I tug my hat onto my head. He was sweet and ran to my car to get it for me. He pulls a scarf from the closet and gently wraps it around my neck.

His gooey marshmallow insides are showing, and I like it. So much.

"No. I know I planned on coming up with them, but I think I need some time to myself." And I need to process everything that's happened without my sister or Angelo constantly telling me how wonderful Greer is.

Because they will. Rosemary would be so ecstatic if she knew something had happened between us. And I want time to pick apart my thoughts and figure out what this is without her influence. Figure out how to navigate it before I see him again.

"Okay. I'll walk you out, then."

At my car, he hands me a small bag through the window. "It's not much. Some fruit and a sandwich."

My heart melts.

He brings his head close to mine through the open window. "You'll call me when you get home?"

His amber irises flash deep gold as he reaches in and pulls me close. It's like he can't stop touching me now that he knows I'm heading home. A "Please" rumbles against my lips right before his crash onto mine. He sucks my tongue into his mouth, inhaling my breath before slowly retreating. His eyes are still closed when he leans his forehead against mine. "Kit?"

I nod, and instantly, a deep, happy sigh hits my cheek. When I look up, he's staring at me, his dimples on full display.

Please don't let this be a game. Some stupid way for me to trust him before the real him shows up.

Even knowing that Rosemary set this up isn't enough. Ethan tricked the people around us into believing that we were a happy couple.

I don't want to get it wrong again.

I'm getting in too deep, and if I trust Greer and let him in, and he rips my soul apart, it'll be the end of me.

His gaze searches mine. "Are you sure you won't stay?"

Even though I enjoy his pestering, I nod. "I want some time to process everything."

"I can come back early..."

"Then I wouldn't be processing." Laughter bubbles up from deep inside, joyful and resonant. "You stay. I'll see you in two weeks."

"Okay. Two weeks." He nods. "Goodbye, Kit."

With another nod, I leave the property. The drive to Stirling Harbor is long, and with every passing mile, my chest caves in a little more.

He showed me what life could be like: a happy life, a whole life. He's given me a glimpse of what I've been fighting to gain: an unbroken version of myself.

He sees me as whole.

Scarred, but whole.

I tighten my grip on the wheel, wanting to take the next exit off the highway and turn back to the mansion in the woods. Back to him.

But I don't.

I won't be consumed by my false feelings and naivety again. If my time with Ethan taught me one thing, it's to take it slow. And every moment I spend with Greer, all I want to do is rush into the life I'm almost certain he can give me.

One without nightmares or pain, where my past no longer consumes me.

I've only just regained control, and I don't want to lose it.

And so I drive the next mile, and the next, until I'm home.

Pulling into my driveway, I click the button for my garage. As soon as I park, I dial Greer.

"Did you make it?"

"Yep. I had a lot to think about, so the time disappeared." I throw the key in my purse.

His smile bleeds through the earpiece, making pleasant zings skirt down my spine. "Thank you for a great weekend. It's the best I've had in a long time."

"Me too." I bite my lip to keep the grin off my face. It's so weird to be happy. To have something other than restless energy running through my body.

"Are you sure I can't come back early? I'd like to take you out." He's persistent, that is for sure.

I chuckle. "Hm. I need the time, Greer."

"How about next Friday?"

Will that be enough time to figure things out? One full week to decide what the hell is going on in my brain and heart.

A sharp pang fills my chest.

Will I miss him?

Yeah, I will. But I told him I needed time. Would giving in show him that he can walk all over me? He's asking, though. It's not an order. And that means more to me than he'll ever know. "What time?"

"Seven?"

"I'll be ready."

After we've said goodbye, I text him my address and get out of my car with a pep in my step. A stone walkway with lush green ground plants lining it leads from the garage to the house. Today, they are peppered by spots of melting snow. My house is on two acres with trees that back up to the ocean.

It's a small place. A main-floor kitchen, living room, dining room, bedroom, and bathroom. Straight through the entry, there are stairs leading up to the small top floor. An attic, really, with my own bathroom.

It's perfect for me, and it's right off the water, so I wake up to the crashing waves. I painted it in neutrals with deep blue and green accents, which pair well with the rustic dark mahogany woodworking. It is vibrant and lush, giving me a sense of peace whenever I walk in.

I pause at the front door.

Odd. It isn't latched. I know I locked it when I left for that date. My heart stutters before racing again.

Okay, no reason to freak out. Let's think it through. I gave a key to Mom and Rosemary.

I dial Mom first. She answers on the second ring. "Hi, love."

"Hey, Mom. Were you by chance in my home over the last few days?"

"What, Kit? Sorry, I'm getting into the store, and it's hard to hear you." A loud humming sounds through the earpiece.

"Were you in my house over the last week?" I ask louder. My skin prickles. My spine itches as sweat drops form on my temples. I clench and unclench my free hand as my heart pounds in my chest.

Calm down. It was probably Mom in the house.

"Oh! I was. I stopped by and dropped some things off. Your dad came with me and put together your new bed frame."

My shoulders drop, and blood returns to my fingers. Simply Mom watching out for me. I bite my lips to stop the smile. "Thanks, Mom. Did you forget to latch the door?"

"Sorry, love, I might have. I was in a hurry toward the end. Your dad had reservations for dinner."

"Thanks, Mom. I love you."

"Love you too, Kit-Kat. Bye."

I shove the phone into my pocket as I scan the area, looking up and down the street. Nothing. *Not that I'd know.* I haven't been here long enough to learn which vehicles and people belong.

I turn back to my door and push it open, looking inside for anything out of place. Nothing.

Ethan is dead. Get a grip. That doesn't stop the knot from forming in my gut. Ignoring the light switch, I look at the oranges and reds of the setting sun streaking through the window, the natural light calming my nerves. That tranquility stays with me as I walk into the kitchen and place my keys in the bowl on the counter.

With the tension gone, I kick my shoes off.

It's nice not having to worry about putting boxes away. *Thank you, Mom.* Picking up the key bowl, I place it on the new mahogany table by the front door. *Thank you, Dad, for putting this together.*

I head up the stairs to sort the clothes myself. Mom probably put most of them away already, but I can see to what else needs doing. Stepping into the room, my jacket half-off, I freeze, and ice pours through my veins.

A solitary black dress is laid out on the bed, its skirt dangling over the edge. It was the one I wore to Ethan's funeral, but I don't remember packing it with my belongings when I left California.

More items are on the other side of the bed, thrown haphazardly into a box. Mom must have forgotten to mention it.

I pick the dress up. Its weight more emotional than physical. I'll never wear it again. I'm not the woman Ethan demanded I be.

I rush down the stairs, the fabric burning my fingers, and grab an empty box. Swiping a pen off the counter, I write "Donate" in large letters. After I toss the dress inside, I scrutinize it one more time, and then close the lid.

I need a hot bath and sleep, stat.

Climbing back upstairs, I head into my favorite room. The white ceramic clawfoot tub placed against the wall is delicate and clean. The entire room is relaxing and pure.

While I wait for the tub to fill, I wander back into my bedroom and grab a small box labeled "Jewelry" and bring it to the bathroom. The lid is heavy, the inside lined with velvet. I untangle necklaces and pair up the few earrings I own. My wedding band and engagement ring stand out, blaring in their loudness. I pick them up slowly.

In my palm, they're a metaphor for my marriage.

Cold.

Pain burns through me, singeing and searing me from the inside out. He stole so much from me.

I wanted to carry a child, to feel the growth, the aching hips, the pain of childbirth. I slide a shaky hand over my stomach and let the ache fill me.

I hate him. "Do you hear me?" I shout to Ethan's ever-present ghost. "I hate you!"

The rings clank as I clench them in my fist. "Fuck you, you worthless asshole." Trembling, I curl in on myself, my body too heavy to stay upright. Resting my hands on my thighs, I suck in what I can through the lump in my throat.

The burn bubbles from deep down, pouring out from every crack in my soul. It races up my throat and out through my mouth. It's harsh in its eruption as I stand and scream.

Raw and crushing and long. So long it makes my throat hoarse.

I take a breath, and the tension starts again, kicking open every door I closed, pulling free every memory I kept buried.

The scream erupts louder this time, pulled from depths I didn't know I had. My tears start again, giving me whiplash from how quickly my mind twists between emotions.

I hate him—hate what he made me into. What he took from me. And what he stole.

Then it ends, all my energy expended, my body spent.

"Shit." Out of energy, my voice a ghost of its former self, I open my palm. The rings glint in the light. Rings I never want to see again.

I throw them as hard as I can.

As they sail across the room, I turn away, ignoring the clinking sound they make when they hit the bedroom wall.

No longer having their weight on my shoulders, I drop to my knees. My chest is heaving, my shoulders racking. My whole body pours out the poison it's held in for so long.

Greer

The two jackasses and the rest of the group are due up here in the next few hours. Fuck, what was Angelo thinking sending Kit up here in a snowstorm? And why am I just now hashing it out?

I grit my teeth, raking my hand through my hair. I shove open a cupboard door and push around the various teas and coffees, looking for my beans.

Damn it. I'm not comfortable yelling at Rosemary, but today might be the day that changes.

The coffee bag crinkles as I pour a scoop into the grinder. The routine helps to calm me. So does breathing deeply.

Fuck, she has been through so much. No wonder she's on edge with everyone and everything.

I shove my hands through my hair again.

If that man were alive, fuck, I'd end him. I told her I'm not violent, and that's true, but I'd want to hit that son of a bitch and let him know how it feels. Give him pain. End Kit's agony. My blood boils. Kit, bruised and broken, floats through my mind.

It was a blow for me when she said she couldn't have kids. The heartache she's endured makes me want to pull her into my arms and take her pain.

To take away all her heartbreak.

I want kids. I've always wanted several kids, but it's not a dealbreaker. If she wants kids and wants to adopt, I'll do whatever. It hurt, though, shocking me like a punch to the gut.

But only because when I think about kids now, I see them with her fiery spirit and her red hair.

Here I am, thinking about her long-term, and I don't even know if we will work out.

But at least I have the chance to find out now. I'm still reeling over her saying yes to a date. I half chuckle into my coffee. My fingers itch to call her again, and I force myself to give her the time she's asked for.

"Greer?" A voice calls from the entryway.

I set my coffee down and stare into the dark liquid for a moment, thankful I can remain calm. *Don't yell. They were only trying to help.*

Rosemary steps in, and it's easy to see how I never realized Kit was her sister. They are opposites with her brown hair and brown eyes. "Hey! How are...things?" She sets down a bag without looking away from me.

I raise my brow at her. Whatever Kit wants her to know, she can share. I'm not about to out her to her family. I obviously have to acknowledge she was here, but that doesn't mean I have to do so right away.

"How was your drive?" I sip the coffee, letting the burn dance around my tongue before I swallow.

"We made it." Angelo slips past Rosemary and picks up the coffee pot. "Decaf?"

I nod.

"Fuck, I need something stronger."

"There's whiskey in the cabinet."

"Not that strong." His laughter tumbles out. He pours himself a cup of coffee, then leans back against the counter. "So...how was the weekend?" With an innocent expression on his face, he smiles.

"Long. The snow was heavy, so I had to wait for the weather to warm up and melt some away."

"And the company?" Angelo meets my gaze as he sips.

Rosemary can barely hold in her energy as she bites her lip. She's practically bouncing on her toes. They are invested in this, which is sweet. But it makes it even more imperative that I don't betray Kit's confidence.

My lips are locked better than Fort Knox. I settle with something bland. "Kit is nice."

"But how did it go?"

"How did what go?" I hide my smile behind my mammoth cup, hopefully giving Rosemary an innocent eye. She's practically salivating; she wants to know so bad. "She's a nice girl."

"Kit isn't a girl, Greer, and you know it. Did you guys get along?" Rosemary is like a dog with a bone.

"Jesus, Rosemary. Leave the guy alone." Angelo's laughter softens his harsh words.

Clearly, he thinks Simon will get what happened out of me later, and then he'll get the details. Simon won't tell him shit.

"She's nice, and we had a relaxing weekend. She headed home a couple of days ago."

Rosemary frowns at me. "Why wouldn't she stay? Did you say something to her?"

No, but I did something to her. Wonderful things.

Angelo gives her a frustrated look. "For fuck's sake, Rosemary. You know Greer would never do anything to hurt her. Now drop it."

"Thanks, man. What was with sending her up here before everyone else, anyway? She could have been in an accident."

Rosemary's face drops, and regret flashes across her features. "I didn't know it would snow the way it did. I didn't think. I only saw the opportunity to get you two together." She wrings her hands together, watching me. "Thanks for taking care of her. I know you're a good guy."

Angelo grins at me. "He sure is." He walks past, slapping me on the back a little too hard.

I glare as he continues on, but his eyes are still dancing. *Fuck, they won't let this go.*

Now that my siblings—minus Troy, Han, and Harrison—and my parents are here, I'm hiding in the entertainment room. I have to make an appearance at some point, but right now, I need mental rest.

It's blissful. And I hope it stays that way as Simon clip-clops in. Man, he is never graceful.

"Theo all tucked in?" After a day of incessant chatter and dodging questions, I'm finally ready to relax. I shuffle back into the couch, the exact spot that Kit and I sat on our "date."

Simon sits and throws his feet up on an ottoman. "Yeah, it took him a while to wind down, but he finally crashed." He releases a tremendous sigh, tucking his hand behind his head. "What are we watching?"

I toss him the remote. "I hadn't picked anything yet. You can choose."

He scrolls through the guide channel. "Action?"

"Whatever you want."

He settles on *John Wick*—classic—and I let my mind settle long enough to enjoy the movie.

Simon shifts next to me. "You know at the beginning of the movie when he pulls the plug on Helen?"

Nodding, I glance his way.

He mutes the TV and clears his throat. "I hope no one else ever has to go through that. Even though I didn't love Eden that way, it was still hard watching her life end like that. Especially knowing that Theo will never see his mom again."

"Shit. I'm sorry, Simon. I wish I'd been there for you more."

"Hey, it's okay." He shakes his head and shoots me a small smile. "You helped with Theo. When I needed help, you were there."

"Whiskey?"

He looks up, a sad half grin on his face. "Yeah, that sounds fucking spot on."

Moving to the bar on the opposite side of the room, I pour us both a drink, then settle back into my spot on the couch.

The first sip of whiskey burns straight down to my belly while also smoothing out the ragged edges of my mind.

"She wasn't the person I thought I would end up with. Our time together wasn't easy. And I won't ever say this to anyone else. But she was sick, Greer. Her mental health issues were so deep, and nothing I did pulled her out."

The flash of the screen reflects around the room, and I study Simon. He's peering into his glass, his brows furrowed.

Mental health issues are hard, and I know this firsthand now with Kit. "I don't know much about it, but I've learned a little. Patience is important, and giving them space when they need it."

"With Eden, there wasn't space, you know. Not for me, anyway. She wanted to be with me every moment of the day. *I* needed the space. If I asked for a night to myself, she assumed I was out with someone else."

Fuck, that would be agonizing. "How did you deal with it?"

"Not well, truthfully. It was hard to stay positive."

"You were always joking." I never noticed that he seemed more down.

"Yeah, but despite that, I was down, and we fought all the time. I wanted her to get help, and every time I pressed, her family was there pushing back against me."

"Why?" I swirl my glass, the liquor moving smoothly around and around, catching the flickers from the screen.

"I'm not sure. But there's nothing I can do about it now." He takes another sip. His eyes, identical to mine, glance up toward me. "How did you learn about the patience and space?"

Bringing the glass to my lips, I take a sip, ignoring him for a moment. I don't share much with him, but he gave me a huge piece of himself. It was my fault that we lost what it was like when we were young.

I can still read his mood, and he can read mine, but we lost the talking with a look.

My heart pangs, and I sigh, squeezing my eyes shut for a moment. I want that back. I miss Simon and that closeness we shared.

"Kit. She has some anxiety issues." I clear my throat and look his way.

His brows rise, and he nods, giving me a half smile. "Do you like her?"

Fuck yeah, I do. Nodding, I give him a smile of my own. "Yeah, she's funny and smart. Beautiful."

"Wasn't Angelo trying to get you to meet her?"

If I weren't still pissed at how reckless the two of them were when they sent Kit up here, I might chuckle, but damn it. Those two blockheads could have hurt her.

Simon must sense my sudden mood shift. "Why the frown?"

I almost growl but cut it off at the last second. "They sent her up in a fucking snowstorm, trying to play matchmaker. Anything could have happened to her." My body trembles with the image of her injured or worse.

Fuck.

I shake myself to erase the image from my brain.

"You really like her." Surprise tints Simon's words.

I nod and press my lips together. "I want to know more about her, how she grew up, what she likes. Who the hell her husband was."

"Was? Well, you know her name, right? If she told you his, you could look him up."

"Hmm." Why hadn't I thought of that? I pull my phone out of my pocket and search his name.

"What's his name? I'll look for an obituary while you look up the rest."

"Ethan Piece Of Shit Finney."

"I'll keep out the piece of shit, and if I can't find him, I'll type that in." He chuckles a moment and then whips his phone out.

My google search turns up a shit ton of hits, and I scroll through.

American CEO Missing in Brazil Flash Flood; Reward for Information on Missing American; Missing American Declared Dead after Two Years; New CEO for Finney Financial Firm Named Colette Finney.

I click on the first one and skim the article. It discusses the missing body and the reward offered for information.

"The obituary says the usual: preceded in death by loving father, Walter, left behind mother and wife, no children. Instead of gifts, send a donation to one of the houses for battered women in California. Do you want me to look that charity up?"

For battered women? Piece of shit is apt. "No, I can't see why it would matter. This article says he went missing in Brazil, which she told me, but nothing else that tells me what kind of person he was."

"The kind of person who gives money to charity."

Fuck that shit. A growl rumbles through my chest. "That doesn't make him a good person."

"You're right. He could have been completely black inside."

"He was." Seriously, the urge to kill that fucker is strong.

"Well, then, it's good she has you."

"Why's that?"

"Because you might be all hard and stuffy on the outside, but I think the marshmallow you used to be is still in there."

A smile tugs at my lips. I did used to be pretty gooey on the inside. Maybe he's right.

Twenty-One

Kit

"I'M WALKING IN NOW." I close the door behind me and drop my keys in the bowl, then bend to take off my shoes. There are a few envelopes at my feet, having been shoved through the letterbox, so I scoop them up as I rise.

Setting my bag on the counter, I smile at it, a little thrill buzzing through me.

New scrubs for a new life.

Shopping for myself is usually a chore, but I couldn't pass up the cute little bears, rainbows, or dragons, so I got all three. Can't forget the scrub top with little dachshunds on it. That one will be my favorite.

A crinkling rustles through my earbud, and then Mom's voice echoes through loud and clear. "So? Did you get the job?"

An excited squeak escapes me, and I barely contain the happy dance my feet want to do. "I did. I got the call this morning."

She squeals loud enough to pierce an eardrum. She's such a champion, always in my corner.

A small chuckle escapes me. "I picked out some scrubs today. And since I have nothing but time on my hands, I convinced them to let me start right away."

"What's your schedule going to be like?"

"I'm going to pick up full-time hours for a few months, get comfortable with the clinic. After that, I'll scale back to my two to three days a week."

"I never asked how you got away with working while Ethan..." She trails off, clearing her throat. Does she regret asking?

"I didn't. I wasn't allowed to work. After I finished my degree, I sat on it for years. It was only last year that I took my boards and got a job."

"Wow, that must have been terrifying." She exhales heavily into the phone.

Going out into the workforce after being isolated for so long was nerve-racking. But this feels right. Nursing has woven itself into every fiber of my being. "My therapist helped me with that. She encouraged me to pursue something outside my comfort zone. That was the first thing I picked."

"It was a big thing."

Smiling, I switch the phone to the other ear and drop the envelopes next to the bowl. "It was excruciating. It took months before I felt okay going to work every day."

"We need to celebrate. Would family dinner be okay? Sunday at noon? And you can say no."

"I know I can, Mom." My heart warms at her thoughtfulness. She continually gives me control over situations. "I'll be there. Thanks, Mom."

"Absolutely. I want you to be happy."

And that is the truth. Looking back, I never realized how lucky I was to have my parents. They were always so supportive. My stomach clenches. I missed that so much.

She clears her throat. "What types of things are you decorating your house with? When I stopped by, there wasn't anything on the walls."

"Nothing yet. Still trying to get a feel for what I like." Or who I like.

Would she think I'm crazy for being interested in Greer even though I just met him? I lick my lips, my mouth opening to tell her about him.

"No worries, love. When you find a piece that speaks to you, you'll know."

"Are you sure?" Greer speaks to me. My soul recognizes something profound in his. "Sometimes I wonder if I *should* listen to my gut. Stupid thing told me Ethan was a good guy."

"I know, love, and I don't think there was anything wrong with your gut. I think you were catfished. You were painted a portrait of good Ethan but were given bad Ethan. You can't help that he took advantage of you."

"I think if I had met him when I was a little older, I would have been able to see it better. But he was so charming in the beginning. He made me feel special and beautiful and alive."

Mom shifts, the creaking of cabinets traveling through the phone. "If you had been older, he would have used another tactic. There is nothing you could have done, Kit-Kat. You remained strong; you lived. Now it's your turn to show the world who you are. If you want to." The last part is added hastily like she's worried her pep talk will scare me off.

Not anymore. Maybe she's right. My body will tell me when I need to be on guard. After living that way for so many years, always on edge, always wondering when someone was going to jump out of the shadows, living in the light is liberating.

I grab the scissors in my junk drawer and snip the tags off my scrubs. "I'm learning to be myself, and loving who I'm becoming, finding the woman I lost."

"Can I ask you a question about Ethan?"

A pit forms in my gut, hard and fast. "Yes. I can't promise I'll answer."

"Why did you think he could hurt us?"

I shift, fighting the urge to change the subject. "Ethan showed me pictures of you guys out and about, doing stuff. He showed me how easy it would be to get to you."

"But that didn't mean he would hurt us, love."

"I've felt his anger, his abuse. I knew what he was capable of. He had guns and a security detail that would monitor the house. It took two years to get Colette to drop the security after he disappeared. I know she still had someone watching the house, but it was easier to breathe without the constant oversight."

"Why would you need a security detail?"

"Ethan was the CEO of a financial company. He said that if clients lost large amounts of money, we'd be targets for their anger. Colette agreed.

Ethan said it was through the security guards or clients that he'd find people willing to make you disappear."

My mom is silent for a while. "Hm. That seems..."

"Impossible, I know. But you didn't see these people, Mom. It was enough to make me believe what Ethan said. He knew the dark souls of California, and if I didn't listen..." I shake my head. "I couldn't risk it."

"Oh, love. I'm sorry."

"But it's over now. I don't have to worry about that anymore." My gut twinges. It's been three years since he disappeared, but I can't help but expect him to show up on my doorstep at some point.

My pulse races, and my palms grow sweaty.

Focus, Kit. He isn't here. I'm safe.

Let your body relax, unclench, and unwind. Miraculously, I do.

"But I think I'll be able to move on. Being home has been the best thing for me, and Rosemary has been helping me."

"Oh, how? She didn't say anything about helping you."

"That's because I asked her not to say anything. She's set me up on a few dates, but they didn't mean anything." Do I tell her I have a date coming up? "But I-I have a proper date next Friday."

There's silence on the other end of the line, and I worry she's upset, but her voice is bubbly when she responds. "That is lovely. Is he a nice guy?"

"Incredibly nice. I've met him a few times, and..." A sigh escapes me. He's seen me at my worst. "He is very patient, and he's going to take things slow with me."

"Oh, Kit. Love. I'm so glad."

"Me too, Mom." The smile on my face physically hurts because it's so wide. He did this. He makes a happy future seem possible. "Well, I'm going to get these scrubs in the wash so they are ready for tomorrow. I'll call you later this week and tell you how my first day went."

"I'd love that. Love you." She makes a kiss sound through the phone.

I chuckle. "Love you too, Mom."

We hang up, and my fingers hover over my contacts. I want to call Greer, hear his voice.

Hurrying, I put my new scrubs into the wash and scarf down a sandwich.

I settle on the couch and pull up my contacts, find Greer's name, and click call.

"Hello, beautiful."

Greer

"UNO." Angelo shouts, beating Violet's stealthy, secret version.

"Shoot." Violet pouts but picks up the necessary cards.

With six cards spread out in my hand, I survey my opponents, then glance at my watch. Another thirty minutes, and then I can call Kit. This is the fourth round of the game, and they can play until midnight, but I've already invested more time than I usually do, trying to keep my mind occupied.

Thank fuck it's not one of the *championships* we do around Christmas.

My phone buzzes in my pocket, and my heart skyrockets. It can only be her.

I pull my phone out and catch the flash of her name on the screen. In less than a second, I click the answer button with a giant grin.

"Hello, beautiful. Give me one second."

"Hi. Okay." The smile in her voice makes my insides do that buzzy thing. She's happy. I could fucking fly right now.

Not glancing at my family, I turn my cards over and stand.

"Hey! You can't forfeit." Someone yells.

"No fucking way, not in the middle of a match." Simon chuckles. "Unless she's worth it, then I'll give you a pass."

I turn back to the group. They're all watching me, their eyes expectant, waiting for me to snap like I usually do.

Instead of losing it, I smile. "She's totally worth it. I'd give up UNO any day of the week for this."

Angelo laughs. "Does she make you all giggly and twitterpated?" He shows me his best Bambi face and then jerks in his seat, reaching under the table.

Rosemary gives him a death glare.

"Ow. You didn't have to kick me." He winks at Rosemary, then turns back to me. "No, seriously, do you like her?"

"Oh my god, shut up. Let them get to know each other." Rosemary elbows him.

Simon looks my way, a half smile on his face. My parents are looking at me like I've grown horns.

I shrug. "I like her enough to teach her our version of UNO one day." I turn back around and head out of the entertainment room. Their hoots and hollers and "What the fuck just happened?" follow me out the door.

I smile to myself. "Hey, again."

"Hi, again." She exhales softly. "How was your day?"

"Good, I had to haul more wood in today. There was no one to ogle me, though, so it was disappointing." I glance around the kitchen, not putting it past any of those fools to come out and listen, but I'm not upset about it. They can listen. I won't hide Kit away.

Her laugh flows through me like a jolt of electricity. That is something I want to hear all the time. "I didn't ogle you. I just had to watch to make sure you didn't drop any pieces."

"Is that what they call it these days? Watching out for my welfare?" I bite my lip, smiling at no one and letting the banter settle deep into me.

"Somebody has to do it."

"Are you applying for the position?"

"I think I already have an interview. Friday, if I'm not mistaken." She laughs again.

"Your preliminary interviews were stellar, so you're a shoo-in for the position. How does a movie night sound?"

Silence stretches on the line, but when she finally speaks again, it's with confidence. "Yeah, I'd be okay with that."

"I can promise there won't be any suspense or thriller movies that night. Unless there is a Michael Jackson 'Thriller' replay at the old theater."

"That is the best Halloween song. That and 'What's This?' from *Nightmare before Christmas*."

"Halloween is the best holiday. So yeah, it could be the best song of all time."

"Are you kidding? Christmas is the best holiday. The lights, the festiveness, the snow."

"You're kidding, right? Even after driving up in the snowstorm, you still praise that white shit?"

"You don't like snow?"

"Absolutely not. If I could live without snow, I would."

"You would miss it. I promise, if you lived without it for ten years, you'd swear you see snowmen everywhere. I once saw a snowman walking down the street. Turns out it was a grandma wearing white. She was so perfectly round in three places, but she was magnificent."

Fuck, she's so stinking cute. Laughter flows freely from me as footsteps echo down the hall. My mom walks into the kitchen and snags an armful of water bottles and a few bags of snacks. She smiles at me with a weepy but happy expression.

I smile back as Kit chatters in my ear.

I'm getting an inkling of how distant I've been over the last few years. Maybe Kit is changing it. The need to keep things locked inside is fading.

My thoughts used to be filled with work, planning, making, fixing, and promoting. Doing everything I could to make the business flourish. It was compulsory, but it closed me off from everyone around me.

Work hasn't crossed my mind since she left, and I haven't been this refreshed in ages.

Mom turns to me, her voice hushed as she points to the phone. "Is she a nice girl?"

I cover the mouthpiece and wink. "She really is."

Mom bites her lips, holding her smile in. She nods a few times, then pulls me down to kiss the side of my head. "I'm glad." She leaves, beaming brighter than headlights. Then I focus on Kit again.

Her husky voice is like a serenade in my ear. "What did you do tonight?"

"We played Ultimate UNO."

"I know how to play UNO. I heard you say you had to teach me, but I know how to play that game." She chuckles.

"You've never played it like this. The only way to teach it is to play it."

"Is that a nice way of saying I'm too stupid to play it?" Her voice is teasing, so she's not offended.

"Not stupid, just simple." Her laughter reverberates through my ears, and I smile. "I like simple, though. You are simply beautiful and simply unique."

And hopefully, one day, simply mine.

December

Twenty-Two

Kit

THE METAL LOCKER IS cold against my fingers as I push it shut. I made it through the week.

A smile bubbles up from my effervescent depths, and I grab my phone. I click on Rosemary's name and dial it as I clock out.

"Hey! How was training?"

More importantly, where did the week go? Between Mom's dinner, the new job, and phone calls with Greer, it flew by.

"Busy. I got to do vitals on kids today, which is the best. That and the squishy thighs on babies. I'm getting to know some of the doctors here. Everyone has been so nice."

"Any favorites yet?"

"Favorite what?"

"People, doctors, friends?"

Laughter escapes me. I push my bag over my shoulder and palm my car keys. "Not yet. Everyone is nice, though."

"Are you excited about tonight?" Rosemary laugh-asks through the phone.

"Why?" The work door bangs behind me as I exit the clinic.

"Greer left today. He was all smiles. You're seeing him tonight, aren't you?"

I grin, reaching into my purse to dig for my keys. "I have no idea what you are talking about."

She snorts. "You talk for hours every night. Are you trying to tell me nothing happened between you two when you were here?"

"There is nothing to tell, Rosemary."

"I know that's not true, Kit. Greer is smiling more than he has since I met him, and Angelo even caught him singing to himself."

I roll my lips, biting back a grin. "That's interesting. What is he singing?"

"I don't know. Some dark lullaby about death and lovers."

"Morbid. Sounds like he's depressed." I can't stop the grin. He is proving to be more and more fascinating. If he isn't cracking me up on our late-into-the-night phone calls, he's making me think.

Warmth spreads through my body from how he touched me and the deep resonance of his voice. The way he laughs at my stupid jokes liquefies my heart, molten lava pouring through my veins.

I pull open the door to my SUV as Rosemary continues to chat. Clinic staff are exiting the building in varying degrees of loudness. Some groups are talking, some are alone.

Laughter echoes through the car lot, and my blood freezes. My heart pounds in my ears. Goose bumps pebble along my skin.

That laugh.

It's maniacal, frantic, absolutely crazy. Eerily familiar.

I whirl around, scanning my surroundings.

My skin prickles, and sweat forms at the small of my back while I search every face. A group of people make their way through the lot; some I know, most I don't.

Another laugh, the same agonizing cackle.

I zero in on one of the doctors I haven't met. I've seen him in passing. His dark head is thrown back, and a woman stands in front of him, her hand on his arm. He isn't Ethan. He's not waiting for me to make a mistake so he can hurt me.

He's not here. I'm safe.

I force my heart to slow, but the ice continues to flow through my veins, my skin tingling.

It was nothing. Only the doctor.

The fluorescent lights flicker in the parking lot, and I can make out most of the cars and people, but something nags at me. Nothing looks out of place, and everyone is setting out to get home, so I force my body to relax.

Not a goddamn thing seems out of place.

For Pete's sake, it was one of the doctors. Ethan is dead. And even if he's not, he has had nothing to do with me in over three years. He has Francesca and a daughter he's never met but always wanted. I wouldn't be his priority, and Colette would call me if he were alive.

I pull my phone away from my ear and check it. No missed calls or texts.

Breathe, Kit.

I put the phone back to my ear.

"Kit? Where'd you go?"

"I'm here." I make one last sweep of the lot, searching for the cause of the spine-prickling sensation, then slide into my car. I place the phone in its holder on the dash and start the engine.

"I was saying if Billy gets handsy one more time, I'm sending him to the office."

I chuckle as I put the car into drive. "You should have slapped his hands on day one."

"You can't do that anymore, Kit. It's considered abuse."

"The next time he pinches your booty, fart on him."

On the thirty-minute drive home, I keep up a conversation with my sister. Her voice is at the max as she talks about her school year so far and getting to work with Mom on projects.

I pull into my garage and we say goodbye. In the house, I rush up the stairs to shower. I have about an hour to clean myself up before that hot, sinful god is at my door.

I shave everything and put on soft lounging clothes. This camisole, cardigan, and super soft cotton pants are my go-to. I hope Greer isn't looking for someone primped to the nines, because I'm not that type of girl.

Once I'm dressed, I head downstairs and into the kitchen to see what I have to drink. As I reach for the cupboard, I freeze and glance back at the door. *Something is missing.*

I turn fully toward it, my hand on the cupboard. What am I not seeing? Shit.

Keys? In the bowl. Badge? Next to the keys.

What am I—

Ding-dong.

I jump. Greer. The tension leaves me, and I practically skip to the door.

Pausing before it, I sweep my hands down my shirt, smoothing out any wrinkles, and then open the door. "Hel–Oh. Hi. Can I help you?"

The man at the door is almost as tall as Greer and is wearing a stocking hat so low it covers his brows. All I can see are his brown eyes and a part of his nose. He's bundled up tighter than a burrito. I pull the edges of my cardigan closer together at my chest, ignoring the icy cascade running up my spine from his presence and the cold wind.

"Hi, sorry to bother you." His voice is deep with a lyrical twang, slow and soft and pleasing on the ears. "I ran out of gas in front of your house. I don't have a phone. Can I come in and use yours?"

"Um...let me grab my cell. I'll be right back."

He moves to take a step inside.

No way, guy.

I put a hand up to hold him off. "Please wait there. I'll be back in a moment." I pause to make sure he stays. A set of lights pulls into the drive, and my heart jumps, beating frantically as I prepare to slam the door shut and lock it. The lights turn off, and recognition flares.

Greer. My muscles weaken, and my hands drop to my sides.

"Actually, my boyfriend is coming in. Maybe he can help you."

Greer walks up the path, another set of peonies in hand. Skirting around the stranger, he stands next to me.

"Kit?" Greer smiles, then nods his head toward the stranger.

I move closer to Greer, wrapping an arm around his waist. Warmth bubbles in my belly when he mirrors my affection. "This gentleman said he ran out of gas and is asking to use my phone."

"Greer Winters." He holds his hand out, waiting in silence as the man shifts his attention from Greer to me, slightly squinting.

Maybe it's a scowl, but it's hard to say with him bundled up that way.

Finally, the stranger sets his hand out, and they shake briefly. "John Wilson."

Greer hands the man his phone. "You can use mine."

My stomach is in knots the whole thirty minutes it takes for someone to come rescue John. Thankfully, he didn't push when Greer insisted they wait outside together.

With my flowers in a vase and popcorn popping in the microwave, I lean over the kitchen sink and peek outside at the car that pulls up next to John's. The guy gets out and pulls a gas can out of his trunk. The two work on filling John's car while Greer stands outside and does something on his phone.

When they're done, John shakes Greer's hand and gets in his car.

The microwave beeps, and I pull the scalding bag out by the corner. "Shit." I hot potato it until I have it on the counter.

Mmm. The popcorn's buttery scent fills the air as Greer shuts the door. I pour it into a bowl, then turn to face him.

He looks so good. He shrugs off his suede jacket and pivots to hang it by the door. His black sweater fits his body like a glove. His jeans mold to his delicious behind, faded where his pocket holds his wallet. I smile as his gaze moves to mine. Every piece of me is primed, ready and waiting for him to touch me.

He moves gracefully through my home toward me.

I want to rush him, throw myself in his arms, and inhale every piece of him—absorb all of him into my body. Instead, I bite my lip as his face turns to a smolder while he prowls toward me.

"Keep looking at me like that, and we won't be taking it slow. You'll be taking it hard and fast."

Oh yes, our conversations over the phone have bypassed casual innu-endoes.

I shiver at the growl in his voice. Biting my lip hard, I try to remove the smile from my face.

His eyes burn as he reaches me.

"You still look like you want to eat me."

He wraps his arms around me, hugging me close and warming me up. "Will we still be taking it slow if I kiss you?"

"Yes, absolutely, yes." His lips slam over mine. He sucks in my breath, stealing it while giving me his tongue. It moves against mine, stroking, teasing. Mesmerizing.

Shivers rack my body, pouring through me as he slows his movements and pulls back, rubbing his lips over mine.

Whoa.

That is what kisses should feel like. Mastered.

He runs his nose along my jawline, his hum magic in my ear. I shift, my core becoming achingly wet. "That's the way to greet your boyfriend. So...boyfriend?"

My cheeks hot now, I hold back hiding them behind my hands. "It made me feel safer."

"Let's keep it, girlfriend."

This is the precipice where I either lean into the relationship and fully trust that he won't rip my heart out and steal my soul. Or I run.

I search his eyes. They are beautiful and warm and strong.

And despite feeling like I could drown in them, there is safety in the depths.

I lead him over to the couch. Handing him the remote, I settle in beside him, his big body firm and familiar.

"So what are we doing tonight?" He laces his fingers with mine and kisses my knuckles.

"Eating, movie, snuggles, making out."

"And nothing else?"

My toes curl at the desire in his gaze.

Breathless, it slips out husky. "And nothing else." I want to know we have a foundation other than lust.

Pulling me close against him, he rests his chin on my head and whispers, "I'll take it. What do we have to eat?"

"Pizza should arrive soon."

"What flavor?"

"Pepperoni with banana peppers on one half."

"What the hell is a banana pepper?"

"Are you serious?" I pull back, searching his face. He has one brow cocked. "A pickled pepper, and you are in for a delight."

"I'm in for heartburn."

I turn back to the television. The doorbell rings, and we both jump.

"I'll grab it." He hops up, smiling at me before heading to the door. His voice carries back to the room, and soon the pizza delivery guy is gone. I grab some plates while he sets the pizza on my coffee table. "Can we eat here?"

With a smile, I hand him a plate, grab my piece, and sit. "What do you want to watch?"

"You up for something different?" His smile is contagious as he plops a piece of pepperoni pizza onto his plate.

"What did you have in mind?" I point to a piece with banana peppers. "You have to try one."

"*Monty Python*. Are you going to give me CPR if I choke?"

"If you choke, I'm giving you the Heimlich. Back to *Monty Python*. I've never watched those. Most of the people I know say they are boring." I give him a goofy smile while I wait for him to take a bite.

He turns to me, his eyes incredulous, his pepperoni-banana pepper slice poised in front of his lips as his mouth drops. "Their movies will stand the test of time. Those people are narrow-minded fools. *Monty Python* is the epitome of perfect British sketch comedy."

"As long as the test of time doesn't put me to sleep."

"If you fall asleep, we have to break up."

My heart pangs for a moment, my pulse flaring, and then he winks at me. The beating returns to normal, and a smile settles on my face.

He smiles, dazzling as he watches me take his joke. "We can stream it."

"Do you want to get it ready?"

While I cool down, he sets it up, and before I know it, we are both laughing while finishing our pizza. The movie is funny and keeps me entertained for a while. Eventually, the pull of sleep is more than the sweet chuckles coming from my date.

I blink, fighting to keep them open.

I can close them for a minute, rest one minute...

"Where's your bed?"

He rubs my arm, and I point upstairs. Then I'm weightless as he carries me up the stairs. I snuggle against his chest, inhaling his woodsy, smokey scent. His chest rumbles under my cheek as he whispers, "Thank you for this evening, Kit."

I'm lying in bed with the blankets up around me. "Greer?"

"Yes, love?"

My heart stutters. *He called me love.* I struggle to get out of the depths of sleep, blinking against the grittiness in my eyes, but I can't keep them open, and I'm in too deep.

"Stay. Sleep with me." I roll to my side, tucking my legs up. "The night-mares stay away when I'm with you."

Twenty-Three

Kit

I'VE BEEN ON PINS and needles all week while waiting for this date. We're actually going out tonight. I primped myself to within an inch of my life because tonight is going to be special. I've been anxiously waiting to have sex with Greer and I want him with every fiber of my being.

Not that we aren't spending almost every night together. Many nights Greer comes over late because he's worked on something into the wee hours. But I almost always wake up next to him. And nothing has felt better.

Ding-dong.

When I open the door, Greer's face drops, and my heart pounds. I'm smoking in this dress; I made sure of it. Loose waves fall gently over my shoulders, and my makeup is subtle.

Rosemary helped me pick the dress out—a tight black boat-neck sheath dress with an open back and long sleeves. It ends at my knees, and I'm wearing a pair of aubergine suede pumps.

He gives me a full-body scan, starting at my feet and traveling slowly up, burning a delicious trail over my body. His eyes blaze when they finally meet mine, and he lets out a long exhale.

That's more like it.

He is so outlandishly tall that I have to look up at him, even with heels on. His unruly hair hits his shoulders, framing his trimmed beard. He's dressed in black slacks that hug his thick thighs, a cream shirt, and a wine-colored sports jacket. Even his shoes are stylish.

I hope he's on the menu because I want to start the first course now, or maybe just skip to dessert.

He leans in, and my body stills as his lips lightly touch mine. That's it. That's all he gives me. Like he knows it will leave me wanting the rest of the night. It will.

If he'd given me any more than that, we wouldn't make it to the end of the date.

He grabs my hand. "You look so beautiful, Kit." He holds my arms out so he can look at me again, smiling as he shakes his head. "Now let's go. I've got a full night planned." He pulls me gently forward, drawing me to a white sedan with blackout windows. It is sleek but not overly expensive, sporty without being flashy—like Greer.

Like a true gentleman, he opens the door, then when I'm settled, reaches across my body and grabs my seat belt. I still, my heart hammering in my chest as his hand casually brushes along my breasts. Very faintly, the latch clicks.

Deep, gravelly, and skirting every inch of my body, his voice makes me shiver. "Safety first, Kit."

Then he's hopping in on his side.

"So where are we headed?"

He gets to the main road before his hand settles on my thigh. He smells good, his usual woodsy scent gone, replaced with something fresh and clean, like he showered in Irish spring wood shavings.

"It's a surprise." He peeks at me, trying to watch the road at the same time. He casually brushes along my leg, his pinky inching up my thigh.

Arousal pools in my core, spiking it with a heavy dose of lust, making me drunk with desire. I squirm as minutely as I can, hoping to relieve some of the ache forming there. "I'm nervous."

"I'm easy. Get a few drinks in me, and my pants come off pretty quick."

A chuckle erupts from me before I can cut it off. "Is that what you tell all your dates?"

"Hell no. They'd go running. But I've already tasted you and had my fingers inside you. I know you want more."

OF LILIES AND LIES

His mouth, seriously. "That's what I mean. You've done"—I gesture wildly—"all of that. I'm still getting to know you."

"Well, like I said, I'm easy. So ask away."

I stare out the window as he parks in the lot of an expensive-looking restaurant. "Le Délice. I've never heard of it."

"It's only been around for about a year. I think you'll like it."

He slides his hand along mine and laces our fingers together. I suppress a shiver, my knees weakening for a brief moment. With his long legs, he walks swiftly, and I shuffle, almost running to keep up.

Like he can't take his eyes off me, he looks back. His brow rises a moment before lowering under his wolfish grin. He devours me as he slows his pace. He is so good at that, catching me before I'm going to fall, adjusting himself to fit me so I don't get out of breath running.

And then we are at the doors.

Oh for the love of blessed Pete.

We step through the doors into the most extravagant place in Stirling Harbor. The walls are gray brick, painted in a warm glow from the black-trimmed sconces on the wall. The chandeliers look like glowing candles with a black accent. The tablecloths are pristine, with a candle at each table and glasses set.

It's incredibly romantic.

Greer lays his hand on my lower back as we follow the server to our table. That small touch sends desire to pool at the apex of my thighs.

My body is primed, and we haven't even had dinner. I wanted to take things slow, but we've already passed third base, and now I'm sprinting down the home stretch.

The menu is in French, and I stare at it wide-eyed. "Can you read French?" His menu rests on the table, his hands over it while someone takes our drink orders, leaving as quietly as they came.

I lean forward when he does. His voice is soft and deep. "To be honest, I usually tell them I want a steak, and they bring me something delicious." One side of his mouth creeps up in a sexy-as-sin half smile.

Appetizer, maybe?

The server appears out of nowhere, handing me a white wine and Greer a cognac. We listen to the specials, and then Greer orders his steak.

"And for you, Miss?"

"I'd like a traditional French meal. Surprise me."

"If you are sure?" Clearly surprised, he watches me closely.

I nod, trusting him to bring me something delicious.

"What if he brings you a raw fish head with brussels sprouts?"

"I like raw fish and brussels sprouts." Maybe, but I miraculously keep my face straight.

His face contorts as he curls his lip on one side and scrunches his nose.

My laughter erupts. "I'm kidding. I don't think I can eat a raw fish head, and I'm allergic to brussels sprouts."

"Truly?" He taps his glass with his thumb.

"Yup. Any time I eat them, I gag uncontrollably." I peek at him from under my lashes, biting my cheek.

"That's not an allergy." His dimples pop, his white teeth gleaming in the candle glow.

I grin. "Are you allergic to anything?"

"Women who make my emotions riot."

"That's not an allergy. That's an aversion."

"It should be an allergy. The thought of it makes me itch all over." He playfully scratches his chest.

I sip my wine, the cool white slipping past my tongue. "So you are saying that I make you emotional?" He always seems so in control.

As he talks, I'm mesmerized by his mouth. "Something like that. I've had a lot more to think about."

What does he mean by that? I open my mouth to ask, but his steak glides in front of him, and he beholds it like it's his last meal. I swallow when my plate is set gently in front of me. Minced meat with a red sauce, a raw egg, and greens.

"*Tartare de boeuf* for the lady."

Greer's laughter erupts.

"What?" I stare at him and pick up my fork. It wavers in the air, and his laughter continues. I don't know if I can eat this, but I'm going to try.

"Take a bite first. Tell me if you like it, then I'll tell you what it is."

"So you do speak French?"

He raises a brow, pointedly looking at my meal.

"You know"—I slice off a sliver of meat and dip it in the red sauce—"I don't want you to tell me. It will ruin it."

My stomach does a flip-flop as I bring the fork up. I stare at it a moment before placing a bite in my mouth.

My face drops.

The texture is buttery smooth, but the taste is off. I force my jaw to move, trying to swallow as I smile at Greer. Mirth dances in his amber gaze as he watches me.

The bite of food isn't going down. *Wine. I need to wash it down.* I take a sip out of my glass.

Ooh! That is not better. Nope. That is worse. So much worse. I try to prevent the gag from coming up. *Swallow. Swallow. Swallow.*

The wine slips down, but that is it. *Ugh.*

I gingerly bring my napkin up to my mouth. Wiping my lips, I push the hunk of meat into my palm and napkin. Greer is no longer smiling. Instead, his laughter is loud as he watches me lay my napkin down.

Damn, I wasn't sneaky enough.

"Okay, you can't ruin it now. What the hell is this?" I gesture with my fork to the pile of meat and greens.

"Did you find some brussels sprouts?" He is tearing up now as he shoves his hand through his hair.

"Seriously, what is it?"

"It's steak tartare—raw meat. It's a French delicacy, and most people love the flavor."

"It must be rotten meat, then. Maybe it has an STD from going raw all the time."

"Likely. Let's give it a sheep's skin. Or an antibiotic."

"For Pete's sake." My chuckle fills the air as he takes my plate and puts his in front of me. "Really?"

"Yeah, of course. I mean, I love steak, but I also adore it raw."

The mouth on this man. And I like it because it's making me a smidge breathless and more than aroused. I hold back a smile before taking a bite. Oh, the steak is good. He finally puts a forkful of the tartare in his mouth, and I can't stop staring at him.

His face suddenly changes, and he stops chewing while his eyes glaze over.

"Good?"

His swallow is audible. "So good." He watches it like it is going to leap out and attack him.

It's my turn to fight a smile. "Do you want your steak back?"

He shakes his head as he stabs another piece of meat. Fortifying himself, he shoves the fork into his mouth before scooping another helping. He's like a Hoover now, shoveling in each bite, barely chewing before he swallows.

Sweat forms on his forehead, and his eyes turn glassy, but he makes it through the beef before the server brings a crème brûlée with two spoons.

"Is that how it's supposed to taste?" I ask.

"I don't know."

"Then why'd you eat it?"

"I wanted you to have a good meal, and I'm hungry." He shrugs.

This man. He's like a big roasted marshmallow. Like crème brûlée—all charred and crusty on the outside and sweet inside once you crack into him.

"What is next?" I stare at him, licking my spoon.

His eyes follow the trail of my tongue on the metal. "Dancing. But we have to brave the cold to get there."

I hold myself back from jumping out of my seat. I drop the spoon. "Really? What are we waiting for? Let's go."

He laughs as the server brings the bill over, and I reach for it.

He grunts. "Don't offer to pay. I'll be offended."

I swipe my hand back from the table. "Okay, I won't. How 'bout I cover the tip?"

"I've got that covered too. Your job tonight is to have fun."

"Okay."

He beams as I lead him out of the restaurant. He squeezes my hand, linking our fingers. "Hope you don't mind that we have to walk a little to get there. They have dancing in the park in the evenings. Don't worry, though, you won't get cold. They always have it closed in and heated."

As we get close to the park, the music can be heard over the street noise. Slow strings pour through the night, and the sultry tunes of Etta James echo against the buildings. "Ooh, this is my song. Hurry!"

We rush around the corner, my hand still in Greer's, his long strides eating up the pavement while I run behind him. We stop inside the closed off gazebo, and I gasp at the dance floor and the willowy woman singing on stage, a jazz band behind her.

"Oh my goodness."

Strings of light cast a warm glow on the couples on the floor. I sigh, a sweet pang filling my chest. The woman is singing "I'd Rather Be Blind."

Greer pulls me forward onto the floor. "This is kind of a sad song, Kit."

"I know. But it's the best one." His hand slides along my back, touching the bare skin there, the rough pads of his palm shooting shivers up my spine. He pulls my hand up, linking our fingers.

Chest to breast, hip to hip, we sway. My head hits below his chin, thanks to the heels.

Tonight, I'm so freaking high, nothing can bring me down. He brushes a thumb against my spine, sending goose bumps over my skin.

I've never danced this way, without the weight of the world on my shoulders, with the gentle rush of wind through my hair as he twirls me.

This must be what coming home feels like.

He lays my hand over his heart, setting his on top and tapping with one finger to the rhythm.

I don't want to break the silence, but I can't stop myself. "You know this song?"

"I adore Ms. James. We'll have to listen to her music on vinyl at my place. So do you approve?"

"I so approve."

His thumb is doing that thing again, brushing slowly, and my heart flutters, my body rejoicing as I lay my head on his shoulder.

His heartbeat reverberates through his body and into mine, flitting down to my core, more potent than anything I've experienced. His voice vibrates through his chest as he sings. It is sultry and slow, deep and romantic. I move my hand, curling it against the nape of his neck and threading it through his hair.

I lose track of the number of songs we dance to. He sings most of them to me while his hands move sensually over my back, building me up in a way I'm learning I need.

"Greer."

"Hmm, Red?" He leans back to look down at me.

"I'm ready to go back to my place."

His eyes turn, the darkness of his pupils taking over. His voice is an octave lower, settling deep inside me. "Then let's go."

We stand on my doorstep as I enter my key code to unlock the door. "Fancy."

"Someone told me it is safer than a lock and key."

"Only if you don't give away the code."

Stepping inside, I hold the door open, inviting him in. "Well, good thing I've only given it to you."

I need to lick his skin and feel his hands on me soon.

My heart is pounding at his proximity. All I want is to have him above me, on me, inside me. "Do you want a glass of red?" I slip off my heels, sighing as the ache in my arches eases.

Greer unties his shoes before kicking them off, then slips off his jacket. He hangs it on the hook, then rolls up his sleeves. *Mmm-hm, arm porn.*

"Sounds great."

With my focus on him, I slip into the kitchen, aching deep inside. "I'll grab us glasses. Make yourself comfortable in the living room." Head turned to the cupboard, I pull out two glasses. When I turn to grab the wine, I bump into a rigid body. "Oof."

With my hand on his chest, I catch myself. His eyes are alight, fiery in the dim room, and I'm instantly breathless. "Or we can make ourselves comfortable in the kitchen."

He nods as his warm hands settle on my waist. Then he lifts me effortlessly and places me on the counter.

All the air is gone. My chest constricted.

He brushes my hair back from my face and tilts my head so I'm looking at him.

"This is cozy." His deep voice vibrates all the way to my soul. "I like cozy."

My lashes flutter before I exhale softly. Then he's there, his buttery lips against mine, drawing mine open so he can slip inside. I stroke my tongue against his, rejoicing in the groan erupting from his mouth. His skin is smooth under my palms, and I need more. Grabbing my skirt, I hike it up around my hips so I can cradle him.

I suck on his tongue, nipping it gently when he steps closer. He grows stiff against me. Hands on my hips, his fingers clench, his cock straining against me as I shift.

I break away for a moment and stare breathlessly at his bee-stung lips. "I've been waiting all week for this."

"Do you want me to go slow and savor it, or do you want me to fuck you?" He pulls me tight against his groin and thrusts.

Delicious friction erupts against my clit, the soft cotton panties providing almost no barrier. His fingers dig into my hips rhythmically as I rock against him.

I tremble, a broken moan escaping from my lips. "Fu-uck." I drop my head back, I meant soft and slow. But having said it? Now it's all I want.

His soft chuckle fills my ears.

That is becoming one of my favorite sounds. That, and when I scratch his beard or neck and he moans in ecstasy. I peek at him from under my lashes. The tiny crinkles at the corners of his eyes fill me with a buzz that wants to bubble to the surface. I want to make them permanent residents on his handsome face.

I move my head to his neck and inhale, missing that smokey cedar smell. At least I can taste him. His stubble rubs against my tongue on my way up his neck. *Mmm.*

He stiffens, then hefts me into his arms and wraps my legs around him. "Fucked it is, Red."

I point upstairs, my arousal already pooling between my thighs, coating my panties. I'm ready and need his mouth on the rest of my body.

Squirming against him, I whimper with each contact of his shaft against my core as he moves. His tongue rubs against mine silkily. Rhythmically.

Shit, he's everywhere.

One hand lands on my neck; the other holds me so close there's no room for air between us. When he stops at my bed, I drop one leg to the ground, but he holds the other up around his hip.

I'm drowning in the onslaught of desire. My pussy is so freaking wet, my heart is racing, and my soul is flying. It's been three years since I've felt someone this way, and he keeps moving us forward, helping me lose myself so I don't overthink it.

He grinds his hips against me, bringing me closer and closer to orgasm. I push back, fighting for the friction that will make me explode.

"Not yet." He shifts back, dropping my leg. His hand ghosts down my neck to settle on the shoulder of my dress. The cool air hits me as he pulls it down, then the other follows. Dark hair floods my vision as he leans down, kissing my collarbone.

I shiver, standing there, a ball lodged in my chest as he exposes my breasts. Fingertips drag down my skin, pulling the dress past my simple black panties. I step out, one hand on his muscular shoulder.

He is the opposite of me. Hard where I'm soft, rational when I'm not.

And he's moving too damn slow.

I grab his shirt, ripping at the buttons at his collar. He attacks those at the bottom. We meet halfway, and then his shirt is lost somewhere behind him. As he shoves down his pants, I can't do anything but watch.

His cock—thick and irresistible—bobs when he slides his boxer briefs down his hips, and my mouth waters; my core aches. He watches me, intense, that wolfish grin still in place.

My pussy clenches so hard I almost come from that alone. He nudges my chest, forcing me back against the edge of the bed, and I stumble onto the mattress.

"Ooh."

He prowls closer, stalking me. Pulling me to the edge of the bed, he glides his palms up my thighs. His head disappears, and then he's licking against the cotton, that tongue making me dizzy.

It's encompassing, shattering every piece of me with the intensity of our feelings. It's been years since I've felt this good, this cherished, this free. And I need more.

He dips his fingers into the band of my panties, pulling them down past my knees. Then he's on me. His tongue slides through my slick lips, and I arch into him.

"So wet, Red. So luscious. You know how fucking beautiful you are, right?"

His tongue brands my skin, taking everything I have to give as I gasp, moan, and arch beneath him. He slides up to my clit and blows on it as he thrusts his fingers inside.

His mouth is so damn intense. I'm going to come so damn hard.

He nibbles as he pumps three fingers inside, pulling my body taut and so blissfully, achingly clenched that I almost come from that alone.

The pressure centers there, pushing out against the walls where his fingers work to bring me higher.

He thrusts them hard. So hard that I move against the bed, and my headboard hits the wall. Then he nibbles on my clit and growls.

"Oh, yes. Yes. Yes." I shoot up, doubling over as my body tightens, and I spasm around his fingers.

"Yes, baby. That's it, Red. Come all over me. Let me feel it." His fingers continue to move, riding me hard while I come down. I tremble, arching against his face.

With our gaze locked, he removes his fingers and licks them, then dips them back into my pussy for another swipe before bringing them to my mouth.

I part my lips, allowing my essence to coat my tongue before sucking his digits deep into my mouth. I taste tangy, slightly sweet, and musky.

"You are so fucking magnificent when you come, Red."

"More, Greer." I reach for his cock, sliding my hand over his rigid length. "I want more." I lick his bottom lip, then bite and tug on it gently.

"I'm big, Kit. We'll start slow, but once you're ready, I'm not stopping. I'm going to fuck you hard." He nudges against my entrance, smearing himself against me, teasing me.

"Start it already." I need more.

He bites my lip, and my core spasms.

I lean up on my elbows when he pops up from the foot of the bed. His hair flies as he rips open a foil packet with his teeth. He rolls the condom over his hard length, and then he's on me.

He threads his fingers through my hair and guides the head of his cock to my entrance, and then he's pushing, intensely stretching me in all the right ways.

Holy shit, holy shit.

I squirm at the intrusion. He grabs my hips, holding me in place, and gently slides in another inch, fitting us together slowly.

I suck in a breath, biting my lip and grabbing his shoulders. Shifting my hips, I try to adjust to his size. "Big, Greer. Really big."

I brace myself for another push.

He nips my lip and moves his hips from side to side, then around, stretching me. "I'm not all the way in yet, Red. Can you take more?"

"Mm-hmm." I bite my lips harder to keep from crying out.

"Open for me, baby. Relax and let me in." He pulses his hips against me.

It's so much, so full and tight and I try to loosen up to let him in. I look up into his molten, blown-out eyes.

"One day, we're going to watch your pussy eat my cock. Every inch, nice and slow, until you come all over it. Right now, though, I'm going to fuck you."

Yes, it's what I want. To be consumed by the electricity that engulfs us. Fierce. He can love me tenderly another time. Lost in his gaze, I wrap my legs around him and let myself relax.

"Holy fuck, you are tight, woman." A guttural moan vibrates through his chest as he slides all the way in.

Circling his hips, he gives me time to adjust. Thank god, because I'm filled to capacity.

And as the sting disappears, he pulls out.

I whimper at the tug, my every nerve ending alive as he drags along my slick walls. *It's exquisite.* He pushes back in, slow and steady, his hips rocking into mine. "Kit?"

"So good." So deliciously good. It's like feeling light inside my soul after years of darkness. Like flying after being chained to the ground and having never felt wind under me, freeing me.

It's more than I thought it could be.

I watch him closely: his hips poised and ready, his grin blooming on his face, his brow cocking up. Then, he thrusts deep into me, and my whole body erupts. *Oh, shit. That is so much better than exquisite.*

He's stretching, pushing, pulling, and filling. And I want it all. "You fill me to the brim."

"And you take it so well. More, Red?"

"Shit, yes, more. Everything."

He pulls out slowly, agonizingly.

"Holy shit, I feel everything, Greer. Every. Damn. Thing." Veins, the head, the long length of him. Another deep thrust in, and my core ripples, making me shiver.

"Has anyone told you that you have a potty mouth?"

"Stop talking. Start fucking, and yes."

He nips my chin. "Kit, I fucking love it."

He pounds so hard, I know I'll have bruises in the morning. But my body is rejoicing like this is everything it needed. Releasing all the pent-up terror of sex, pushing me past my limits, and reminding me that it can be mind-blowing.

The slap of his hips reverberates through the room, and the rub of his balls on my ass is heaven.

My core is wet, pulsing, squeezing, changing me from the inside out. Weightless in so many ways. I wrap my arms around him, holding on. My moans blend with the slams of the bed against the wall.

He spreads his legs, widening mine and deepening the angle. Clenching at his arms, I arch as his thrust hits a new area.

Each pass of his dick is stringing me taut, winding me up. My body is alive, outside, inside, everywhere. Delicious friction builds up until I'm tense all over, and then he shifts, hitting the right spot.

Holy shit. "There, yes, there, deeper." I moan and grunt and pant. It's so good. So fucking therrrre. Yes, that is the spot.

He leans back on his knees. Grabbing my hips, he keeps up the pace. His abs flex. His cock slides in and out of me, glistening with my wetness. Pulling my hips into his, he watches me, his hair swaying with every thrust.

He drives into me so hard, and all I need is a bit more. *More.*

"Come, Kit. Fucking come. I'm about to lose it, and you have to go first." He grits his teeth and shifts his hand to thumb my clit in tiny circles.

Oh god. Yes. Yesss.

My core spasms, tightness exploding through me. I'm flying. He continues to circle and pump, each movement keeping me longer in rapture.

Slowly, the energy fades, and I collapse, breathing hard. Leaning back down, bracing on his elbows, he moves to kiss me, swelling inside me as he comes. I smile at his loud groan.

I wrap my arms around him, stroking his back as his body winds down. When he finally pulls out, he's still semi-hard, and I shudder.

I lean up as he pulls off the condom and ties it off. "There's a wastebasket to your right."

Shifting onto my side, I face him as he rolls back toward me. Then he pulls me into his arms, resting my head on his shoulder, positioning my thigh up over his lower abdomen. "This good?"

"Better than good. I'm going to be sore tomorrow."

"Good, then I did my job."

"Holy shit, you did your job. I think you need a raise and a new schedule."

"You have full liberty to change my schedule as needed. I'll sign you on as the new head of HR."

I'm floating on air. I'm so...everything. I laugh and hug him as close as I can get him. I'm relaxed, sated, and safe. I take in the pleasure, the excitement, the hunger, and the bubbling giddiness.

It's never been this perfect.

Twenty-Four

Greer

PAIN RADIATES THROUGH MY lower abdomen, and harsh rumbles echo from my stomach, dropping into my lower gut as sweat droplets form on my head.

Fuck. I'm going to be sick.

I shrug out from under Kit, who's still got her head on my shoulder, and clutch my stomach. *Please stay sleeping, please.* Sneaking down the steps, wincing at the creaks as my feet hit the cold tread of the floorboards. I clench my cheeks and rush into the bathroom. My stomach cramps as I sit. Sweat dripping from my temples, I bend over my knees.

"Greer?"

I jerk up. *Fuck, why didn't I close the door?* "Ugh, go away, Kit." Of course, the headstrong woman doesn't listen. She steps inside.

"Hey, it's okay. I see this every day." Even though her palm is cool when she touches my forehead, it stings, and I jerk back. My body is a massive pin cushion of pain. Every inch aches like a hot poker has been stabbing me for the last hour.

"Please get out. Shut the door behind you."

She squats down in front of me.

"I'm begging you, Kit, please. Get out. Now. I'm going to be sick." My body relaxes when she finally leaves. *Thank fuck.*

I lace my fingers together, putting my hands between my legs, my head down. An empty ice cream bucket enters my line of vision.

"In case you're sick from both ends."

I groan. "Fuck, Kit. You should not see this."

"You've got food poisoning." Her footsteps fade away again.

A plate settles on the floor. Two bottles follow. "Some crackers in the bag for when you are up for it. An electrolyte drink and a bottle of water. Do you want me to stay down here?"

"No, I don't know how long this will last." My stomach cramps. I glance at the ice cream bucket, hoping I don't have to use it until she leaves. "You should go back to bed."

"I'll put some blankets and a few pillows on the couch, but you can come back to my room if you want. You don't have to stay down here." She settles down beside me.

"I don't want to keep you up."

"I'm already up. You're not keeping me that way."

"Is this where you wait until I'm delirious so you can get that secret ingredient out of me?"

Her tinkling laughter slightly eases my tension. "I wish it would be that easy. You won't get delirious. Most likely, you're going to be miserable for a few hours, then uncomfortable for six to twelve."

"That long?" I groan, dropping my head. My energy drains like a leaking balloon.

"That long, sweets." I stiffen when she reaches out, expecting pain, but her touch is cool against my head. As she lightly ruffles my hair away from my eyes, I slowly relax.

"Go to bed, Kit."

She leans down and gently brushes her lips to my forehead.

Tingles, and not the good kind, spear up my spine. The sharp pain makes me gasp. "Out. Now."

As soon as the door closes behind her, I bend over the bucket and let the sickness overtake me.

My eyelids are crusty, and my side is cold.

I reach out.

More coldness and wetness. Puke?

I pop my eyes open.

Oh, thank fucking Christ. I'm touching a sweating toilet bowl. My body is bulldozed, and my throat is sore. Fuck, my guts still ache, and my ass hurts worse than spicy food butt burns.

But at least round one is over. Food poisoning one, Greer zero.

My legs are shaky as I stand. Turning on the faucet to rinse out my rancid mouth, I look around for toothpaste and grab the sample tube sitting on the marble counter. My finger is all I've got, but I do the best I can with it.

With a minty taste on my tongue, I shuffle out to the couch, throw a blanket around my shoulders, and roll onto the cushions.

Something brushes against my head. I snap my eyes open, blinking against the soft light. The blanket is twisted around my body, and my teeth are chattering. My stomach clenches again.

I push the blanket off and run to the bathroom. Round two.

"Greer, sweets." Kit's cool hand brushes my forehead. "Greer, babe, we need to get you in the shower."

More rustling. The shower is loud as it starts, then the fan. *Fuck, it's too bright in here.* I bring my hand up to shield myself from the lights. "Let's get you in the shower, and then the light won't bother you so much. Can you stand?"

It takes a shit ton of effort, but I'm on my feet. My body is weak, but I won't go down in front of her.

I finally look at her, and my stomach does that stupid flippy-do thing that only happens around her. She's naked, her cheeks pink like she's still embarrassed to be naked around me. Opening the curtain, she pulls me into the lukewarm shower. The spray hits like pin prickles along my skin.

Groaning, I lower my head and allow her to push me under the stream. She kneads my skin gently, her soapy fingers tenderly working out the knots. Suds slide down my body into the drain, taking the tension from my muscles with them. I groan again as her hands travel up my neck, then briefly leave me before a fruity scent hits my nose.

"Hope you don't mind. This is all I have. No manly scents. But we need to wash your hair." Her hands are light as they work in the shampoo. She pulls my hair back, and I tilt my chin so she can reach better. "Thank you."

"The pleasure is mine." And it is, despite the burning in my cheeks and weird constriction in my chest. No one has had to care for me in years. I like it, but does it also make me a bit unmanly? I'm supposed to care for her, not in a sexist way, but in a take care of your partner way.

That's my job.

"That feels...painful but incredible." I moan. Her hands are perfect. The pressure is perfect, and her nails score against my scalp in a way that shoots tingles through me. "What time is it?"

"It's after three in the afternoon."

Holy shit. Has she been watching me the entire time? Damn it.

When I tense, her hands do too. Her voice is soft behind me. "What?"

"I don't like that you've had to take care of me."

"I enjoy taking care of people, Greer. It's what I do. Ready for more heat?"

I nod, and she makes the water hotter.

My shoulders drop, the stiffness releasing. *Fuck, she's a miracle.* She moves me to rinse my hair, and I close my eyes, basking in her magic hands. Tugging on her hips, I dig in as I groan. "You're so good at this."

"I always thought I'd be a doctor, but that didn't work out. I love being a nurse, but I feel like a little something is missing." There's a smile there, her voice a little bubbly.

"Why don't you do the doctor thing?" The shower is exactly what I needed. My strength is coming back, and my energy is too.

I grab the soap and slowly lather up her body—around her hips, her breasts, paying special attention to her nipples. She moans, rapture flickering across her face. My heart topples right into my stomach. My cock jumps to attention, surprising me since the illness wore me out, but I'm learning I'm never too tired to touch her.

"I wasn't allowed to. I was getting my undergraduate in human biology when I met Ethan. Before we got married, he pushed me to get my nursing degree rather than continuing on for my medical degree. He convinced me the extra stress wouldn't make up for the monetary gain because I could never make more than he already did, that I didn't need to 'prove myself' to be 'enough' for him." She trails off, her face tight.

I smooth my fingers down her skin, drawing her back from whatever terrible memory she's clearly thinking about. "Would you do it now if you could?" I slide my hands down her abdomen and brush against her with my thumbs. Goose bumps erupt on her arms. "Cold?"

She shakes her head. "No, not cold. Your touch is fire." Her face grows serious, then she whispers, "It's too late to do it now. I'm too old for med school. I love working with kids, and as a nurse, I can still do that. There are always avenues in nursing. I can do education or get my doctorate."

I slip my thumbs between her legs, brushing back and forth. She's so smooth everywhere, and I can't stop myself from touching her. Her hands slide over my chest, and I shiver as she scratches my nipples.

"Mmm, then I can treat patients like a medical doctor. Obviously, it's not the same training. They work closely with doctors, though."

I twirl us and put her under the water. Pushing my hand through her hair, I tilt her head back. The shower helps wash the last of my illness down the drain, giving me the energy that I desperately need.

"You should do that. I can pay for it if you need the money." The energy changes, and despite the hot water, she's cold, almost frigid, and tense. Her eyelids scrunch closed. Her chest rises faster. Her hands stop moving. *What the fuck just happened?*

"Hey, baby. Look at me, please."

She peers up at me, and her fingers relax against my abdomen, but her chest still heaves with every breath, and a slight wheeze rattles from inside her.

"Kit, baby, take a deep breath." I put my hand on her chest, right above her heart. Its thunderous beats are heavy against my palm.

"Red?"

Her head jerks up, her eyes wide as she searches mine. She swallows, and I watch her war with whatever is in her head.

"Let me in, Kit."

Her throat works a few times as she struggles to find the words. "I don't want your money. You can't buy me, force me to do—"

Shit. "I'm sorry, Kit. I didn't mean it like that. In no way will I ever tell you what to do. I'll encourage you, push you, but never force you. Not now, not ever. I promise." Her pulse paces out before she tips her head back to look at me. She's still working through it, though, because her hands keep clenching on my back.

She nods, still wary. I wait, deliberately breathing slowly as we focus on each other. It takes a moment, but she follows my lead, hers easing, becoming even and steady.

She drops her head to my chest, placing her ear against my heart. "Thank you. I'm sorry."

I kiss her head as I wrap my arms around her. "What do you have to be sorry for?"

"I lose my shit so easily sometimes, but I can't go back to that, Greer, ever. Having my decisions taken away from me broke me. I won't be with someone who wants to control me, regardless of the reason. I can make my own choices and take care of myself. Being a victim again is not an option."

"I understand. I promise. I won't ever make you do something you don't want to do. And I won't ever expect anything in return for whatever help I give you."

I tilt her chin up, watching the water cascade down her body. She shudders, and then her palms glide along my skin as she moves them up my chest. My pulse races headlong toward my dick.

Leaning up on her toes, she pulls my head down gently.

I press my finger to her lips. "Hold that thought. Unless you want my vomit breath to kill you when I fuck you, I need some toothpaste. And a condom."

We're both laughing when she hops out of the shower.

"No extra toothbrush. Where are your condoms?"

"Wallet, back pocket. I'll use my finger. Now hurry because I feel so much better, and all I can think about are those pouty lips of yours parted while I take you against the wall." She pulls the curtain back, and I hold my finger out so she can squirt some paste on it.

It's only a moment, and then she pops back in, putting a foil packet on the ledge. I cup her breast, brushing her nipple with my thumb, then lean down and take it in my minty mouth.

"Shit, Greer. Oh." She threads her fingers through my hair and holds me right where she wants me.

I suck deep, my tongue flicking her nipple as I pinch the other. With my free hand, I slide her leg over my hip, then move my fingers between her thighs. With a gentle touch, I cup her pussy, sliding my fingers into the slit. She's already so wet. "You're so responsive, Kit. Are you sore?"

"Yes. But I want it. It's never felt this way. It's a delicious hurt. Don't stop." She arches back, her hips driving against my fingers.

I push her against the wall, using it to hold her up so I can pump her deeply. Curling my fingers up, she moans. It's loud, and gloriously written on her face.

"Greer, oh my god. That's—Yes—the spot." Her body moves against the wall. Her hips rock against my hand. "Oh, shit. I'm going to come already."

"Good." I pump harder, the squelch of my fingers in her pussy soft in the thunder of the shower. I slip my thumb over her clit and circle it, delighting when her body tenses around my fingers. She's close. And never in my life have I wanted to make a woman feel good so badly.

Every aspect of our time together should reflect me worshiping her body, showing her what it means to have someone take care of her. "Yes, Kit, yes. Let that pretty pussy come all over my fingers."

And she shatters. Her core spasms around my digits, her breasts heave, her cheeks pinken, and her eyes darken to the deepest green I've ever seen. "You are so fucking beautiful. So beautiful."

She reaches for the condom before I even put her leg down. Ripping it open, she slides it on my cock. Her finger scrapes my chin as she leans up to kiss me, her tongue plunging inside to claim me. With my hands under her ass, I hike her up against the wall.

"Wrap your legs around me, Kit." Her thighs grip my hips.

I groan. I'm enveloped in desire. Her hands around me are the most erotic thing I've ever felt, and I'll never get enough. Not of this, not of her.

Forever.

I want her to want it forever too.

Her groan catches my attention, her voice hesitant. "You sure you're feeling well enough for this?"

I lean in, licking up her neck. "Fuck yes." I nudge her opening with my cock. "I'll go slow again to start, but after..."

"Fuck after..." She bites my lip. My hips surge in, out of control with the pleasure-pain. "Ooh. A moment." She pants against my mouth.

"Kit, baby, you okay? I'm sorry." I let her acclimate, shifting side to side and circling around to stretch her out.

"Yup, okay, getting better by the minute." Her lips are warm on my shoulder, her tongue rough against my skin.

Then she bites down hard.

Tingles zing down my spine straight to my balls. Her moans spur me on as I pull out and push back in fast and hard.

I could fucking come now. I could come inside her pussy forever.

Keeping up the rhythm, I massage her ass as I push in and pull out. Her breasts bob with every thrust. I shift, tilting her hips and pinning her to the wall with my chest. Her thighs grip me hard. One hand above her head for leverage, I move back a bit to give her space to breathe.

"Kit?"

"Harder."

Her head is against the wall, tipped up, lost to how it feels. One hand is on her nipple, squeezing, and the other is grabbing my wrist like an anchor.

She's so sexy, my cock throbs. My balls pull taut. Shit, I won't last much longer in her tight channel. I bite my lip, and hints of copper bloom on my tongue as I struggle to hold my orgasm back.

Fuck this. She needs more, and I'm giving it. I pull out, chuckling when she groans. "Put your hands on the wall."

I curl my fingers between hers and keep them on the tiles. Bending her over, I line up my cock and thrust in.

"Yes. Yes, yes, yes."

"Keep your arms locked, and don't move." I hold still inside her. My cock twitches a few times. Sliding one hand down her arm and under it to grab her breast, I squeeze gently before moving to her hip. I hold firmly, my fingertips digging in, then I pull out and ram back in.

Her gasp urges me to do it again and again. I keep up the frantic pace as she shatters. Her pussy is tight around me, strangling me as I pump furiously. I slide my fingers between her thighs, find her clit, and stroke it. Her legs twitch against me.

"Oh..." That sweet pussy pulls me in, gripping me perfectly, milking me as she peaks. My balls tingle at the sound of her moans and the slurps of wetness as I slam against her. My body tenses, my cock twitching, my pulse racing.

I thrust again as my cum shoots free on my release. Every aching inch of my cock rejoices as I unleash inside her, rocking, jetting into the condom over and over. Finally, I slow, dropping my head on her back.

"Greer, you are seriously going to kill me."

"That or my dinner dates. Glad I ate that meal and not you." I pull out gently. Sliding the condom off, I tie it up and throw it over the top of the curtain. It plops on the tile floor somewhere in the bathroom.

"You did not just do that."

"Whaaat? I'll pick it up when we get out there." I give her my best attempt at a sheepish look. Her laughter lights a spark inside me, and I smile at her happiness.

She wraps her arms around me, letting the water hit us. "You're definitely feeling better."

"I'm never eating that again."

"Maybe it was bad raw meat?" Her eyes twinkle as she teases me.

"I'll give you raw meat."

She snorts as she cleans herself. I do the same before shutting off the water and grabbing a towel.

"What's on the agenda for the rest of the day?"

She looks at me, a warm smile blooming on her face. "You want to stay?"

"If you'll let me. But I don't want anything to eat yet. My stomach is a bit sore after that workout. Damn, you're a lusty wench. I was too sick, but all you wanted was some cock."

She smacks me hard on the ass.

Rubbing it, I turn to her and wink. Her eyes fade to a soft, rolling green. Damn, she looks sated. "I did a fucking excellent job. You look just-fucked dreamy."

"I've never heard that before."

"That's because it's only said by the ladies I've been with."

"Oh my god, Greer, shut up. Wait, did I bite your lip?"

My laughter fills the bathroom as I walk out.

Twenty-Five

Kit

THE ENGINE DIES, AND I pull the key from the ignition. Shoving the earbud in my ear so I don't miss anything Rosemary says, I get out and head to my house.

"Billy got handsy again. I sent him to the principal today." Rosemary's cackle bleeds through the earpiece.

"Oh." A parcel sits in the doorway, propped against the siding. "I have a box. It's big and long."

"Gross, Kit. But seriously. Boyfriend?"

I let a chuckle escape and fight a grin. "How do you know already?"

"Angelo talks."

"So does Greer, apparently."

"Angelo and Simon had to trick it out of him, and trust me, it took a lot. It was hours of drilling him. Besides, we all knew you were together. We were just waiting for the label."

I pick up the white box with the thick red bow. It's hefty, but I lug it inside, then drop my keys in the bowl and bring the box to the counter before putting Rosemary on speakerphone.

A rancid smell permeates the room, and I glance at my scrubs. Right. The last kid of the day had an accident.

"Hey, I'm going to shower quickly. One of the patients threw up on me during the last appointment. I want to wash the stink off, and then I'll open the box."

"Call me before you do. I want a play-by-play."

I click off. After stripping off my scrubs and throwing them in the wash, I make my way upstairs, a smile tugging on my lips.

Greer is more than anything I thought possible. So incredibly patient with me through everything. His gentle dominance is the most attractive thing about him. I wonder if he sent flowers. The box is kind of big like that.

My heart racing, I shower faster than I ever have in my life. I throw on my favorite loose T-shirt and a pair of joggers.

Downstairs, I dial my sister.

"Yo."

"You are weird, Rosemary. Who answers with 'Yo'?"

"I knew it was you. Now stop stalling and open the damn box!"

"Hold on to your panties." I use both hands to pull up the large lid.

"I totally knew something happened at the cabin." Her voice is smug.

"I'm not telling you anything about the cabin."

A loud "Ha!" hits my ears. I'm still pulling up the lid when a scent hits my nose.

What the hell is that smell?

I know it...it's familiar. Ice flows in a slow cascade down my body.

"What is it?" Rosemary's voice is high-pitched.

The lid is off, and I look inside. My limbs tremble, and then my hands and feet go numb. All of my insides clench, and a knot forms as I struggle around the rubber band squeezing my lungs. I stagger back. "No, no, no."

"Kit?"

I gasp, doubling over.

"Kit, are you..." Her voice fades into the background.

"No...he's back." I curl in on myself as the flowers' scent fills the air. My heart beats frantically in my ears, the pounding obliterating all other sounds. Blackness creeps into the edges of my vision, amplifying the pink of the petals. My body shakes.

Those aren't from Greer.

Shoving the box off the counter, I run.

⌐... . .⌐ ⌐. ⌐ ⌐ .. .⌐. .. ⌐ .⌐.. .⌐.. ⌐.⌐⌐   ⌐... .⌐. ⌐⌐⌐ ⌐.⌐ . ⌐.

Seven years ago

I hum along to the music in my earbuds as I clean the toilet. When I turn to rinse my rag, Ethan lounges in the doorway. Lilies sag in his hand, their heads angled toward the floor as if he doesn't have the energy to keep them upright.

I meet his gaze. Today, they are cold, sub-arctic blue, not the warm color they used to be. Such a change from when we first started dating.

I hesitate because he's never hurt me, but sometimes he'll work out his frustration with his punching bag. He'll yell and rail at me, terrify me, but he's never hit me. I've learned to try to defuse the anger and walk on eggshells, but lately, he's been going down to our gym more and more.

Pasting on a smile, I drag the earbuds from my ears and place everything on the counter. I try to inject cheerfulness into my voice. "What is the special occasion?" I point to the flowers.

His eyes glint in the bathroom's light. "Today is lesson day."

The blood leaves my face. My palms prickle in the heat of the room.

"White lilies mean I'm sorry. That I did something wrong." He casually taps the flowers against his thigh. "Are these white lilies, Katherine?" His other hand fists against his side. A vein throbs near his temple.

"N-no. They are pink." I move my hands in front of me, twisting them frantically as my mind races.

What does pink mean?

He takes a step forward. I strain my muscles, forcing them to remain where they are. If I run from him or shy away, the yelling and name-calling are worse.

His voice is low and controlled. "Pink means that you did something wrong, Katherine, and you need to apologize for it." He takes another step closer. There are only a few feet between us now.

My lungs are tight. The atmosphere is stifling through the energy radiating off him.

"Any time I bring you pink lilies, you will have five minutes to apologize for what you did, and you will tell me what it was, so I know you are learning from it." He steps closer. Slowly bringing his lips down to mine, he kisses me so gently, so tenderly.

I want to wipe my lips clean. But I don't dare move.

He steps back. His fingers brush my cheek and then slowly trail down my neck. "Since this is our first lesson in lilies, you can have some extra time tonight. I'll go downstairs, put your flowers in a vase, and make myself a drink. When I come back, you can tell me why the lilies are pink today. And then you'll thank me for them."

Sure-footed, he walks away, his steps carrying down the hall. The liquor cabinet squeaks, and ice clinks into a cup.

The walls close in on me.

My hands grow cold.

My feet turn numb.

My mind blanks.

For how long, I don't know. I'm finally getting myself under control when his footsteps announce his arrival.

Leaning against the doorjamb, he stands with his hands in his pockets. "Why did I bring you pink lilies, Katherine?"

My lip trembles, and my heart is in my throat. Think Kit, think.

What did I do that I'll need to apologize for? What have I done in the last few days? Nothing. I don't even work.

He takes a step closer. Sweat pools in my palms, between my breasts, and around my temples.

Shit, slow your heart rate down.

"I-I don't know, Ethan."

His hand shoots forward, and he grabs the hair at the top of my head, his tug harsh and hard. A few strands pull free with a sharp pain as I blink back tears. He hauls me forward as he bends down, his face mere inches from mine.

"You do, Katherine. Think back very carefully. What happened on Saturday?"

I jump from the low, malicious voice. Shit, shit, shit. Saturday.

We had dinner with the Rogers on Saturday. I was friendly and presentable since they're potential clients.

They are a lovely couple in their forties. Mrs. Rogers was pleasant and cordial. Her husband was a gentleman. He held the door open for me and caught me when I tripped over a loose tile.

"I'm not sure, Ethan. I'm sorry, though, whatever I did."

He jerks his hand, yanking my head sideways. I grab on to his wrist to leverage myself. "Let go, Katherine. Now." His voice is icy, crystalline, and his mouth is pinched.

Oh shit. This is going to hurt.

I let go of his wrist, bracing myself. The tension drains from my body when a few seconds pass without incident.

"What happened Saturday?"

"I don't know." I hold my eyes open wide, trying to prevent my tears from falling. He shoves me hard into the shower wall, and my head bounces off.

A whimper escapes as my temple throbs, and I land in a heap on the floor. A trickle of something hot oozes down the side of my head toward my neck.

He is coming toward me.

I curl into a ball, trying to escape as he looms over me, dark, dominating. He grabs my hair again and drags me toward the bedroom. I grasp his wrist with one hand and scramble after him, half crawling to catch up.

"Please, Ethan. I don't know what I did. I'm sorry. I'm so sorry." I can't stop the tears now. He lets go suddenly, and I sigh with relief as the pull on my scalp is instantly gone.

Pain and force, sharp and tearing, explodes in my cheek, and my head rebounds to the right.

"Look what you made me do, Katherine." His voice never changes inflection, remaining a cold, calculating monotone. "Stand."

I whimper, struggling to stand. "Please, Ethan, if you tell me what I did, I promise I'll never do it again."

"What happened Saturday, Katherine? I'll give you one last chance to tell me."

I stare at him, trembling so hard I can barely stand. I shake my head, racking my brain. Still, I have no idea what the hell he's talking about. Nothing. I didn't do anything wrong. I lash out. "I don't know!"

He tenses, his nostrils flaring, his mouth tightening even further. Shit, shit, shit, now I've pissed him off. He grabs me, bringing me close, and I hold on for dear life.

It's coming.

A rippling, agonizing force hits my stomach. The meal I had for lunch comes up and plants itself on the floor. Twice more, I retch before I'm able to breathe through the blinding pain. My vision blurs, and my ears ring as I glance at him, trying to understand.

He sighs heavily. "You will clean that up later. Now it's time to show me how much you love me. How sorry you are. On the bed."

Gasping around the lingering hurt centered in my stomach and the spasms in my diaphragm, I wheeze, "I promise, Ethan, I promise whatever I did, I won't do it again. Please, tell me. I can learn."

"You are going to learn your lesson tonight." He grabs my arm and hauls me up beside him. "Lie down."

No, no, no. "Ethan, please, please, not this. Anything but this. You don't have to do this to make me learn my lesson. I've learned it. Whatever I did, tell me, and I'll never do it again."

He picks me up. Throwing me onto the bed, he follows me down. "Never, ever, let another man touch what is mine, Katherine. Never."

My pulse buzzes in my ear. My heart is beating too fast.

Not this, not this. Anything but this.

I don't know if I'll survive this.

Twenty-Six

Greer

MY PHONE BUZZES IN my pocket. Turning off my sander, I pull off my safety goggles and mask. I wipe my hands on my jeans, dig out my phone, and hit answer without checking the number.

"Greer Winters." I push the phone between my ear and shoulder as I unplug the sander.

"Greer, it's Rosemary." Her voice is high and fast. "You need to go to Kit. Go to her house. Something happened. I can't get to her. You have to go."

I grab the keys and run toward my truck. "Slow down, Ro. Tell me exactly what happened." My heart skips a few beats, and nausea churns in my gut. I start up my vehicle and throw it into gear. My tires squeal as I jump the curb to get onto the side street. Fuck, it's a twenty-minute drive to get there.

"Kit got something in the mail and opened it while we were talking. She screamed. She said he's back and then stopped talking to me."

I swerve around another car. *Fuck! I need to pay attention to the road.* "Gotta go, Ro. I'll call you when I know something."

My heart hammers in my chest. *Motherfucker!* If he is alive, he won't be for long. I'm not letting him anywhere near Kit.

Fuck, what if he is there? I don't know what I can do legally.

My throat constricts, and sweat forms on my palms. I swipe them off one at a time so I can still hold the steering wheel. Spine tingling, I glance at the clock. Four minutes.

Fuck. Hold on.

Please let her be there. Let me make it in time.

What am I going to do when I get there? Fight him?

My legs ache, and my stomach is a tight ball of worry. I'm still minutes away.

Hold on, baby. Please.

Fuck, I can't lose her.

Scant moments later, I pull into her drive. Her front door is shut, so I approach it slowly and knock. When I don't get an answer, I enter her key code.

"Kit, love. Baby, where are you?" I scramble through the main floor, stopping in each room to look. I flash through all the areas, my focus darting to every nook. My body is out of control, and my pulse spikes as I take the stairs two at a time. "Red? Come on. Tell me where you are."

I skid to a halt at the top of the stairs. Nothing.

Where the hell is she?

There is no sign of her anywhere. I start toward the bathroom but pause when I reach the door. A dull thud echoes from somewhere else, slow, hard, rhythmic.

Waiting in the doorway, I sway, searching for where the sound is coming from.

Following the noise, I step into her bedroom again.

The closet. My hands tremble as I grab the knob and rip the door open.

Kit. Alone.

"Oh, Jesus, Kit." I step inside, hunkering down on my knees, edging close to her curled-up form. Rocking, she hits the wall. Everything about her is tight, closed off, shielding her from the outside as tears stream down her face.

"Kit?"

Her head snaps up, and she focuses her blown-out green irises on me. Her voice is so faint. "Greer."

And then she's launching herself into my arms. I pull her close, holding her in my arms, trying to subdue the trembling.

Hers and mine.

She sobs, her body a wreck as I try to get as close as I possibly can. Her arms are choking around my neck, her legs around my hips. I stand and step out of the closet.

Knowing she's safe, my body settles.

"Kit." On the bed, I pull her close and rock her. "Tell me what happened, love."

"He sent me flowers." Her whole body shakes so hard I have to hold on tight.

I smooth my hands up and down her back, moving them in a pattern, forcing my body to relax as her sobs continue to shake her.

"I got you, love. I've got you." Fuck, I need to absorb her into my body and show her she's okay.

I rock her, our bodies pressed against each other until her sobs fade and her pulse slows. Her hands feed through my hair, stroking and smoothing mindlessly. My heart slows, and I let out a shaky breath.

I lean my head against hers, waiting for her to talk. She stays silent, and I hold her, letting her tears stain my beaten-up old cotton shirt.

"I don't want to be here."

Of course. "We can go to my place?"

She nods against my shoulder, and I stand, keeping her around me as I head out to my truck. I buckle her in the middle seat so I can hold her as I drive—not only for her, but for me too. "We'll be there in a few minutes, okay?"

The drive seems like it lasts forever, but she's safe.

I'm so out of my element, but beside her is the only place I want to be. Her strength is a balm to my soul. I want to absorb every piece of her, the good and the bad, and love the shit out of it all.

Love. I'm undeniably in love with her. Every aspect of this courageous woman.

I pull into my drive and get us into the house, then settle on the couch, keeping her tucked against me and straddling my hips. I kiss her head, her neck, and her shoulder, showing her I'm here. My hands are steady with the knowledge that she's whole and in my home. She tilts her head back, and I wipe at her tears.

"Start at the beginning, love. Tell me what is going on."

Her trembles rack through her body as she talks. "There was a box outside waiting for me. I thought it was from you, so I brought it in. When I opened it, it was pink lilies." Her eyes are red from crying, and the emerald green is coming back. "Pink lilies were his way of saying I did something wrong, that I needed to ask for forgiveness. When I saw the lilies, I-I couldn't stop the memory. I think I started running. That's the last I remember before looking up and seeing you there."

"Do you know if anyone was in the house?"

"I don't think so. For a long time, I have had weird feelings. Sometimes I get a shiver down my spine, or it feels like I'm being watched, or things move. I believed it was me transitioning and forgetting where I put things. Do you think he's following me?"

"He's dead, Kit."

Her voice is loud, screeching at me. "They didn't find his body. They searched for years. Nothing. Not even a hair. He's out there. I know he is. He's pissed." She closes her eyes and drops her head against my shoulder. "He is so pissed."

"How do you know he's alive?" I push my hand under her shirt, running it over her skin. Her body melts, falling into mine.

"I don't. But I don't think he's dead."

"My brother owns a security and PI business. Maybe he can help. They do this sort of thing all the time. I can have him look into it and see what they can find."

"They won't find anything. Colette and I searched for Ethan for years."

She looks so tired. All I want is to take it all away. Absorb it into me and keep it from her. I keep up the soothing strokes on her back. "Tell me about the memory?"

She bites her bottom lip. "Lilies, pink ones, are his way of saying I fucked up. It was the first time he ever brought them home for me. We had dinner with two clients the weekend before, and the man had caught me when I'd tripped. Ethan was furious, thinking that I had instigated the whole thing. That I asked for the man's hands on me." Her voice is strained. "He forced himself on me. I belonged to him, and he wanted me to remember. I didn't forget after that."

My heart plummets to the floor. This strong, courageous woman has been through so much, and I don't know what to do for her. "Did he rape you more than once? You don't have to tell me if you don't want to."

Her eyes are glossy as she nods. "I know. You don't push me for more than I can give. It doesn't hurt so bad thinking about what happened. A lot of that has to do with you, Greer. The way you handle everything is so different from the way Ethan did. I'm lucky." She swallows, trying to get closer to me, like she's trying to disappear into my body.

"The first time was the worst. I didn't know what he was capable of, how long it would last, or what he'd do afterward. I learned quickly, though. At the end, he always told me how much he loved me. He made me say it back to him every time. Every damn time. So sick and disgusting. I thought I was over it, that I could move on. I thought I was strong."

"You are strong, Kit. I don't know anyone who could go through what you did and come out functioning and resilient like you have."

She nuzzles her face into my neck. "I didn't know what it meant to be happy until I met you. What will I do if I lose you, Greer? You're so important to me. It happened so quickly, and I couldn't stop it. I liked you even when you terrified me. Now I don't want you to leave. I don't want to lose you."

"You won't."

"What if he comes after you?"

"You don't know it's him."

"There is no other explanation, Greer. He is the only one who knows about the lilies. I never told anyone."

"He won't hurt me, Kit."

"You don't know him." She sighs, the exhale hot on my shoulder as, finally, her trembles slow. "I want to move on, forget him and the memories."

Her skin is smooth under my hands, and I keep rubbing, letting her know I'm here for her. When her body finally stills, I settle my hands on her hips. "Better?"

She nods, her arms wrapped around my neck. We sit a moment, holding each other.

"What do you want to do now? Snuggle, warm bath, read a book, whatever you want, I got you. I'll take care of you."

"I want to sit with you for a bit. Be close to you." She slides her hands under my shirt, rubbing against my skin in gentle sweeps. Her hands become more insistent, smoothing, stroking.

I bite back a moan at the way her fingers graze my skin. "Your touch feels so good. It's never felt this good. When I'm with you, I go up in flames."

She nods against my shoulder. "You're the kindling to my fire." She brushes my cheek, and I lean into it. She shifts, leaning back so I can see her emerald eyes. They are deep, the pupils blowing out. Her gaze dips to my lips, and without a thought, I lick the bottom one. The tension shifts, and I tighten my fingers.

Waiting.

I won't push. She has the lead, and I'll gladly follow her into hell if it means staying by her side.

"Greer." Her voice drops, husky and sending shivers down my spine. She bites her bottom lip as her hands rhythmically massage my back. Her hips shift on my lap. "Replace my nightmare. Give me something magical instead."

A deep groan vibrates from my throat as I thread my fingers up through her hair. I angle her head how I like it and then plunge into the magic that is Kit.

Headfirst, I spiral. My lips brush against hers. Her taste explodes against my tongue as I lick her lips to get her to open. I smile against her mouth, my beard brushing her chin as she gasps.

Standing, I carry her into my bedroom and sit on the bed.

She tastes so good. My tongue brushes hers, and I open wide to taste more, to give her all of me.

She pulls on my shirt, her fingers gliding against my sensitive skin. Our lips part, and I lift my arms so she can pull my shirt over my head. When I'm free of it, I bring her mouth back to mine by gripping the back of her neck.

I'm desperate for her. I want to consume her like she said I would. But I don't want to steal her life. I want to consume her and fill her with joy at the same time.

Breaking the kiss, I skim my hands down, sliding them under the hem of her top and pulling the flimsy material over her head. I smirk as she shivers, and goose bumps form along her skin from my touch.

Kissing the swell of her breasts over the cups of her simple bra, I reach around to undo the clasp. When she's free, I bite my cheek, holding back my gasp.

She's magnificent. Her nipples are rosy, pink, round, and perfect.

I brush them with my thumbs, loving her gasp when I lean down and suck one into my mouth. It hardens, pebbling against my stroking tongue, and she moans. The sound is dark and delicious. Her hands spear through my hair, holding me closer to her breast as she arches against me.

Flipping us, I lay her on her back and brace myself above her, staring into her eyes.

She's exquisite. Her fucking breasts are sinful.

Palming one, I lean down and lick it.

I need to see the rest. To get rid of every terrible memory. Right. Fucking. Now.

I settle back on my heels. "Lift your hips."

Kit

His excitement is contagious, building the fierce need in me. The weight of his attention is heavy as he watches the reveal of my body. Then I'm naked, aching under his gaze.

"You are every fantasy I have ever had all rolled into one remarkable woman." His rough palms glide up my legs, and I shiver as he inches closer and closer to my core.

Yes, this is what I need, his touch erasing every horrible piece.

His thumbs brush along my lips, opening me. I arch back, focusing on how his breath hits me. Then he pushes my knees wider, keeping me exposed.

Needing an anchor, I slide my hands up the bed and hold on to the bed frame. His tongue attacks me, sliding up my slit and flicking my clit.

"Oh my god." His tongue is magical, moving in a dance my body recognizes.

He smiles against my thigh before leaning back in. *How does he do...Oh, Jesus. That. Yes, that, right there.*

His tongue is rough in places I want it rough, yet gentle when it flicks around my bean. His strong hands hold me down when my body betrays me and starts to thrash.

I'm so close. So freaking close to peaking, to overcoming every bad emotion in my body, replacing it with love and acceptance.

"I want you inside me." I grab on to him and pull him close. "Greer." His expression is intense and focused as he rises. His lips glisten, and my pussy clenches when he licks his mouth clean and moans at my taste. "Are you clean?"

I want him bare. I want him to erase everything that has come before him. Every tear and rip and scream of pain Ethan inflicted on me. "I haven't been with anyone but you since Ethan. I'm clean."

His eyes flash, his pupils so large and black. *He's as lost to this as I am.* He nods. "My test came back this week. I'm clean."

"Clear it all away. Take away the last of the memories." The burning, searing torment, the rough hands that gripped to cause pain, the harsh movements of Ethan's body in mine, the glass-like splinters of my soul as it broke apart every time.

The agony of having to knit myself back together.

I won't have to this time. It's my choice to take someone into me this way. My choice to fill my life with something loving and complete.

"Kit. Fuck." His arms wrap around me. Craving more contact, I press against him as he climbs my body. His arms lock, and he planks against me as I lay my hands on his muscles, then slide them up his back.

I exhale, letting his weight settle over me. I'm not caged in, like times in the past—before Greer. Stroking his skin, I focus on the smoothness, the way my body melts into him, the pleasure of the hint of his weight on me.

He nuzzles my neck. "Okay?"

I pull him closer, his weight pushing me into the bed. I know that this is different. I'm safe in his arms, cherished.

Testing his response, needing to know I have the power, I slide my hand to his abdomen and push lightly. His whole body eases off me. Sharp relief and a chuckle escape me before I pull him back down.

No matter what happens tonight, I'm in control, and if I want it to end, I know Greer will stop.

"Better than okay."

He groans against me, his weight settling again. Then his mouth is on my skin, and all I can do is let the desire take me, move me, steal my breath.

Everything intensifies, and I ache to have him. He grinds against me, his hips rocking and his hand stroking. His touch is sending my body higher, climbing with every brush.

I'm building, flying, and if he doesn't hurry, I'm going to finish without him.

His cock slides through my wet lips, and I wrap my knees around him, so excited I can barely stop myself from arching up to feel him there.

His eyes shine with something deep and meaningful that stills everything inside me. It's warm and tender and everything that I wanted with lovemaking but never received. This is more than sex.

Trust.

That's what this step means. That's what giving him my body this way means.

It's a level far beyond anything I thought I would be ready for. But Greer is more than anything I'd ever hoped for.

My stomach drops as he thrusts home, his cock hard, deep, and so big.

"Oh, shit. Greer." I hiss around the delicious sting as he shifts from side to side.

"Stop?"

I shake my head wildly. *No. No, don't stop. Oh shit, yes, that's it.* He slides out then back in, and I shut my eyes as he pumps in a rhythm, slow and steady.

"Thank god, Kit. You're fucking wonderful, beautiful, and strong. I never thought it could feel like this."

He rocks again, slowly, letting me get used to his size. He dips his lips to my neck, and I race my hands over his back, his arms, anywhere I can touch. This is how it should be, safe in your lover's arms.

Connected. Sharing the experience.

"Still okay?"

I nod into his shoulder because, right now, gasps are the only sound I can make.

"Good. Let it feel good, let it surround you, consume you. Let me make you feel wonderful. Let every touch take away your pain and heal your heart. Let me love you, Kit."

Oh shit.

Tears prick my eyes, and I swallow around the ache in my heart. He's moving everything inside me. Filling up all those cracks with the brightness inside him, healing my inner turmoil and replacing it with something strong. Gluing me together. Painting me in golden rivers.

He pulls my leg up and over his hip, dragging it high so he can shift deeper. The way he moves inside me is like a perfect symphony of movement and depth. Restoring my soul, pulling away all the darkness. Unable to control myself, I moan against him.

"With me, love?"

Love. I nod, the tears falling now. He is so good inside and out, and he doesn't even know it.

He thrusts slowly. "You feel so good. It's like every time I move inside you, I can feel parts of myself."

"Me too."

He moves with reverence, his hand leaving my leg to worship the rest of my body, stroking my skin and my breasts, tugging at my nipples. He leans down to lick one of them, driving me slowly insane.

He's not fixing me—he's giving me the strength to take back everything with meaning, everything joyful and mesmerizing and beautiful. He's giving me the strength to be whole.

The man gives. With his body, his laughter, himself.

He's a giver.

He shifts again and hits something delicious inside me.

"More, Greer."

His hips grind against mine, moving his cock deep and slow but hard.

I gasp as his cock swells, filling me almost mercilessly. But the ache is so good, showering me with bliss and serenity. It takes away the last lingering remnants of the pain I felt before, ripping it away forcefully but tenderly.

The pressure builds. His body rubs against mine. My nipples pebble against his chest.

Hooking my ankles over each other, I dig my fingers into his shoulders and rejoice in the strength of his body, the hard thrusts, and the way he makes me lose my mind. "Damn it, Greer. It's too good. This. Everything is so perfect." I tighten around him, grabbing on to him as fiercely as possible. I trust him to take care of me, to love me through my racing pulse and aching heart. He'll catch me at the end of this and hold on to me for the rest of our lives.

"I know, love." His hands brush across my cheeks, his attention completely on me. "I've never been consumed this way, either."

His words rocket me into bliss. My core spasms, and the rest of my body shudders. "I'm going to come."

I throw my head back, my body pressing against his as I explode around him. My hips rock into him, meeting him motion for motion. I cry out, my voice breaking as I ride the waves of pleasure.

And he lets me, drawing it out until my heart stops racing.

I lean up, needing his lips. His body tenses as he holds back. And I can't help it, I clench around him, loving his groan as he drops his head to my shoulder. He grits his teeth; he's still hard inside me, still waiting for his release.

My heart is at ease, and my body is calm. Everything inside me is languid and smooth, not jagged and broken. It's pieced back together in a way only Greer could have done. In a way that I never thought was possible—completely.

It's freeing.

A heavy weight from deep inside me slips away.

And when I need it, soft lips settle on mine, pulling me back to Greer. He licks my lips, and I open to let him in as he continues to move.

Our tongues mesh, stroking, sliding, gliding against each other as I settle. I need him close to me, want him to feel the way my heart is beating only for him.

He shifts back; his hand grips my thigh as he slides my leg up his body, then settles against it so my foot is by his head. "You ready for the rest?"

"You want me to come again?"

His chuckle brushes against me as my body bends in ways I've never been bent before. Nodding, he pistons in and out of me hard. "As many times as I can."

"Oh, holy shit." He's hitting that spot from earlier, the one that makes me see stars.

Ooh, he's big. Every thick ridge, every hard vein of his cock, creates delicious friction as it rocks into me. He is persistent, making me gasp as the tremors begin again, the pleasure overtaking me, my skin tingling from the inside out. It's fast, my body furiously climbing the peak, and I can't stop it.

I cry out as I come around him, spasming almost painfully, deliciously, agonizingly.

He thrusts deep. And I know he's with me, the way he loses himself, the moans in my ear. I palm the back of his head, holding him as close as I can as tears prick my eyes. Basking in his movements, I wait for my body to come down.

"Kit..." He pumps hard, his body tensing against me. He groans, and a rush of heat settles deep inside me. He twitches as he comes, pushing his head into the crook of my neck.

His mouth moves against my shoulder. I hope it is a smile. I hope he feels what I feel, this earth-shattering, heart-melting intimacy. For the first time, I'm full. My heart is full, my mind is at peace, and I'm loved.

I hug him with my legs before letting them relax, loosely holding him. Curling my lips, I bite down on all the words I want to say and instead enjoy the beauty of this moment.

I ruffle my hand through his dark hair, scratching his scalp. His head pops up. *He is gorgeous.*

He studies me for a moment, and then he smiles . "What I'm about to say is without expectation. That means I don't expect you to say it back, and I don't expect you to feel that way for me. If you ever want to say it, I'll be happy to hear it." He tilts my head up and brushes a thumb over my cheek. "Without expectation, without wanting anything in return, I love you."

His smooth lips brush mine. Sweet bliss fills me, clearing away the remaining memories of the past.

Crushing him to me, I meet him kiss for sweet kiss, stroking his tongue languidly with mine until he breaks our contact.

His smile brightens as he shifts, and I let go so he can get up. He disappears into the bathroom and comes back with a washcloth.

"You don't have to...I can do..."

He doesn't let me finish, just pushes my legs open and cleans me, and then he's gone again. I roll onto my stomach as I wait for him to come back to my side.

Standing beside the bed, he smacks my bottom, the sting playful, then holds his hand out. My heart leaps to my throat.

Is he expecting the words back? Do I feel that way about him? Holy shit. Holy shit. Holy shit. I tremble. My vision blurs. I might.

My heart sputters, dropping into my gut. It was the perfect thing for him to say, but me not saying "I love you" back makes me ache.

Hopping off the bed, I throw myself into his arms. His laughter is contagious, and I let it pour through me, washing away the ache of holding back words. Letting it delight me, dizzying me as he catches me effortlessly.

He always catches me, whether I know it or not. He's a rock—a foundation that is so resilient.

I plant my hands on his cheeks as he cups my ass in his hands, his palms lifting me off the floor. I pull him close and kiss him, my lips lingering on his as he laughs.

His stomach growls.

I laugh at the sound. "Hungry?"

His beard tickles my skin as he carries me around. Smiling, I squeal and hold on as he bounces us back onto the bed.

Settling on top of me, he smiles. "Yeah, I'm hungry." His lips trail down my chin, his tongue licking me as I laugh. "I'm so hungry, Kit. Feed me, baby."

I close my eyes, enjoying the tickle of his beard as he moves down my body.

He loves me.

Twenty-Seven

Greer

"Tell me again how long weird stuff has been happening." I bite into an apple while sitting at my table. She flits around my kitchen, cooking spaghetti. Her red hair is in a ponytail, and her curvy body is in one of my white shirts and a pair of sweats so big, she had to roll them at the waist.

"I'm not sure. When I got back from the cabin, my front door was unlocked, but Mom had been in and thought she hadn't shut it properly." Her movements turn short and jerky as she rubs the back of her neck.

"But you don't think it was her?"

She shakes her head.

"Anything else?"

She looks down at the pot while she stirs, a red flush creeping up her neck. "I've had the feeling of being watched a few times, but there's never anyone there. Other than the lilies, there hasn't been any..." She pauses. Her face pales, and she freezes.

"Kit?"

She blinks, focusing on my face. "Someone took a box of belongings I was going to give to charity."

"Do you know when?"

"I'm not sure. I had it in my kitchen. The only thing in it so far was a dress that I thought I had gotten rid of once already."

My heart stutters. Someone may have been in her home.

"The other day, when I was leaving work, I thought I heard Ethan laughing. I thought it was one of the doctors, but I couldn't shake the feeling of being watched after that. It wasn't until I left the car garage that it faded away."

And then there was the guy who showed up at her house. "Did the guy who ran out of fuel look familiar at all?"

She scrunches her brows together as she thinks, setting noodles in a pot of boiling water.

She points to the French bread. "Would you cut and butter that, please? I'll throw it under the broiler. The garlic butter is over there."

I set about my task. "So...the guy."

"Right. I don't think he looked familiar, but there are a lot of unknown faces when you're back home. Do you think we need to be worried about him?"

"I don't know, Kit. But if you're okay with it, I could have Maddox and Asher dig into the guy. I can call Maddox tonight." I finish slathering garlic butter on the last piece, and she takes the cookie sheet from me.

She frowns but nods, and I go sit on the other side of the counter, pulling out my phone to dial him.

He picks up on the third ring. "Greer. Hey, man, what's up?"

"Hey, we need your help." I spend the next few minutes briefly going over her piece of shit husband, the box, the car garage, and everything that has happened that might be useful.

"Is she okay?"

"Yes, we are checking in on things."

"Do you have a name or plates or anything from the guy at the house?"

There is a whirring in the background of what I assume is his computer starting up. And then a furious typing of keys. He has the longest password ever.

"I took a picture of his license plate while standing out there. I'll send it over."

"How'd you get it without him noticing?"

"I liked the grill on his vehicle; it sparked some ideas. I took it when he and the other guy were filling up his tank. Hold on."

"What's his name? I'll look that up too."

"John Wilson."

He types furiously in the background while laughing. "Fuck, Greer, do you know how many people have that name? I'm not going to get much of anything off that, but I'll look into it and the license plate number. What did he look like?"

"Brown eyes and half a nose is all I can tell you because the rest was covered. He was bundled up."

Another round of furious typing and a moment or two of silence.

"Well, unfortunately, the car was stolen. And without more information to go on, I'm afraid I have little on John Wilson."

Every dead end is erasing the relaxed energy we've had. There are too many things happening for them to all be coincidences.

"She got lilies today from a random person; they are...They have significant meaning to her past. Only her dead husband would have known about them."

She glances at me with a worried look, and I wink to let her know that's all I'll say. I can't take my attention off her as she turns back to the stove to pull out the bread.

"I can search him and see what I find."

"He disappeared three years ago in Brazil."

"That helps. I can go from there. Has she received any threatening messages, phone calls, anything?"

"Nothing. Other than the implied ones with the lilies."

"What about people she knows back in California?"

"I'll let you talk to Kit. She can tell you about them." I pull the phone away from my ear. "He wants to know about the people you knew in California. Can you give Mad their full names and any info you think might be relevant?"

She nods, wringing her hands. "Why do we have to check them?"

"We're covering everyone who knows you."

"No one knew about the lilies. Ethan is dead. He has to be, but it can't be anyone else. How can it be anyone else?"

"I don't know, love, but we have to check everything. Maddox?"

"Hmm, lover boy?"

Fuck. I should have hired a different firm to do all this for us. Maddox is the worst gossip in the group sometimes.

"Here's Kit; be nice."

She puts the phone to her ear and introduces herself to Maddox. She laughs, her belly chuckle one, and it makes me smile—even if I'm not the one making her laugh, I want to hear it all the time.

"Mm-hmm."

Damn it, her cheeks are turning pink. What the actual fuck is he saying to her? He can be more of a flirt than Simon. I strain to listen but can't hear anything over the buzz of the refrigerator.

"I don't know. That's not a compelling argument." Her eyes shine, the green turning a deep emerald. "Maybe, one day, if...Oh my god. Stop." Her laughter is deep and joyful.

I smirk as she covers her mouth with her hand. "Tell him to shut it and get to the good stuff."

She covers the mouthpieces and whispers conspiratorially. "He says this is the good stuff."

I reach for the phone and pull it away from her ear.

"—and he wet the bed until he was thirteen. That should be reason enough to dump him and go out with me."

For fuck's sake. I scrub my hand down my face. "You don't even know what she looks like. So shut it. Now take the names and leave us alone."

"Damn, Greer. You are testy. When do I get to meet her? Or are you afraid she'll dump you for the better brother?"

"I'll text you the info. Goodbye, Maddox."

"No, I'll be good. Hand her back, and I'll be good. Scout's honor." Mad is stifling a laugh on the other end of the line.

I hand the phone back. "You should mention the brother, Liam."

"Do you think we need to?"

"They might be watching him as well." Or he could be the watcher.

"Francesca said Colette and Liam didn't get along. Yeah, good idea."

She relays the information, and then she's silent again. Seconds, then minutes pass as I watch her face twist in horror, and then her laughter erupts. I grab the phone back.

I should have put it on speakerphone.

"—two pumps, and then he's done. I've seen it with my own eyes."

What a fucker. Seriously. Next time I see him, I'm strangling him. "Mad, find your own fucking woman."

"Ooh, I've got plenty to keep me company. I like teasing, you know. But, seriously, Greer, if you need help with the sex department—"

"For the love of fucking Pete. Shut it, Maddox. She's plenty happy with...that."

"That. Oh, Greer, I knew it." He practically crows.

"Bye, Maddox." I end the call and put my phone down before looking up at Kit.

"He sounds fun."

"Yeah, he and Simon are a riot together. Trying to get a reaction out of me is their favorite thing."

"Will I get to meet them?"

I would love for her to meet my family, but I wasn't sure she was ready. "You want to?"

She nods enthusiastically.

Now that she's said it, the deep desire for her to meet them courses through me. "Just know that I can't promise they'll be on their best behavior. In fact, I can guarantee that at least one of them will say something inappropriate."

"They sound great." Her cheeks are pink again, and she's biting her lips to keep the smile off her face. Damn, she fills me with peace. My whole body is relaxed for once. Actually, I haven't been restless or twitchy since the moment I got my hands on her.

"Would you want to come to Christmas?"

She gets thoughtful and stares at me for a moment. "I'm not sure when my parents celebrate, but I'll check. If it works out, I'd love to come." She places a plate in front of me.

Moaning at my first bite of spaghetti and meatballs, I point at it. "What's in the sauce?"

"It's a secret." She settles next to me and pours a glass of wine for both of us.

"Ah, I see. I'll have to teach you mine so you can teach me yours." Sliding my hand behind her neck, I pull her close and brush my lips against hers. "I like that." I kiss her gently before pulling back and digging into my spaghetti. "Tell me about Francesca. Who is she?"

"Ethan's mistress."

I barely stop my jaw from dropping. What a fucking piece of shit. Somehow, I'm not surprised by this. "I'm sorry, Kit." How anyone could cheat on this woman is a mystery to me.

Her smile is sweet as she pokes at her spaghetti. "He had a secret life with another woman and a child he never got to meet. His daughter's name is Harper, and she is about three now. She's brilliant, like all children her age. When he died, she was left with nothing."

"So you left her with something." Her soul is far too gentle to have left them with nothing. She would have watched out for a mother and a tiny kid.

"I'm working on it. I sold our house or whatever it's called. You know, the penthouse of a building. There is enough for me to live off for years. I don't have to work, but I want to. I want to do something for Harper, though, too. Maybe give her half or something, but keep it in a trust fund until she's eighteen."

"You hardly know them, and you'd give them half?"

She shrugs and looks my way. "I have the money from the house I sold and our accounts, and Harper has nothing. She was part of him and deserves something." She slurps up a noodle the same way I did, grinning the entire time.

"Who's running the business now?"

She toys with her fork, swirling it in another pile of spaghetti. "Colette oversees everything, but I guess his business partners or a board of directors? I'm not entirely sure what he did or if he even had a partner, but..." She shrugs. "It was some company that handled big corporations, so I imagine he had a board."

"What about Colette? Does she run them?"

"I don't see her having any active interest in them. Most of the time, she attends charities and galas. She might only be the face of the company, not actually do work." She shrugs as if it's completely normal that she didn't know what he did.

It makes my skin crawl. "Did she know about his abuse?"

Her smile falls. She shakes her head. "I don't think so. Maybe suspected. But she never said anything. Ethan was charming and knew how to hurt me without leaving bruises—well, never where people could see them, anyway."

They may have been hidden, but now that I know about the scars—emotional and physical—they linger in my mind. Her alone in her house, a target for that psycho; she's not safe.

She'd be safer with me.

If something happened to her, if I didn't make it there in time, that would be an agony worse than the most painful death.

My stomach twists. "Will you stay with me until we can figure this out?"

"No, I'm not going to run or hide."

"You won't be. You'll be with me. Safe."

"Greer, I spent my whole marriage allowing someone else to decide for me. I won't let you. You care about me, I know that. I care about you too. But I'm going to make the tough decision and prove I'm stronger than I was before. I won't be that person ever again."

"That's not what I'm trying to do, Kit. I don't want to make your decisions. But I want to know you are safe. What if I get Maddox to have a few of his workers patrol outside?"

She scrunches her eyes shut, her shoulders hunching as she shakes her head. "I don't want to feel like I can't be in my own home."

"That's not what this is about. No one is running you out. We're just making sure it's safe."

She hesitates for a moment before responding. "And only Maddox or his group?"

I nod. Please say yes. Please say yes, because I won't take away her decisions, but I'll be sick with worry. Every. Fucking. Day.

She wrings her hands together for a moment before she realizes she's doing it and forces her hands down. "And that will make you feel better?"

"Immensely. Please, Kit. I'm not telling you, I'm asking. You can say no, and we will go on as we have been." *And I'll worry.*

She smiles and finally nods.

Kit

A squeal hits me, and I'm engulfed by the slim arms of a woman who is a smidge shorter than me. She's bubbly, bright, and sweet. His little sister, I'm guessing.

Greer laughs as he shoves her off me. "Violet, let her breathe."

My stomach tightens, and my heart races. She's too close. Too loud, too cheerful. It's almost suffocating. I want to get away from this wild excitement.

I might be healing well, but these are all people I don't know, and having her up in my space is overwhelming at the moment. It's been easy to relax around my family and Greer, but being around other people is always tricky at first.

She bounces on her toes, waiting. The ball in my stomach compresses to an almost glass consistency—heavy and hard in my gut as I wait for her arms to come back around me.

Space, I need some space.

Greer growls and gives her a stern look. "Give her some space. Let her get used to us."

A blush creeps up my neck, blasting my cheeks, and I try to hide it. Greer grabs my hand to pull me in, and I tuck my face into his shoulder for a moment. Something presses against my head and lingers—like a kiss.

When I move back, someone grabs my free hand, and I'm being pulled somewhere else. When I look up, it's Violet who's pulling me into another room. I'd be panicking, but Greer's behind me, my other hand tangled in his, keeping me grounded in the moment by rubbing his thumb over mine. I peek behind me, and his smile is sweet and relaxed.

I can relax. So I do, smiling back at him, then he nods before leaning in. His voice low, so only I can hear. "I got you, Red."

Yes, he does. But I'm strong—or at least learning to be. Turning back to the kitchen, I'm ill-prepared for the awe that is Virginia's kitchen.

It's enormous, a true chef's kitchen. Two stoves, two ranges, and a huge refrigerator. And it's comfy, cozy, and sweet with gray and white walls and cabinets with glass doors.

It's beautiful and, much like Greer, calming.

"Violet? Can you make sure the table is set, dear?" The short woman's voice is smooth and melodic as she stands at the sink.

"Sure! Hey, Mom, look who's here." With that, she lets me go and is gone, out the doorway where there is a loud hum of noise.

His mom turns. Dang, she's beautiful. I see where Violet gets the blond hair, petite body, and excitement.

"Kit!"

I jump as Greer's mom rushes toward me, taking my free hand in hers. It's warm and gentle but strong as she grips it. "I've heard so much about you. I'm Virginia, but everyone calls me Mom or Ginny." *Shit, woman. Real subtle.*

Her eyes—the same color as Greer's—sparkle. Her brows arch the same way too. It looks like those are the only things he got from her, though.

Leaning down, he whispers, "I'd be happy with you calling her either." *Did he propose?* Because I can't call her Mom unless we are married. *Do I want to get married again? Shit on a biscuit, push those thoughts away.*

He shifts closer to me, enveloping me in his warmth and happiness.

Virginia beams at us. "Merry Christmas!" She leans in and kisses Greer's cheek, then wraps us both up in a hug. She looks so blissful, but there's still a bit of a tear that lingers. "Come in, come in. Let me take your coat. Go to the living room and introduce her to everyone."

With a palm on one of Greer's cheeks, Ginny pulls him down so she can kiss his other. When she walks away, Greer turns back to me. "I think she likes you."

That's a lot of pressure. What if one day she doesn't like me, or I break his heart, or worse—he gets hurt because of me? I swallow the lump in my throat as Greer turns back to me. It's so much. They are so full, so brimming with life, while I'm still learning what makes life work.

She walks ahead of us, and he grabs my hand, pulling me back a moment. Big, powerful arms wrap around me, locking me in place pleasantly.

"You're tense. Do you want to go?"

I tuck my head into his neck. "No, it's okay. But I need a minute or two."

He nods, his nose brushing against my neck. He settles his hands at my hips, his thumbs digging in and finding a knot I didn't know I had.

He inhales deeply, scenting me. "You always smell so good." His breath puffs against my neck, and I shiver.

Calm, girl. You're at Christmas with his family. No need to think about jumping his delicious bones. Heat rises up my cheeks.

"What are you thinking about?"

"Stop it. You're making this incredibly hard."

His hands slide down my hips to the swell of my ass. "I'll give you something hard."

Laughter bubbles out.

Amateur. Those innuendoes have got nothing on me. He presses his hips into mine. *Oh, but that is delicious.* Now I'm hot and bothered and ready to head back to the car. A quick moment in the car where I can ride him fast and hard and–

He lets go abruptly, swinging his hand around to grab mine.

He's leading me into his life with open arms, and I'm falling so readily. No doubts that he'll catch me and keep me safe.

"Greer." His dad saunters over. They would be twins if not for his hazel eyes and softer brows.

"Hey, Dad, this is Kit." Greer's arms stay wrapped around me, a perfect cocoon. "Kit, this is my dad, Ed."

Ed holds his hand out, and I slide mine into it.

"It's a pleasure to meet you."

Then Greer is taking me to meet everyone else who is here.

Simon is in a constant state of merriment. He never seems serious. And he keeps adjusting his man bun like it's a badge of honor or something. Man buns. I chuckle a bit at that. His son, Theo, is climbing all over him like a monkey, with the same dark hair and eyes.

Maddox is fun-loving but also rigid, if that's possible. He cracks a lot of jokes, but he hides a lot behind his teasing.

Han is calm. His family is from Georgia, his parents are from Korea, and he's like a goofy little kid.

He smiles my way before telling me more about himself. "My wife and kids are back in Georgia right now. I'd be there, but my father-in-law hates me." He laughs, not at all perturbed by this. We chat a little longer, and then Greer steers me over to his other brother and Violet.

Asher is quiet but seems smart with his quick responses. The tortoise-shell glasses don't hurt, either. He and Violet hang out in the corner. Violet is as bubbly as Ginny. A mini-Ginny, actually.

"We're missing two. My brother Harrison is currently in prison, and that is kind of a long story. But I can assure you he's the best guy you will ever meet. And then Troy. He's out on assignment right now. He's quiet and takes things in. Troy and Han are the two I told you about—our siblings from another mother, honorary Winters. They were a part of Maddox's crew when he was in the military."

It's a whirlwind as we move around the room, talking and chatting to people, and before I know it, dinner is served and cleaned up.

We're all sitting at the table and I'm stuffed to the brim when someone throws down an UNO deck, and the words pop out. "That's cute. You guys play UNO on Christmas."

Maddox laughs maniacally. "Oh, sweet stuff, we don't play UNO. We play Winter's UNO."

Right, Greer mentioned it.

"You don't have to play if you don't want to." Greer sits me on his lap as the rest of the group gathers around, taking chairs and making sure there is space.

Maddox throws out his elbow, hitting Violet. "Move, Violet, or you're going to run to Mom crying when you get a black eye."

Are you serious? I whip my head to Greer. "Should I grab my med bag? I'm sure I can scrounge up an Ativan." I bring my anxiety meds everywhere, though I haven't used any since Greer started sleeping over.

"Who needs Ativan?" Maddox cuts in. "Not me. No, she knows the rules. Stay out of my way or don't play."

Holy shit. He's serious.

Violet laughs, then glares at him good-natured. "It's on, pea brain."

Maddox shakes his hands, pretending to be scared. "Ooh, I'm terrified."

What is wrong with these people that the threat of violence makes them giddy?

"It gets intense, sorry." Greer pulls me closer. "Maddox has been champion the last few years. It's a sore spot for Asher."

Asher looks up, glaring at Greer.

Greer raises his chin, his voice traveling in Asher's direction. "Hey, I'm not going to lie to save your feelings."

"So what are the rules?" I pick up the cards I'm dealt.

Greer wraps his hands around mine, shielding my cards from spying eyes.

"Oh, we are intense, aren't we?"

"Honey, you have no idea." Simon throws down another card, and it slides my way. "Have you played UNO?"

I nod. Of course. Almost every child of my generation has.

"This is nothing like that. We play by normal rules but with a few extras thrown in."

That's when I notice the stack of cards is at least three times the size of a normal UNO deck.

"Maybe I should sit this one out?"

Simon slowly grins at me, his brow up and his gaze intense. "It's now or never. You in or out?"

I turn to Greer, who is staring at me with a blank face, but his eyes say it all. This is more than UNO, more than a game. He wants to know how much I'm going to invest in this. Something he's never asked, never pushed for. But with Simon saying it, he doesn't have to. He simply has to wait for the answer.

The room is quiet as I study Greer. Too quiet. I look back, and they are all watching me. Warmth sneaks up my cheeks.

"Well, which is it?" Asher pipes up.

I turn back to Greer, who's still smoldering.

I give him a small, hopeful smile. "I'm in."

He settles a hand over my neck and pulls me in for a kiss, brushing his lips to mine, not caring that his family is watching. They hoot and holler, but then it's silent when Greer deepens the kiss. Tightening his grip, he holds me in place while he stakes his claim on me.

When Greer finally pulls back, he drops his head to mine, and we both try to slow our ragged breaths. Heat colors my cheeks. His whole family is watching. I should be mortified, but instead, I'm so turned on for this man, I have to stop myself from pulling him out to the car.

"Find a room."

"Not mine, please."

"I'm ready to finish explaining the rules."

He smiles, dispelling my embarrassment. "They sure know how to kill a moment, don't they?"

Laughter erupts from me, and I look back. "Okay, I'm ready to play. I'm warning you, though, once I get the rules down, that crown is coming off, Maddox."

The room quiets, and surprised faces turn to Maddox, who watches me. My heart races. *Shit, did I say the wrong thing?*

Then everyone laughs, and comments fly from every direction.

"She's gunning for you, Mad."

"Holy hell, are you ready?"

"Shit, Mad. I can't wait to see your face when you lose."

Greer hugs me close and leans down to whisper in my ear. "You better beat him now because there is no way in hell you can live that down."

I bite my lip, smiling as the rest of the cards are dealt while Simon explains the rules. Standard UNO rules, plus extras thrown in.

Twenty minutes later, I've got two cards left, and Asher plays a red card. *Hell yes!* I lay down my red draw two, holding it there for a split second before screaming, "UNO!" A chorus of Unos rises as I pull back, but I've beaten them all.

Everyone groans, especially Maddox. I give him a moment, waiting as he draws two cards. Ed, who's next to him, gets ready to lay down his card, but I invoke Winter's UNO rule two, slamming down the second draw two.

I wait a moment, biting the smile off my face.

The aftermath is a whirl. Maddox demands a rematch. Someone slaps Greer on the back. People jump and shout and cheer. Pulling my head to him, Greer kisses me.

Furiously.

Madly.

Lovingly.

When we finally come up for air, the room is silent and empty. My heart is so full, it wants to burst. Is this what love feels like? Happiness is being lost in the moment. Love is feeling like you're going to burst. I want to say those three big words but hold back. I'm not ready, even if his whole body says I can. "What's next?"

"It's probably time to open presents."

We head to the living room, and I settle on one of the many couches. With a family this big, they need a few.

A group of them are fiddling with the TV, hooking up some old cam-corder. "What are they doing?"

Simon is almost gleeful as he connects wires and winks at Greer. Greer groans. "Whatever you see on that video, I was ten. I had no excuse to get out of it."

"Shhh, shhh, everyone, find a spot."

Once everyone is settled, Simon stands up. "We are starting a new Christmas tradition. We have to watch *A Christmas Story*."

Damn, I hate that movie. I look at Greer, who has his brow cocked, an unimpressed look on his face.

He growls. "Really? This year you start the tradition? Fuck you, get on with it."

"Ooh, testy." Simon winks at me. "Don't worry, next year you'll get to see the one where I'm the star."

"Sex tapes are not Christmas appropriate." Maddox quips.

"Hardy har har." Simon groans.

I lean into Greer, looking up. His arms wrap around me. "I thought you said presents."

"Usually it is."

For the next thirty minutes, we watch a school play that is indeed a version of *A Christmas Story* with Greer as the lead. It's adorable and freaking wonderful to see him playful like this as a kid too.

Greer trips on-screen unintentionally, and everyone laughs. He pops up, yelling, *I'm okay*, and the show continues.

This happens a few more times until I realize Maddox and Simon were in the background moving the rug so when he walked, he tripped. It's plain as day on the screen.

Stinkers.

When that is over, everyone laughs, moving into groups and talking until Ginny stands and waves her arms around.

"I have been informed by my wonderful grandson that it's time to open presents."

There is a whirlwind as presents are handed out and everyone chats.

Christmas Eve with my family was quiet and relaxed yesterday. And Greer had fit in easily because he knew almost everyone anyway. It was effortless. Kind of like my family. Surprisingly, they didn't make a big deal out of it. I thought it would be twenty questions and lots of comments about me moving on too quickly, but no one raised a brow when I mentioned he was coming.

It was exactly what I needed—a completely calm Christmas.

Where my family is quiet and more reserved, Greer's is loud and chaotic and always in each other's business. I kind of like that, the way they know each other so well.

It's two different Christmases, but they are both wonderful. It all blooms in my soul, creating a little bubble that wants to burst in a good way.

Ginny hands me a beautifully wrapped gift box, her sweet smile touching my heart. "I hope you like it." She winks and then hands more presents out.

Greer nods at it. "Why do you get a bow on yours, but mine is still wrapped in old funnies?"

I laugh.

"Go ahead. You don't have to wait here. Once Mom hands it out, it's a free-for-all."

I rip open the paper and pull out a box holding a beautiful silver chain bracelet. There's a lobster and a tree attached to individual links. A note sticks out of the box. *To making memories.*

A charm bracelet to hold the memories.

I fight back my sudden tears. When they are defeated, I look around the room, taking it all in. The Christmas tree is decorated simply and bright in the open room. Everyone is laughing and ripping into their gifts. They are all so blissful, deliriously joyful. It bubbles inside me, wanting to break. *Shit, the tears are back.*

Grabbing Greer's hand for a moment, I squeeze it. "I'll be back."

In the bathroom, I shut the door gently and sit on the toilet. My heart is stuffed, as is my head. Christmas hasn't been this way in so long. Every year I spent it with Colette, and while it was sweet, it wasn't filled with love the way it is here or with my family. It was always a show to people around her.

This year has been full of changes.

It's perfect.

This Christmas, I've spent time with family, laughing, loving, and living in the moment. Not having to worry if my hair was out of place or if my makeup was smudged or if the dress was too tight.

Everything has shown me what it means to be surrounded by people who love and accept me.

That's what started the tears—the exponential love that I've been given not only from my own family but by Greer's too. These people barely know me, but because Greer is important to them, I'm important to them too.

I've been accepted for every piece of me, perfect or not.

It's more than I thought was possible when I came back here.

It's so much more.

A soft tap sounds at the door. "Love?"

"Yeah?" Now he's here, checking in on me instead of being with his family. He slips in. His brows knit as he shuts the door, and he drops onto his heels in front of me. I spread my legs so he can scoot in.

"What's wrong, love?" He cups my cheeks and wipes away the tears.

"Nothing. Absolutely nothing is wrong." The tears are falling harder, and I laugh and shrug. My breakdown is confusing to him; it's as plain as day on his face. I put my hands over his and drop my forehead until his dark jeans line my vision.

I can't name these emotions because I know I'm not ready. If I look into his eyes, I'll see his heart on display, and I'll freak out.

So I settle for sharing a less intense emotion. My voice trembles but I get it out. "I'm so happy, Greer. I didn't think I'd ever feel this way again. This is more than I ever could have hoped for. I feel safe, adored, whole." My shoulders shake, and sobs form. I don't know what the hell is wrong with me.

Seriously, I'm so happy.

Palms on my hips, he pulls me down. Then he scoots backward to the opposite wall and leans against it, holding me. His hands move up and down my back. Mine twine around his neck as I sob into it. He peppers the crown of my head with kisses, and that moves me more. This marvel of a man is so big and rough and deep, and he loves me.

Another tap sounds at the door.

"Yeah?" His deep, rumbly voice vibrates against my cheek.

"Is she okay, honey?" Ginny's voice is sweet and soft with concern.

"Yeah, Mom. We're taking a moment to be happy."

I laugh, snorting through the snot of my ugly crying. He rubs up and down my back, soothing me. His chest rumbles, jostling me when he laughs too. I want to stay here forever, but after a while, I'm better and put back together.

He stands, helping me up. His lips come down to nibble, his mouth telling me how much it means to him that I'm here. I hope he can tell how much it means to me too.

He opens the door, and everyone crowded around in the hallway scatters like they weren't there. Suddenly, there's talk about random things from everyone at once.

Everyone except Ginny. She pulls me into her embrace, hugging me gently, then kisses my cheek softly. Her whisper is for my ears only. "Thank you, Kit."

The rest of the evening is spent *oohing* and *ahhing* over everyone's gift while I swipe my hand over the chains of mine. Eventually, Theo falls asleep, and Simon ushers him upstairs, and people get their jackets on or make their way to the door.

My body stays attuned to Greer as we make rounds, my hand tucked in his. The hum inside me is pleasant and blissful from the evening and in anticipation of the rest of the night.

On the car ride to his place, I can't keep myself off him.

We rush into the house, and he pushes me against the door, scrambling to get our clothes off. Over and over, he worships me with his lips, his hands, and his body. I try to show him what my heart screams but can't say.

This is the best Christmas I've ever had.

Thank you for bringing me into your family.

I'm happy, safe, home.

I love you.

January

Twenty-Eight

Greer

"ARE YOU SURE THIS is the movie you want?"

She nods, though her hand is wrapped around my arm tightly. Instead of watching the ball drop last night, we stayed in making love. And tonight we picked a movie. "Red, we haven't even started it, and you are already tense. Are you absolutely sure you want to do this?"

I pick up the movie we were supposed to see on our first date. I have no idea why she wants to do this, other than to prove to herself that she can without another attack. She's trying to be brave, trying to force herself to stop reacting to her triggers. It'll take time, but if it were left up to me, I'd say fuck it and move on to a different movie. I have half a mind to chuck it in the garbage.

"Have you ever seen *Spaceballs*?"

"Yep, I've seen it. And no, I'm not sure I want to, but I also don't want to live in fear that we'll pick another movie that will send me off my rocker."

"Okay, but we don't have to do this tonight. We can do it another night." Or years from now, when the love I give has firmly solidified in her mind that she's safe.

She sighs. "I don't want to."

Kissing her head, I nod. "When you're ready, let me know, and we can try it."

She looks up at me, grabbing my cheek to pull me in. I zero in on her mouth. Her fucking delicious mouth. Our lips move and tangle until she finally comes up for air.

My phone buzzes, vibrating obnoxiously in my pocket.

"Don't answer it."

I pull it out, and *Maddox* flashes across the screen, turning it so she can see his name. "He might report something."

She smiles, nodding. "Water?"

"Sure." Accepting the call, I put it on speakerphone. "Hey, Maddox."

"Hey, Greer, you with Kit?"

She hands me a water bottle and uncaps her own. "I'm here." She takes a swig and then settles back next to me.

"I've got a few guys who can monitor the place. Sorry it took a few extra days. I had to wait for them to get back from their assignment."

"No worries, I've had a guard animal here the whole time I was waiting."

"Yeah, a big Doberman?"

"Naw, a colossal bear." She winks at me, then leans in to kiss me. Her voice is soft, for my ears only. "I like you big and growly."

His laughter pings through the phone. "She fits in great, Greer. I'll have Roman and Troy come by starting tomorrow."

Good, that makes my insides less volatile. I hate having her here alone, so I've been sleeping over every night, kind of like normal. And really, she hasn't minded, thank goodness. I worry about her when we are apart.

"Troy is the one I was telling you about at Christmas." I sip my water, then place it on the end table.

Maddox chimes in. "Yeah, if you thought Greer was quiet, Troy is stoic. He doesn't talk much because he likes to blend in with the crowd and watch. He's a perfect ghost."

"Mad brought Troy and Han home when he left the military..."

"And Mom took to them. Troy doesn't really have anyone. Han has his family but sticks with Troy on missions."

I shrug but nod. "What about Roman?"

"He's a good friend. I'd trust him with my life, Kit. You are in excellent hands. I can vouch for all the men I hired, having been with them in the worst situations."

"Maddox has brought a few of them around. They are all great guys."

Maddox chuckles. "They are. Okay, on to other things. I found Ethan's brother, Liam."

My pulse stops for a moment, and Kit's hand slips into mine, squeezing.

Maddox continues. "His birth certificate says his parents are Walter Finney and Clair Ernst. Liam is still in California. I have a contact out west who is looking into him more. I only had time to find that, but he'll be able to do more while I work on other things."

Kit drops her head to my chest and when I wrap my arm around her, she relaxes a little. "Thanks for everything so far, Maddox. You've spent a lot of time on this."

"Oh, I'm not done. I rechecked the license plate on that car to see if anything else came up. The car was found in an abandoned lot, set ablaze. When they ran it for prints, it was wiped clean."

He waits, letting that all sink in. Kit frowns, looking up at me. "If they wiped everything down, then they knew..."

Maddox finishes for her. "What they were doing? Yes, most likely the person who stole the car is a professional—cop, military, or private investigator."

"That or they watch a lot of *CSI* or *Forensic Files*."

I chuckle a moment. It's true, though, they either know what they're doing, or they know enough to be dangerous. That cuts my chuckle off instantly.

This *is* dangerous; we know that.

I can only guess that John Wilson was a fake name. Needing reassurance, I hug Kit closer to me. She's safe right now, here in my arms. "Did you find anything out on John Wilson?"

"Nothing, which makes me think it was a bogus name. And I have nothing else to look for with him."

I clench my jaw as the churning starts.

"Asher looked into the accounts for Ethan. His personal accounts flagged nothing for him, but he's digging into the accounts for the financial firm he owned."

Kit sits up. "Stocks and portfolios, that sort of thing? I knew it was a financial firm, but he kept me in the dark about everything."

"Yeah, exactly that sort of thing."

She looks back at me, shaking her head, questioning. "At least it wasn't something bad."

"I wouldn't say that. So far, he's only dug into a few of the accounts. What he's found wouldn't flag an investigation, but it's enough to make me suspicious." Maddox sighs into the phone.

He sounds tired.

She scrunches her brow, her body curling into me.

"A few of the accounts are moving money, trickling, but it's to at least fifty accounts in Brazil. Asher is trying to find out where the money trail is leading. He's getting closer."

Money has a trail, and if it's buried that deep, there must be more than a few people involved. My gut tightens.

Whoever is harassing Kit might be more than her husband. Maybe someone thinks she knows something she doesn't. Ice burns through me. "What does that mean?"

Maddox continues. "Money laundering, or worse. If it's innocent, then it's clients who are picking their own investments."

"Worse? Are you thinking shady investments or insider trading?" Kit's working through everything, trying to connect the dots.

But she's thinking too easy, not looking dark or deep enough. I lay it all out there. "Worse like drug dealers, cartels, or weapons."

Her face is a myriad of expressions, and she gasps. "Or sex workers. Those poor women."

Maddox jumps in. "Yeah, exactly. The list is limitless for where the money is from, and unfortunately, that includes people. Ash says the trail is buried so deep that it's taking a while to weed through it all, but he's going to find it."

Kit looks at the phone quick. "Thank you for doing all this."

I kiss her head. "It's what they do, love."

Maddox speaks again. "You're welcome. Last thing, my contact says there is a lot of talk on the streets. People are missing, more than the usual runaway, and the whispers say that Ethan has something to do with it. We can trace one missing person to an account he serviced, and Ash is waiting on names to check the rest. Be careful."

"And we have no idea who it could be, unless you have a list of his clients?"

"Unfortunately, no, but I'm working on it."

We say goodbye and then click off.

The television still flickers in the background, the glows reflecting off her face. She lets out a long exhale and then stands to pace. Raising to my feet, I stand by her, brushing her hand as she passes.

She looks up at me and then steps into my arms, her head dropping to my shoulder.

"This is so much, everything. I feel like I'm putting you in danger, Greer."

I nod against her because there isn't a lot I can do. "I'm safe. And I'll do my best to keep you safe. I got you. I won't let him get to you. We're sticking together."

She pulls me closer, wrapping her arms around me.

"We're safe, Kit. Maddox and his crew are watching. If anyone comes, we'll know."

Twenty-Nine

Greer

IF I HAVE TO yell at Simon one more time to get his stuff to me, I'm firing him. Not that I can, but it's a nice thought. It's been a week already, and I'm missing the design inquiry for the next project.

Where last month my desk was chaotically messy—like my insides—now it's clear, and everything is put away nicely.

Everything in my life right now fits.

I glance at the clock. I've got until five to finish this, and then I'll shut things down for the day.

Fuck, I hope Kit likes this hiking spot. Who knew she'd love hiking? She's pretty fucking miraculous.

It's easy with her. The way we laugh and love. And the urge to take care of her as much as she takes care of me.

Simon knocks on the door and then steps inside.

"Well, I found it in...never mind, you don't want to know where I found it." Simon slaps down a folder on my desk, glancing around and taking it all in. "What happened in here? For the last six months, this office has been a hovel."

Without preamble, I snatch up the folder and flip through it, grabbing the page I need.

"Seriously, what happened?" Simon flops in the chair in front of me and slouches back lazily, feet out and crossed.

"I'm not sure what you're talking about."

"Really? Because it looks like Mom came through here and ripped you a new one for leaving dirty cleats on the floor."

I chuckle at that visual. Yeah, Mom is a terror when she wants to be. "I've felt more focused and collected."

I set aside the graphics in the folder, styles that the Mertins want for their home. Classic with a twist. I can work with this.

Simon is awfully quiet. I glance up at him, waiting for him to say something.

"Is she the reason you don't work late anymore?"

That stops me. Because honestly, I hadn't thought of it that way. But if I had to say what makes me more vigilant of my time? Yeah, it's Kit.

I still have the drive to work hard. I think that's evident in my work. But I'm happy to let the day end at five. The urge to get back to her as fast as possible makes me work more efficiently.

My priorities have changed, and it all stems from a little meeting outside of a gas station months ago.

He is still waiting for an answer, so I nod. "Work was my staple before Kit. I needed to have something solid to stand on before starting a family. Now..."

"Now you are happy and realize that life is best lived in emotional chaos."

"Yeah, something like that. This business is doing great. It's not going anywhere. I still want to work hard, but..." I shrug at him, smiling. "I want Kit more. I love her."

He beams at me. The twin bond is like nothing else. He gets me, even when I was being a driven, hard bastard.

"Where are you taking her tonight?"

"Hiking."

"To the spot?"

"Yes."

Simon gets up, smiling like a freaking loon, then heads out the door.

Kit grabs my hand, and I pull her up gently. This part of the hike is especially rocky, but the way the ocean looks when we get to the top will be worth it.

"I can see the top. We're almost there."

"This is a serious trek." Her voice is lyrical, soft, and so happy. I'm doing that—adding to the joy.

"It can be. It's more snowy than usual, but I promise when we get to the top..."

"Right, you're going to tell me all your secrets."

"Every one." I kiss the top of her head, pulling her into me.

She loops her arms around my neck. "Tell me again why we're wearing headlamps."

"So we don't break our necks on the way back."

Fuck, I'm so blessed to have her here with me in this moment.

When we are almost on the cusp, I stop her. "I want you to close your eyes."

She gives me a skeptical look, and I watch her war with herself before she nods, doing what I asked with her hand held out.

A ripple of warmth radiates from my chest. That thought lights me up, that she can feel me when I'm close. Sense me when she can't see me.

This is by far the most real thing I've ever had with a woman. It's never been this easy, and I've never wanted to bring a woman here. But I was eager and excited for Kit to see this place.

Fuck, she's beautiful, trusting me, cheeks pink, a fucking bonnet-like stocking hat. Her red hair flowing, and that adorable lumberjack coat. She's fucking perfect.

I tug her hand into mine, guiding her up the path.

Energy dances along my skin. I've wanted to share this with her for a while—something that's a piece of me that no one knows about. Other than Simon.

Simon calls it the spot because once we found it, it was our place. It's hidden from the rest of the world unless you know where to look.

295

I tuck us under two enormous trees and turn her so she can face the ocean.

"All right, open." I wrap my arms around her waist, smiling at her gasp.

"Wow, oh wow." She brings both hands to her cheeks while she stares at the view.

I stand beside her, hunching down so my head is level with hers, taking in the sight. Trying to see it through her eyes.

It's getting dark, and the city's lights glow against the water as it churns below us. The moon is half-hidden behind clouds, but it plays off the ocean like magic. The lighthouse I told her about is just visible if we look north and east.

I point it out, and she nods. It's possibly the second most beautiful thing I have ever seen, but it pales compared to Kit.

When I glance at her face, she's in awe, and it stops my heart.

The colors dance as the water moves. It's ethereal and magical, and all the things I forgot I loved about the water. The beauty in its changes, the way it can be calm and forgiving or raging and cagey.

"This is simply amazing." Her honey scent and the ocean salt meld together, and I like it. A lot.

"My dad used to bring us to the beach where we started our hike. Simon and I would explore all around, and one day we found this spot. We marked it so we could remember how to get to it any time of year."

"How old were you?"

"Thirteen. It was a hard year for us, and this place made me forget it sometimes. My family owns a mill; we harvest trees upstate. That year, my granddad died and passed it on to my dad. But there were some stipulations with the will, and Dad ran into financial trouble paying for leans and levies. Granddad hadn't taken care of it like he should have. He took out illegal loans to cover new equipment and repairs."

I swallow, wetting my mouth before I go on. I hadn't planned to tell her about this part of my childhood today, but now that I started, I can't stop. Not that I want to. She should know all my ins and outs.

This place is sacred to me. It's where I figured out what life meant when I was thirteen. It's where I'm discovering how that meaning changes when I have someone that I love.

Deeply.

"Dad borrowed against everything, emptied their savings. It was many years before we could afford something so simple as new shoes. There were weeks when my parents barely ate because they saved it for us kids. We wore hand-me-downs or donations from other families. We scrimped and saved, though Mom would probably argue that we lived lavishly with what little we had. But it hit me how important it is to have something stable for my family."

"When I was fifteen, Simon and I were horsing around and we spilled a whole gallon of milk. Mom cried, though she tried to hide it by rushing to the bedroom. I vowed I'd never put my family in that position."

I clear my throat, squeezing her, needing to get it out so she understands how much she means to me, and how she changed me too. "Simon started the business with me because I asked. But for me, it was a way to prove myself. I pushed myself, letting go of everything around me. So focused on making my life worth it, I stopped being a person and became a machine."

"You stopped feeling. That's why your brother said you were quiet. You're not quiet."

She gets me. I kiss her temple and continue. "Yeah. I stopped being part of the family, and I worked and worked and worked. I wanted a family, but I needed to know I could care for them. You know?"

She swallows and tenses a moment.

"Kit, if you want kids, I'll make it happen any way you want it to. I want what you want if we get to that." And we will. I know we will. I've never been more certain.

She relaxes against me, and everything is right. "You didn't want your wife or family to ever feel like there might not be enough money for something."

"Yeah. But I suffered, and so did my relationships. I became closed off, losing myself to work, trying to tell myself I needed to do more. Push more—one more hour, one more project. Until I met you. Now I want to enjoy what I have, take chances, and spend the evening doing something other than work. It's the first time I've felt this shift. It made me crazy at first, and it was so much worse when I saw you again. I thought I was having an allergic reaction to life."

She sputters out a laugh at that, then turns to face me.

"But what I wanted to say is that we're both learning something new. Learning to be the people we were always meant to be. And as corny as this sounds..." Yeah, it does sound corny now that I'm saying it. "I'm glad it's with you. I love you."

She searches my face, then grabs my cheeks, pulling my mouth to hers.

I take over, caressing, licking her lips, stroking against her tongue gently. Trying to show her how much she means to me.

When we break apart, we both turn to look at the water. Letting the ocean soak away all our history and showing us our future, how it could be. Choppy but clear, always changing, but beautiful when the right person is by my side.

My heart flutters, strong and insistent under my sternum as I pull her close.

I smile against her hair and squeeze again.

When she sighs and relaxes against me, I know I'm not the only one falling.

Thirty

Kit

THE LAST MONTH HAS been bliss. Greer and I are melding well together. Our lives balance each other out.

I glance up and shield myself from the brightness. Day five of five, and I'm finally done. I clock out, swiping my badge against the timekeeper.

"Good job today, Kit." Dr. Hart touches my arm briefly. I tense and then force myself to relax against it. Regardless of the decrease in anxiety attacks, the touches from random people still get to me. I still see Ethan's hands flying out of nowhere before I remind myself he can't hurt me. I can't seem to control that, despite trying. "Don't tell anyone, but you're becoming my favorite. And don't tell Pattie." She chuckles a moment. Yeah, her personal nurse would probably not like hearing that.

"Thanks, Dr. Hart."

"It's Ophelia. And you are welcome. I'm so glad they hired you. Seriously, my kids are so relaxed when I walk into the room. Thank you." Her permanently sad eyes light up for a moment. And then she's gone.

Her words bubble along my skin and bring a smile to my face. She's my favorite too.

At my locker, I grab my things and shove my backpack over my shoulder. I exit the doors and head to my car, looking around to make sure I recognize all the people trickling out as coworkers. No one seems out of place, but I monitor my surroundings as I get to my SUV.

I check the windows to make sure there is no one in the back and get in, locking the doors as soon as I'm inside, like Greer and I talked about.

That man. He's so protective, but not in an oppressive way.

I throw my backpack on the seat next to me and place my finger on the start button. Before I can press it, my backpack buzzes.

Greer, I bet. Checking on me. That big, gooey, roasted marshmallow. No, not even roasted anymore, he's a gooey marshmallow.

Colette's name flashes across the screen, and my heart stutters. We've chatted weekly since I left California, and it has been pleasant, but I haven't told her I've moved on. For a brief moment, it's a heavy weight that sits on my shoulders.

"Colette, Hi."

"Hello, Katherine. I mean, Kit. Sorry, darling. I always forget to call you Kit now. Forgive this old woman."

The hum of her words is slow and long and different today. Like she's sad, or she's been crying. I frown as I glance around the car garage. It's filling with people leaving for the day. A few people wave goodbye, and I wave as they pass by. "How are you, Colette?"

The sadness in her voice turns slightly bubbly but hesitant as she answers. "Really well, actually. That's why I was calling. I finally met Harper. You were right. I should have met her when she was first born. My mistake means I've missed out on so much. Thank you for helping me to realize I needed her in my life."

Is she serious? "Colette! That is wonderful. I'm so happy for you."

"She's such a joy. We've had lunch quite a bit recently. I've taken her shopping, and we go to tea. Mostly shopping, but I adore her."

"How about Francesca?"

She's silent for a long moment before she clears her throat. "It's been rocky. I didn't treat her the best in the beginning. It's taking her time to open up to me. I'm not pushing, but I hope that eventually, we can have a good relationship. Like you and I had. I miss that. The closeness. I miss you, Kit." Her voice drops, sadness returning to flood through the line as she finishes.

I slide my hand over my stomach, trying to hide the ache there. Our parting was easy, but still, I've missed her too, even if it wasn't as strongly as she missed me. "I miss you too, Colette."

She sighs into the phone. "Come back, Ka-Kit. Please."

The ache grows stronger, and my body softens at her words. "I can't, Colette. This is my home now, where I belong. I'm making a life for myself, meeting people. I have friends here." More than friends, I have Greer, and he means so much more to me than anyone ever has.

"It broke my heart to hear that you wanted to leave, but I knew I couldn't keep you here. You've always been more than a daughter-in-law. I tried so hard to keep you safe, and—"

"What?" Coldness spreads through me as I struggle to understand what she said. I scrunch my brow. "What do you mean?" Did she know he abused me?

"Ethan was a terrible husband. I saw the way he handled you. I tried so hard to take the brunt of it, to protect you. I begged him to hit me instead. He did. So many times. I tried to keep you away from other men at the galas so he wouldn't get jealous."

My brow drops further. That is true, she always kept me close to her side, and when men came over, she'd pull me away, usually to one of her female friends. She often gave him a look when he'd get angry. She'd take him aside, and it would defuse things for a while.

Could it truly have been worse had she not been there? I swallow around a lump in my throat. I don't want to picture what worse could have been. What I experienced was agonizing enough.

She sniffles through the phone. "When you miscarried, he wanted to pull you out of the hospital after the D&C, bring you home, and try again. I convinced him to wait, to give you time to heal."

A bomb detonates inside me, shooting ice through my body. Those three months were the most blissful months of our marriage. Goose bumps form on my skin, pins and needles pricking me, making it tingle. "I didn't know."

"I didn't want you to know. I felt so guilty, Kit. I couldn't help you. When he disappeared, I was distraught—he was my son, but all I could think was that you were finally safe."

Me too. Wow. "I didn't know, Colette. I'm so sorry that you suffered for me."

She sniffles again. "I would do it again and again, Kit."

Does she know about his business too? Maybe she can explain what is going on. Those transactions are more recent. "Do you know much about the firm Ethan ran?"

"Yes, darling, I've been helping to run it since he...died."

"He never told me what they do. I was always curious. Would you tell me?"

"We're a financial firm, darling. We do stock, trading, portfolios, retirement funds."

"Oh, that sounds way over my head." And doesn't explain any of the money that is moving around. "How do you pay people or move the money? I've always wondered how that works."

"We have access to their bank information, and the client has access to their account. They can sell or move money at any time, so we have to move money to their account."

"Does it have to be certain amounts? Can it be small amounts?"

"Oh, any amount, truly. We have a company right now that moves small amounts frequently."

"Why the small amounts? Wouldn't people want to wait until they can transfer a bigger amount?" I hope I get an appropriate answer. A ten-pound weight sits in my stomach, waiting to either drop or disappear.

"Well, in one case, we are moving small amounts to bank accounts for women who have been battered or victimized in Brazil. It's a pet project for me. When Ethan disappeared, and I spent time in Brazil, I discovered just how many impoverished women and children are in need there. Many have been victimized. I wanted to do something, so I take money from my own accounts, invest, and then use the money I earn to transfer to them."

Like the charity for battered women when Ethan died. "Colette, I'm so amazed by your charity. You're such a good woman." The goose bumps and pebbles form on my skin again, and the weight disappears. Truly, she's done so much for me, for other women, and I never realized. Never knew. "Thank you. What you are doing means so much to me—to them."

These women have a chance now. They have hope. It was disparaging when Ethan disappeared, living without hope, in pain, and in terror that he would return.

"I'm trying to make up for not doing enough when you were here."

"You don't have to make up for anything. I didn't know, but I'm so grateful you were around."

"Me too, Kit. I've missed you so much. Will you please come home?"

My heart breaks. She was the only other person in my corner for so long, even if I didn't know it. "I can't, Colette. I'm so sorry, but I promise I'll come and visit."

She sighs in the background. "Okay, I thought you'd say that. But I would be thrilled with a visit." She finishes by telling me a little more about Harper before we say goodbye. When I look up, most of the people in the car garage are gone. I punch the start key and head home.

Music blasts through my speakers, and I sing along loudly until I hit the exit for the highway. I hit my turn signal and turn onto the highway to get back to my place. Maddox's group is following me. Adjusting the rearview, I note the car behind me. They follow me home until Greer gets there, and then they leave for the night if he stays.

I turn onto my street and into my drive. I check the area before I get out and head into the house without waiting for my protection detail. Maddox said they would patrol outside and keep watch.

Inside the house, I do a quick sweep through it. Everything is clean and clear. Now it's time to relax a bit before Greer gets here.

Work has been short-staffed, and I've been picking up extra shifts. It eases my racing mind to get out of the house and help, but some days are long, and some doctors are needier than others.

Dang, my feet ache tonight. I need a bath with some mineral salts to help soothe the ache, and maybe a steamy book.

Sinking into the hot water is heaven for my aching muscles. I let it pull me under, removing all the tension in my body, and close my eyes. The steam billows in the room. There is immeasurable joy in a hot bath.

Despite the chaos, my life is happy. Something that would be further out of reach if it weren't for Greer. I know I would have gotten there one day, but it happened faster because of him.

He is coming over later and I need him. My heart flutters everytime his *I love you* replays in my brain. I know I love him, but am I ready to say it back?

I want to. Some days I almost choke on the need to say it back.

Greer is so much more than I ever thought I'd have. He's calm and rational and not at all like the rest of his family. They are all so tight-knit and part of the Winter Package.

It's not something I would give up, though. I can get used to the chaos when they are all together. And I'll have to learn when to say *no*, or *I need space* because they obviously don't know what space means. Especially Violet.

It's not a bad thing. The hug at the party threw me off because I wasn't ready for it.

Okay, so mental checklist: get used to the family, accept that they are loud, and try to not get overwhelmed. Figure out how to say I love you to Greer.

Fuck, what if something happened to Greer, or if Ethan somehow hurt him?

Sharp, stabbing bolts of ice pierce my heart as my stomach drops. I don't know what to do if something happened to him. I'm putting him right in the path of an oncoming Mack Truck. Maybe Maddox can protect him too. And his family.

And my family.

Fuck, this is getting bad.

There are so many unsolved questions, and I'm sick of not having answers.

I'm not going down without a fight. Not when I have somebody who finally sees me. Someone who loves me as much as I love him.

It was his patience, the way he always knew to give me space, then the laughter, the stupid movies he and I both love, the way he supports me when I want to try something new. He's invested in me, but in a way that makes me feel cherished, not controlled. He makes me feel loved.

Love.

My heart stutters, and peace blooms inside me.

I'm ready. Tonight I'll tell him.

I pull the drain. This is my favorite part of the bath, letting my body cool before hopping out.

Luxury towels are the stuff of dreams, all soft and fluffy, and I wrap one around my body, the other around my hair. Now I need to brush my teeth, and my routine will be complete.

I stop at the sink to grab my toothbrush. Looking up, my hand poised to wipe away the steam on the mirror, I freeze. Pain blooms in my chest. *Holy shit.* I gloss over the letters written on the glass.

My lungs seize like a band is constricting them. There isn't enough air, and my hands have gone numb.

The toothbrush slips from my fingers, the clink of metal in the sink bowl drawing my gaze down.

My wedding rings.

In the sink.

He's coming for me.

I look back to the glass, the words blaring. *Tell me what you did.*

Thirty-One

Kit

"KIT?" GREER'S VOICE DRIFTS up the stairs, followed by his racing footsteps.

My attention shifts away from the mirror for a moment. He's here.

Acid burns deep down, and I shake my head, my chin trembling. I don't want him to see my past, this horrible reminder of how it used to be. How weak I used to be.

My hand is poised, hovering over the words. No, I want Greer to see it. I want him to know. I clench my fist instead, letting it fall to my side. I'm strong, and I won't go down without a fight.

His body is a hazy image through the mirror as he strides up behind me. Warm arms wrap around me.

Tell me what you did.

I stiffen and glare at the words.

"What the actual fuck is that about?" He points at the words. His body tenses behind me, rigid like he's ready to fight. Growling, he brings his arm back around me, tightening his hold. He knows. "It's that fucker, isn't it?"

He doesn't wait for me to answer. "Get dressed, Kit. We need to call the police *now*."

Yes, it's time. It's time to show Ethan that I'm not weak. This scares the piss out of me, but I know I need to let people help me.

I'm not the weak woman I used to be. I'm strong and capable. And I won't give in without a fight—won't give up my family or Greer without a fight.

I can't do this alone. I don't want to. And I'm not fucking going to. It's enough. I'm not running from this asshole anymore. Turning to Greer, I nod. "It's time."

I dress as Greer calls, and eventually, there is a loud knock on the door. Greer opens it to two officers.

"Good evening. We've been told there was a break-in."

"Yes, officers. Come in, please." He lets in a short and squat man with a thick head of hair and a tall, muscular, balding man. I smile at both of them and offer them a seat at my kitchen table.

I spend the next fifteen minutes explaining what has been happening. Greer is beside me, offering comfort as I tell my story. He nods from time to time, but he doesn't butt in.

As always, he's supportive, lending me strength when I need it. If having him means I had to suffer through all the manipulation and abuse Ethan put me through, I'd do it again.

I finish with the officers, and Greer holds my hand while they speak.

The second officer turns to us, shoving his notepad back in his pocket. "At this point, we can send a patrol car out a few times a night, but we have nothing to go on."

Considering they scoured the house and checked the windows and latches, it doesn't seem like they would have found much anyway. "Don't you dust for prints or anything like that? Check them against a database?"

The first cop turns, his mustache wiggling as he talks. "Nope, not enough manpower, and most people who break in wear gloves. Like he said, there is not a lot to go on and not much we can do."

"Fuck me." Greer stomps into the kitchen, his posture rigid as he paces in my line of sight.

The officers study me again. "It might be best if you stayed at someone's house or a hotel for the next couple of days, in case he strikes again."

I shake my head. I don't want to give Ethan a chase. I don't want him to have any kind of control over me ever again. "I appreciate your concern, but I'll stay here. You can send the patrols." Not that it will help. Ethan has not been seen or heard from in three years. A patrolling officer won't catch him. And Maddox's team is already making the rounds.

I close the door softly behind them, engaging the lock as they leave. The old Kit would be hopeless, scared, but me? I'm contained, my pulse is regular, my stomach is all right, and my head is clear.

But I'm not in shock.

I'm ready for that asshole to grow a pair of balls and come for me. Not threaten me, terrify me, or make me nervous. I'm ready to defend myself, and I can't do that if he keeps hiding. I'm prepared to fight in a way he's never seen.

Slipping his phone back into his pocket, Greer heads toward me. "Maddox says his guys didn't see anything, but they're not a constant surveillance. He can arrange for them to cover you twenty-four-seven."

"Do you think I need it?"

"Yeah, I do. Are you okay with it?"

"Will they prevent me from doing anything?"

He shakes his head.

"Then yeah, I'm okay with it." I'm willing to do whatever I need to stay safe. To stay free.

"Great. I'll text Mad to have them come by tonight to introduce themselves. They'll watch at night when we are sleeping and monitor things during the day. I'll take some time off work and–"

"No."

"What?"

"You can't rearrange your life to stay with me all the time. You have a company to run, people to look after. I won't disrupt your life. Who knows how long this will go on?" I smile softly, stroking his cheek. "And if you're here with me all the time, you are going to drive me nuts."

His smile is sweet as he drops onto the seat next to me. Greer might be great to lean on, but I need to stand on my own too.

I'm ready.

Let the bastard come.

Greer

"Kit, this is Marcus, but we call him Roman. The guy next to him is Troy. They'll be your shadows when I'm not around."

"Nice to meet you, Roman, Troy. " She shakes each of their hands. I have to hand it to her. She's looking at Troy without blanching. His ragged scars make most people pale at the sight of him, but he's a great man, and he'll watch out for Kit like his life depends on it. Same for Roman; I can't leave the guy out. They're both ex-military—brothers in Maddox's unit.

She slips her arm around my waist and leads us into the house.

"Very nice to meet you, Kit."

I look at the two of them, trying to see them from Kit's perspective. Roman is smooth. When he blinks, his green eyes disappear behind a massive set of black lashes. His head is buzzed on the sides, longer on top, and black.

Kit turns to me, baring her teeth like she's going to bite and arching her brow.

I stifle a chuckle. He is kind of vampiric looking. They should have called him Dracula instead of Roman.

Troy is tall and muscular, with deep blue eyes and blond hair. He keeps it longer on top so that the patches from the scars on the left side are not so noticeable.

Roman looks around and pulls out a notepad. "What type of security do you have in the house?"

She looks at me and then back to Roman. "None."

Shocked, he looks at me. "No video cameras, alarms, nothing?"

"No." I shrug. In hindsight, we probably should have installed some when we realized something was going on, but it never occurred to me.

"Hmm." He purses his lips, writing something down on his notepad. Probably how much I suck as a boyfriend since I didn't install a security camera.

We walk through the house while they check windows, doors, upstairs, and the perimeter. All the while, Troy is quiet, and Roman is jabbering our ears off but being nice. When we finish, we stop in the living room. Kit turns to the men, her body a tad tense. Probably as tight as mine is.

What the fuck else can we do? It's killing me. I can't go out and find this guy and end him. I've never thought about murder before, but I contemplate it with this guy. Acid burns deep in my belly when I think about him, wondering if he's out there right now watching us.

And there isn't a goddamn thing I can do about it.

Fucking all I could do was call Mad. And I'm thankful I could do that, but this doing nothing is eating me fucking alive. I'm scraping myself raw at night when Kit isn't looking.

On edge, tense, ready to fight anything that growls at me. But the monster we fight is currently a ghost.

A fucking ghost.

How the fuck do I fight a ghost?

How do I protect the woman I love? I shove my free hand through my hair, biting back the groan.

Kit started out tense with these two being here, but now, chatting with Roman, her body has relaxed a little.

It's a far cry from when we first met and she couldn't stand to be touched. She's such a fighter, and I fucking love that about her.

She glances at Roman. "Will you both be with me at all hours?"

"Maybe, have you ever had two men at the same time?"

I whip my head around. *What the actual fuck?*

Surprise paints Kit's face, and if I hadn't had my arm wrapped around her, I wouldn't have noticed how her body stiffens. After a few seconds, she laughs softly, then it gets louder as she relaxes against me.

He puts both hands up, palms out, his smile popping into place. "I'm kidding. Maddox said you were touchy when it involves Kitty over here."

"Kit. No 'Kitty' here for you." Kit's voice is smooth as honey, and her eyes sparkle. "Why do they call you Roman?"

"It's boring, actually. There were two Marcuses in Maddox's group, so he started calling us by the names of famous people. He said I looked like a hockey player or something. It stuck."

"Weird they picked that over Dracula. Everyone got a name?"

Roman laughs, eyes sparkling. "Funny. But no, only people with similar names. Except for Ayers here. Troy got his name from his pretty boy face."

Kit blanches and looks to Troy, who manages a slightly less than dead stare and a halfhearted eye roll. He looks like he could be a famous movie star, minus the massive scars on the left side of his body.

"Why Troy, though?"

Troy speaks his first words of the day. "The movie."

"Should I call you Troy, or do you want me to call you by your real name?"

I don't even know his real name, so if she gets that out of him, she's a freaking miracle worker.

He's tense as he looks her over, but that isn't new. The guy is tense all the time. His lips soften around the edges, barely kicking up at the corners.

"Troy is fine."

"What's your real name?"

"No need to get personal; I won't be." His voice holds no trace of malice. It's direct because he's stating a fact.

She takes it in stride. "Troy, it is."

I pull her close to whisper, "He doesn't let anyone in. He's even quiet with Mad."

"I think we have enough for now. I'm going to propose some changes, but I'd like to get specific items and write them down before I send them over. Is that okay?"

Kit nods and puts her hand in mine as we guide them to the door. My pulse is racing. I want them to leave—*need* them to leave—because

I need her in my arms right now. This not being able to do anything has made me tense and kind of lost.

I need her.

She shuts the door with a click and turns back to me.

Pushing my hands into her hair, I tilt her head and press my lips to hers. I need to taste her, feel her, wrap her up inside me and keep her safe. Invading her mouth, I stroke her tongue with mine before nipping her bottom lip.

Her body shudders, and her pulse flutters under my thumb.

She moans against me and slides her arms under mine to dig into my shoulders. Her fingernails are sharp as they grip my shirt and pull me closer.

My hands glide down her neck, past her chest, to her ass. I haul her up, and she wraps her legs around me. She whimpers as I rock against her, pushing her hard into the door.

Her legs pull me close as she grinds against me. I run up the stairs, not even trying to draw this out. We get to the top, and she pulls back to throw her shirt over her head, then tears her bra off. Her hands spear back through my hair, scratching, then dragging my head back down to hers.

I groan as her mouth lands on mine. Her tongue deep in my mouth, she bites my bottom lip hard. My cock twitches, the pleasure-pain spearing through me.

Fuck. Me.

I toss her gently on the bed and reach behind me to pull off my shirt.

Her sultry voice sends shivers down my spine. "Take your pants off. Now."

She needs me too, needs me to show her I can protect her. "Greedy girl. You need me like I need you?"

She nods at me.

Thank god. I can't do anything about what's going on outside the world, but here I can make her feel safe.

Here I can love her. Make her feel good.

"You want my mouth on your pussy? Or my fingers in that tight cunt? Tell me what you want, Kit."

"I want you in my mouth."

I want that, too, but I want to taste her more. The need to have her is overwhelming, but so is the need to give her what she wants.

She has complete control here.

I slide my hands into the waistband of my sweats as she shimmies out of hers. No panties. She's been walking around without panties all evening. I close my eyes with a groan. *If I had known.*

She sits up and focuses on my hands as I slowly push down. My cock springs free, hard, thick, and so ready for her. She licks her lips, then bites them.

Kicking my sweats to the side, I stand before her. Her smooth hands slide onto my hips as she scoots close, her legs wide open and her pussy glistening. Pulling me into her mouth, she swallows me with a groan, and I moan, drowning in ecstasy.

I'm slayed by the magic of her luscious lips.

She's killing me with the suction of her mouth, the swallow of her throat, and the vibration of her moan. My hands tangle in her red locks while she anchors me in place, pulling the tension out of my body.

Shallowly, I thrust until I can't take it anymore. "I want to come in you, Kit. I want to fucking fill you up." She pulls back, the pop of her mouth making me twitch.

"Yes, I want that." Panting, she shimmies back, her gorgeous fucking body undulating against the bed.

"Put your hands on the headboard and hold on. Don't move them."

Her nostrils flare, and her eyes dilate. She likes it when I'm demanding, but she's too slow, so I grab her hands and push them up, curling them around the rungs of the headboard.

I lean down and scrape my teeth against her neck, growling at the way she smells. The way she tastes. "Don't move them."

Her breath hitches.

"Too much?"

She shakes her head. Thank god because I want her to feel safe with me. At all times.

Fuck, I need to show her how much I love her.

That asshole could be out there, but in here, she's mine—mine to worship, to adore.

I slide my hands down her arms, feeling her skin pebble beneath my touch.

This, this right here, is what she needs, to feel loved, cherished, and worshiped within an inch of her life.

I love her, and I'll keep showing her until it wipes out any fear.

I want to fuck her until she forgets everything but me and us and how we are together. I can't get rid of her monsters, but I can at least erase her nightmares.

I slide my lips to her breasts, to her luscious nipples. Popping one in my mouth, I pull deep. She groans as her hips buck against me. My fingers trail down her side, brushing against her hip as I continue to tug and suck her pebbled buds.

The skin at the apex of her thighs is like silk. It drives me insane as I run my fingers over it. It's so sexy to see her fall apart, to see that I do this to her. I slide a finger between her folds and watch her face as I trace the seam of her slit. Her wetness coats my fingers, and I've barely touched her.

"You're so fucking responsive, Kit. Do you know what that does to me?" I bring my hand up to her mouth and trace her lips with her wetness, letting her taste herself, then lean in, licking her bottom lip. "So sweet, tangy. Divine."

I delve back into her, my fingers sliding through her lips to find her clit, already so hard and pulsing. I brush it gently with my fingertips as she lets out a shattered moan.

"You're worked up already, love. What do you need?"

"You inside me, a part of me. Loving me." She arches her hips into me. Her arms tremble, ready to come down. I watch her let go of the headboard.

"Oh, baby, if you want me to keep touching this pretty pussy, you're going to have to put your hands back."

She does, grabbing so hard that her knuckles turn white. She bites her lip, her body bucking again. My fingers rub around her clit now, circling with firm pressure. Her legs twitch next to me. "Softer?"

Her hair flies as she shakes her head. I slide my hands down to her slick opening and pump two fingers inside.

Holy fuck, she's so damn tight. I drop my lips to hers, sucking down her moans, then twist and move my fingers in and out slowly. I add a third. Her pants are music to my ears.

I can't stop stroking her—my fingers in her clenching pussy, my tongue in her mouth.

I pull one finger out and change my angle, searching for that fleshy spot with my other two before pressing hard. I tap my fingers against it, pulsing and rubbing as my thumb strokes lightly on her clit.

"Oh shit. Your fingers are...Oh, shit." She hitches against me, her pleasure building, her core clenching my fingers so intense, it's almost painful. I keep it up. Red blooms all over her skin, her cheeks turning a beautiful shade of cherry.

"Greer..." She bucks against me. "Greer..." Panic laces her voice.

"Relax, Kit. Relax and let it happen." Let me take away every bad memory, let me love you tonight.

"Shit..."

I press harder, my fingers twisting and rotating on that little spot. She spasms around me, clenching and unclenching on my fingers, her head tossed back, her neck arching, her pulse fluttering chaotically at her neck. She falls apart.

All. Over. My. Hand.

Wetness floods my palm. I can't get over this—her being here in my arms, trusting me to let her shatter safely.

I ease the pressure, letting her orgasm ride out gently, slowly letting her body come down. Her channel flutters as I remove my fingers, and I bring them to my lips to taste her.

Her laughter is music to my ears. "What the hell was that?"

"Did you like it?"

"Um, yeah. Can we make it mandatory that you do that every time?" Her smile lights up my heart, and I can't stop mine from spreading across my face. She pulls me close and tilts her hips.

Leaning down, I kiss her and thrust into her. She arches back, her mouth falling away from mine as she gasps. So I do it again, pulling out and sharply sinking back in. "Oh. Fuck. Me. This is so good." She's so close, so fucking tight, and I won't last much longer.

I lace our fingers together. In. Out. I watch her face, memorizing it. Did I say she's beautiful? I meant glorious.

She's glorious.

"Harder." Her voice is ragged, broken, ethereal.

I slam against her. She clenches her cunt, squeezing me. She's tight and hot and wet and perfect. My spine tingles, and her body stiffens. "Come with me, Kit." I pound into her harder. The headboard bangs against the wall. Our bodies slap together. She leans in and bites my shoulder.

Hard.

So fucking hard I see stars.

My cock twitches, and she squeezes again. I can't hold it anymore. She cries, and I explode, the tingle in my spine taking over as I thrust as deep as I can, over and over. Jetting myself into her, I fall over the edge.

Her skin is golden, her cheeks red, her chest rising and falling rapidly as she returns to earth.

Our hands are still linked together and I suck in a breath. "I love you, Kit."

And then she cries, pulling me close to her.

Despite the chaos of everything, my guts tell me she's happy.

Kit

Wanting to keep life as normal as possible, date nights are still on. My guard and I go on walks because if I don't get outside, I'll go crazy. I still go to the grocery store, and I can still have coffee with my sister, but it's all kind of surreal.

Tonight they are off, and Greer is downstairs sitting on the couch, waiting for me. It's still early; the sun hasn't even set yet. And I prefer these in-home date nights, but getting away once in a while is nice too. The real joy is the desire that builds in Greer's eyes when he knows he gets to unwrap all the pretty I put together.

Greer nods at me on my way down the stairs, my phone up to his ear. He switches to speakerphone when I hit the bottom step. "It's Maddox. I've only been on for a minute."

I slide next to him, snuggling in as his arm winds around me.

"Sorry it took so long." There is some mad clacking in the background, like Maddox is typing. "I had to be a bit of a supersleuth to figure some of this out. Is Kit with you now?"

"Yup, I'm here, Maddox."

Greer presses his lips to my head and laces his fingers with mine.

"All right. I'll start with Ethan. He still has accounts offshore. There is nothing we can do about it in the US. He has four bank accounts in Brazil. Two have been accessed as recently as last month, with money being transferred to the US and into Colette's account. Which wouldn't be odd since they were moved to her name when he disappeared."

"Why wouldn't they go to me?"

"Not sure, but all his US accounts transferred to you. Maybe it had something to do with business, and that's why she got them. We'll dig deeper, but as CEO, she would have access to those business accounts and could transfer what she likes when she likes. So that could be legitimate."

I lean into Greer's touch. "I talked to her last week. She mentioned putting some of her own money into investments and distributing it to women in Brazil. Victims of crimes, abuse, you know... people like me."

There is silence at the end of the line while he digests that. Maybe she took some of the money from the accounts in Brazil since that is where he was storing it.

Or maybe she didn't know about them until recently. Maybe Ethan was doing things illegally, and she turned it around.

Helping the battered women's groups sounds like something she would do.

"A contact in Brazil tracked Ethan's last whereabouts to Rocinha, where rebels or the cartel grabbed him. It's hard to determine which one it is. His brother Liam was with him on that trip, but I haven't been able to reach him to verify what happened. My calls go to voicemail, and my contact can't seem to get close enough to talk to him."

Greer squeezes my hand, and I drop my head to his shoulder.

Holy shit. Rebels or drug cartels. If it was drug cartels, did he piss someone off enough that they are coming after me?

No, if it were them, then we'd be dead already. They wouldn't play games.

So maybe the rebel forces. Did he owe them something? Or was he a random pick from the streets? Those areas are incredibly dangerous.

But what if they made it look that way? He could have paid someone to make him disappear for whatever reason. Maybe it was the money laundering for a cartel he was down there visiting in exchange for freedom or invisibility. From what, though? Me? Seems like he could have solved our problem by killing me. Feds then?

I have no doubt that what he was doing was wrong now, but I don't know the extent of it.

Maddox continues when Greer and I don't say anything. "Liam stayed in the area for weeks after. It looks like he exhausted his funds and had to return to the US."

I frown at Greer. "I thought they hated each other. Francesca met him once, and Ethan ushered him out and told her never to talk to him again. Why would Liam spend so much money if they hated each other?"

"Other motives?"

"Or...shit. What if Liam was the one who killed Ethan? Maybe that's where his money went."

Greer nods. "I don't suppose you know why Ethan was in Brazil?"

"No, he never told me. How do you know Liam exhausted his funds?"

"I hacked into his credit cards. He had enough left to get him home. I can see that a lot of his money was spent at a hotel, but the rest of the money was taken out as a cash withdrawal. Maybe he paid people on the street for information."

Greer is thoughtful a moment then adds. "Or for other things—rides, local search parties, random kids for information."

He's right. It could be any of those things. "How do we know for sure which one it is?"

"There isn't a way. I can't track cash." And Maddox sounds pissed about that too.

"Did you find out anything else about Liam?" My insides are seriously about to become my outsides, and the only thing tethering me to this spot is the fact that I refuse to go down without a fight anymore.

"Liam is a few months older than Ethan. Clair and Colette grew up together, attended the same finishing schools, and ran in the same circles. Walter married Colette, then years later in their marriage, he and Clair got pregnant. A few months later, Colette was pregnant too. It looks like they kept things quiet until Liam and Ethan were about two, then Walter started paying child support after that.

"Liam was sent to boarding school at age ten, paid for by Walter. In college, he studied electrical engineering. When Liam was eighteen, Walter died from a heart attack. A few months later, Clair died in a car accident, and Liam was on his own. He works at a corporation in California and is single with no children. He makes a hundred and twenty grand a year. No outstanding debt or arrest warrants. But he was listed as a suspect for murder."

Everything in me quakes, and a cold sweat beads on my neck. "Do you think he's the one following me?"

Greer takes my hand and laces his fingers through mine, offering me comfort and strength.

Maddox's voice bleeds through the speaker again. "If it is, he has someone helping him. We've been watching his location, and he's remained in California this whole time."

"It makes sense why Colette wouldn't want to talk about him. Or why she was so against Francesca. She had been cheated on. She knew how it felt." My mind is swimming, but I can understand her pain.

Greer squeezes my hand gently. "What about Colette? What has she been doing all this time?"

"What? Colette would never..." She wouldn't. She's done so much to help me.

Greer shakes his head. "She knew about the abuse and did nothing to stop it, Kit."

I swallow, fighting back nausea as my hands sweat. "She's as much a victim in this as I am. He abused her too, she admitted it to me. She tried to protect me, tried to take the brunt of his actions many times."

He lets go of my hand to shove his through his hair. "Why didn't she reach out to the police then? Why didn't she confront him, do something more, anything more?"

"If Ethan is as bad as we think he is, maybe there was nothing she *could* do. Maybe she tried in the past and was told that it was a family issue and to solve it at home." I don't know if I'm grasping at straws, but it seems like something valid.

I search Greer's eyes, imploring him to understand that. His body deflates a little. "I need to keep you safe, Kit. I'm not overlooking anyone."

"Greer is right. We are watching all four of them." Four? Who else are they watching? "You said Colette referred you to your therapist, so we are digging there too. Dr. Brigham has a lot of high-profile clients. We are literally watching everyone you knew back in California."

Shit. "Was there anything concerning about Dr. Brigham?" I roll my shoulder, pausing, waiting for their denial to ease the tension from my shoulders.

They suspect the two people I trusted most in California. It makes my insides want to rebel and reject everything I ate this evening. Shaking it out, I force the nausea back down.

"A lot of her clients were associates of Ethan's. Most of them. A few of them have disappeared or suddenly died. She knows many people, so we are busy tracing everyone."

Maddox clears his throat. "Back to Colette. Last week she was in California. This week she's in the UK. Next month she'll be at a spa in Colorado, booked there until mid-February. Besides that, she's doing what she has always done: attending public events and charities and making donations to organizations in the state. With her deep pockets and long reach, she touches almost everything."

"What about psych or violence in her past? Any mental health issues?" Greer pushes.

"No, never. Our last meeting was sad, but I was leaving."

"I've found nothing in her records to suggest anything. But I uncovered Francesca's history. Drug addiction, a few stays in rehab, and jail time. She's currently on methadone for opioid dependence."

My body trembles, and my throat constricts. A burn climbs up through my chest and cheeks.

There was nothing wrong with me. He can't control me anymore; he can't make me feel like I'm less than I truly am. I won't give him that power.

Shaking out the tingles in my hands, I look up to find Greer watching me.

"Okay, love?" He leans in to kiss my temple.

I nod.

"Hey, guys, I've got a call coming in. Don't hang up; it's my contact in Cali. He's watching Francesca. I'll send over a picture of Liam, too, so you can see if it's John Wilson."

Maddox switches over and we sit processing until I need to move.

"Do you need some water?" When he nods, I stand, heading to the kitchen. His footsteps are soft behind me. He grabs my hips as I pull water out of the fridge. He fills our cups and puts the pitcher back, then lifts me onto the counter and steps between my legs, pulling me close.

He wraps himself around me like a Greer burrito blanket. "I don't know about you, but I need this. I need to feel you."

"I do too." I smooth my hands up and down his back, my legs locked around his hips. "It's a lot."

"It is."

"I just...I ache for Francesca. You know? Why was she doing drugs? What was she escaping from? Was it Ethan? Someone or something else? I've taken care of babies with addictions, and their moms have no control over themselves. It's heartbreaking to see when they can't pull out of it, then have their babies taken away."

He hums against my shoulder, his hands massaging up and down my back in a supportive way.

"I'm glad she got treatment. I should reach out to her, check in and make sure she's doing okay."

Greer leans back, smoothing the hair off my face. He leans in and brushes my mouth with his. "You're such a good woman, Kit. I'm so lucky." His phone buzzes, and we both focus on it. "It's the picture."

He opens it and turns the phone so we can both look. It's an okay picture, and we can make out his eyes but not the color, though they look dark.

"Does it look like him?" Greer shoves the picture around, trying to see his features better.

"I honestly can't tell. I didn't see enough of the guy at the door to know for sure."

"I can't either." He sighs and clicks out of the picture. "How are you doing with all this?" He tucks some hair behind my ears, brushing his thumbs against my cheeks while he watches me.

The smile I give is small and tentative. "Okay. It's so much. I feel like I'm betraying people who were looking out for me or treated me well by spying on them." I want to hang my head in defeat, but... "I know we need

OF LILIES AND LIES

to, but I hate this. And what if I am putting you in danger? If something happened to you, I'd be heartbroken."

He softens and drops his forehead onto mine. "I would be heartbroken if something happened to you too, Kit."

It's the closest I've gotten to telling him I love him. I pull him close, opening my mouth—

"Hey, sorry. I'm back. You there?"

I cough, redness creeping up my cheeks again.

Greer smiles, rubbing his nose on mine, and then answers. "Yeah, we're here."

"My contact saw Liam leave Francesca's house."

Thirty-Two

Kit

GREER'S PHONE BUZZES, AND he looks down, frowning before he glances my way. "Unknown number. I'm going to grab this."

I nod and then take Maddox off speaker. "You probably don't know why he was there, but any guesses?"

Maddox sighs into the phone. "No. We'll monitor them and then try to figure out what they are doing together."

"Shit, Violet, are you serious?" Greer all but growls into the phone. "I can't." Greer looks my way, his eyes torn, frustration painted all over his face. He starts pacing and the growl erupts again. "Why didn't you call Dad?"

Maddox's voice pierces my brain. "Kit? Sounds like you're busy, I'll let you go for now. Call me if you need me."

"Right. Bye." I end the call and look to Greer.

"No, stop crying, Violet, I won't call him. Fuck. What about Simon or Mad?" He shoves his hand through his hair, his focus on me. He looks wrecked and nods like Violet can see him through the phone. "No, I get it. Asher, maybe?"

She's sniffling so loud it's traveling through the speaker.

"I'm just...yeah, I do...Nora." He sighs. "I don't want to leave Kit right now."

I restrain myself from going over to comfort him. He keeps looking my way, worry evident on his face. "What do you mean you're in Prescot? That's the next county over."

324

He stops, his legs planted in the middle of the floor as his face drops while he stares at me. "I'll be there as soon as I can." He hangs up and shoves his hands through his hair and pulls, his knuckles turning white as he growls.

Okay, so something happened to his sister.

"We need to call Roman. I have to go down to the Prescot police station. Violet was arrested."

"Is she okay? Do you know what happened?"

"She's okay. I don't know; she won't tell me over the phone."

"Okay, I'll call Roman." I pull up Roman's number while he gets ready.

Five minutes later, Greer has his stuff ready and drops it at the door. "I'm so sorry, Kit. Shit, I don't want to leave."

"It's okay. Roman is coming over. We'll be fine." It'll all be fine.

Greer pulls me into his arms and kisses me. His lips are soft and sweet. I open for him, letting his kiss fill us both with peace, something neither of us feels at the moment.

"I have to bail her out, then I'll be back."

"I'm good."

Five minutes later, Roman walks in and slaps Greer on the back. Greer kisses me one more time, then with a tortured look on his face, he heads to his truck.

It's a long while later that I stare at the teacup in my hands, going through all the reasons Liam would be at Francesca's house. Is she seeing him? Are they stalking me together?

I'm shaky and cagey, like I'm crawling out of my skin. The anticipation is killing me. The waiting game is Ethan's calling card. Sometimes he'd bring me lilies, and then it would be days before punishment. Not knowing was the worst part of it all.

He liked to strike, let things fester, strike, let it abscess, and then he lanced everything with a deep and stinging knife, letting it bleed and seep out.

He didn't repair it, either. He let it heal in a jagged, puckered scar.

"Did Greer say when he would be back?"

I shrug, my mind not on Roman.

"Great, we have time to get to know one another." He waggles his brows at me and winks, which makes me roll mine.

"He's only a call away, and I told him to go." Besides, I need time to think about everything. And he was Violet's only call since she didn't want her parents to know she'd been arrested. For what, I have no idea yet.

"Don't think so hard. It'll ruin your brain."

"Holy hell, you are annoying. Shush it, Dracula." I smile at him to soften the blow, shaking my head when he grins at me. "I'm thinking. Trying to connect the dots."

I just hate not knowing if there is something I missed, something that could make everything crystal clear. The suction of the fridge opening pulls me out of my thoughts. I glance up to see Roman halfway inside of it, digging around.

"Kitty, are you making us dinner tonight?" Roman is actually funny—in an annoying big brother kind of way. His head pops out, and he looks at me expectantly.

"Nope, I'm thinking about drinking my dinner tonight. You are on your own." I nod to the small glass of wine I haven't touched yet. It's a calmer, so it's not like I'm getting wasted.

His whine, however, is not funny. He has some serious ass-backward ideas of how men and women work. "It's the woman's job to feed the man."

"Not this woman. Order in something."

A huff sounds from his direction. *Ahh, he's annoyed.* Music to my ears. He is off in the corner, though, ordering something. After a few minutes, he smiles and puts his phone back on the coffee table.

"What did you decide on?"

"Chinese—enough to feed four people. I got you some shrimp, too, that kind you like."

Okay, that's nice. Maybe he's not an annoying older brother, but a sweet one.

He smiles. "I'm going to walk the perimeter before the delivery arrives."

After I nod at him, he walks out the door. The chilly air hits my skin, and I shiver before he shuts the door.

Ping.

My phone. Greer is probably telling me goodnight or that he's on his way back.

My heart swells, heat blooming in my cheeks. I love him. Now I need to say it to him.

Unknown Number: *Did you see my gift to you? A little late for Christmas. But you are having such a grand time. I needed to make sure I got you a gift.*

What in the hell? A furrow knits my brow. My scalp prickles, and my stomach quivers. I glance up, looking for Roman. I look out the front door window, trying to see him. Nothing.

I yell through the door. "Roman?" No response, but he could be on the other side of the house. "Roman, are you out there?"

Shit. I dial his number and my heart hammers while I wait for him to answer. Seconds seem like hours as I wait. Fuck, he's not answering. Okay, barricade the door, lock myself inside.

Now, who do I call? Cops? Last time I called them, they had nothing to go on. And a text message isn't going to tell them shit. Maybe they can trace it, but Asher can do that too.

Maddox, then Greer.

It rings, vibrating almost violently in my hand. My pulse skitters, but I'm not trembling. My jaw is so tight, the clench makes my teeth hurt. I brush over *accept*.

I should be trembling. My gut should be sucker punched, my lungs tight and struggling.

But I'm not. They aren't. I'm in control.

I brace myself and answer the call.

"Hello, Katherine. Have you missed me?" His voice is low, gravelly, and choppy. Like he's pieced together and almost indistinguishable, but I hear it.

Sweat wets my palms and beads on my forehead. My body tenses as every terrible memory rushes back.

Forcing down the pain, I wipe my hands dry. I won't let him control any part of my life any longer. "Ethan."

"I've missed you. I'll be there soon." Now he's cheerful, like he's having the grandest time.

He's trying to shake me, but I won't let him. "What do you want, Ethan?"

"I'll see you soon." The line dies.

Shit, shit, shit. "Roman, wherever you are, I need you right now!" The door stays closed as I stare at it, waiting for it to miraculously open.

What gift is he talking about? The lilies are long gone, dead and destroyed in the trash.

Okay, text the men, then stall Ethan. I quickly text Greer, Roman, Troy, Maddox, and Asher.

Me: *SOS, emergency. Need you—he's here.*

Now it's time to keep him on the line.

Me: *What gift?*

I wait, my fingers itching to tap the keyboard to ask again and again. I could call him back, but I don't want to hear his voice.

My phone vibrates. Maddox is twenty minutes away. He's called the police. Asher wants the number, so I text that back to him. Greer doesn't respond. I wish he would, but he might not be able to with being at the police station and all. Fuck, this is shitty timing.

Troy is on his way but doesn't say how long. And nothing from Roman. Oh, fuck.

Focus. Staying strong is about breaking the overwhelming pieces down to make them manageable. I grounded when I panicked.

Now I need to compartmentalize to keep my wits about me.

I need to keep him busy. If he's busy, he can't hurt me, Greer, or anyone else. I tap my fingers on the phone, ignoring the sweat beading on them. Finally, I text.

Me: *Where is the gift?*

Unknown Number: *Upstairs. I left it on the bed for you.*

My blood runs cold.

How did he get past Roman? I glance out the window. There's no movement. Not a sound. No Roman. My pulse spikes, loud and harsh in my ears.

Me: *When?*

Roman and I walked the block a few hours ago, and he checked doors and windows before we came back in. There was no sign of forced entry. *Does Ethan have a key? Does he know the code?* Roman checked up there but maybe didn't realize something was out of place.

If I don't go up, he knows I'm not playing the game, and if I'm not playing the game, then someone gets hurt. Where the fuck is Roman?

Glaring at the steps, I head toward them. The railing is cold as my hand skims it. My steps are heavy and slow as I climb. The top landing is like a beacon of death pulling me toward it.

This is so easy for Ethan. I have no clue where he is or what he's doing, but he knows enough about me to know my habits and how to get into my house.

Each step is more painful than the last, and the pit in my gut sinks deeper and deeper.

I glance behind me, willing Roman to rush back into the house. Where is he? "Roman! If you can hear me, I need you."

Play the game; save my family. Paying attention, I turn my back to the wall as I reach the top of the stairs.

The pit of despair in my stomach tells me to run. The woman I want to be says *look and see.*

I want to be strong, so I look.

My black mourning dress lays across the bed.

Ethereal, cold. Its presence is marked by the solitary light painting it in an innocent glow.

Unknown Number: *Merry Christmas, Katherine. Do you remember when you wore it last?*

Like it was yesterday. I thought that day was a joke, and now I know it was, and I'm not letting him get the best of me.

He won't get the last cruel laugh.

Unknown Number: *I do. So beautiful, regal. The way you should still be. Not a tear fell down your cheek. A wife should mourn her husband—should mourn what she lost. Weren't you sad? No, you were already planning your escape, weren't you?*

It pulls me to it. Clutching it with white knuckles, I wring it through my hands and twist.

Yes, I wanted to escape. But he's wrong because, at that point, I still didn't know it was possible.

I know now, though, that life can be beautiful, and I'm not broken. I know what love is—what *actual love* is. I know what a real *man* is, and it's not him. He's a monster.

And he wants me to beg and plead for my life.

I won't, but that doesn't stop the choking feeling from cutting off my air. For three years, he's played this game. Kept me waiting on pins and needles. I used to be able to guess the severity of my punishment by how long he'd force me to wait. Three years...

He's going to kill me.

It chokes me, the pressure building inside me, pounding in my head and throughout my body.

My eyes skirt to where I keep my gun.

Then I tap out another message on the phone.

Me: *Leave me alone.*

Unknown Number: *Tsk tsk tsk, Katherine. You betrayed me. You let someone dirty what is mine. You are no longer pristine. There is only one way to change that. How should I start? Your boyfriend? Do you know where he is?*

My stomach twists. Does he have Greer? Is that why he didn't respond?

He is a sociopath. I know that now.

My phone buzzes twice.

Maddox: *Fifteen minutes.*

Asher: *I can't locate the number.*

I take a step toward my gun.

If he hurts Greer...if Greer dies because of me, my life will be over. He is the light in my darkness. I love him.

Walking over to my bedside table, I pull open the drawer. The gun is still there. Nine millimeter, loaded with hollow points. I pick it up and walk over to my window.

Me: *See this? Leave me alone.*

I lift my arm, my reflection waving at me. The trembling in my hands is uncontrollable, but I try to keep the gun from shaking anyway.

I can't see anything out there. Only me, staring at myself in the window, shaking like a freaking leaf in the breeze.

My hands sweat, making it difficult to maintain a tight grip on the butt. I drop one hand and wipe it against my pants, then do the same with the other.

For the love of Pete, what is he waiting for? It's eating at me. I wish he'd end it, get this over with.

My phone vibrates.

Unknown Number: *<<Me and Greer in his shop>>*

Oh shit. Greer. He knows where he works. How long has he been following me? The pressure in my belly expands, forcing nausea up hard in my throat.

Unknown Number: *<<Me and Greer walking down the street holding hands>>*

Unknown Number: *<<Me and Greer in my bed sleeping>>*

My stomach drops. How the fuck did he get the last one? Another shows up on the screen.

Unknown Number: *<<Me sitting on Greer's lap as I beat Maddox at UNO at Christmas>>*

A gasp escapes me, and I cover my mouth with a hand.

No, no, no.

Greer's family. He knows where they live.

Nausea boils over, and I rush to the toilet. My stomach heaves as I empty everything inside me.

The gun clanks against the toilet as I struggle around the burn in my throat and mouth.

When I can breathe without my stomach rolling, I set my gun on the counter and clean up.

Unknown Number: *See this? I can play games too.*

My hands tremble so hard it takes three times to send the text.

Me: *See what?*

Greer is at the police station. There is no way Ethan would attempt to take him down there.

He's safe.

I know he's safe.

And if he's not, if Ethan has him, I'll find him. I'll fix it.

Unknown Number: *Look out the window, Lilliput.*

Ice stabs through me, my whole body quaking. Lilliput. That stupid nickname meant to make me feel small.

No, I don't want to know what's out there. Please, don't let it be Greer.

My pulse pounds in my ears, and my hands tremble like crazy.

I grab my phone and dial Greer's number. What seems like hours pass, and then his voicemail kicks in. "You've reached—"

I click off and scroll to my sister. It goes straight to voicemail.

The only noise in the room is me and my heartbeat as I scroll to my parents, but they don't answer either.

"Fuck." I scream, my throat burning from the force of it.

I race to the window and pull back the curtain again. A body is on the ground, unmoving, with a small dark puddle pooling under him. Greer?

Dropping my phone, gun in my hand, I run.

Thirty-Three

Kit

LET HIM BE OKAY.

It has to be Roman. He was the only one out there, and he should be back by now.

My stomach twists in knots as I reach the front door.

I unclench my fist, keeping the gun in my other hand, and turn the knob. The dim exterior light barely illuminates the body. It's Roman. Frantic, I look into the darkness.

Inky blackness and the sound of nothing greet me.

No cars, no dogs, not the hum of a street lamp.

My legs tremble, but I need to get to him. Sprinting to his side, I drop to the ground.

"Roman?"

His breaths are shallow but audible.

"Please, be okay."

I check for his pulse. Then look up and around me again, though I can't see shit. It's still black. Still eerily quiet.

His pulse beats strongly against my fingers, and for a moment, all the tension leaves me in a whoosh.

But we are still sitting ducks.

My hands shake, and I force them to steady. Focusing on what I can control, I force my body to relax and scan the path back to the house.

Get it under control. Get him inside. Freak out in the house, not here.

The puddle of something under his head isn't getting any bigger. With a gentle touch, I comb through his hair, looking for the gash or laceration on his head. Something sticky coats my fingers when I get to the back.

Shit. It's tacky, though, so it probably clotted off. Some tension leaves my shoulders.

Get him inside.

Hand on his shoulder, I shake him gently. "Roman, please. I need you to get up."

My pulse spikes, and pins and needles prickle along my spine like someone is watching me just out of view. I should have called Troy.

Roman moans and slowly brings his hand to the back of his head.

Thank you, Jesus. "Roman, can you hear me?"

"Ow, mother...fucking..." He shifts, struggling to sit.

My spine tingles, and I look around again. Heart thundering in my ears now, I grab for his hand. "Come on. I need to get you inside."

"Suck a dick, this hurts. What the hell happened?" He staggers to his feet, and I slide my shoulder under his armpit.

It's so dark out here. Why didn't I install more lights? Or move somewhere with closer neighbors? "Roman, I need to get you inside, and then I'll check your head. Can you walk?"

He gropes the back of his head but walks forward, stumbling a few times and almost taking us down.

Please don't let him fall. I don't know if I can get him back up.

He rebounds, and we get to the door. I pound on the keypad to get in, the beeps loud as I press each button harder than I need to.

"Shit, Kit. What the fuck happened?"

After shutting the door, I get him to my kitchen counter and help him ease onto the stool. "I'm not entirely sure. Someone hit you from behind and knocked you out? Maddox and Troy are on their way. I can't reach Greer."

That wakes him up quickly. He squints against the light. "Holy shit, seriously?"

Standing back up, he fumbles to the door. "Roman, you need to—"

"Check things." And he does, the locks and the windows. Then he makes his rounds through both levels, checking everything everywhere. He's holding his head when he gets back to me, his eyes running over me. "Are you okay?"

I nod.

"I'm sorry I let someone get the drop on me."

"It wasn't your fault. I'm pretty sure it's Ethan. He's been watching me. Does it still hurt?"

"Yeah, but I'm sure it's a scratch. Got some booze or something to kill the pain?"

Gun on the counter now, I grab my first aid kit from under the sink and a bowl of warm water with a washcloth. Then I point to the chair, so I can check out his gash.

Roman shakes his head. "I don't know how the fucker got me, but damn, I went down faster than fresh gyoza."

If my heart wasn't still hammering inside my chest, I'd probably laugh at how much this guy loves Asian food.

Shit. What if it had been worse than a head wound? He could have been killed. Shit, my gun. "I need to go put this away." He nods, and I rush up the steps. I shove my gun back into the drawer beside my bed.

Five minutes is all I need to recover from this.

I shake out my palms, forcing my heart and breathing to slow down. The adrenaline is wearing off, and everything in me deflates.

Greer. All I want is Greer.

Everything is numb, and I need to know he's okay.

Searching around the room, I finally spot my phone on the floor next to the bedpost. Greer's name is first in my contacts, and I call him again. It rings to his voicemail. "Hey, babe. Call me back."

Then I call my mom. "Hello?"

"Mom." The dead weight in my belly lightens, my shoulder tension dropping a fraction. I need to know they're all safe. "I, uh." *Simply check in; see how she's doing.* Don't freak her out until we know what's going on. "I wanted to check in and see what you and Dad were up to?"

"You caught me at a good time. We are at the symphony concert tonight, and we just reached the intermission. You doing okay, Kit-Kat?"

"Yeah, Mom. Wanted to hear your voice."

She sighs happily into the phone, and then there is a loud noise overhead. "Intermission is over. Do you want me to call you after the show?"

"Yeah." I'll tell her what's going on then. At this point, the action is over. It's not his MO to attack twice in one night. He wants me on pins and needles. He wants me to make mistakes. I truthfully don't think that he'd do anything more tonight.

"Will do. Love you."

"Love you, Mom."

I click end and pull up Rosemary's name. "Hey, Kit, I can't talk right now. Milo is testing for his orange belt tonight. Sorry I didn't answer earlier."

Another pound eases from my stomach. "No, it's okay. Tell him Auntie Kit said good luck."

"Will do. I love you."

"Love you." I'll call her back later and fill her in. No point in scaring people tonight.

Three down, one to go.

My phone buzzes, Greer's name flashing across the screen.

Everything in me drops—the tension, the sinking in my gut, every-thing—as a cool wave rushes over me. My legs wobble, and I fall onto the bed and close my eyes. The thunder of my chest eases, and I press my palm to it and smile.

Everyone is fine.

"Kit, babe. Are you okay?"

"I am now. I was terrified for a moment. Ethan texted me, called me, then knocked Roman out. We're fine now—"

"Fuck. Kit, are you sure? What's going on? I'm leaving now. I'll be there as soon as I can."

"It's okay, I promise. Maddox and Troy should walk in the door soon. Drive safe. I'll explain it all when you get here."

"I love you, Kit."

"I love you too."

I sit on the edge of the bed, letting the last of the numbness fade away.

I've never in my life felt so helpless. I couldn't reach any of them, and Ethan knew it.

Shit, I've been so stupid, believing that he was gone.

He's not gone. He's been waiting for a moment like this. Once I felt safe and able to move on, he returned.

I stand, shaking the tingling feeling out of my hands.

He's out to kill me and hurt everyone I love.

Roman. His cut might still be oozing. It needs to be addressed.

When I get downstairs, he's using a washcloth to clean up the blood on his face.

"Sit down. I'll clean it up." I wash my hands, then grab clean gloves and my first aid kit. With the bowl of warm water ready, I set it and a clean washcloth next to him. "Do you have any STDs I need to be aware of before I start? I'd hate to be surprised."

His deep laugh is music to my ears, deflating some stress of the night but we're both still on edge. His shoulders are tense, mine too, but it's nice to laugh some of it away. "Hell no, I always wrap it. I'm not an amateur."

Moving to the back of his head, I set out a clean towel and lay my things on it.

He sits quietly while I pat around his injury. He's got a pretty good goose egg and a cut about the length of my pinky. Head wounds bleed like crazy, even if they're superficial. "I think you need stitches, and you've got a lump back here."

"Do you have the glue stuff for cuts?"

"No. Although maybe I should buy some if I'm going to be hanging with you guys more often."

"How about super glue?"

My stomach plummets. "Yeah."

"Use that. It's the same."

"It's not the same, different chemical makeup. One's safe for skin, one's not."

He whirls to face me, then groans, gripping his head. His eyes burn into mine. "Listen, Kit. I'm not leaving here tonight. Either grab the super glue or watch me bleed to death."

"You stopped bleeding." Okay, I'm lying. It's not bleeding much. Mostly oozing.

"Then why do I need stitches?"

"Because it's deep enough that it might not heal right."

"Just fucking super glue it."

Fine, fucking baby. I grab my super glue from the junk drawer and dab away the blood again, and then I dry it as best I can and glue him up.

"Don't touch it for a while. It has to set." I keep my fingers pushing it together, giving it time to harden.

The front door opens, and we both swing our heads to it.

Troy. He cocks his brow at Roman. "I leave you alone for two minutes."

Roman's hearty chuckle is music to my ears.

Greer

"I love you, Kit."

"I love you too."

The phone clicks off, and I stare at it, my body buzzing, feeling light.

She loves me.

Holy shit, did she even realize she said it?

We have plenty of time to talk about it, to build a life together.

As long as that asshole doesn't get to her.

Fuck. The euphoria ends abruptly.

It's like a bomb detonates in my chest, and every inch of me is in ruin, on edge, on ice. I need to get to Kit.

Ethan was at her house—he was at her fucking place—and I wasn't there.

I want to annihilate him so he can never hurt the woman I love again. Fucking damn it.

I've never driven so fast while praying so hard there weren't police around than on the hour drive to her house.

"Kit?" I drop my things at her front door and hang my jacket up. Until I see her, physically have her in front of me, feel her in my arms, and make sure she's safe, this frantic pounding in my chest and head won't cease.

A flash of red rounds the corner.

It all eases, everything chaotic in my body and mind.

She's safe. She said she was when we talked, but seeing is believing, and I'll fucking fall and worship at the feet of any deity as long as she's safe.

"Greer." She runs to me and jumps. I grab under her thighs and hoist her up to my chest. Her legs wrap around me, and I slide my hands across her back, hugging her to me, inhaling her scent.

She trembles slightly, and I settle against the back of the couch. "I'm not letting go." I growl, and she shivers against me, nodding for a moment.

Someone taps my shoulder, and I look up from where my head is tucked into her neck. Maddox. "Better?"

She nods into my neck.

"I think the next step is to go through the house. I know we swept it once initially, but we need to again."

Rubbing up and down her back, I nod.

Her head leaves my shoulder, and she peeks over my shoulder. "Do what you need to do."

For the next twenty minutes, the three of them go through every nook and cranny of the house, delicately but thoroughly, so her house isn't destroyed.

I gaze around, looking for Maddox. "Mad?"

His head pops up from behind a door frame. "Yeah?"

"Safe to talk?"

"Not yet." Moving to the kitchen, I sit Kit on the counter and push the hair off her face.

As quiet as I can, but loud enough for her to hear me, I lay my feelings out there. "I want you to move in with me. I can't protect you here, Kit. And I need to. I need to be able to protect you, or I'm going to go crazy."

The warmth of her body leaves me as she shifts back. Her face falls, and she drops her forehead onto mine. "I can't. I won't run, Greer. I'm going to be smart. We're going to do this right, but I won't run from him. I won't show weakness."

I grind my teeth and force my hands not to shake as I continue stroking her skin. How can she not be as frightened as I am? "Aren't you scared?"

"Terrified. But I'm healing, Greer. I won't let him control me like that anymore." She scans the room, stopping on my brother and the other two guys before focusing on me again. "I won't hide again."

"Fuck." I swipe my hands through my hair and pull the strands. "*Fuck.*"

Someone taps my shoulder, and I whirl around to Maddox at my back.

He points to all the gear. "It's all clear down here, but you need to keep it down a bit. We're still cleaning up things upstairs in case we missed something."

Feeling caged in, I pace her kitchen and dining room. "Then we have to bring people in to help. We can set up something so you have a group of people watching twenty-four seven."

"How many people are you thinking?" Her voice is biting.

I stop to face her. "As many as it takes."

"How many?" She snaps at me, something she never does. She's as riled as I am.

"I don't know, three, five, as many as it takes to make sure you're safe. Fuck, Kit, if I lost you..." My heart dies a bitter death in my chest at the thought before starting up again.

Her eyes soften, and she holds her hand out. I rush over and pull her into my chest.

"I know. If something happened to you or your family..." She jumps back, her hands flying to her mouth. "Shit, Ethan has pictures of you and your family, of us at your family's house. He has been in my house when we're sleeping."

Heart in my throat, stomach rolling, I clench my teeth and hold back a growl. "Show me."

Regret flicks across her face, and she hands me the phone and his texts, then the pictures.

Motherfucker. Molten lava boils through my blood. He's threatened everyone I hold dear with those pictures. I'll fucking find him and tear him apart.

End him.

Massive pressure builds inside my body, aching to get out. I grab on to the countertop and grip with all my might as I clench my teeth. The urge to destroy flows through me, and my body shakes as I rage against the countertop. A soft hand strokes my arm, and I look up.

Concern is etched across Kit's face as she watches me. No fear, thank fuck. She doesn't fear me.

I nod at her. I'll get it together.

It takes every ounce of my strength to relax my muscles and calm my breathing, but when I do, Kit pulls me in and wraps me in her arms.

This is peace. Knowing she's safe.

I can work around the rest, force the powerlessness down and figure out what to do.

Troy and Roman hurry down the stairs, the steps creaking once in a while as they get to the landing space.

"Well, the psycho had cameras set up in a few places and a recording device."

"Her bedroom?"

Roman chirps. "Yeah." He waves a little wand over the devices. Nothing beeps. "Deader than roadkill now."

Troy smacks him hard in the arm. Maddox chastices him. "Fucking idiot, you're insensitive. Don't say shit like that." Maddox turns to Troy, irritation winning out. "He was raised in a barn."

Troy arches a brow and then looks at Kit. "Okay?"

She nods. I pull her back into my arms, and she lets me. "What is all that?"

Kit hops down to look through the pile Maddox brings to the table top. He picks up a tiny-looking cable. "This is a video recorder, transmitter, listening device..." he flips through more things.

"These are what they found upstairs. These were down here." He points to a small stack next to it.

Holy shit. He's been watching and listening to her for who knows how long. My body tenses again. "Where did you find them?"

"The places that were easy to find—decoys, really—lamp shade buttons, smoke detectors. Then there were the places that were harder, like the peephole. I have to ask Asher how he managed that one because we could still see out of it."

Maddox picks up a few tiny, shiny, button-looking things. "This one was on the curtain rod. Some in outlets, the hook by the door, a recording device in a few pens, and a button on the TV."

Jesus.

Kit's hand strokes my back. "How long have they been there?"

"Hard to say. We swept through the first night and found nothing but didn't check after that. Judging by what we have here, though, it probably took hours to set it all up."

Maddox pauses a moment, his brain churning like crazy.

"Guys, go check her car." He pulls two guns from his back, checks the safety, and hands them and the wand to the guys. "Recheck the perimeter."

When they are out the door, Maddox turns to us. "We need a plan."

"What do you have in mind?" Kit stands in front of me, her back to my chest, trembling slightly.

This freaked the shit out of her, but she's standing tall, standing her ground, not letting that asshole bully her into hiding.

Even if I want her to.

"I think we need to amp up security."

"Agreed." I slide my hands to her shoulders and squeeze gently.

She tenses slightly. "I'm not going to be followed by a flock of men everywhere I go."

A boulder forms in my stomach, filling the massive pit that's been there since this started. I'd love nothing more than a flock, but she won't agree to that. "What about three?"

"No, we keep it as is."

"It needs to be more than that." I turn her to face me and look deep into her eyes. "I mean it, Kit. You mean everything to me. If something happens to you…" I can't finish the thought.

Maddox covers his mouth, grumbling under his breath. "And we've already seen that. We don't want a replay."

Throwing him a glare, I growl as well. "Shut it, asshole."

Kit pats my chest. "You keep me grounded, Greer. You're my rock." She leans up, her lips touching mine briefly, then wraps her arms around me.

I exhale slowly, forcing my body to release the tension. This situation fucking sucks, and it makes me want to lock on to Kit and steal her away.

I grit my teeth. "Okay, so not an armored escort service every time you go to work. Can we do twenty-four-hour coverage?"

"We could do that."

"Will they be walking over me, sleeping on top of me?"

"I'm the only one sleeping on top of you."

Maddox grimaces. "Too much, gross. No, they'll work like shadows when you are out and about. At work might be an issue. Can you drop your hours for a while?"

"I'm casual, so I can pick up what I want. I'll stop picking up shifts. For how long, do you think?"

Maddox shrugs. "Hard to say. I'm finding nothing on Ethan, and it's hard to track a ghost. A few weeks. If that comes and goes, we can discuss more."

She turns to look at me. "A few weeks?"

It's not enough. How will they protect her? "They need to carry guns."

Kit nods, thankfully. The boulder shrinks a little, but I still don't like any of this.

She points up to her room. "I have a gun. I can carry it if needed. It's in my bedside drawer."

Troy and Roman walk in with a few more devices, which they drop on the table. "Car is clear now."

Roman fiddles with a few of them and throws them on the pile. "More tracking and a listening device."

Kit scowls. She picks one up and flicks it back into the pile. "Jerk."

Maddox grabs a bag and starts shoving them all in. "Well, at least we know that his eyes and ears are gone."

"For now." Roman quips.

Irriation flashes on Maddox's face and he scowls at Roman. "Jesus, you sure know how to kill a mood when you enter a room, don't you?"

"That's not what the girls say."

Stomach flipping, I find a smile for the first time. So does Kit.

Maddox shakes his head. "No, it's usually when you drop your drawers that they say it."

"You're jealous that my dick slays."

Troy grunts. "From STDs."

Roman grimaces, and I fight back a smile as he whines. "I'm thoroughly tested."

Kit smirks, hiding a chuckle behind her hand, her expression relaxing a bit. "He assured me he's clean when I glued him up tonight."

"Virgin." Troy coughs.

Her laughter spills out, and so does mine.

Maddox cough-laughs. "Enough. Okay, Roman, Troy, we're starting a twenty-four-hour watch. We'll need another person for rotations."

"You got it." Roman looks at Kit and winks.

She shakes her head, despite the big smile on her face.

Maddox addresses Kit. "How good are you with a gun?"

"Pretty good." She stands taller against me, and I drop my lips to her head, kissing gently.

There's a knock on the door then, and we all turn. Kit starts toward it, and I grab her arm until she smiles. "It's probably the police since Maddox called them."

The next hour is spent telling the police what happened and taking report. Roman doesn't want to go down to the station, but Maddox says he'll take him so everything can be documented.

Troy and I spend the rest of the evening talking about rotations, what they'll carry, and how often they'll monitor for devices.

Troy grabs his jacket. "I'm going to check the perimeter."

I nod, and Kit grabs a few things to make for dinner.

It's quiet in the house now, and the only sounds echo from the kitchen as Kit scrapes together a meal.

Now that the danger is passed, I want to talk about *it*. Talk about how she said she loved me. If she's not ready to say it again, if it was a slip of the tongue, then I won't press, but I hope she feels that way.

Her skin is soft in my palm as I slide my hand down her arm. She sets her spatula aside and looks my way. She smiles. It's still strained, but not as stressed as it was before.

"Are you okay?"

She nods, turning completely to step into my arms. Her arms are tight as they wrap around me, her head resting on my chest. I tuck her hair behind her ear and run my hand down its silky softness.

"Yeah, I'm okay. It's a lot. I never thought it would come to this. It was a little paralyzing at first. And when I thought it was you lying on the ground, I about died."

I reach around her to turn off the burner.

"I never want to feel that again. I worry that he could take you from me."

Those are things I worry about too. Gravely. I press my forehead to hers and nod. "You said something to me earlier. Do you remember what you said?"

She nods, her forehead rubbing against mine, and I pull back to look at her face. She smiles brightly with a beautiful blush painted across her cheeks.

She pulls my face to hers and brushes her lips against mine briefly before the puff of her breath hits them. "I love you, Greer. So much. Without expectation, wanting nothing in return."

"I love you, Kit. Always without expectation, wanting nothing in return."

And despite everything happening to her right now, despite the chaos of the unknown and the shit happening, everything with Kit feels right.

February

Thirty-Four

Greer

MAYBE I SHOULD START drinking coffee. I yawn as I shift my car into park. The last three weeks have been calm, but my body is restless because I know something is coming.

I don't like that I have to go to Prescot today, but apparently, because I bailed Violet out of jail, I have to be at the arraignment. Violet better get her ass in the car soon.

"Good morning, Greer. Thank you." She hops into the passenger seat and gives me an apologetic look. I head out of her parking lot and make my way to the highway.

"I love you, Letty. You know that." It's just shitty timing.

She sighs, her eyes tearing up a bit. "I know. I'm so sorry, Greer."

"Do you want to tell me what happened?" Because we are still in the dark, Asher threatened to hack into the government database, and she almost stabbed him with a fork.

Her swallow is the loudest noise in the car, and that says something because we're surrounded by semis and road noise. "I can't. That's why I called *you*. I thought you'd be least likely to pry."

"You know, none of us are going to judge you. We've all made mistakes, some of us more than others." Me, I'm the one who's made a shit ton of mistakes, but I'm figuring it out and letting my family in.

She shakes her head and looks out the window, effectively ending the conversation.

I'm left to think and fester for an hour. I don't want to leave Kit, and each mile away from her is ripping my heart out a little more. It's going to be shredded by the time we get to Prescot. I clench the wheel tighter, my left leg bobbing as we draw closer and closer to the county line.

My stomach drops as I park in front of the government building. Sweat beads on my temples, and my heart races. We'll be here until they call her name, which Nora says can be at any point throughout the day.

I don't like this at all.

Kit

The oranges and apples look delicious, and after picking a few, I lay them in my cart. I hate grocery shopping with Roman, but Troy wasn't available. Seriously, after this many hours stuck in Roman's company, I'm ready for a break.

And dinner. I'm hungry. More so than usual.

"Do you think my love life will go back to normal after this?" He grins at me.

Uh. No. I can't talk about this today. I smile at him, making sure it's saccharine as hell. "I'm pretty sure that you're not missing out on anything, and neither are the women you date."

He grins at me. "Sounds like someone is jealous."

My "Mom eyes" bulge out, even though I don't have kids.

He throws his hands up and chuckles. "I'm kidding. I know you and Greer are solid." He looks me up and down and winks anyway. "But just in case."

Jesus. But he's right. Greer and I are solid, even after the last few weeks.

He's kept his cool and shown what a remarkable person he is. I'm freaking lucky.

And then there's whatever's happening today. He couldn't tell me yet, and I get it. It's not his secret to tell, but he had to be there for Violet.

It's been three weeks since Ethan made an appearance, and we've been waiting for him to pop up again.

One of the things I miss is freedom—me time, solitude. Another hour of shopping with Roman, and I'll go crazy, but I smile anyway. "Don't you need something for dinner?" I make a shooing motion with my hands.

"Can't leave you. You know the rules."

Indeed, I do.

I know they are keeping me safe, really, I do, but I'm just...ready for whatever is coming. Because something *is* coming.

Ethan has to be salivating at the anxiety he's caused me. Double and triple checking doors, looking closer at every person who passes me, hiding in my home instead of working.

It's been exhausting, and I think I might be imagining things. Like when Roman popped out of the bathroom, and I hadn't realized he'd even gone in. I screamed before hitting him hard in the chest.

He laughed. I wanted to cry to release some of these pent-up emotions.

My pocket vibrates, and I pull out my phone. Greer's name flashes on the screen. "Hey, love." I can't help the smile spreading across my face. "I'm grabbing groceries. Did you need a last-minute something?"

"Kit." He draws my name out with a happy sigh. "No. We are the last ones in line with the judge, Jesus. I didn't realize I'd have to be here when I bailed her out. I hope this doesn't take long, but it might be late when I get home."

Frowning, I nod. "I'll keep your dinner warm, all right?"

An enormous sigh echoes through the phone, and I bet he's running his hand through his hair. He's frustrated that he can't be home with me.

"I hate this. I hate not being there. Are you okay? Should you be at the grocery store?"

"Yeah, Roman is watching me like a hawk. He's even threatened to eat me." He hasn't, but I love Greer's growl through the phone.

"Put him on." His voice is only mildly serious.

My heart flutters. He's wonderful.

"Will you call me when you leave?"

"Always. See you soon, love."

"Bye, babe."

Roman turns to me, holding three frozen pizzas. "Greer?"

Nodding, I blink as he tosses the pizza into the cart. "Dinner tonight?"

"Nope, it's a snack for later. Doesn't matter what you order, I'm going to be hungry after."

"I could order you double."

"Nah, I want the pizza too."

Cocking my brow at him, the smile still slips out, even if he's annoying. "You remind me of Jack so many years ago."

He grabs a box of corn dogs. "Your brother, right?"

I nod. That looks like a heart attack on a stick. "Are you sure you want those?"

"Oh yeah. I'm having a few tonight. Appetizers." He waggles his brows.

We grab a few more things, and Roman talks my ear off the whole time.

When we are finally home, he has me wait in the car while he checks around outside, then inside the house too.

He trots back out, his arms swaying gently. "All right, Kit. Coast is clear. Head inside; I'll grab the bags."

The rest of the evening is spent putting things away, then reading a book while Roman watches TV at a low level. It's almost six when I text Greer.

Me: *Hey, love, how's it looking?*

I read a few more pages of the latest mystery romance. Somehow, reading about someone else's tension and crazy life makes mine feel not so isolating.

My phone buzzes.

Greer: *Another hour, at least. Nora is working us through the charges. I want to be on the road.*

Me: *<<Sad face emoji>>*

Greer: *Eat without me. I'll call you when I'm leaving.*

Greer: *<<Kiss emoji>>*

Roman and I end up ordering something, and then it's almost nine when I realize I still haven't heard from Greer.

There's a knock on the door, and Roman gets it. Troy saunters in and nods my way.

He's not much into teasing, so I wave back and dig back into my book.

One of their phones rings, and my ears perk. I look up, waiting for someone to grab their phone. Troy pulls his out and sets it on speaker. "Maddox. Hey."

"Hey. Is Roman with you?"

"Yup, gang's all here. Ready for the bang."

He's such a man whore. Grinning, I turn my body, waiting for Maddox to start again.

"Liam is in Maine."

Thirty-Five

Kit

LIAM IS IN STIRLING Harbor. Holy shit. Everything I ate attempts to retch back up as the words sink in because I still have no idea if he's the good guy or the bad guy. And this makes it seem like he might be the bad guy.

Maddox's voice breaks through the haze of thought. "We lost him sometime between his lunch break and three. By the time we found him, he'd boarded a plane already. We had someone waiting at the airport, but somehow he slipped past the man I had there. Asher is combing through security to find out how he left the airport."

More than that, they have no idea where he is right now.

Seriously, shit.

I shoot a text to Greer, giving him the update. He doesn't respond.

If Liam is coming for me, I need to be prepared.

The skin on my neck and back prickles.

"Roman, Troy, keep your eyes open and your guns out. Asher is frantically trying to get a visual on him. I'll let you know what I find out. In the meantime, Roman, are you okay working longer?"

"Yes." Roman puts his game face on and pulls the gun from its holster as Troy does the same.

"Put in coms so I don't have to call you and disrupt something. Kit, would you want to call Francesca and see if she knows anything? Be subtle."

When both men are set up with their earpieces, Maddox clicks off. Troy looks my way. "Going to do a perimeter check."

Roman moves, already checking windows and locks before heading outside. "You okay? I don't want him out there alone. He's good, but so am I, and someone got the drop on me. I'm going to lock you in and follow behind."

Shaky but nodding, I pull out my phone and wave it at him. "Going to make my call."

He nods, giving me another hard look before he whistles at Troy.

Francesca, Jesus. How am I going to start this conversation? Act naturally, be subtle. Yeah, I'm about as subtle as a hurricane.

Steeling myself, I calm my trembling hands. I can do this.

I pull up her name and click call.

"Kit? Hi."

"Hey, Francesca. It's been a while. I thought I would call, check in and see how things are going." Yup, that's a good start.

Be subtle.

The restless energy bubbles inside me. My feet carry me from one side of the room to the other, and I force myself to sit.

Francesca chuckles nervously, it seems. "Things are good. Weird, but good. How are you?"

"Still working on getting my life back together here. I've got a job and bought a house." Might be obvious, especially if she already knows that. But I don't know how far into this mess she is, so I play it like she knows nothing.

"Wow, that is great. I couldn't imagine moving somewhere to start over. It was hard enough moving out of my parents' house when Harper was a baby. Now I'm starting over in a new way."

"I talked to Colette the other day. She said she was getting to know Harper and trying to get to know you. I'm glad she finally changed her mind."

She sighs, then gives a small laugh. "At first, it was weird. But she's seen Harper a handful of times now, and it seems like it's getting easier to be in her presence with each visit. Colette wasn't nice, you know?"

I arch a brow and half chuckle. "Yeah, she wasn't. But hopefully, she's changing her attitude. She said you're taking a bit to warm up to her. Which I get wholeheartedly."

On her end of the line, she harrumphs. "She's asked me to go to luncheons with her a few times. Then asked me if I was ready to date anyone. Even tried to set me up when Harper and I were doing a lunch thing with her once. "

An elegant man that Colette brings over to introduce to her. Yeah, I can see that 100 percent. "She never introduced me to other men. Probably out of respect for Ethan."

"So weird. Maybe she realizes that her son is dead."

"Could be, or she wants you to be happy and stay around California." Because I didn't.

"I suppose. She and Harper seem to get along well. Colette doesn't like to be called Grandma, though. She's Nan or Colette."

Francesca has to be rolling her eyes right now.

"It's galling, you know. I was never after Ethan's money, and now the men she introduces me to all seem from money. Pretty sure one of them does coke too. He had a white smear under his nose at an event."

"She's from money. She doesn't know other people. As for the drug use, I've seen a few men who miss the clean-up. It's never been something I've been interested in, though."

"Me either. My cousin had a horrible addiction to painkillers after a football injury. He did recovery with methadone and everything. It was incredibly sad, but he's doing well."

"Your cousin?" Is she for real? Either she's lying to me, or someone falsified her health records. Which isn't impossible if they can find someone sneaky enough to do it. And why would she bring it up unless she knows we are looking into her past?

She has to be setting me up.

"It was horrible, Kit. We watched him through it all. The addiction turned him into a completely different person. He lied, stole, and was unreliable. He was my best friend until that happened. It broke my heart.

Our relationship was never the same. I don't want to go through that again."

Were those even her files, then? Because she sounds earnest. Not that I was ever good at detecting lies before, but now my radar is more tuned in.

She's telling me the truth.

Where the hell did that information come from, and why?

Francesca continues like I'm not stuck in a cycle of revelations and concern. "I should tell her thank you and let her know I've met someone. I want to explore what happens with him. I...I like him."

Liam? Or someone else. Thank the lord the conversation steered here. "I met someone too. Greer. What's your guy like?"

She's silent for a moment on the phone, her swallow audible through the speaker. "Oh...This is so weird. It's, uh, Liam."

"Wow. How?" If she and Liam were in on this together, she wouldn't have mentioned him, right? She would have lied to me.

"He came by to meet Harper, and we started chatting more. There was this tension when he would look at me—it was so...right there, deep down."

"Tension?" Sexual tension? I'm-going-to-kill-you tension? Where-do-I-stuff-the-body tension?

"A good kind. We're taking things slow, which is hard. He is sexy, kind of dominating, but not like Ethan. But he's only like that in private. Otherwise, he's so sweet."

My pulse spikes, and I push down the nausea. Oh, shit. She has no idea. "Do you feel safe with him?"

"Yeah, as safe as I can feel with someone I've only been dating for a couple of months."

Do I tell her? I have to tell her. "Did he know about me?"

"Yeah. He asked about you a few times. Where you were, how you were doing, what made you move. He wanted to meet you. He's so nice, Kit."

"Oh, shit. Francesca, I don't know if I should tell you this. But I think he's stalking me."

OF LILIES AND LIES

Silence rings out on the other end of the line, and then her breaths turn harsh. "Why would you say that?"

I tell her everything that has happened since I started noticing the strange things around here.

Her voice trembles. "Are you serious? He asked for your address, and I figured it was no big deal. You sent me that card, and I held on to your return address. What if he isn't a nice guy? He seemed a bit off lately. Colder than normal, but I figured it was because I called him Ethan by accident. They sound so similar on the phone. It just popped out."

"He sounds like him?" My throat dries up, and my hands turn clammy. The thud of my heart pounds in my ears.

"Yeah, almost like twins."

"I got a call from Ethan, saying he was coming for me."

"Could Ethan be back?"

"After all this time? I thought so, but now there are things that point to Liam." I go into detail about the things Maddox found.

She inhales sharply, her voice wobblier now. "Oh my god. What have I done? Are you in danger? He knows where you live. You need to leave, Kit."

The pulse that has been trying to break free and run away from me finally does. I fight the urge to clench my hands, shaking them out instead.

"Liam is in Maine. We're trying to find him." And, at this moment, it doesn't seem like it's enough.

She sounds frantic now, matching my thumping heart rate and the tingles under my skin. "You need to call the police. Oh, fuck, Kit. I sent him to you. What if he's crazy? What if this is a jealousy thing? He wanted what his brother had?" She sobs softly into the phone.

My hands tremble, and I look around the house. I need something, anything, to keep myself safe.

"Can you call the police? Kit, I'm so sorry."

"There are guards in my house doing a perimeter check. I should let you go so I can find them."

"Call the police first. Get someone over there. If he came to Maine, it's not good, Kit."

"When did you give him my address?"

There's a long pause. "A few weeks ago. He said he wanted to meet you. I'm sorry."

"It's okay. It's not your fault. You didn't know."

"I'm hanging up. Call the police. Please."

"Okay." She hangs up, and I look around the room. The guys are still outside, and I'm a sitting duck alone in this house. Shit.

My gun, I need my gun.

I rush around the couch and head for the stairs. I'll call the police when I have my gun. "I can't believe Liam is the bad guy."

Something bangs, and wood skids across the floor. "Damn it." A rough growl comes from behind me.

Everything in the house disappears as the lights go out.

Holy motherfucking shit. What's left of my heart flees, bursting out of my chest.

It's pitch-black. The air in my lungs stutters as I frantically search the room for anything—light, movement.

Anything.

Something hard and large barrels into me with the force of a tornado. It's heavy and massive, and I can barely breathe.

Shit.

He rolls off me enough to grab my arms and pull me up.

Fight, Kit. Don't just stand here.

Once my feet are firmly on the ground, I thrust my foot out and kick as hard as I can. It connects with something hard and warm. Pain shoots up my shin, and I wince, shaking it out and preparing myself.

"Oof."

Not thinking of anything but safety, I kick again. It's soft this time, and then a massive weight hits the floor.

I'm free, and I suck in much-needed air.

Run.

Frantically, I charge to the wall and flick on the light, but the room remains dark.

Think.

I flick on my phone light. A massive body kneels on the floor. His hand is on his stomach, and he's struggling to stand. He looks up, and his piercing blue eyes meet mine.

Holy shit. Holy fucking shit.

The pounding in my chest quakes, making me shake. He looks like Ethan, but not like Ethan. Liam.

It *has* to be Liam.

Why the fuck aren't I moving?

"Roman! Troy! Where the fuck are you?"

Fucking move, Kit. Don't wait for them.

I force myself up the steps, tripping and coming down hard on my wrist. Fierce and sharp pain shoots up my arm.

Ignore it.

Scrambling, I get up and stumble toward my room.

I need to get there. Get there, get the gun.

"*Kit.*" The bellow ping-pongs through my brain, loud and harsh. His heavy footsteps pound the stairs below me.

Almost at the top, I grab the railing, using it to propel myself across the room. I jump onto the bed, shoving my body across it, and pull the drawer open.

The wood scrapes against my fingers as my hand closes around the butt of my gun, and I jerk it up into the air.

His body hits me hard, forcing me down onto the bed. "Turn over. I—"

I swing an elbow, hitting his stomach or something. The gun is cold, and my hands are slippery, but I hang on, trying to draw it closer. Heavy weight settles over me, pushing me into the bed.

Oh, Jesus. My pulse is obliterated. I don't know how it can get any faster. My body is trembling. I buck against him. He forces me over, grabbing a hand and a leg to flip me easily.

Shit. He is strong.

Too strong.

I throw an arm out, trying to hit him with the gun. One solid hit. That's what I need. I can barely see in the dim light upstairs.

"Stop it! Now! Fuck, ow. That"—he grabs one hand—"is"—then the other—"enough." He squeezes, struggling to get them over my head as I fight back under him. His fingers pinch blood flow to my wrist, and I lose feeling as the gun clatters to the floor.

I won't make this easy. Greer will know I died trying.

Greer.

My heart aches, shattering as I fight back. I want to cry because we were so close, so close to happy and together. I won't let this be the end.

A surge of energy moves through me. I pull harder, my body twisting, moving, anything. I snap my teeth, looking for something soft.

"*Enough.*" His growl, deep and dark, sets off a torrent of ice-sharp spikes down my body.

Pulling hard, I struggle to get my hands loose. I have to get free. He's going to kill me.

Then Greer and Roman and Troy. All these deaths will be because of me. "No, please."

"Stop fighting me." He straddles my hips now.

All his weight presses down on me, blocking my movement and constricting my chest.

Gasping, I wrench down again, trying to pull my hands free.

Fuck.

Sweat pours from my forehead.

He's on me, forcing me down with both of my hands in his grip.

I'm going to die here. This is the end of me.

"Please, stop." I beg. Something I swore I would never do again. The tears fall. "Please." I'll beg all day, if it means I have a chance of staying with Greer.

"Stop fighting."

I jerk again under him, pressing my hips up, trying to dislodge him.

"Stop moving, stay still." His harsh pants are loud. "I need a minute." He slides his hand down my body, and I buck again, tugging as hard as I can on my arms.

Is he copping a feel? He pushes hard and leverages up.

He's going to rape me, then kill me. Sadistic, sick bastard. That would be worse than death—to be given something beautiful and have it taken away, only to die.

My repaired body and soul broken again by rape.

Thwap.

He falls forward, crushing me. All the air is pushed out of my lungs with his massive body weighing me down.

"Arrruuughhh." Comes from beside me, and Liam's body rocks on top of me.

I squeeze my eyes shut, but then the weight disappears, and I take the first full breath of air into my lungs.

Sobs rack through me, but I force them down and let the tears fall.

Breathe.

It's quiet, only the sounds of my harsh breathing and someone else's. Someone quiet. Troy.

Thankfully Troy was strong enough to pull him off.

Exhale.

He's giving me a few moments to gather myself, and I take them. Letting the weight of everything that happened flow over me.

Swiping the tears off my cheeks, I sit up.

I almost died. It would have been the end of Greer and me, of my new life, of everything I worked hard to reach.

I rub my wrists, massaging against the pain.

The room is quiet while I calm down.

Liam is alive. So am I.

I want to cry again but force myself to calm down. My savior's still quiet in the corner.

Troy saved me. I drop my gaze to the floor and let the tension leave my body, waiting for the calm to flow through my veins.

When I can move without trembling, I look to where Troy's body is barely outlined in shadows. "Thank you." I trace the faint, swollen marks from Liam's fingers.

He nods, and boneless, I sit on the bed and rub my hands down my legs. Something sticky coats my fingers, and a metallic scent fills the air.

Oh, shit. I look up, my heart racing. "Are you bleeding?"

Thirty-Six

Greer

THIRTY MINUTES EARLIER.

"I am sorry, Greer." Violet turns to me, her hand on the door handle as she stalls getting out of my car.

"I know you are, Letty. Nora will take care of it. I promise she'll do everything she can to help. What a fucking mess." Whatever happened between Nora and me, Nora is the best at her job, and she will solve this.

"I swear it wasn't me."

"I know." Well, I don't know. I mean, the charges are harsh, but I still don't understand how it happened, and she won't tell me the story. She's only talked to Nora. Whatever the charges are, they could be enough to get Violet kicked out of med school.

Doo wop, doo wah.

My ringtone blares through the Bluetooth. I point to it. "It's Maddox."

"I'll get out. Thanks, Greer." She leans over, kisses my cheek, and rushes out the door, looking behind her before escaping into her house.

I hit answer.

"I need you to get to Kit's now." His voice is frantic, and there's a rustling in the background like he's playing with clothes.

My pulse spikes, and ice shoots down my body. "What do you mean?"

"Liam showed up in Maine this afternoon. I've been trying to get a hold of Troy and Roman. I lost them on the coms ten minutes ago and can't get through to Kit. I think someone has used a signal scrambler on the house. I'm on my way over there, but I'm forty minutes away."

Fuck me.

363

"I'm on my way."

"Hurry the fuck up. I don't know what's going on. I already called the police."

My hands are shaking as I pull onto the highway.

Fuck. What the hell is going on? Let Kit be okay. Let her be safe. "Siri, call Kit."

It rings straight to voicemail. I keep trying as I drive.

Fuck, if Liam is the stalker, then she could be dead by the time I get there. Trembling overtakes me, and I gasp in the breaths I desperately need.

No, no, I won't let anything happen to her. Whatever powers are out there, let me make it in time.

The speedometer says I'm going almost a hundred now. I've never gone this fast, but it's not fast enough.

Her body, coated in blood, floods my vision. Limp, lying on the ground. Bile churns in my belly, poking hard, trying to escape.

Red and blue lights flash in my rearview and off the dashboard, and the rush of my heartbeat drowns enough for the blare of a siren to reach me.

I glance at the speedometer.

Fuck.

I growl, grabbing the steering wheel and clenching with all my might.

Do I keep going or pull over? I'm going a hundred and twelve in a seventy zone. Fuck, this is reckless driving.

Reckless. Yeah, the shit coursing through my veins right now is reckless.

Fuck, fuck, *fuck*.

"Ahhhh!" I shove a hand through my hair and then signal that I'm pulling over and slow to a stop on the side of the road.

I sit with my hands on the steering wheel, window down.

The cold air blows in.

Please let me get an understanding officer.

"Hello there, license and registration, please."

I look at the young cop at my window. Fuck. There is no way he's going to let me go. He's almost crowing at the thought of giving me a ticket with the smug look on his face. Officer Harrigan.

"It's in my wallet in my back pocket. Okay if I grab it?"

He nods. And I do everything slowly before handing over both.

He reads through everything at an agonizing pace while I force myself not to bark at him. "I'm sorry, officer, I'm in a hurry."

"I can see that." He flashes the light on my license, then back on my face. "Why?"

"Emergency. My girlfriend is in danger. She has a stalker, and he's at her house."

He cocks his brow at me. "I haven't heard that one before."

I tap my fingers on the steering wheel. "Please, you can give me a ticket. You can follow me, but I need to get to the house now." My leg bobs as I wait for him.

He's looking at me like I'm the stupidest person he's ever met. "I'm going to run your license. You were going pretty fast."

"Right. My girlfriend's husband or brother or someone is at her house right now. I'm trying to get there before she dies."

His brows flash up. "You are invested in this, aren't you? Have to say, I'm mighty impressed."

"Here's her address. Go check. My brother called in a disturbance." I rattle off Kit's address. "Please, write it down and check on it."

The steering wheel squeaks as I squeeze it, rotating my hands around it. The cop looks at my hands, then looks back at me.

"All right. I'll be back in a moment."

His walk back to the car is faster than his walk here. Thank fuck. Because it took everything in me not to reach through the window and shake some sense into him.

Still, it doesn't stop me from dying a thousand deaths while I wait for him.

Five minutes pass while I sit in this fucking truck.

Do I leave and then hope he follows me?

Jesus.

Fucking.

Christ.

Knocking on the hood of my car pulls me from my thoughts. "You were right. I said I'd check it out. Let's go. You follow behind me. I'm running sirens. If we get there and nothing is going on, you're getting one hell of a ticket."

Whatever. I push into drive and follow his lights.

Thirty-Seven

Kit

"A COUPLE OF FLESH wounds. And you're welcome." A slow, soft, southern twang fills the air. Not Troy, not Roman.

Shit. I know that voice. It's the man who supposedly ran out of gas outside my house. "John?"

"Wow, I'm impressed you remembered that name. Not my real name, but that's irrelevant."

I scoot back on the bed. "Why did you save me?" Trying to keep my attention on him, I pat around for my gun.

I scuttle backward on my hands. I'm so close; I just need an inch.

He lunges, landing on top of me and pushing me down onto the bed.

I don't have the energy to fight any longer, but I won't lie here and die. Lashing out, I throw punches, barely glancing off his body as he sits.

"Who says I did? This is nothing personal." Rough hands grip my wrists, and he wrenches them away from his body.

The bed shakes as we both buck. Liam groans next to me.

Using all my energy, I propel myself, rearing up hard. The bulk of his weight pivots forward, and then he straddles me.

This is it; this is where I die. I thought I was dead before, but that was a taste.

"Such a waste." John clucks, his hands tightening on mine.

Liam groans, then growls, and the bed shifts between the three of us.

John looks his way for a moment, surprise flashing across his face. Then a blur flies across my vision.

All the weight leaves my body, and the two men fall over the foot of the bed and land on the floor with a hard thud.

The sound of pounding flesh reverberates through the room.

I watch in a daze for a moment. Fists are flying, and the men are shoving into each other, trying to get the upper hand.

What am I doing? Move!

I need my gun.

I lunge over the other side, my hands slipping against the floor before my body follows.

The cold metal greets my fingers.

It's hard to stand with shaky legs, but somehow, I manage. The room is still dim, and the men are at the end of the bed, still a mishmash of bodies as they grunt and snarl.

I raise my gun and drop the safety. "Hey."

The impact of my raised voice is nothing. I need to be louder. "*Hey. I have a gun, and I'll use it! My safety's off, now back off each other.*" I'd fire a warning shot, but the thought of accidentally hurting someone because a bullet flew through my wall makes me sick.

John glances my way and takes a step back.

Liam turns and stares down the barrel of my nine millimeter, his body instantly moving to a surrender pose.

"Downstairs, now." My voice is loud even to my own ears, drowning out the thunder from my heartbeat. "Slowly."

They both stand. Liam watches me with a wary expression while John stares me down.

"Move."

They both take trudging steps toward the stairs as I keep my hands fisted on the butt. Thumbing the safety, I click it back on.

"Into the living room and stand there."

"Sure." John drawls. "In the chair?"

What? No. "Stay standing. Where I can see you both. Stand over there." With my back to the wall, I keep my attention on their movements as they turn to face me.

"Roman? Troy?"

The thundering in my ears continues as I wait for confirmation. Anything from the two of them. John smirks and quirks a brow, his arms crossed over his chest.

Fuck, he's big. Bigger than Liam.

"Why aren't they answering?" I wait a moment, and when neither responds, I shout, "I don't give a shit who answers. Someone tell me what the fuck is going on."

My hands tremble, and I force them to still, holding the butt a little looser to bring blood flow back into my hands.

Do I go outside and check on them? Are they out there lying in pools of their own blood? I glance at the door.

The urge to wring my hands together is strong, but then I'd have to let go of my only chance of survival.

One of the men in front of me moves, and I swing back and aim my pistol at Liam, who shifts on his feet and shoves his hands in his pockets.

"Hands out!"

He nods and holds up his empty hands.

Damn it, I can barely function. The room is stifling, my heart is racing, and I still have no clue what the hell is going on. And the two men outside could be hurt, dead, or dying, and I'm doing nothing to save them.

Tears prick my eyes, and an overwhelming sense of loss fills me.

I can't lose it. Not now.

What do I need to do? Stabilize them somehow. Tie them up? Yeah, that works. How?

My gaze shifting from object to object, I look for something to bind them.

Shit.

Where's my phone?

My hands tremble again.

Okay. We need power. Tie them up, find a phone, call the police, call Greer, find Roman and Troy.

Lights blind everything as they flicker back on, and then the floor creaks to my left.

I turn, blinking against the brightness and look into my kitchen. A shadow slowly moves into the living room.

A body slams into me and grabs on to my hands, jerking them down. I throw out my elbow, almost smiling at the grunt. My hair is flying in my face as I turn.

I can't tell who it is.

A hand settles on my wrist, squeezing painfully. One hand on my shoulder forces me down, and then I'm on the floor holding my wrist, and they have my weapon.

Liam shifts in the corner, well away from me.

John. Damn it.

John has my gun, Liam looks pissed, and I'm on the floor in my living room, having lost my only means of survival.

A gaping hole fills my chest. I'm going to die here. And I could cry, but what's the point right now?

Think. And stop shaking.

How do I get the weapon back? That's my aim.

"Katherine?" The kitchen floor creaks again, and I turn my gaze that way.

"Colette?"

Heat sprints down my arms as she nods. She's pointing a pistol at John. "Drop your gun."

"Sorry, lady, I can't."

"Drop it now, or I'll shoot."

Bang.

She shoots into the wall, and the plaster shatters, spraying everywhere. Small shards hit my cheeks and arms, the sting slight.

John drops his firearm slowly. Watching Colette closely.

"Come here, Kit. I'll help you."

I stand on shaking limbs.

My body is weak with the dizziness of having someone here to help me. It washes through me, melting away the tension. I exhale in a sigh and move on jelly legs. It's slow, like I'm walking through waist-high water.

She stands there, her body stiff and watching, her gaze swinging between John and Liam. It's ice cold and such a reminder of Ethan.

For whatever reason, that look roots me to my spot.

"Kit, please, come with me. We'll call the police, file a report, whatever we need to do, but I promise I'll keep you safe."

"Kit, she's not who you think she is." Liam's voice whispers from the corner. .

"What do you mean? Why are you here?" Colette looks at me. "Has he hurt you? He broke in here, tried to kill you, but *I'm* not who I say I am? Kit, I'm your mother."

She takes a step toward me, her free hand out. "Extra mother. I love you. Please, I'll help you. Come here." She signals me closer with her free hand. Her face softens as she looks at me, but worry is still etched across her face as she switches her focus between the two men.

"Don't do it." Liam all but growls.

I look his way. He's calm, his body relaxed as he watches me closely. Almost too closely. Those eyes, so like Ethan's, are beseeching, and I think if he could reach out to me, he would.

Thank god Colette showed up. Thank god she was in Maine.

She was in Maine. Like Liam. Like John.

Why?

Ice shoots through my body, and I shiver around the freezing of my heart. Hair whips around me as I shake my head.

If she knew Liam was in Maine, then she was watching him. But why?

She's not who you think she is.

I thought she was there to protect me, keep me safe. At least she made it out to be that way.

But was it?

The lilies, the phone call, the texts, the pictures. Was that her? Or Liam?

Frowning, I look between them. Colette's face is pinched tight, and Liam is mostly relaxed and watching me. Not creepily. He gives a surreptitious shake of his head. I don't know him, but I know her, our history.

How many times did she run to Ethan when I broke a rule of society or my hair wasn't right? Too many.

How could I forget that?

Or the time I dropped the teacup at the gala, and the teacup broke? She told me not to worry, but Ethan learned about it. There was only one person who knew. She was the only one, and he confirmed it. No, there is no way Liam knew about the lilies, the beatings. He couldn't. Or the Lilliput.

Ethan wasn't close to him, so he wouldn't have told him about them.

But who is John to her, and how is he involved? I glance at him. His stance is rigid as he watches Colette and me.

He gives nothing away.

I stare at my hands, slowly forming fists. I clench them to control the trembling.

It was her. It had to be her. My gut eases, the twisting and turning ceasing.

Trust myself.

It was her.

So how do I get out of this? She has a gun, and I have nothing. A pit forms in the middle of my stomach, rock hard and aching with the knowledge of my stupidity.

"How?"

Colette shifts. "Stand straight, darling. How what?"

Nodding, I slowly take a step away from Colette and John. It's almost impossible to school my features, to neutralize the urge to flee as I look at her.

"How did you know to save me?"

"What do you mean?" She slowly lowers the weapon.

"How did you know I was in danger?"

"Mother's intuition, darling. Something told me I needed to get to you, so I came as fast as I could."

I search the floor for invisible answers. That could be true. She has a private jet; she can go anywhere. I nod slowly.

"Why?"

Her brows raise. "I don't know what you are talking about, darling. Can you explain?"

"You had me followed. You sent me the flowers. The phone call, texts."

Colette shakes her head. "No, darling, I've been watching Liam. I saw him in a flower shop." Her eyes are imploring, begging me to believe her. "It was him. He and Ethan must have been closer than we thought. When he flew out here, I knew he was trying to get you. It's always been a game. So I followed him."

Oh, that is horrible. I swing my gaze to Liam, wrapping my arms around myself.

Blue eyes bore into mine, and he shakes his head slowly. He looks back at Colette with wariness in his gaze and his hands still up.

"Darling, please. All I want to do is take my daughter home." She motions me over again, her look almost pleading.

I look at Liam, who remains stoic. Then at John, who looks bored as hell standing there. He watches me with cold intelligence. He's not worried. I have nowhere to go.

It'd be comical if he lifted his hand to examine his nails or something, but his attention doesn't leave me.

She takes a step toward me. "Now, Katherine. Be an obedient daughter and come here."

Instinctively, I step back. The gun in her hand slowly trembles, despite her body's calmness. Ramrod straight, like normal, but tension lingers around her mouth and eyes like she's trying to hold something back.

"It *was* you." The air is tight as I edge closer to Liam, the only one at this point I have a chance of surviving with. I hope.

"I don't know what you're talking about. Get over here. I'll keep you safe." Anger flashes before she adjusts the grip to her other hand, shaking the free one out.

"You followed me. Did you send John here?" I turn to him. "Were you the one who sent the flowers, broke into my home? Called me Lilliput?"

John cocks a brow and crosses his arms over his chest but says nothing.

"Why?" It still eludes me. The how is present and blinding, but not the why. "Tell me why." Turning back to her, I beseech her to answer me.

Colette clenches her jaw, her nostrils flaring as her eyes blaze that ice blue. Familiarity flares inside me. I'm moments away from witnessing her explosion, like all those times with Ethan.

My chin trembles, and my hands shake so hard I have to squeeze them together so it doesn't show.

Escape. That's what my body is saying right now. I need an escape plan.

Ha. Fat chance of that. I'm in the middle of the most fucked-up family reunion ever. I need to provoke her somehow, risking my life in the process. "Tell me what you did." I throw her words back at her. Those stupid tears trying to fight their way out.

She freezes, her whole body like a steel bar as she stares at me. And then she cracks. Her voice is bitter.

"Everything. I did everything to have a daughter."

Greer

The harsh lights of the city are gone, and the blue and red of the police vehicle screeches to a halt a few hundred feet from Kit's home.

The first floor of her house is lit up, but the shades are drawn. Anything could be happening in there.

Officer Harrigan gets out with a hand hovering over his gun. He turns back to me, raising his hands to his lips as I close my door.

It's eerily silent as we advance on the house. It's like the world has shifted, telling me to shut up and pay attention.

Frantically, I search the exterior, looking for anything out of the ordinary.

Fuck! There are three bodies outside near the trees, one tucked off to the side, the other two close together.

One of them struggling to get closer to me, and I run, Officer Harrigan behind me. The ground is cold when I drop to it, and through the dark, I can make out Troy's features.

I rip the duct tape off his face.

"*Fuck.*" He rubs his mouth against his shoulder. "They're inside." He turns to the other body. "Not sure who that fucker is, but I found him. Roman was questioning him when another man joined us."

He rolls, offering me his zip-tied hands. "I've got a knife in my boot, but I couldn't reach it."

I help him free while Officer Harrigan helps Roman. "Shit, I was not prepared for this."

"Yeah, no one was." Roman wipes his mouth then grabs his shoulder. "Fuck, he dislocated it. Who's that guy?" Roman nods to the man who's out cold.

I shrug. "Did you knock him out?"

"Well, yeah, he lunged for Troy. I shot at the one fighting Troy a few times. I thought I hit him but he didn't go down. That guy was huge. He pounded Troy like he was nothing. I mean, I thought we were big, but he's massive."

Officer Harrigan rifles through the unconscious man's clothes and pulls out something that looks like a wallet. "Says he's FBI. Special Agent Noah Forsythe."

Why the fuck is the FBI here? I look to Roman, who is grimacing. "Any ideas?"

"Fuck if I have a clue. Troy?"

Troy grunts, clutching his ribs as I pull him to his feet.

Bang. A shot echoes through the trees.

A shot? "Officer?"

The blood drains from every part of my body, and ice shoots through my veins.

Kit. Is she hurt in there? Terrified? Dead?

Don't let her be dead. Please.

Nausea forces its way up my throat, and I swallow it down and take off toward the house.

"*Stop!*"

I freeze, looking back at Officer Harrigan. Fuck. I need to get in there. My pulse pounds in my ears, thumping out of my chest.

Does he know how hard it is to stand here?

Finally, Officer Harrigan hits something on his shoulder and speaks into it, throwing out codes I don't understand. "2418 Summit Lane. Unsure if there is a casualty or injury. Multiple ambulances requested."

He whirls around, surprise on his pale face. "I need you to stay out here, stay in your car. I'm going to wait for backup and then head inside."

"Fuck that. I'm not waiting. If he shot her, if she's hurt—I'm going in. She could be dying."

"Don't be stupid. We have no backup."

"We are backup." Roman swings a look at him and Troy. "Push my shoulder back in." There's a grotesque squelch, and Roman bites off a howl of pain.

"You're hurt; not a help. Sit."

Motherfucker. I'm not stupid, but I'm desperate for the only thing that made me value anything other than work in my life. I need her.

More than I need air.

And it's never been clearer than at this moment that she has to *live*.

"I will arrest you." He palms his cuffs.

"Her fucking husband has been stalking her, and you say you're going to arrest me? I'm sorry, that's not a threat." I point at the house. "Whatever is going on in there, that's the threat. I'll do what I need to, with or without you."

OF LILIES AND LIES

I sprint to the kitchen door, moving as quietly as I can. The keypad is cold as I punch in numbers. It beeps loudly, the lock disengaging, and I wince.

A hand grabs my shoulder, and then there's a harsh whisper in my ear. "You should let me go first. I've at least got a vest for protection."

I nod, but only after I grit my teeth.

Finally, the officer gets inside, signaling me to be quiet.

There's a low hum coming from the living room. Angry, bitter words spew from the mouth of a woman I've never seen before. A man's body is on the floor, and another man is standing close to Kit.

I hold back my gasp. I want to sag into the wall and thank fuck. The wobble in my legs gets better as I take another step forward.

She's alive. She's fucking standing in front of me, whole.

She's trembling, her hands out in front of her. A myriad of emotions crossing her face: fear, disgust, anger, and more fear.

Who is the man? Ethan? But wouldn't he have a weapon on her or something?

As we inch closer, I skirt around Officer Harrigan to see Kit better.

The woman's words pierce the haze hanging over me. "Katherine, please come home."

Home. To California? Colette?

Kit shakes her head. "No."

At that, the woman aims the gun at Kit.

I run.

Thirty-Eight

Kit

I SHAKE MY HEAD. "I'm not yours."

She laughs, bitter and breaking as she loses her shit. "Oh, but you are. You *are*. From the beginning, you were supposed to be mine. For years, I wanted a daughter, and I tried desperately to have one. But Walter had his mistress Clair, then they had Liam, and then..."

She shakes her head like she's trying to rid herself of a memory. "He wanted nothing more to do with me. Not that I would have him after he betrayed me. And kept betraying me."

She bites off a laugh as she looks at me. "Do you know how long it took to make you perfect? Years. You fought it so hard. But all it took was a word from me, and Ethan brought you in line."

Nausea churns in my belly. The years of abuse were all orchestrated by this woman in front of me.

"Why? Did you hurt Ethan too?"

"I did what was needed to make him perfect. If it involved violence, so be it. When I couldn't physically hurt him any longer, I had to get creative." She twists her hand like she's digging into something with pinpoint precision.

"It didn't take much for me to push him in the direction I wanted, a few words were enough—he was always eager to make me happy and prove his love. And then I met you, and it was like a ray of sunshine in my dark world. You were perfect, and everything I wanted in a daughter—smart, beautiful, funny. But you were so provincial with your mannerisms, that harsh accent, and dear lord, I needed to fix the way you dressed."

She tsks and shakes her head as she waves her pistol around. "You could easily have been classy, but you dressed like a vagabond. You were everything I wanted and so eager to please, and then eager to stop the punishments. You complied so well. And I couldn't have any more children, so it was just easier to fix you."

She points at Liam, who has edged closer to me. "Stop moving."

Like a statue, he stops, frozen.

She leans toward Liam. "I absolutely despise you. You took everything from me. Everything. John, keep eyes on him."

Confirmation. The burn of her betrayal singes my body.

"Sure thing."

"Where are the guards?" Colette barks at John.

"I tied all three up outside."

Liam jerks in my peripheral vision, and I look at him. I only had two guards. Is one of them helping him?

She waves her weapon. "Three? Who was the third guy?"

"Pretty sure they came together." He points to Liam.

Colette rages. "Who is it? Who did you bring?"

Liam watches her, his hands still by his side, calm.

"Who did you bring?"

He grits his teeth. "My partner."

Colette watches him, shrewdly assessing him. "You've been watching me."

Liam nods. "For years. I've been trying to get the pieces to put you behind bars."

She laughs almost maniacally. "Which one?"

A pregnant pause fills the room like he's debating telling her. "FBI."

She shakes her head, her gun wavering heavily with her trembles. "How did you find me?"

"We knew a few of the aliases you've used in the past. Lilith, Achlys, Carman. So we have them flagged. I knew your itinerary when you left California."

"Well, isn't that wonderful." Her ice-cold gaze swings to John. "What in the actual hell do I pay you for? Are they dead?"

"Nope, wasn't paid to do that. Let's discuss that for a moment. We're going to add a flesh clause. If I bleed, you pay more." He pokes at one of the holes in his shirt, which is still oozing slightly. "It wasn't easy getting them down. The guards took out the agent, thank fuck. Otherwise, it would have been harder. As it is, I've got two bullet wounds, a broken nose, and possibly a broken rib or two."

Colette gasps in outrage. "You didn't kill them? And you want more money?"

John shrugs. "Hey, lady, whatever you think of me, I'm not free. And I have an ethical code."

"A killer with an ethical code. How lovely." Liam titters.

"Yeah, exactly." John whirls back to Colette, his face stern. What the hell is going on? "You didn't pay me to kill them or this girl. Scare her, yes. Hurt her, sure. But kill her? Not yet."

"You are utterly useless. I'll be terminating our contract soon."

He perks at that and drops his hands to his sides.

"But first, I need you to finish everything we started."

My mind swims with everything she and Ethan had done to change me. And all the things that have happened since. The texts, the flowers, the dress, rings...phone calls. I search her face. "How did you have Ethan call me?"

"Oh, that was actually John. He's brilliant. I said I wanted you home; he said scaring you would probably help get you back to California. He had free rein to do what he needed. I gave him all the voicemails I had, and he spliced them together."

Liam shifts again, closer to me now, and Colette swings the pistol toward him again. She squeezes, shooting above his head, and he ducks. "I said don't move."

Swallowing against the tightness in my throat, I force myself to remain calm. My pulse is pounding out of control.

"I'm not moving." And he doesn't, his feet planted firmly in place.

"For once, you listen. For once, you do as you're told." The furry causes spittle to fly out of her mouth.

Frowning, I look her way. "What does that mean?"

"He never listened or fell in line. It means that I sacrificed to do what needs to be done."

"What sacrifices?"

Colette turns toward me slowly. "I killed his mother." Her words are venomous, spilling out like the poison stewing in her soul. She turns to Liam. "You didn't know that, did you? I detested the very air you breathed, you and that cunt of a mother. I fixed that, though."

The air drops from my lungs.

Liam's anguish paints across his face. The sucker punch to the gut hits me like I'm sure it's hitting him. He's almost next to me now. I could reach out and touch him, and I ache to console him.

"What do you mean?" He starts forward, and I grab his arm to hold him back.

"Your whore of a mother came to my house to tell me she and Walter were going to run away together, but there was no way in hell I was going to suffer through the embarrassment of a divorce. I did what I needed to do. They had to die."

"What did you do?"

"Walter was diabetic; it was easy to give him extra insulin. Heart attacks." She smiles as she waves the gun at them. "And car crashes are easy to create. It pays to know the right people, and darling, I know the absolute best."

"Why?" Liam's voice shakes, his body tense under my hand.

"She was pregnant. Again. *Again*. I thought I took care of that after you were born by having her stabbed during a mugging. The end result was beautiful and poignant. If I couldn't have more children, then neither could she. But somehow, it happened. After eighteen years of believing I'd marred her life as much as she had mine, she proved me wrong. She reached out and killed any piece of me that was left."

Colette is so, so sick.

Her body is stiff, and her eyes are blazing but somehow soulless like she's nearly dead inside. "I could have withstood the betrayal of their affair. And I did—*for years*. But that was too much. How could she have a daughter, but I couldn't?"

Despicable, that is what she is, and the things she has done make me sick. "Francesca?" Her name slips from my lips before I can cut it off. I slap my hands over my mouth, not wanting to reward her more than I already have.

"It was all working out great. But then you miscarried. It killed Ethan. He wanted a baby, and when you couldn't get pregnant again, he started looking at other women. *Francesca* was the start of the downfall. I told him to adopt, that it would be fine. But he said no, he wanted a baby of his own. So he got that stupid girl pregnant instead of surrogacy. Another idiot move."

"Was she a drug addict?"

"What are you talking about now?" Colette asked.

John snickers, a smile plastering his face. "God, no. She's a saint. Truly. That was Ethan's idea. We were going to stage another accident and then take the baby."

Colette waves her firearm wildly at him. "What are you talking about?"

He shrugs. "He didn't love her; he just wanted the baby. That was my job, take the baby, kill the mother. Nothing unlike what you've had me do. That battered woman's sh—"

Bang.

Colette shoots, and I flinch.

John drops.

"Can't have him spilling all my secrets. He'll die soon. It won't hurt for him to suffer first. There are always more like him."

I drop to my knees, my throat constricting. His body is right there. Close enough to reach my hand out, check his pulse, and ensure he's okay. Somehow my fingers stretch toward him.

"No, let him die."

Snatching my hand back, I watch Colette. They are certifiably fucking insane. Colette, Ethan. The whole family?

"Then Ethan screwed it all up. He planned on leaving you for Francesca. He'd fallen for her, exactly like his pathetic, useless father. Ethan was weak and proved that he couldn't be trusted. And I wasn't going to live with another unreliable male, so I told John to kill him."

But John just said Ethan was going to kill Francesca? I can't reason with Colette, so I'm not going to bring it up. Whatever was going to happen didn't, and I need to keep my head about me here.

She glances at John. "A pity John had to die for no reason. He was incredibly talented at his job. A bit of a hardball with extras, kept wanting me to pay more and more."

Colette looks at me, her brow cocked as she laughs. "John hired rebels to kill him because I had to protect you. It was made to look like an accident. But when he was supposed to bring the body home, there was a flood, and Ethan was swept away with everything else. John assured me it was done, though."

She hums softly for a moment, watching me. "But it was supposed to be both of them—him and Liam. I'd convinced Ethan to get to know Liam, to take him on the trip." She turns to Liam. "Somehow, you escaped, and I couldn't kill you right away. It would have been suspicious."

My heart is in anguish. All of this because of the infidelity almost forty years ago. Because she wanted more children, especially a daughter.

Me. She wanted me.

Her eyes blaze with something crazy, and she stops pacing. She raises the gun, both hands around the butt to hold it steady. She's shaking so badly.

"All I ever wanted was a daughter, someone to laugh with, share stories with, and love." She softens for a split second, imploring me to understand, to agree and give in. She holds a hand out to me.

Then she shifts. She lowers the pistol for a moment, her head down. "You were so happy here. So carefree while I was in California, miserable without my daughter." She shakes her head. When she looks up, tears are about to spill down her cheeks. "Katherine, please. Come home."

She's still trying to manipulate me. Trying to make me fall for her bullshit.

"No."

"I'm sorry to hear that." She points the pistol at me.

Ice pours down my veins, and my heart roars in my ears. I won't go down without a fight. Feet heavy, I move forward. Her brows raise, and she turns her head to the kitchen.

My gaze follows hers.

Greer. He's running. No. *NO.*

Bang.

Thirty-Nine

Kit

I FREEZE. EVERYTHING HAPPENS in slow motion. Colette looks from Greer to me. He's running for me. Yelling my name. Time slows, and I pray as I watch her finger inch over the trigger. I close my eyes.

I try to calm, striving for peace, and open myself, making wishes I'm pretty sure will get me nowhere.

A loud bang reverberates through the room. Someone large hits me, knocking the air from my lungs, spasming before landing on me in a heap. They're heavy and warm, and heat blooms all over my chest.

There's a loud yell. "I need her alive!"

Bang. Bang.

Bang. Bang. Bang.

Bang.

There's a loud shuffle of people around me, multiple bodies hitting the floor, and people crying out. And then nothing because Greer is over me.

"Kit. Love. Baby. Tell me you're okay." His voice is harsh, coming in pants, and I open my eyes. His arms are around me, pulling me to him and rolling us so I lie on top of him.

My head pounds, and Troy is speaking into a phone. "Shots fired, suspect down. We need another ambulance..." The rest drowns out in the chaos. I look down at Greer.

"I'm okay. I'm okay. Oh, god, Greer. I was terrified for you." I shove my hands through his hair and pull his lips to me. He grunts but opens, his tongue reaching out to stroke against mine. His hands are on my hips, gently pulling me down on him. "I love you, Greer. I love you."

385

"I know, love. I know. I love you too." He sputters under me, coughing. I put my hand on his chest.

Wetness pools under my palm.

My heart stops. I lift my shaking hand. Thick red liquid drips from my fingers. Shit. He's bleeding.

"Troy! I need towels." He's shuffling behind me, and I'm ripping apart Greer's shirt, looking for the wound. There's so much blood everywhere. There's a hole barely an inch under his left clavicle.

The blood flows out, not spurting. Not an artery. I hope.

My heart is pounding in my chest, and my hands are shaking. Troy lays towels next to me. I scramble for one. "Help me roll him over. I need to find the exit wound. Sit there, hold him up so he's not on his face. Use this and put pressure, steady pressure." Troy nods, and I get to work on his back.

I rip his shirt and pull it away from the wound. There's so much blood I can barely see his skin. I run my hands over his body. But no hole.

There's no hole.

The bullet is in him somewhere. Ripping, tearing, thundering through his chest area.

Stop. Calm down.

I take a deep breath and let it out slowly. Focus on my training.

"Keep pressure on that spot." Troy pushes harder, pushing me back a little.

Greer's so pale, and he's panting. "Greer?"

"Hmm."

"Stay with me, love. Stay with me."

"Tired...You're safe...now." He doesn't open his eyes. With a finger against his neck, I count his pulse. Weak. Not thready yet, but weak. One. Two. Three. "I love...you...Kit."

"Shush, love, keep the energy. Stay awake."

"You were everything...I wanted. Nothing..." Tears burn, and I try to blink them away before I start counting over. "... would have...changed that."

"Jesus, don't, Greer. Just shush. You can tell me all this stuff tomorrow or the next day, when you're stronger."

His lashes are stark against his cheek.

Fuck counting. I lean down and press my lips to his again. "You're everything I wanted too."

He chuffs. "...perfect...for me."

The tears drop, and I set my forehead on his. "For me too. I love you."

"Love..."

Pulse frantic, I wait for the rest. Did I miss it with the pounding in my ears? Noooo.

I run my finger down his carotid, thready now. So weak.

And I blink away tears to stare at his face, taking in everything. Memorizing the spattering of freckles I never noticed. The small scar on the side of his nose. I run my hand through his hair, letting the silk texture commit to my brain.

My heart stutters.

The pounding in my ears drowns out everything else around me. I run my hand down his frame, his pale skin clammy.

When I glance up, two uniformed people are rushing toward us. Two gloved hands cover mine, and voices yell at me to move away; they've got it.

My tears are blinding as I glance up. Paramedics. "Gunshot. Under the left clavicle, no exit wound."

The one nods, ripping open his bags, and the other rolls him to his back so they can get him on the gurney.

As I watch, two hands help me stand and then curl me into a chest. My tears fall. There are words, but I don't register them. I look up, catching the scars on my helper's face. Troy.

My gaze sticks on the paramedics as they rush him out on a gurney, an oxygen mask over his face with an Ambu bag attached. I know this is standard. I know they are prepping, calling ahead.

They'll start an IV in each arm, and if they can't get enough fluids in him, they'll give him an intraosseous line. They'll transfuse him with blood, platelets, and colloids to help with the blood loss. They'll stabilize him in the trauma bay, then give him a CT scan to find the bullet before rushing him into surgery. They'll open him up and suture what needs to be sutured. They'll stop the bleeding, patch him back up, and put him on some painkillers.

In a few days, he'll be released home, and we'll start our life together. I know it. Every day, I see miracles.

Please.

Please.

A two-way radio beeps. An ambulance calls to dispatch, the echo blaring from the walkie-talkie of a paramedic team here, covering those of us in shock or needing first aid.

Troy tenses, like he knows something I don't. I focus on calming myself, the roar in my ears slowly easing. Pieces of the conversation hit me. Gunshow wound. Blood loss: Substantial. Pulse: None. Time of death: 0246.

2:46 a.m.

I sob, and Troy holds me. There is screaming, someone is screaming over and over, and it doesn't stop.

Me.

A paramedic rushes over and pricks my arm with something. I don't give a shit what it is, as long as it blackens the noise in my brain.

My life is over.

At 2:46 a.m., all life inside me died.

Forty

Kit

IT'S BEEN TEN DAYS since he died. Ten days since the hole inside my chest opened, and the weight of my guilt threatened to swallow me whole.

His death is because of me.

I'm the reason for the gathering under another canopy of trees in a cemetery. But this casket isn't empty. My heart aches, even with the support I have beside me. Simon and Troy stand on either side of me, their hands firmly in mine as we watch the coffin lower into the ground.

I didn't know it could hurt this bad—that the agony of loss could eat at me so much. Not that my agony compares to his parents'. They stand across from me, their hearts on their sleeve, their eyes red and angry from the tears they shed.

I wanted to be here, but I wasn't sure I'd be welcome. I'm the reason he died. It tears my soul apart every day.

Every day since his death.

Every day that I've gotten out of bed, and he hasn't.

It's agonizing to know that I get to live the rest of my life, and he can't. That his life ended that night.

Another sharp stab of pain ricochets through my heart, and my chin trembles as the tears start again. Simon squeezes my hand, and I drop my head on Troy's shoulder.

The pastor clears his throat, and his calm, strong voice begins.

"Honor, duty, love. These are the things that made Jeremiah the man he was. Since he was a child, he wanted to be a police officer. He wanted to provide for the community in the same way his father did, honoring the Harrigan name by being the best police officer he could be. He will forever be with us."

That he was such a good man makes this so much more painful. He died because of *me*. His life was spent to save mine.

The pastor continues, "Mr. and Mrs. Harrigan wanted to thank everyone for coming out today. They are honored by the outpouring of love from the community. At this time, please step to the front and say your goodbyes to Jeremiah."

The pastor steps away from the casket, and Simon, Troy, and I linger as people go through the line, saying their goodbyes. These people will go to the church and celebrate his life, truly remembering an honorable man. A man who deserves all the love and praise of this amazing goodbye.

Well deserved.

When Officer Harrigan's parents are free, I swallow around the lump in my throat. It's agony knowing that he died for me. I can't imagine how these people must feel. Tears burn a trail down my cheek, and I make my way forward.

She's a beautiful woman. Her hair is streaked with gray, and fine wrinkles surround her eyes. He towers over her, providing support as she dabs at her tears with her handkerchief. He's regal and poised. Jeremiah probably went into the police academy to make his father proud. Judging by the sadness that lingers around his mouth, Jeremiah did just that.

I reach my hand out, expecting to be rebuffed. Instead, his mother draws me close and hugs me. When she lets me go, the tension leaves me too. "I wasn't sure if I should be here."

She smiles around another set of tears that fall. "We are so glad you are. Jeremiah died doing what he loved most, protecting people."

His father places his hand on her shoulder. "He would have wanted it that way. Thank you for coming."

We spend a few more minutes talking, and I make a promise to come visit from time to time.

Simon, Troy, and I say our goodbyes, and they drive me home. Troy hops out first, opening my door. "Are you heading to the hospital now?"

I nod. "I just wanted to put on some comfy clothes first. Thanks for coming with me today."

He nods, watching me. He pats me on the shoulder and then gets back in the truck. Simon kisses my cheek, and then they leave me to myself in front of Greer's front door.

Inside, I change quickly and rush out to his truck.

Fuck, we were so lucky. It could have been so much worse. Liam stopped by a few days later, and we discussed Colette and the charges against her and John—or whoever he was. Liam wanted to make sure I was okay, and honestly, after everything that happened, I am. There isn't anything that could happen that was worse than almost losing Greer.

The walk to his hospital room is quick, mostly because I'm anxious to get back there. I didn't want to leave, but I needed to honor Officer Harrigan. It makes my guts ache to think that I may have missed one of Greer's wakeful moments. They are happening more and more, and his strength is slowly returning, but it's been a slow road to recovery.

When I reach his door, it's open, and I can see his legs through the doorway. My heart drops into my chest. The undeniable thankfulness lingers whenever I think of still having him. It could have gone so differently.

I step in. "How's my favorite patient?"

He's upright in the chair, finally detached from all the tubing and telemetry units. His amber eyes eat me up, stalking my steps as I reach his side. He puts his hand in mine and pulls me down with his good arm.

Our lips touch, his devouring, mine savoring, our tongues meshing as he pulls me onto his lap. He grunts slightly but laces his good hand through my hair to pull me closer.

When we come up for air, he rests his forehead on mine. "How was the funeral?"

"Beautiful. It was absolutely perfect, and such a good way to honor him."

"Good. We'll have to go to his gravesite when I'm finally out of here. Dr. Everette checked on me while you were out. He says I'm healing nicely, and I can go home in a few days."

My heart stutters, warmth blooming through all of me. "I'll take such good care of you, baby. You're going to have the best one-on-one care."

He quirks a brow and brushes his nose to mine. "I'm going to need a sponge bath every day, Kit."

Laughter erupts from inside me, deep and resonant and so incredibly blissful. "I promise to do my best."

"I'll make sure—"

I slam my lips on his, shushing him. The last week without him has left me craving his touch. The need that pours through me is strong as our lips mingle again.

When we part, I move off his lap, allowing him room to breathe. And me room to settle my stomach, which has been so queasy lately. I was hoping that with the chaos and tension gone that it would settle, but it really hasn't.

"Kit, I still don't remember everything that happened that night."

I bite my cheek for a moment. "Your doctor said not to talk about it yet."

He pushes himself out of the chair and sits on the bed, scooching in gingerly, making sure not to hurt himself.

I shake my head as he does it. "You're supposed to get help with that."

"If I baby myself, I'll never get out of here. Lay by me?"

He scoots his body over as far as he can without falling off, leaving me a sliver of an inch to settle in, but I do, being careful of his injury. I brush my fingers over the bandage there, tracing around the outside of the tape before I move up to scratch his jaw.

Damn, he needs a shave, but he groans in delight as I drag my fingers through it. "What do you want to know?"

"Why was Liam there?"

These are the easy answers. "Liam works for the FBI and was watching Colette. Her flight itinerary was flagged. She used an alias, and he was watching for it. When he saw that she'd had a sudden flight to Maine, he thought I was in danger. He said she'd been more erratic, her contact with her hired gun had increased, and he could see that John was in Maine. When she came here, he did too."

"Why did he tackle you? You said the other day your bruises were finally starting to heal."

"He said he tripped. He came into the house because he saw John enter. He fought me for the weapon because his training kicked in, and he needed to disarm me."

He nods a moment, the frown still on his face as he traces the healed spot on my wrist. "And the third man outside?"

"His partner."

We talk more, going through the events of the night, the people who died, and who was there. "What about Francesca? Wasn't he dating her?"

I give him what I hope is a chagrined look. "Liam said he was getting close to Francesca to get more information on Colette. It wasn't romantic."

Greer grimaces and shifts so he can rub my shoulder with his good hand. "Did you get your stuff moved in? I told Simon to make sure you didn't do any heavy lifting, and Maddox owes you, so he better have enlisted some help."

"They did everything. I just stood around like a dictator while they brought everything to your house."

"Thank you for moving in with me."

A chuckle escapes me. "You didn't have a choice."

"True. I am a kept man now. You own every piece of me, my home, my body." And one day, hopefully his name, but we haven't talked about that, and I told him I'd never marry again.

He groans, his body tightening for a moment before he forces himself to relax.

"Bad memory?" I do that. When I think of the worst that could happen, I tense, then try to shake it off.

He nods, his lips brushing my forehead before he tilts my head back so we can look into each other's eyes. "Fuck, Kit. If I'd have lost you..." His swallow is loud, even through the noise in the room. "I wouldn't be able to go on. What I feel for you is everything. I've never felt this way about anyone."

Tears burn again because, damn it, I'm emotional lately. "I love you too, Greer. I can't believe that we get to live with each other, love each other, and be happy."

He angles my head, his lips touching mine briefly. "I am so fucking lucky, Red. No matter what else happens, even if it's only ever you and me, I am. So. Fucking. Happy. And in love with you."

"Without expectation, without wanting anything in return, I am always yours, Greer."

September

Forty-One

Kit

IT'S COLD. COLDER THAN September fifth usually is, but I'm out here anyway. With my feet tucked under me, I sit on the blanket I've laid out.

"Happy Birthday." I lay a flower on the gravesite, clearing away a few freshly fallen leaves. Fall can be bitter in Maine, and this might be one of those years.

"There aren't enough words to tell you how thankful I am or how I feel. You saved us that night. I'll be out to check on you frequently. I'll bring you flowers. No lilies, though. Your mom said you liked daisies, so I'll bring you some of those." I chuckle softly.

My skin is kind of prickly, but not how it used to be. It's different now. Prickly because I don't know what to say. I don't know how to end this. Thank you doesn't seem like enough.

I lay a kiss on my hand and touch the grave marker gently. "Rest."

On all fours, I push off the ground to get up. A strong hand grips me, pulling me the rest of the way.

Greer's deep, gravelly voice fills the peaceful silence. "You ready?"

I nod and rest my hand on my lower back.

"This kid needs to get her feet out of my ribs."

He smiles softly, then sets his hands on my stomach and rubs, his eyes moving down to my enormous belly.

"How's my boy?"

"It's a girl, Greer."

His laughter pangs my heart. "You don't know that."

He's right, but it's still fun to think of her as a girl.

"Officer Harrigan wouldn't expect you to visit out here, you know." He tucks my hand into his arm gently.

"I had to bring the birthday gift. You didn't have to follow me out here."

"You're far too pregnant to be out here alone, so yeah, I had to. I made a promise that I would always keep you safe. If you go traipsing off whenever you get a harebrained idea, I'm not liable for what I do next."

"I'll kick you from here to Saturday if you don't knock off the Macho Man shtick. I'm not afraid of you. But thank you for driving me. I really appreciate it." As for being afraid of him? Really, I'm not. I'm not afraid of anything anymore. The worst has happened to me, and I've lived through it. There's nothing else I can't face.

A smile spreads across my face as my baby kicks me again. I shift, trying to make room for her. She's going to be a big baby, like her daddy. Tall, strong, fierce.

My miracle baby.

I have no idea how she is possible. My biggest fear, after everything, was that she wasn't safe in there. Maybe she'd grown over scar tissue and wasn't getting the nutrients or oxygen she needed because the placenta didn't have enough surface to absorb what it needed.

Every checkup, they assure me she's doing well. The placenta had attached to the back wall of my uterus in an area that was completely safe.

The worst always plays in my head at those doctor visits, waiting for the words—no longer viable.

Waiting for them to tell me to end my pregnancy.

I wipe away the shivers.

It still gets to me, still triggers something when I go in for a checkup. But it's always been okay. Every time they walk out of the room like I'm a miracle. And we are—she is.

I didn't even realize I was pregnant until almost five months in. She'd been nestling her tiny embryo in during every stressful event that happened in February. Even after all the chaos, she'd hung on, digging in for the long haul. She'll be a fighter.

Greer ushers me to his truck and drives me to our house. I claimed his home as mine. No one minded, least of all him.

It helps that everyone who wanted to hurt me is dead or locked away. Colette's trial will start in the winter for things I never thought were possible from her, but Liam says the list is long, and she'll never get out. She will never hurt me again.

Neither can Ethan.

They found his femur and some of his ribs on a shore in Brazil. They ran it against Liam's DNA, and it was a match. It was a lucky happenstance, one that I readily welcomed. No more looking over my shoulder every night.

Francesca's fake medical records were corrected by Asher, even though Liam said he could do it. Asher said it was easy and proved he could do it faster than Liam. As soon as it became a game, the two bonded like crazy.

As for Liam, I've forgiven him. He asked me to name the baby after him. He thinks he's hilarious.

Maddox is sucking up big time, and I have to say I love it because I can't get enough of the prenatal massages he's been springing for. Although he shouldn't, he carries guilt for not catching Colette's aliases and tracking her when she flew to Maine.

After all of that? I've never breathed so easily in my life. Well, I'd breathe easier if baby's feet weren't in my ribs.

"What do you want for dinner? I can run and grab something. Dill pickles with ice cream? Fried chicken?"

"You sure know my vices right now. Maybe some tomorrow. I have plenty for tonight."

"Are you sure? It isn't a problem."

He all but carries me into the house and sets me on a stool at the counter. Overprotective marshmallow of a man. Shit, I love him.

"Greer, you have been walking on eggshells around me for the last week. What is going on?"

OF LILIES AND LIES

"You're due any day now; I just want to make sure I don't upset you. I wouldn't be able to stand it if something happened to you."

I grin, shaking my head. "You need to go finish that crib so it's ready for when this baby arrives. I'm going to eat some cereal and watch TV until I crash."

He finally kisses me and makes his way to his work area. I snack, then head into our bedroom to rest so I have strength for tomorrow.

In bed, I pull out my phone and dial Greer's number because he doesn't like me in the man cave with all those machines. He won't hear it anyway. I leave him a message, clicking off after telling him I love him.

I pull the sheets up and over me and my bump, then slide my hands across my belly while baby kicks. "You can't get crazy tonight. I need rest, and you need to show me how well you behave." Eventually, I settle into my favorite dreams.

Greer grabs my hand and squeezes it rhythmically.

"It's going to be okay."

He exhales, slowly shaking his head. "I was not prepared for this, Kit. Not at all."

I would laugh if he weren't so serious.

"I know, love. It'll be okay. We'll go in and check it out, make sure everything is perfect."

"I was reading on google about scars and pregnancy."

"Oh, Jesus. No wonder you're worried. It's going to be okay." And despite telling him this, I can't help but send up a brief prayer to whatever deity is up there.

Then we are in front of an ultrasound machine.

"Do you want to see your baby?" the technician asks.

Greer swallows loudly and nods.

The buzz of the machine drowns out my fears, and then our baby appears on the screen. The heartbeat is strong, and I can't hold back the tears.

A huge weight fills my chest, and I can barely believe the enormity of what I'm seeing.

Life.

We created this baby.

"And here's the heartbeat." Doc flips a switch, and the loud lub-dub fills the room.

Greer gasps, and the tears fall down my cheeks, sliding over my temples.

When I look at him, his cheeks are wet with tears too. He doesn't even hide them, just watches and listens, holding my hand.

"We made that." He points to the screen and sniffles a moment, then looks at me with the most loving expression I've ever seen.

He swoops down, his lips brushing mine in an achingly wondrous kiss. He drops his forehead to me. "This is our love. We made this."

"Yes, we did." I laugh, smiling against his lips as he kisses me again.

Then we are home, in bed, where his hands slide against my skin, his rough palms gliding up my body effortlessly.

His movements send me into bliss, his body moving hard and deep. He rides me, his body claiming me, loving me as we move together. When it's over, he slides his hands down to my softly rounded stomach, his thumbs brushing the bump.

"Are you sure it's in there?"

"Safe and sound. I promise, the doctor said she's safe."

"She?" His face is full of wonder.

"Only a guess."

"Miracle, Kit. You are so much more than I ever hoped for." He leans down to kiss it gently. "Hello, sweet baby. I can't wait to meet you. I already love you."

He leans back up, his gaze intense on mine, his hands on my belly. "I wanted this so bad. So bad, Kit, only with you." His eyes well with tears again.

I gasp awake.

Shit, that dream always kills me.

My body hums, like it's in tune with the change in energy around me. The bed dips, shifting me, and my pulse races. Greer's warm, strong palm slides over my hip, settling over my belly. Lips kiss my shoulder.

The clock says it's just after ten. I roll onto my back and cradle his neck in my hand. "You're done earlier than I thought you'd be."

"I couldn't stop thinking of you in here by yourself, lonely and needy. As needy as I am." His deep, gravelly voice ricochets down my spine.

"Mmm. Did you finish what you wanted to?"

His gaze eats me up, and warmth pools in my core.

"Yeah, but there is still stuff to finish. Nothing more for tonight, though. Everything has to dry." He kisses my shoulder and smooths a hand down my hip.

"How's your shoulder?"

"It bothered me today, but nothing more than normal. No more talk. I need you, Kit."

His lips are on mine, and I open for him instantly. I missed him. I need his touch, his love, and I long to give him mine in return. My hands brush over scars, scars that could have changed our whole life, but somehow, miraculously, they didn't.

The bullet caused fluid to build up around his heart. His right lung needed suturing. He needed a pacemaker because of his slower heart rate due to the damage. He spent nearly two weeks in the hospital, followed by six weeks of intense physical therapy.

It took twelve weeks before he could use any of his power tools, and he was worse than a hormonal teenager during that time. Itchy, twitchy, and pissy.

Then, once his hands were lovingly moving along the wood, he was back to his usual self. I nuzzle into his chest, my head resting over his steady heartbeat. "I love you, Greer."

His lips graze my shoulder, moving my T-shirt down off my shoulder. Shivers rack me as I arch into his touch.

Damn it, I need him.

He moves slowly, touching, savoring every inch of my body. Rolling us so that I straddle him. Then he primes me in the way only he can with dark sighs and powerful hands. His fingers slip through my slit, then slide deep inside me, preparing me.

"Look at your pretty pussy, already wet for me." Then he laughs, his fingers stalling. "Sorry, love, I know you can't see it." He wiggles his digits, tapping them deliciously on that spot that makes me explode.

"Mmm. Not fair." I rock my hips against his hand. "Greer, I need you."

He pumps his hand again, twisting, and it rockets euphoria through me. The pleasure moves through my body, making me arch my back. I brace my hands on his legs, my body spread wide as I grind against him.

"Please, baby, I need you in me."

"Come first, Red. I want you to coat my fingers. Come all over me."

His words send delicious pulses through my body. I scoot back and grab his cock, stroking up and down. I lift my body, angling it at my entrance, and slide down, rocking slowly as I do.

"Ohh, Jesus Christ, Kit. You are going to kill me."

"I tried, love, and you came back."

He laughs until I clench around him. Then he groans, his hands digging into my hips as he rocks me on him.

Long, slow, fast, hard. He gives me everything, making me finish so hard I see stars at least three times.

He grabs my hips, guiding them, lifting me, and sliding me back down on him. His cock hardens, and then he's pulsing a hot stream deep inside me as we both return to reality in the quiet room.

Out of breath and energy, I drop onto his chest. He holds me, settling me snug against him. "Fuck, I missed you, love."

He rolls me to the side and then gets up so he can clean me up. After he's done, he climbs into bed, draping himself over me, wrapping us up in a Greer burrito. Rough fingers move the hair away from my face. Gentle lips take mine, and then he presses his forehead against me.

I love him, every inch of him, every part of his soul. He's such a good man, and all mine. "This is more than I ever thought I'd have."

His hand slides to my belly, stroking it. "I know, baby, we're lucky. So fucking lucky. I love you too."

Epilogue

Greer - September 20

"Hey, love?" Kit calls from the living room.

I turn to her, my sandwich shoved into my mouth as I take a bite. She grimaces as she tries to stand from the couch, her body a gloriously, ridiculously beautiful ball of belly, sweet curves, and plump breasts.

Fuck, I love those things.

I swallow around the salami. "What's up?" I rush over, grabbing her hand with my free one to help pull her the rest of the way off the couch.

"I have to go to the hospital. Can you drive me?"

Oh, yeah, another appointment with the OB. "Sure, love. Wherever you want to go. If you want a massage when we get home, I can do that for you." And maybe plug her at the same time. Fuck me, pregnancy sex is the fucking best.

She nods, her face pinching as she braces her hand on her back, then she sucks in a breath as her body tightens. She looks like she's counting in her head, like she's done for the past few weeks. Every time I ask, she says it's that fake contraction thing. Braxtonian Hippocampus, or whatever they fucking call it. I'd look it up, but I've been banned from googling pregnancy stuff. Apparently, it makes me a bit panicky.

"Are you sure it's not the real ones this time?"

She shrugs and starts waddling to the door while I shove the rest of my sandwich in my mouth, trailing behind.

I tuck her into the seat, making sure she has plenty of room.

"Thank you, baby."

I drop my forehead to hers and bask in the glory that is Kit. I've never been so inclined to worship someone like I am with her. She has given me everything I could have ever wanted in life and doesn't even know how much it means to me.

At the hospital, I help her out at the door so she doesn't have to walk from the parking lot.

She leans up to kiss my cheek. "Greer, bring the bag in with you, just in case."

I stare at her belly, which she's holding on to as she grimaces. "Another contraction?"

"Heeeee....Mm-hmm..." Her face is tight, lips drawn back, and after a minute, and despite her whispering her voice carries. "This one was stronger than the last one."

Oh, fuck me. "How far apart are they?" This is it. She didn't say anything. This is it.

She looks at her watch, then starts waddling toward the door. "Two minutes."

"Holy shit, Kit. The doctor said to come in at five."

"I know, love, but it's okay. I didn't want to lie in the bed forever waiting. Park the car and bring the bag."

Fuck that. I scoop her up, bridal style, and head into the hospital. My pulse is frantically racing faster than my legs can carry me.

"Sir, would you like a wheelchair?"

I whiz past the person who asked me, making a beeline for the check-in station. While Kit gives them all the information, my heart is a fucking mess inside my chest. We are bringing a baby into the world right now.

"We should get her to a bed. Can you get her a bed?" She needs to be on a bed to push. Fuck, I should have paid attention. Should have brought her in sooner.

"It's okay, sir, the nurses are on their way, and we'll take great care of her."

"Greer." Kit's hand pats my arm. I'm still holding her. I wrinkle my brow and glance at her. "Baby, it's okay. Put me down, go park the car, and by the time you get back, we'll be ready to go upstairs."

I pull her closer, and my stomach flops. A fucking whine escapes me, and I'm sure I look like the most fucking pained soon-to-be father in the universe. "I don't want to leave you."

"Well, we need the car to get home, so park it so it doesn't get towed."

I clench my jaw and force myself to let her down so I can park the fucking car. "Next baby, we're taking an Uber."

It's a whirlwind while I park the car and rush back, then I follow Kit and the nurses upstairs.

My fucking glorious, beautiful pregnant wife. Who, throughout this whole fucking thing, has remained calm and controlled and radiant. Once she's hooked up to the machines around her, I drop into the chair by her side, the adrenaline from earlier finally easing.

She reaches out, and I grasp her like a lifeline. I have no fucking clue what I'm supposed to be doing, but when they tell me to jump, I'm going to fucking jump.

Her eyes glow, her brow and mouth pinching as her body tightens through another contraction. I count in my head as she tries to relax through it. When it finally eases, I bring her hand to my mouth, kissing it, loving the way she wraps her fingers through my beard, offering me comfort when she's the one in pain.

"You look miserable." It comes out as a half pant half chuckle.

"I hate that I can't help you."

Her body stiffens again after a minute or two, tightening up as she moans around this contraction while she grabs my hand. It hurts. Not that I mind, I'll take all the pain I possibly can if it saves her from it.

When she finally calms, I grab the washcloth tucked beside me and wipe her forehead.

"Thank you."

"I love you, Kit."

"I love you too, babe."

Rat-a-tat-tat. We both turned toward the door as Dr. Larue walks in. "Well, I hear you've decided it's time to get this baby out. Should we see where you are at?"

A nurse dims the lights, and peace fills me. Dr. Larue has been doing this forever, and the fact that he's so calm and easygoing made choosing him a no-brainer.

Kit tenses while he checks her, and he hums and smiles when he's finished. "You're doing so great, Kit. Baby is presented nicely, and your cervix is fully dilated."

Dr. Larue spends the next minute walking us through the plan for when the baby is born.

And it's not instantaneous. At this point, I'm thinking I need to swing into the bathroom for a piss break, but I know Kit won't get one, so I'm hanging in there, holding her back, supporting her with my chest and arms and legs, almost wrapped around her like a burrito. A baby-delivering support burrito that keeps its head up by hers.

"Push, Kit. You're doing so great. Four. Five. Six. Seven. Eight. Nine. Ten. Relax."

"Fuck, this hurts, Greer."

I wisely keep my mouth fucking shut. Epidurals are there for a reason. I know she's strong and brave and courageous. She didn't need to prove it to me. I press on her hips like they showed me, offsetting the pressure.

"Fu-uck, this *hurts.*"

Dr. Larue looks up, patting her leg to get her attention. "Again, Kit. The baby is right there. You're past the point of no return. A few more pushes, and this baby will be out." He continues to massage something, at least I think he is. "Baby has a full head of hair."

"Is it red?" I want to go down and look, but fuck I've been told it's a death sentence. I hope the baby has red hair.

"Oh yeah, it is." He smiles up at me and then at Kit.

I drop my head onto her shoulder, tears pricking my eyes. Our baby is almost fucking here. She looks back at me, tears and sweat trailing down her face.

"On your next contraction, I want you to give me your best push."

With her game face on, she nods at me. "This baby is coming out."

I nod, encouraging her. "You're doing amazing. I love you so much."

"I love yoooooo-ooohhh." And then she's pushing as hard as she can, her face red with her exertion. Soon there is a wail, and Kit laughs.

"Congratulations."

They place the baby on Kit's chest, and we both stare at the scrunched red face, red hair, and angry fists. I lean down and rest my forehead against Kit's, tears streaming down my face, and my heart fuller than I ever thought possible. We peek under the blankets, checking out what we've been wondering this whole time.

Every bit of me is floating, warm and completely whole.

"We have a girl." Kit whispers, one hand stroking our girl, and one hand stroking the tears from my face.

"We have a girl. Welcome to the world, Ellie."

AN EXTENDED EPILOGUE IS available for my newsletter subscribers. Among other perks. :D

Click here: Extras

Or

Get the Extras

If you like the story, please consider leaving a review at your favorite place to buy books. It would mean more than you ever know.

About Author

Authors rely on readers to help us. **If you loved the story please share it with someone you think would like it, or consider leaving a review.** :D Even if it's something as simple as: I liked this book. :D The more reviews we have, the more visible we are to other people (who might love the story).

I'd always wanted to write stories and spent most of high school day-dreaming about being an author (after writing umpteen thousand poems about romance).

Stuck in a nine to five and dreaming about something that would give me more time at home with my husband and kids, I wrote my first romance novel in the summer of 2020 and didn't stop. With three books written, it's time to edit them and get them out to the world.

I am an avid fan of romance in any genre, but love contemporary, sci-fi, PNR and fantasy most. You might find me penning another name under one of those genres in the future.

I like to create vulnerable characters who "find" themselves in the story and get their HEA.

Thank you for reading this book. :)

Newsletter

You can find me at MargauxPorter.com and subscribe to get all the details: Margauxporter.com/subscribe

Printed in Great Britain
by Amazon

11683396R00237